The SECRET LIFE *and* CURIOUS DEATH *of* MISS·JEAN MILNE

Also available from Black & White Publishing
by Andrew Nicoll

The Good Mayor

The SECRET LIFE and CURIOUS DEATH of MISS JEAN MILNE

ANDREW NICOLL

BLACK & WHITE PUBLISHING

First published 2015
by Black & White Publishing Ltd
29 Ocean Drive, Edinburgh EH6 6JL

1 3 5 7 9 10 8 6 4 2   15 16 17 18

ISBN: 978 1 84502 982 1

ALBA | CHRUTHACHAIL

Typeset by Iolaire Typesetting, Newtonmore
Printed and bound by Nørhaven, Denmark

To Alexander Samuel Valentine, keep your feet dry etc.

ACKNOWLEDGEMENTS

Thanks are due to the staff of Dundee Central Library for their assistance with the files on the Elmgrove Murder. Newspaper cuttings and the diagram of the murder scene come from their files of the *Weekly News*, published by D.C. Thomson & Co. Ltd.

1

IT WAS THE first winter of the war and we had no idea how many other winters there would be before we settled with the Kaiser, how much mourning, how many dead.

I went through the pend under our rooms, and up the wooden stair that twisted back on itself like a high gallows, up to the door and the painting of the Pile Light on the wall beside it. It is a very fine painting. I have often admired it, both on nights when I attend to do our work and, from time to time, as I pass in the street. Look out from the pier or along the beach and the Pile Light is there, a mile off. The artist has captured it well, sturdy on its thick, square legs, buttressed against the tide and the surge of the sea wave. It is a worthy symbol of our lodge, embellished and adorned only by the addition of the square and compasses and the all-seeing eye. It is unsigned of course. None may know the name of the artist, as he gave his work in a generous outpouring of charity and the right hand may not know what the left hand is doing. It was Brother Petrie. He is the only signwriter amongst our brotherhood.

I went inside and along the wooden-walled passage to the robing room. I remember the steamy taste of cold rain in my mouth and the warm, burnt toffee of scorched timber from behind the gas lamps.

I laid my case on the table. Brother Cameron's case was already there. My case is made of wood and covered in leather. It has brass locks and my initials stamped in gold leaf. I regard that as fitting and appropriate, as it contains so much that is of value to me: my cuffs and my apron, other materials of which it is not fitting to speak. Brother Cameron's case is made of that thick, red, glossy cardboard they call "whale skin" – which has never been near a whale – all scored and bent into shape and held together with dull lead rivets. I'm sure it serves.

Brother Cameron said to me: "I see your Lieutenant Trench has landed himself in trouble again."

I do not like Brother Cameron. I know he is a brother of the Craft and worthy of all my affection and loyalty, but I am not affectionate to him. I enjoy the fellowship of the Lodge, of course, but in moderation and after we have worked. Always after. Brother Cameron is in the habit of stepping into the Royal Arch to refresh himself even before we meet in Temple. I do not approve of such things. Ours is a solemn rite and it must be entered into with sobriety. I do not like him, though we must rub along.

When I did not answer, he said: "I read it in the *Courier* so it must be right. He's spoken up for that Jew-boy in Glasgow. Trying to say he never murdered that old woman when anybody in his right mind could see he's as guilty as sin."

"He is not 'my' Lieutenant Trench."

"You took a notion to him, as I recall. He made a midden of it when he was here, what now, three year ago?"

"Two."

"Is that all it is? I'd have said longer." Brother Cameron was standing before the glass, fiddling with his tie. "At any rate it's long enough to catch the bugger, if you and Lieutenant Trench were ever going to catch him. He's clean away in Valparaíso, damn this!" He began again with his tie. "Valparaíso or Constantinople or Timbuktu or some such far away place. Kirriemuir, maybe. I hear it's wild enough to harbour any number of desperate men. And there's your Lieutenant Trench making up stories to get a murderer off."

"What stories?" I could have bitten my tongue. I had no interest in hearing what Brother Cameron had to say, but I was interested in Lieutenant Trench. He was right about that much.

"Man, do you never read a paper? Read the *Courier*. It's a fine paper. He's been carrying stories to the investigators that MP hired, telling them there's been a grave miscarriage of justice and claiming there was all sorts of evidence covered up by the police, this thing and that thing that would prove the Jew-boy could never possibly have killed that poor old widow woman and cut her throat or stoved her head in and well they knew it but they conspired together to cover it all up. It'll cost him his job. In fact he'll be lucky not to get the jail for it, buttons pulled off in the public square and publicly disgraced, more than likely. You should be outraged that he could dare to say such things about your colleagues."

"He's with the Glasgow force."

"They are still officers of the law, constables sworn to uphold justice."

"And so is he."

"I might have guessed you'd be the one to stand up for him. Do you not see that makes it all the worse? He has turned against his own. It's a betrayal, a black betrayal. He should have his throat cut across, his tongue torn out by the roots and his body buried in the rough sands of the sea at low-water mark. Do you know what he says? He says the identity parade, where the murdering Jew-boy was picked out from dozens, was all a sham. Can you credit it? It's in the paper!"

The identity parade. The identity parade. We had an identity parade. Two years before, we had an identity parade, one the Chief Constable had organised. I remembered the identity parade. I shouldered Brother Cameron out of the way and took my turn at the glass. "If one says 'black' and the other 'white' only one can have the truth of it. I don't have to judge, thank God, but it sounds to me that Lieutenant Trench is speaking from his conscience. What has he to gain by his accusations? Nothing. And everything to lose. He is a man of great courage."

"Or a Jew-lover. Or in debt to the Jew. Or corrupted by him."

And then the door to the dressing room opened and I saw in the glass behind me Brother Slidders, Postie Slidders, and he looked at me and said: "Hello, John," just the way he had that terrible morning.

2

I AM NOT one of those who likes to say that he can remember when there was nothing to see here but the beach. I suppose it's true, but I don't dwell on it. Things have changed a great deal since I was a boy. The castle is still here, where it's stood these four hundred years, guarding the little harbour, with its roof put back on and all the damage that Cromwell did undone and the batteries manned by smart volunteers with silver buttons. The fisher cottages stand in their rows with the little boats dragged up in front and lines of washing flapping and dancing in the breeze, but where once there were only rough links and bounding hummocks of marram grass with wild, twisted trees appearing here and there amongst them, now we have an esplanade with grand villas along it and a yacht club, granted its own charter by the old Queen herself, and great, towering mansions along the ridge of the hill, each trying to outdo the other in grandeur and the beauty of its parks and policies.

They say (and who am I to dispute it?) that Broughty Ferry has more millionaires in it than any other square mile of soil on God's green earth. They fled here from Dundee, that sink of iniquity and depravity, to breathe deep of our clean sea breezes well away from the clattering mills that made them wealthy and out of sight of the stinking tenements where they stack their workers like firewood for their furnaces.

We have every amenity in Broughty Ferry: fine public parks and bowling greens for recreation; well-supported churches with excellent preachers in both the established tradition and the Free Kirk, and also an English chapel where persons of fashion attend – and public houses just as well supported; a tramcar serving many parts of the burgh, and our own railway station, of which more presently. We have donkey rides and Pierrots on the beach for the summer visitors. We have an excellent Post Office with the royal cypher in stone on the wall, and many of the more substantial houses are connected to the telephone. There is every type of shop supplying every need, grocers, butchers and bakers of quality, fishmongers, fruiterers, ladies' and gents' outfitters, ironmongery, everything is at hand.

And we have our own police station. At one time, not too long ago, we had our own police force too, ten upright men and our own Chief Constable to command them, and our own Provost and baillies and our own court in our own handsome Burgh Chambers, but Dundee looked at us with envious eyes and sent spies to our little railway station and noted down the number of those who travelled daily up the line to work. Then they used that as evidence to justify an Act of Parliament to swallow our little burgh whole.

But, at the time I have in mind, all of that was still to come.

It was November, at the end of a short, bright day that came as a kind of gift before the winter fell on us. I was walking with Constable Brown in Duntrune Terrace, one of those fine broad streets that began to grace the burgh at the end of the last century with cobbled roadways and walks of finely hammered earth to separate foot passengers from the traffic and villas on either side that must cost, God knows, many hundreds of pounds. We walk slowly. That is the expected way of things. We must be seen to pass. We must be recognised, for it is our duty first to deter crime and we must be available so that any, from the highest to the lowest, may request assistance.

As we came down the hill, towards the Claypotts Pond, we met the postman Slidders, with his bag on his back and a grieved expression on his face. He came up and took me by the arm and called me by my name. As a sergeant of Broughty Ferry Constabulary I would not encourage such a thing in the usual course of affairs, but Postie Slidders and I started at the parish school on the same day and we are brethren of the Lodge, so I cannot stand too much on my dignity.

"John Fraser," he said. "I fear there is something sorely amiss with Miss Milne up at Elmgrove."

I took his hand off my sleeve and said to him: "Why would you say that?"

"Because every day I go three or four times through her gate and down the stairs to her back court and there she has an iron box fixed to the wall where I'm to put the letters. It's not been emptied these three weeks. That box is brimful. I doubt I could get another sheet of paper into it.

"And I can say this as God's my judge, that door has never once opened for days. There's a pamphlet from the Kirk that's been left hanging off the handle and it's never moved since last week. She's a queer-like body and I never ring at her bell unless I've a registered parcel, the kind she has to sign for and, even at that she's loathe to answer her door, but there's something far wrong up at that house. I'm not the man to tell the police their business but, if it was me, I'd have that door in."

Constable Brown and I knew Elmgrove well – and Miss Milne, the owner. Her father had made his money as a tobacconist and, like so many others, he came away from Dundee to settle with his family in the Ferry.

But he died and the rest of the family died or moved away and, after a while, Miss Milne was alone in the big house.

I suppose you would say she declined and the house declined

with her. Elmgrove was a mansion of twenty-three rooms with all the additional offices that are to be expected in a house of that size and character. It stands at the head of Grove Road, not many yards from the car stop on Strathern Road, and that whole corner is given over to its two acres of gardens, trees and shrubs in beautiful pleasure grounds, vegetable plots, orchards. Or it was. For, as Miss Milne withdrew from the upkeep of her house and retreated to a few small apartments on the ground floor, she abandoned the garden also until there was not much more than a mossy lawn shaded out by trees and some straggly rose bushes. The rest was a shameful wildness. There was a sermon in it.

I sent Postie Slidders on his way and walked back up the hill to Strathern Road and from there to Elmgrove. The house is hard to see from the road and it was November, mind you, and early dark, but we knew our way, Brown and I. Miss Milne had the money to indulge her whims and fancies and she was forever going away on little trips, but if the house was to be empty for any length of time she would come to the station and let us know so we might keep a special eye out.

There's a high wall around the property – it must be over seven foot tall – a double gate for carriages and, at the side of that, another, narrow door set between pillars for visitors who arrive on foot. They were both shut, but there was nothing unusual in that and Postie Slidders said he had been using the small gate for weeks.

It opened at a touch and Constable Brown and I, we lit our lamps and uncovered them, for it was a November evening and gloomy under Miss Milne's neglected trees. The house was dark. I went boldly to the front door and pulled on the bell. I could hear it jangling in the hall but in a kind of empty, lonely way. The house sounded hollow. I looked at Brown and he looked at me.

"C'mon we'll away round the back," I said, so we shone our lamps at our feet and found our way to the steps that lead down to the back door. All was exactly as John Slidders described: an iron box on the back wall, rammed to bursting with letters and papers, and that pamphlet opened at the middle and folded open over the door handle. A breath of wind might have knocked it off.

We tried to see through the glass, but it was black as Hell inside and we could see nothing but the light of our own lamps shining back at us.

Brown hammered on the door with his fist and he cried out: "Miss Milne, are you in there at all? It's Constable Broon, Miss Milne. Are y'in?"

I left him at it. A man who had passed his sergeant's exams might very well see what Constable Brown could not: that if she had not opened the door to collect her post these last three weeks, the poor woman was not likely to rise and answer at his knock.

But I'll say this for the man, he was dogged, for he was still there, hammering at the door when I came back from walking round the whole of the outside of the house. "Come away, Broon," I said. "There's nothing to be seen here."

"What if she's fallen? Or she's in her bed and no weel?"

"Has she cried out?"

"How could I tell that? I've been hammerin' on this door for ten minutes."

"Wheesht then an' listen."

We stood together in the dark and all the dark and silence of the place seemed to come and make a rushing at our ears and we looked at one another until Broon called out again: "Miss Milne, is that you?" but there was nothing there. Only the sighing of the wind in the trees and the sound of a few dry leaves scuttering along like rats about our feet.

Broon made to take out his truncheon. "I'll knock this glass in," he said.

But I forbade it. "We've had no report of a crime. The house is in good order. We've no business."

He stood looking at me, like a bull looking through a gate, with that half daft expression on his face, as empty as the moon, waiting for me to tell him what to do, which was appropriate and respectful but still, in spite of that, disappointing. Broon will never make sergeant.

I said to him: "Mr Swan across at Westlea has had the telephone put in. We'll away and ask him for the use of it."

And that was what we did.

Now, Westlea is a handsome house. In many ways not so grand as Elmgrove, but it has not suffered those years of neglect. It has a gable end looking out towards Miss Milne's gates and a high window, with coloured glasses, where I could see a light burning. There's no fancy drive and carriage entrance at Westlea, just a pleasant, homely gate between two good, solid pillars of stone, with carved balls on the top, all smartly plastered and painted white.

By that time I suppose it was getting on for nine o'clock in the evening, not the time for calling, but I was a sergeant of Broughty Ferry Constabulary and about my lawful occasion so I had no hesitation. I went through the gate and up the gravel path and rang at the bell – an electric bell I might add. Mr Swan was not one to stint on conveniences for himself or his family. But this time, when it rang, it rang with the warm sound of a house that was full of folk and life and light and warmth and joy.

Mr Swan's lassie came to the door in her peenie and her wee lace cap, and when she saw me and Constable Broon her face fell and she turned pale as the wall, whether from a guilty conscience or from fear of hearing bad news I couldn't say. I can never say, but it's a look I have seen often in my line. A police sergeant is rarely a welcome visitor.

I was about to state my business, but before I could open my mouth I heard a door opening and a voice calling out: "Who is it, Maggie? At this hour!"

Poor Maggie stood gawping and clapping her lips together and it seemed clear to me that she had no more brains in her head than Constable Broon. I very much doubted that the two of them together could have passed the sergeant's exam, and while she stood there, saying nothing, I called out: "It's Sergeant Fraser of the police, sir, come to beg the favour of the use of your telephone."

At once Mr Swan came bustling out, in his shirtsleeves and his waistcoat with his collar off, as well he was entitled to be in his own house at that hour of the evening: "The police? Well come away in, Sergeant, come away. Maggie, get out of the door and let the man in," and then, because he was no more than ordinarily curious, he naturally enquired, "Is there some trouble?"

Constable Broon had enough sense to stay quiet, a respectful couple of paces in the rear as we entered the house, and I said: "There's no reason for alarm, sir, but I would be grateful if you could permit me the use of your telephone until I consult with the Chief Constable."

"Of course, of course," and Mr Swan busied and bustled again and led the way to the kitchen passage, where the telephone instrument hung on the wall in its polished oak box. "There you are, Sergeant."

I looked at him and I looked at the box and Mr Swan said: "Allow me." He lifted the earpiece and clattered on the hook and, after a moment, he shouted into the trumpet in a careful, clear voice: "Give me the police station of Broughty Ferry," and then he stepped back in the narrow passage and held the earpiece out to me. "You are being connected," he said in the same careful, clear voice.

We stood waiting, the three of us in the passage, me and Broon and Mr Swan, with Mrs Swan looking round the edge of the door frame and the lassie Maggie no doubt listening close by, but, in a queer way, I was no longer there as part of the company because I was engaged with the telephone, so Mr Swan turned to Broon and said, very quietly: "But you're sure there's nothing to worry about."

Broon shook his big bull head and mouthed a silent: "No."

"Hello," I said. "This is Sergeant Fraser. Let me have a word with Chief Constable Sempill." And then there was another moment or two of quiet before the Chief Constable came on the line.

"We had a report," I said, and I told him the whole story.

"And you're sure there's no sign of any wrongdoing."

"The whole place is secure."

"You've checked thoroughly?"

"All round the premises, round the gardens, and, as well as I can in the dark, I've examined the upper windows."

"I don't see what else we can do at this time of night," said Mr Sempill. "Leave it for now and take a joiner up in the morning in case we need to force an entry."

"Very good, sir," I said. "Constable Brown and I will resume our patrol and I will engage the man Coullie in the morning."

"Right you are." And he broke off with a loud click.

I handed the telephone instrument to Mr Swan, who put it back on its hook. "Miss Milne?" he said, curiously.

"Miss Milne?" said Mrs Swan.

"And I thought . . ." said Maggie.

But before I could ask her what she thought, Mrs Swan had wheesht her and threatened her with her character and warned her to "be sure those fires are well lit by half past six of the parlour clock" and chased her off to bed.

There were no further occurrences that evening.

3

AT THE STATION in the morning I went in to the big drawer under the front counter and took out the bunch of keys. God alone knows how we had acquired them, but little by little, slowly but surely keys of all shapes and sizes begin to accumulate in a police office. Somebody would find a key, hand it in and it would lie unclaimed in the big drawer. Two or three others would join it until, after a few months, somebody would get sick of them rattling around, taking up room and getting in the way. Then they went on the big steel ring and were forgotten.

But a key is a handy thing and, from time to time, when somebody found themselves locked out, we would help with our selection of keys. From time to time it worked and I decided I would take them up to Elmgrove with me.

First I had to walk the length of the street, fully half a mile to Coullie's. He had a place – he has it still – a fine joiner's shop behind his house along at the far end of Brook Street, opposite St Aidan's Church with a neat white sign hanging on the fence advertising, "Carpenters and Joiners" and, on another line, in a sloping hand, "Funerals Undertaken."

There was no answer at the house so I went up the lane at the side to the big tin shed where the business is carried on, and at first he didn't hear me knocking and calling for the noise of the saw, which I thought inappropriate since it was a Sabbath morning and early. When, at last, he looked up from his work,

I jingled my ring of keys at him and said: "We're needing a house opened up."

"Whereabouts?"

"Elmgrove, up Grove Road."

"It's a fair step."

"The usual rates." I took my watch from my pocket. "You're on the clock, Mr Coullie."

"In that case, Sergeant, I'm more than happy to do my duty. I'll just get my coat."

Coullie was right, it was a fair step. We walked along together side by side, through the deserted streets, quite convivial, two respectable citizens engaged in their lawful duty, me with my ring of keys, jangling at every step, Coullie with his tools held in a sack contraption, a big, folded blanket of jute with handles on each side that bounced off his knee as he strode along. We walked together back along Brook Street to the police station and then nearly as far again along the Dundee Road to the railway bridge, then on a bit again to the West Ferry railway station and up the hill a step to the bottom of Grove Road. But Elmgrove is at the top of Grove Road and, I may as well admit, my hot breath was hanging in the cold November air long before we reached the gate, and by that time I had told Coullie as much of the story as was his business to know.

Constable Broon was waiting at the gate like a faithful hound and he turned the handle and stood aside to let us in, making his respectful "Good mornings".

Coullie walked up to the front door and he saw at once in the morning light what I had not noticed in the dark. "You needn't bother trying your keys here, Sergeant." He pointed through the glass of the fancy front door. "There's a key left in that lock on the inside. It won't accept another."

Broon said: "There's another door down here," and he began to lead the way to Miss Milne's back stair.

That pamphlet was still hanging from the door handle, though sadly limp and crumpled after a night of chill mist. Coullie took it off and held it between two fingers – which he should never have done – saying: "Would you have me break the lock?"

"Don't you be so hasty," I said. "You are here for emergencies only." And, with that, I produced my ring of keys and began to try them at the door, but some were too large and some too small, some had a solid shank when Miss Milne's lock required such a key with a hole in the shank to receive a pin in the lock mechanism and, to make a long story short, in the whole store of keys of Broughty Ferry Constabulary, there was not a single example that would suffice for the task.

"I'll break the lock," said Coullie.

"You'll open the window," I told him.

Coullie looked disappointed, not because he was cheated of the chance to do wanton destruction but because the bill for the repairs would be that much less. Still, he dutifully took off his cap, held it against the top pane of glass and hit it with a hammer he took from his sack. A few tiny, icy broken bits were stuck to the cloth of his cap and he shook them off at his feet, put his cap back on his head and knocked the loose pieces of glass out of the window with his hammer.

"What if it's painted shut?" he said.

"Then you can break the lock."

But it was not painted shut. Coullie reached through the gap, turned the little brass snib, and the window slid up on its runners with barely a sigh.

"What now?" said Coullie.

"Climb through and touch nothing – nothing mind you. We will be at the front door. Come and let us in. Broon, help him."

16

Constable Brown put his hands together to make a stirrup and lifted Coullie up to the stone windowsill. From there it was a simple job to enter the house. A child might have accomplished it.

We had barely arrived at the front door – Broon and I – before we heard Coullie crying out. "She's lying here in the lobby. Oh the poor soul. God preserve and defend us." And then, through the glass of the front door we saw the inner door flung open and there was Coullie, with his muffler pulled up out of his shirt front and held across his face like a robber's mask, a look of horror in his eyes and his free hand waving about in front of himself, like a man blinded, clutching at the air until his palm collided with the glass of the door and slid down it and he waved about insanely from side to side until he found the handle and the key and he turned it and he jerked the door open and threw himself outside with the gasp of a drowning man.

And how little could I blame him, for, when the door opened and Coullie came out, there came with him the stench of a dead thing, the sweet, sulphurous, warm, rotten chicken smell that only ever comes from unburied flesh. I took a deep breath, pushed the door aside and crossed the little entrance hall to the inner door.

That too I pushed aside, gently, with my elbow pressing in the middle of the door so as not to disturb any fingerprints that Coullie had not already destroyed in his stampede.

I will not pretend to you that I noted every detail in those few moments, but I damn well noted every detail afterwards and they remain with me now, clearer than any notebook. There is the front hall where we came in, with a cloakroom to the left, then a pace or two will take you to the glass door that leads to the vestibule. Beyond that there is no door to the lobby of the house, but there is a heavy curtain of green velvet on the right-hand side and a lace curtain on the left. Somebody had taken the trouble to tie them together with a bit of cord, about waist height; it seemed deliberately to obscure the view through the window.

I took out my watch and noted the time. It was 9.20. Jean Milne was lying there, full out on the carpet, her feet away from me and what was left of her head pointing directly towards me. Anybody could have seen at once the poor soul was beyond all earthly help.

The top of her skull was dented out of shape, just a mass of matted hair and black blood, and her face bruised and swollen and grey-green and yellow, fishy coloured. She had been lying for a good while.

Miss Milne was on her right side, her two arms stretched out, as if she had been reaching for the door, her left arm over her right. There was a cloth, like a half sheet, doubled over and covering the base of her skull, but the blood was astonishing – all her clothes were caked and clotted with it and there was more up the walls and in the carpet. Carefully I edged past her body. Her feet were tied together with a green curtain sash and there was a small travelling case opened on the floor beside her filled with ladies' garments, including underclothing and a couple of ladies' handbags, and odd rubbish here and there and a great number of burnt matches. There was a telephone on the wall with its wires cut and hanging loose and beneath it, on the floor, a pair of garden secateurs.

To his great credit, Broon had followed me into the house. He was looking a bit green and nobody could fault him for that. The smell would have choked a horse. "Touch nothing," I told him, "In fact, put your hands in your pockets."

I did likewise, for, sometimes, the temptation to reach out and set something straight or pick something up the better to examine it can be nearly overwhelming. Together we went from room to room, Broon at my back, like a pair of wandering idiots with our hands in our trousers, and I know he did as I did and kept a grip on his truncheon as if, at any minute, we might find the killer sitting amidst the wreck of his work and waiting to leap out and frighten us.

The place seemed in surprisingly good order. The sideboard in the dining room had its three drawers pulled out, but aside from that, and that horrible butcher's yard in the lobby, there was no sign that the house had been ransacked or robbed. Most of the place looked as if it had been deserted for years. There were a few sparse bits of furniture in odd rooms, but most of them were emptied down to the bare boards. The place echoed under our boots with the same, sad, hollow sound the bell had made the night before.

From what we could see it seemed that Miss Milne had retreated to just two rooms on the ground floor: her bedroom and the dining room, which served as her sitting room also. There was a half-eaten pie on the table and, beside it, a scone and a bit of brown loaf. They were all sitting on a copy of the *Evening Telegraph* that looked as if it had never been opened.

Broon read the date: "Monday, October 14."

"Near three weeks. Well, that tells us something. We can check it with the postmarks on her letters."

Carefully, and without saying another word, we went back the way we had come and out into the light and the fresh, clean air.

Coullie was there making a great show of rubbing his eyes red and snorting and clearing his throat and spitting, repeatedly, at a stunted rose bush opposite the door as if he hoped the ratepayers of Broughty Ferry might increase his wages on account of his distress, but I paid him no heed.

"Stand on that step," I said to Broon, and I gripped him by the shoulders until he was exactly where I wanted him but with his nose pointed well away from the half-opened door. "Do not move from that spot, not for your life. I'll away to Mrs Swan and ask for the use of her telephone again. Coullie, you are a witness. I forbid you to shift."

The truth is, by the time I was through the gate I had thought better of troubling Mrs Swan again. I imagined she would be distressed to overhear the news of Jean Milne's murder, so distressed, in fact, that she would probably have to pick up the telephone as soon as I had put it down and share her distress with a few, trusted friends. Naturally, they would also be distressed and quite possibly the lassie working the telephone connector in the Post Office would be distressed and, ere long, needless distress would be flying through every street in the Ferry and perhaps as far as Dundee. I had confidence in Broon's ability to stand still in one place and I trusted that he could keep that up until I returned, so I resolved to hurry to the station and alert Chief Constable Sempill in person.

Naturally, I could not run. A police officer does not run unless in response to an urgent emergency. But I could walk as swiftly as dignity would allow and it was all downhill so ten minutes was all it took to arrive back. For some reason, Mr Sempill was not in his office when I came in but simply standing, collecting some papers from the public counter.

I said: "You'd better come up to Elmgrove with me, sir."

"Of course, Fraser, if you think so. Is there some trouble?"

"Miss Milne's been murdered."

"You mean she's died, surely. The poor soul. Not a good end, alone in that wreck of a house with nobody to hold her hand at the last, but that's the way of it sometimes."

I made no reply and Chief Constable Sempill looked at me

and turned pale. "You mean murdered. What's happened, man?"

"She's lying in the lobby with her head bashed in. It's not bonny."

"Damnation! Is the place secured?"

"I left John Brown there and Coullie the joiner."

"What's he doing there? He's a civilian. Is he a suspect?"

"Sir, you instructed me to engage him to effect entry."

"Yes, of course. I remember." He stood for a moment, one hand on his hip and the other pushing through his hair. "Was she subjected to . . . was there any unpleasantness?"

"Somebody tied her up and cracked her head open, sir."

"Yes but, you know what I mean, man. I'm trying to determine what we're dealing with here."

"Should I telephone the doctor, sir?"

"Yes, Fraser, I was just about to say that. Call Dr Sturrock and ask him to attend. And . . ." he leaned forward and yelled down the passage towards the cells: "Constable Suttie! Who have we with us this morning?"

"George Watson, sir, drunk and incapable – again."

"Is he still incapable?"

"No, sir."

"Then kick him out the back door and lock it up after you. Come with me, I need you. Sergeant Fraser, I want you to telephone to Mr Rodger the photographer and tell him we require his services. I want all this most perfectly recorded – in fact, no," Constable Suttie appeared in the passage, wiping his hands on a rag, "let Suttie do it. Got that, man? We need the doctor, the photographer, and go round to see Mr Roddan, the burgh surveyor, and present my compliments. Tell him we need his assistance with recording the scene."

Suttie looked at me with a raised eyebrow.

"Murder," I said. "Miss Milne at Elmgrove."

Suttie formed his lips into a silent whistle.

Mr Sempill put his hat on and straightened it. "Do you perfectly understand your instructions, Constable?"

Suttie snapped to attention and said: "Sir!"

"Very well, let's away."

4

IT IS MY inclination to tend towards quietness and I think especially so when confronted with our own human frailty. A minister sees people in the depths of their despair, but at least he meets them also at times of joy. A policeman is a minister of misery. We rarely meet folk in happiness. We are never welcome guests. If a man is glad to see us, it is only because he thinks we are his rescuers from some time of trouble or because we have come as avenging angels to right the wrongs done against him, but he would far rather never have had the trouble in the first place, far rather never have suffered the wrong. Indeed, he might be in his rights to blame us for having failed in our duty, which is, first and above all, to prevent crime and to keep the peace.

Those who commit crime and breach the peace hate us because we are the agents of their punishment and shame. Mostly they are ashamed. Men and women brought low by circumstance or drink or poverty, they are ashamed and that is why they hate us. We look at each other and we know that, if the cards had fallen differently, we each might be standing in the other's shoes.

There are some men of my calling who are afraid of that, and it makes them bullies. They like to crow over the vanquished. They think to make themselves big by making others small. Every profession, I suppose, has its share of them, the loud-mouths and the blowhards but, as I said, I tend towards quietness and that did not prevent me from reaching the rank of sergeant in the Broughty Ferry Constabulary.

I was quiet when I arrived back at Elmgrove with Mr Sempill. Mr Sempill, on the other hand, was quite strikingly profane. There was profanity from the moment he saw the body. Profanity as he raised his handkerchief to his mouth and profanity as he stepped carefully around the lobby. Profanity muttered from behind his hand as he examined the scene, and then, when he passed out into the other rooms, he spoke in hushed whispers which, to my mind, he might have been better to save for when he was in the presence of that poor lady.

"That newspaper is an indication of the timing," he said. "A fifth edition. Find out when that's printed, what time of the day. Find out if she had it delivered or if it might have been purchased here or up in Dundee."

"It wasn't delivered," I said. "If it was delivered, there would be more of them at her back door."

"Quite right, quite right. So she must have been out on that day. But three weeks ago! Who would remember?"

Mr Sempill covered his mouth again, left the room, crossed the hall and went down the passage to the kitchen. There was a pantry, but it was almost bare of food, a tin of tea, some sugar, a small store of apples from her own trees and a paper bag with a scone in it, turned rock hard. In the scullery Mr Sempill pointed to a piece of towel flung on the draining board by the sink. It showed signs of having been used; there was a damp sort of discolouration in it and some dark spots that looked like blood.

"Here," he said, "he stood here and he washed off the blood. He was bloodied. And no wonder after that business out there."

We had not been long in the house when Broon called from the door to tell us that Suttie had arrived.

"Stay out there!" Mr Sempill said, and we traipsed through the hall again, past the poor dead woman and outside to where the others were waiting.

The joiner Coullie was sitting on the step looking unhappy and the Chief Constable said: "Mr Coullie, your services are no longer required here – for the moment. You may return home, but I am placing you under a solemn instruction to discuss nothing of what you have seen here, lest you prejudice a future prosecution. And I am instructing you to return here as soon as possible with a coffin and a decent conveyance for the transfer of the remains to the morgue in Dundee."

Coullie knuckled his cap insolently and went on his way, but before he reached the gate to the street, it opened and we could see the photographer Mr Rodger and the surveyor Mr Roddan arriving, each encumbered with the tools of his trade and, beyond them, a little knot of passers-by who had stopped to watch the show on their way to Divine Services.

Mr Sempill gave a nod to Constable Suttie and told him: "Secure that gate!" and Suttie went off like a rabbit, crunching down the gravel path in his big boots.

The Chief Constable welcomed the two gentlemen and thanked them for their service. He said: "You must steel your-selves. It's a Hellish scene, but I am convinced that, if we apply the most modern methods of investigation, we will be able, very shortly, to bring the culprit to book and have him face the awful penalty of the law.

"Mr Roddan, you would oblige me with a full and exact diagram of the hall where the victim is lying and you, Mr Rodger, a photographic record: an exact photographic record is essential. The body of that woman must by examined. She is the only witness to her own murder and we need whatever clue that she can offer us, but that work cannot begin until every scrap of evidence from the scene has been recovered and recorded."

And then he turned to me. "Sergeant Fraser," he said, "I'll have to away and inform Mr Mackintosh the Fiscal."

I told him about the telephone at the Swans'.

"No. This is police business. I'm relying on you to take charge here. Search the place – get the constables to help you if you need them. Be thorough but gentle. Thorough. I want the floors swept and the sweepings kept. Record everything. Modern methods, thoroughness, that's what this needs. I'm relying on you."

So I flung my chest out and saluted and got on with it.

And this is what I found. There was part of a gold earring lying on the floor within twelve inches of her feet and a small brooch lying within arm's length of the body to the south near the door, a pair of spectacles lying on the floor close beside her back and another gold brooch lying on her clothing at her back.

Going round that room, observing, noting, measuring – none too exactly, as I knew Mr Roddan would perform that task far more efficiently – I began to see, as if for the first time. The little bits of wreckage alone meant nothing, but together their whole story was laid out there for anybody who wanted to read it.

There was an upper set of false teeth lying on the right-hand corner of the doormat at the entrance to the drawing room. What a blow must have done that. And there was the lower set flung right across to the other side of the hall lying on the third step of the stair. Two blows in quick succession, back and fore, east and west, her face spinning, her neck snapping round – just to look at it and I could see it happening again as if before my eyes.

There was a shaped pad of sponge, wrapped in silk threads,

the kind of thing ladies use to pile their hair around to give a false and deceitful impression that their own is rather thicker and richer than in reality, lying at her back and partly covered by her clothing. Close by that was a lorgnette with its chain attached, the proof of her failing eyesight. A glass vase lay on the floor, unbroken, not a chip or a crack, where it had fallen from the hall table and close to the front door.

The gasolier that hung from the ceiling just where the vestibule enters the hall was missing one of its glass globes. How could that have happened? A wild swinging blow that smashed it to bits? Was it dislodged somehow in the struggle and shattered in the fall? In any event, it lay there, broken but carefully set aside, on a brass plate lying in the middle of the doorway to Miss Milne's drawing room.

Nearby there was a tangle of cut bay twigs, evidently intended for decoration – there was another bunch artistically arranged on another brass plate on the hall table, and on top of the twigs there was a lady's hat. It was full of blood. The hatpin was in it and it was bent and curved to the shape of her head. The hat trimming was torn off. You could see it lying under her body and trailing out behind her. It was practically covered in blood.

There was blood all over the carpet, four separate pools of it, one where the blood had poured from her head and face, and we found others when we got her body lifted and all round the hall there were the signs of ransack; two travelling cases, opened, one a Saratoga trunk – one of those things that looks like the pirate's treasure chest in adventure stories – and the other a tin cabin trunk hinged in two parts with one side for hanging garments and the other fitted with drawers. There were two handbags, a wine glass – unbroken – lay on the floor along with a cardboard box with bits of lace spilling out from it, and a broken poker. A broken poker with blood and hair sticking to it, the knob glinting out from those twigs on the floor, and the iron rod set aside on a little round table at the bottom of the stair. There was blood all over it, but, truth be told, a lot more of it on the brass knob. He held it the wrong way up and he hit her with the knob end until the knob flew off and then he stopped and he put it down there on the table. It was plain as day. Anybody could see it. The carving fork from the sideboard was lying on the floor, the sort of thing that comes in a case with a big knife and a sharpening steel. We found them later, a matched set of them, with horn handles.

The blood went up the stair. There was more of it on the carpet on the third step of the stair, and further up, on a broad landing, another bit of green curtain cord, like the bit that was tied round her ankles. Everywhere you looked, everywhere, the whole floor was bestrewn with spent matches – dozens of them.

And there was one other thing. At the turning of the stair, in the corner, there was a tall brass vase. It was full of piss and starting to stink. I emptied it down the sink, rinsed it out and put it back just exactly as I found it.

PLAN OF HALL OF MISS MILNE'S HOME WHERE HER BODY WAS FOUND.

PASSAGE TO FRONT DOOR

HEAD of POKER

BLOOD STAINS ON STAIRS

HAT

DOOR LEADING TO DINING ROOM.

WINEGLASS

TABLE

POKER with which injuries were inflicted.

TRUNK

BODY COVERED WITH SHEET.

CABIN TRUNK Miss Milne had been packing when attacked

RADIATOR

DOOR LEADING TO DRAWING-ROOM

DOOR LEADING TO SERVANTS ROOMS

TELEPHONE with WIRES CUT

5

DURING THE FORENOON Dr Sturrock arrived and had an examination of the body. Dr Sturrock is an unusually short man who favours a soft hat. He had been interrupted on his way to morning services and, not being a very diligent attender, he pleaded an emergency and left Mrs Sturrock at the door of the kirk and came away. Of course he had not thought to take his medical bag with him on such an outing, so he was forced to return to his home, gather such things as were needful and make his way – none too hurriedly I may say – to Elmgrove.

Dr Sturrock stopped in the vestibule and had private conversation with Chief Constable Sempill before joining me in the hall, where I stood guarding the body.

"Has she been moved?" he asked me.

"No, sir."

"Nothing has been touched or disturbed?"

"Nothing whatever, sir."

"Sergeant Fraser knows his duties, Doctor." Mr Sempill sounded very ill-mannered and not at all like himself, but I imagine the strains of the horrible discovery and the responsibilities weighing on his shoulders must have affected his temper. "Now, what can you tell me about this lady?"

Dr Sturrock got down on his hands and knees and turned his head. He was looking Miss Milne right in the face, which is a task I would not have envied him, and then, with a grunt and a loud exhaling of breath, he sat up again. "I identify this as the body of Miss Jean Milne of this address and I am prepared to certify death," he said.

The Chief Constable was furious. "Is that an attempt at humour, man?"

"What else would you have me say? The woman is clearly dead. At first glance it appears she died as a result of blunt force trauma to the skull – that is to say somebody beat her head in, likely with that bloodstained poker . . ."

"Not this bit of rock?" Chief Constable Sempill pointed to a large stone that was sitting on the tiled floor. Part of it had broken off and the broken corner was lying there beside it, the two wounds fresh and clean and new.

"It's a doorstop," said Dr Sturrock. "There's not a drop of blood on it. I cannot conjecture as to how it was broken, but it was definitely not the weapon in this case."

"Was there unpleasantness?"

Dr Sturrock got to his feet with a look of indulgent bafflement on his face and stood making notes in a little book with a silver pencil. "Unpleasantness? Unpleasantness? Look about you, man. The unpleasantness is before your very eyes. Speak Scotch or whistle, Chief Constable. You mean 'was she raped?' I can't tell that either, not without disturbing the body. We need to get her into the mortuary for a proper examination and even then it might not be easy. This poor soul needs to be got into a decent grave."

"How long has she been lying?"

"I can't tell. This time of year, not too warm, indoors, not too cool either, not exposed to the weather, not disturbed by animals, a couple, three weeks. But I can tell you one thing for sure and certain: it wasn't a robbery."

Mr Sempill snorted at him. "Do me the courtesy of not teaching me my trade, Doctor, and I will do my best not to teach you yours. Observe the open boxes, the travel cases, the handbags. There has obviously been a rough and frantic search for valuables."

But Dr Sturrock simply pointed with a flick of his pencil and said: "I count, one, two . . . six gold rings on the lady's fingers. The search for valuables may have been rough and frantic as you suggest, but it was none too diligent." He finished making his notes and said: "I'm sending for Templeman from Dundee. He knows his business and if the body's to be lifted to the mortuary then, by rights, it'll be under his jurisdiction."

"But this is a matter of great urgency!"

"Havers, man. This poor lady has been waiting for a good fortnight. She's in no rush. I'll away home for dinner – Mrs Sturrock has a choice bit of beef. I will return later with Dr Templeman. My best advice to you is to ensure that the photographer is finished with his work before we get back and disturb the scene any further."

And, with that, he snapped down the little brass catches in his portmanteau and went out the door again. But no sooner was he out the door than he opened it again and returned for a moment. "If it's any help to you, I can tell you this," he said. "She was definitely alive on October 16th. It was a Wednesday about dinner time, I'd say between half past twelve and one. I was on the tramcar, going along Strathern Road. Just before we got to Fairfield Road I looked up from my newspaper and saw Miss Milne."

"You're certain sure it was her," said Mr Sempill, "definitely on the 16th?"

"No doubt. You know yourself she was . . ." He hesitated. "Well, speak only good of the dead, but she was odd and she went about dressed, how to say it kindly . . . dressed awful young for her years." And then he said: "I'm away to my beef dinner. Good morning," and rattled the door shut behind himself.

I suppose that left the Chief Constable at something of a loose end, and because Dr Sturrock had spoken to him in a less than respectful manner, he decided to take it out on me and the constables.

He had us chasing round the place, beating the bushes in the garden, catching our uniforms on thorns, getting our knees muddy all in the hopes of finding some forgotten clue, another poker that the killer had chosen to discard in the undergrowth or, well I don't know what, and the worst part is neither did Mr Sempill. He was simply casting about for things to do because he had no idea what to do and, I'm sure, because he feared that he might be held to account for having failed to do something.

He ordered me to break Miss Milne's postbox and take out all her letters and sort them into three heaps: one for circulars, advertising materials, newsletters from the church or any societies she may have attended, another for bills and such like, and the last for personal and private correspondence, all arranged by date, all piled up on the kitchen table. I sat there with a wee butter knife from the drawer slicing the envelopes, taking out the letters, glancing through them, piling them up, each with its envelope, each in order. Miss Milne had a wide circle of correspondence. We knew she liked to travel because she would stop at the police office with the key to the small gate and tell us she was away here and there, off to London for weeks and months at a time or on wee trips to the Highlands, and there were letters from the folk she met on her travels. Letters from men.

"Have you not finished that, Fraser? Well stop anyway. I need you out there with me, knocking on doors. Some of the neighbours must have a notion of what's gone on here. Some of them must have noticed something or other."

I scraped the kitchen chair back from the table and put on my hat. I was following, loyally, I knew well enough my duty and yet the Chief Constable's bruised feelings were still chaffing and he urged me: "Come along, man, keep up. What are you waiting for?" in a tone that was neither respectful nor called for.

6

I AM SORRY to have to report that the Chief Constable's energetic plans came to nothing. We hurried down the path, Mr Sempill striding out in front with me coming behind like his wee terrier out for a walk, my hat not even properly on my head yet – and respectable dress is something an officer of the police must give a due and proper regard – but he had no sooner flung open the gate than we found our way blocked.

There was a sturdy man in a long grey coat standing right in the middle of the gateway, as if his hand had been on the handle the minute before the door opened. I knew him at once for Norval Scrymgeour, a reporter from the *Courier* up in Dundee. I've often seen him, hanging about or pushing in whenever there's a fire or a lost child or some other tragedy. I've even spoken to him once or twice up at the Sheriff Court when I've been called to give evidence. I don't say he's a bad man. He has a job to do and children to feed.

But there he was, standing like a mushroom under his brown bowler hat, and if Mr Sempill did not know him at once for a newspaper man, the photographer standing behind him, wrestling with a camera on a spider-leg frame, must surely have given it away.

I cannot say which of them, the Chief Constable or the reporter, got the biggest fright when that door swung open, but I can tell you who was the first to recover.

Have you ever seen a magic show where the conjurer boasts

that "the hand is quicker than the eye"? Well, to this day I don't know how it happened, but it seemed in a single movement the reporter had tipped his hat and produced a card, which he held out to Mr Sempill as a sign of his authority.

"Norval Scrymgeour," he said, "the *Courier*," as if that simple recitation was enough in itself to open the doors of Buckingham Palace. "Is Miss Milne dead?"

The Chief Constable was lost for words and he could think of no better reply than to shake his whiskers and say: "What? What?" before he turned and yelled back up the path for Constable Suttie to "get back here and secure this damned gate, as I ordered!" which was unfair as I had been present when he ordered both Broon and Suttie to search the gardens. Still, a moment or two of glowering and raging and a moment or two more spent filling the gate with his broad back gave the Chief Constable time to gather his thoughts, so when he turned back to face the reporter he had something to say.

"Now then," he glanced down at the pasteboard card in his glove, "Scrimshank."

"Scrymgeour."

"As you like. What are you doing here?"

"Simply investigating a report of a murder, Chief Constable. Have you anything to say?"

"Nothing at all."

"Have you absolutely no clue as to what happened? Not the slightest indication of the culprit?"

"Investigations are at an early stage."

"But you do have definite lines of inquiry, can I say that much?"

The Chief Constable simply glared at him.

"Can you at least confirm that the victim is Miss Jean Milne?"

"Who gave you that name?"

"We have our sources."

I looked at him and shook my head. "You mean the General Post Office Directory. Is that the height of your investigative powers?"

"Sergeant, that will do." I am sorry to say the Chief Constable was very short-tempered that day, but with a sort of defeated sigh he said: "You may write this. You may say that concerns having been raised for Miss Jean Milne, a spinster lady of this address, who has not been seen for some time, entry was effected by the police this morning. The body of Miss Milne was discovered in the house at about . . ." He looked at me.

"About 9.20."

"At about 9.20 a.m. and there is every appearance that the unfortunate lady has been the victim of a cruel and brutal murder. Investigations are continuing. Anyone with any information helpful to the inquiry is asked to communicate same to Chief Constable Sempill of Broughty Ferry Burgh Police at the police office in Brook Street."

Scrymgeour looked up from his notebook and said: "It's a damned shame. I saw her just the other day."

"You saw her? When did you see her? Think carefully, now, this could be vital."

"It's simple enough. It was Trafalgar Day, the 21st of October. Easy enough to remember. It was the day before my birthday. I saw her at the top of Reform Street. She was crossing over Meadowside as if she was going to the *Courier* office, but I don't know whether she went there or not."

"Are you sure it was her? How do you know her?"

"Well, I don't know her at all really. She's just one of those folk you see about the place, what you might call an eccentric. They increase the gaiety of the nation. Harmless enough. She was wearing a light dust-cloth cloak and a hat with some feathers in it. I was staying in St Andrews, and that date was the day before my birthday. That's what fixed the date in my mind, since I came to Dundee to get a few things for a celebration."

"A few things?"

"Aye, a few things. For a celebration. And I said to my wife: 'That's Miss Milne that lives all by herself in that big house in the Ferry. Would you take a look at her?' and she did and we had a wee laugh."

That offended me. "You laughed at her? And what was so amusing?"

"She was just . . . She stood out, you know what I mean. She always, you know, she dressed far too young. And not for the season. Not for the season at all. Far too light-coloured. And girlish. Like a young lassie."

The Chief Constable said: "You'll be required to swear a statement."

"Can we take a picture?"

"As you well know, if you do it from the street I am powerless to prevent it."

"Thank you, Chief Constable." He sounded a bit more humble now. "And will there be any further statement?"

Mr Sempill said: "You'll be kept informed." He nodded at Suttie as if to tell him to shut the gate and keep it shut, and that was just exactly what he did.

IT IS THE case – and I know this to be true because I have made enquiry at the public library – that the seasonal variations of every passing sunset will lengthen or shorten the day by three minutes. Three minutes. It seems so little, but those little amounts of minutes mount up. Half an hour every ten days. An hour every three weeks. In the summer the sky is barely darkened in the far north-west before it begins to glim again in the east, and in the winter it almost seems as if it's never light. I feel that sorely and I am conscious of those three minutes, every day that passes after June. Ere long it is the equinox and then I give myself up to darkness.

It was dark by five o'clock that Sunday afternoon and I was glad of that. When we carried her out of the house there was a decent blanket of darkness to cover our work.

The joiner Coullie came back with his cart and a coffin – not a proper coffin, you understand, as might have been seen in public at a funeral, not the sort of thing befitting the dignity of a lady like Jean Milne but what they call a "shell".

And it was a grim business lifting her into it I may tell you. Mr Procurator Fiscal was there to see it done, as was proper since he would be directing the inquiry and the prosecution, and Dr Templeman, the police surgeon of Dundee, who had come at the invitation of our own Dr Sturrock, was present to give his opinion on anything that might require an opinion, but he had no part in the work of it. That was down to the joiner Coullie, who made a profession of putting the dead in boxes, but it was more than one man could manage. Suttie and Broon tossed a coin for it out on the front step and Suttie must have lost since it was Suttie who came in to do the lifting. Miss Milne's head lay pointing to the front door, but Suttie was too wise for that and he made sure to take his stance at her feet.

With the shell lying close at her right-hand side, Coullie laid a towel across her head and bent to lift her by the shoulders, but she did not come easily. They had almost to prise her from the hall carpet, her hair, thick and matted with blood, her face glued to the floor, her clothes, starched and stiff with blood, set like plaster and that hideous sound of something being gently ripped apart as she came up.

They had no distance to lift her, perhaps eighteen inches, which was all it took to bring her clothing free of the mess of blood on the carpet, but her bloody clothes trailed down and her loose hair and her arms dragged, and with Suttie at her feet and Coullie at her head, her middle parts sagged, and the whole business was just, well, it wasn't bonny.

With the coffin at her right-hand side, they lifted her onto a long plank at her left.

"Down," Coullie said and then, "Lift," and they picked up the plank and carried her across the blackened carpet to the coffin, and Coullie, with a jerk of his head to indicate the direction, said: "Quick-smart now, tilt," and they tipped her into the coffin with a thump. Bits of her clothing stuck out of the top and over the sides, but Coullie tucked them in with a careless flick of the fingers and dropped the lid.

With the remains removed, Dr Sturrock stepped forward to take a look at the carpet, all covered in scabs as if the carpet itself had bled, and tufts and hanks of hair still sticking out if it.

"It would appear from this that the source of the bleeding is all at the head. All this," he pointed with his silver pencil at the lakes of blood soaked into the carpet, "it's all flowing from the same spot. I doubt we'll find other injury when we get her on the table."

Mr Mackintosh, the Fiscal, said: "This carpet is evidentiary," which we all very well understood without any advice from him, and the Chief Constable said: "Make sure this carpet is rolled carefully and labelled and numbered as a production," very briskly, which we also very well knew, but I suppose saying it made him feel better. I must admit, I was astonished at the Chief Constable's failure of nerve, as if he was afraid to go about his business and get on with doing something, lest folk should see him doing it and attack him for leaving something else undone. So I had been obliged to leave off going through the letters in order to begin inquiries with the neighbours, but that came to nothing when he was confronted with the newspaperman, and Broon and Suttie, who had been sent to beat the bushes, were, instead, made to do nothing more productive than securing the entrance.

Mr Mackintosh said: "Now that's done with, Sempill, I'd be glad if you would assist me in an examination of the premises."

Mr Sempill led him upstairs and we could hear them moving about quickly, from room to room, their footsteps echoing across the bare boards. "Quite abandoned," Mr Sempill said, coming back down the stairs, "as you can see for yourself. It seems she kept herself to these few rooms, the kitchen, the dining room, which she used as her sitting room, her bedroom and, well, the usual necessary facilities."

Mr Mackintosh put his head in at the dining room door. "A pie," he observed.

"Indeed," said Mr Sempill.

"The sideboard drawers have been rifled."

"They have been opened. I cannot say categorically 'rifled' nor can I say by whom."

Mr Mackintosh looked into the uppermost of the open drawers. "A carving set," he observed again.

"It's the match of the big fork in the lobby."

"What can that mean, I wonder."

And then they went into the lady's bedroom. There was the creak of a door opening. "Her wardrobe," Mr Mackintosh observed. "Has this been searched?"

"Certainly not!"

"Why not?"

"To what purpose? It's quite obvious that her clothes are in it."

"And what if the murderer had been in it too?"

"Hiding here amongst the mothballs for weeks while she rotted away in the lobby? I don't think that's likely."

"Something might have been removed."

"In which case, my men are unlikely to stumble upon it."

We heard the sound of a drawer sliding open and a few moments of muffled movement. "A purse," said Mr Mackintosh "and . . . seventeen gold sovereigns. Seventeen! A desperate man might think it worth risking the rope for seventeen pounds in good gold."

"Except the gold is still here," said Mr Sempill.

"But we cannot know how much more he took on his escape."

"Absence of evidence is not evidence of absence," said Mr Sempill. Returning to the lobby, he handed me the purse. "Seventeen gold sovereigns," he said. "Make sure they are recorded and numbered."

"They also are evidentiary," Mr Mackintosh said. "I suggest you begin again with a thorough and complete search of the premises as the next stage of your investigation."

But Mr Sempill said that would have to wait since, to him at any rate, the next step in the investigation was clear and that was to take the body of poor Miss Milne for proper examination in Dundee.

We got it on our shoulders, Suttie, Broon, Coullie and I, and we made our way down the short path to the gate, the light from the lanterns throwing up wild shadows everywhere, the wind sighing in the branches just as it had been the night before, the last leaves of autumn flying past our faces. We must have made a mournful sight. But then things became a little awkward, for the carriage gate was still locked and we had not yet found a key and the gate for foot passengers was not so broad as to admit two men walking side by side with a coffin between them, so we were obliged to ship her between us, as if she had been no more than an awkward parcel, and into the back of Coullie's cart, where the coffin could be decently covered with a tarpaulin.

Constable Suttie and I went in the cart to Dundee, he in the back with the coffin, sitting with his knees drawn up and his hands drawn in, careful not to touch it with even the toe of his boot though it had rested on his shoulder only a moment before, and I sat on the bench at the front alongside Coullie.

The Fiscal and the other gentlemen went ahead together in a conveyance of their own and we followed, going by Strathern Road, which is mostly flat, so as not to trouble the horse with going over the brae at the Harecraigs. All around us were the ordinary signs of a Sabbath evening, lights in houses, the sound of a piano from a distant parlour, folk going about on their way to evening observances or to visit friends. Everything was peaceable and respectable, all as it should be, and behind us, under that sheet of sailcloth, we carried the body of Jean Milne with its head cracked open and its jaws all agape.

Coullie's cart rolled quietly over the hammered roads of Broughty Ferry, but before long we were in Dundee, with its black mill chimneys, its public houses on every corner – roaring even on the Sabbath – and its stinking courts and vennels and tenements packed to the gunnels, rattling and bumping over the granite cobbles all way through the town to Bell Street. You know it well enough, I'm sure, with the fine court building in the square at the west end and, next to that, the jail and the police offices and, a little further along, the new burial ground. That was where Coullie stopped the cart.

"We'll be needing the key." It was the first thing he'd said to me all the journey.

I suppose, as the senior man, I could have sent Suttie, but on the other hand, as the senior man, it was fitting and appropriate that I should go to the Dundee Police offices and sign for the key, and when the choice was walk a few yards or sit under the flaring gas lamps with that tragic cargo, I was not sorry to leave my place in that cart.

When I returned with the key, the gentlemen were waiting at the gates of the burial ground and there was another with them who was not introduced to me, but I recognised him for Professor Sutherland from the Medical School, who is quite a figure in the town and, as it turned out, not so much of a scientist and a seeker after truth as Broughty Ferry's own Dr Sturrock.

I must have made an awful sight, like something from a penny dreadful, as I stood under the yellow gaslight, struggling with the padlock on a graveyard under a waning moon, but eventually the chains rattled free and the iron gates opened. I waited for Coullie's cart and locked the gate behind it, and by the time I had caught up, walking alone through the lines of graves, Professor Sutherland had opened the doors of the mortuary.

It was dark in the burial ground and yet not unaccountably so. We had a half-moon that rolled out from behind the ragged clouds, dim street lamps along the cemetery edge that showed the shadowed railings or the glint of polished marble, weeping angels, broken pillars, half-draped urns carved in stone all of the most fashionable design, but the open door of that squat little brick building held a different kind of darkness. Professor Sutherland stepped into that open doorway and it consumed him utterly until, a second or two later, there came the scratch and flare of a match and the hiss of the gas lamps lighting.

Coullie stood at the back of the cart. At the front, Suttie bent over double and heaved and scraped the coffin towards him until there was enough of it protruding to let us drag it off the cart and into the building. We laid it on the brick floor beside a contraption that was halfway between a bed and a bath, made of enamel-glazed stoneware and raised on a pedestal to bring it to the height of a table, but with a deep lip on it, so it might be hosed down if need be.

The professor and Dr Templeman hung up their hats and coats on pegs at the back wall and took down long rubber aprons and red rubber gloves that came up past their elbows, and the rest of us hung back at a respectful distance, including Dr Sturrock, who carried no authority while the body lay in Dundee. Even Coullie was not any longer wanted since Dr Templeman had sent for an attendant of his own from the Royal Infirmary.

For my part, I was more than content to leave them to deal with the business of lifting the body and I stayed well back, close to the door. If it had been permitted, I would have remained in the graveyard or begun the long tramp back to the Ferry, where the air at least was clean. I cannot describe what it was like in that mortuary, with the light of the flaring gas lamps shining back from the white tiled walls and those men, though they worked in silence, grunting and gasping as they heaved that poor woman's body around. The stench was beyond belief. From the moment they lifted the lid on the coffin, the stink of death began to creep out into the room and, once they had her lifted on the table, Dr Templeman turned to the Procurator Fiscal and said: "Gentlemen, normally it would not be permissible, but, in the circumstances, you may smoke."

Mr Mackintosh the Fiscal had his pipe going in no time and Mr Sempill wasn't far behind. Suttie and Coullie both sparked up, but, I don't know, I hadn't the stomach for it. It felt disrespectful. I simply stood there through it all, watching, saying nothing but breathing deep of the scented smoke.

They took off her clothes, but they were not gentle. They were cold towards her. They kept their faces turned from her. They took deep, gasping gulps of air and breathed through their mouths. Every item, as it was removed, was listed and described and dropped in a hamper.

"The body of this lady is tied at the ankles by green curtain cord, which I remove by cutting, taking care not disturb the knot. I remove a pair of shoes.

"A new cloak, bloodstained.

"A linen blouse with lace attached, ditto.

"A camisole or slip body."

They pulled her arms up and twisted them to get her clothes off, and at every move her poor, blackened, battered head lolled and flopped about so she seemed to be looking for comfort in each of their faces in turn, but none of them would look at her.

"Three knitted spencers.

"A pair of corsets.

"A linen chemise.

"A flannelette chemise.

"A blue serge skirt."

Dr Templeman's assistant went down to her feet and hauled it off her.

"A knitted petticoat."

They had to lift her up by the hips.

"A pair of linen drawers."

She was as good as naked. Girlish. Like a young lassie.

"A pair of stockings and a pair of garters."

The worst of it was done. Dr Templeman's assistant stood with his notebook ready and the great man said: "Gentleman, the discolouration of the skin clearly shows that she has lain on her face since death. The bodily fluids sink downwards due to the effects of gravity, so the skin is pale and blanched on her back and it has taken on this bruised appearance on the front."

He lifted her arms, each in turn. "There are no visible cuts or wounds on the hands or forearms, no signs of a struggle or an attempt at self-defence."

The professor nodded. "I concur." And then he lifted up a knife and he cut her throat. He cut her throat. He cut her throat and he pushed his fingers into the wound.

"The hyoid bone is intact."

He took his fingers out of her throat and Dr Templeman opened the wound and put his fingers in.

"I concur. That means, gentlemen, that this lady was not strangled. The hyoid bone is a small structure in the upper part of the throat. In the event of strangulation it is invariably broken."

The professor said: "I can see no possible advantage in examination of the internal organs."

Dr Templeman said: "I concur." And then, as if to justify himself, he said: "There are no signs of any external injury other than the obvious blow to the head. She was not stabbed.

Decomposition is advanced. The internal organs are unlikely to offer anything useful at this late stage."

The Procurator Fiscal plucked up the courage to stop sucking on his pipe for just long enough to ask: "How long, exactly?"

"Hard to say," said the professor: "Have you any idea when she was last seen?"

"We have witness statements confirming that she was definitely alive on the 21st."

"Only eleven or twelve days. Not impossible."

"I concur." said Dr Templeman. "Not impossible."

The Chief Constable said: "Dr Sturrock suggested she may have lain as long as three weeks."

"Out of the question," they said together. "Oh, out of the question."

Dr Sturrock did not seem at all offended by that, but he took his pipe out of his mouth and pointed to the body with the stem of it, as he had with his silver pencil before, and he said: "Would you be good enough to examine the underside of the body?"

"The underside?"

"Aye. Her back."

Dr Templeman and the professor gave each other a look and, gripping the poor woman by the shoulder, they tipped her over a little, but before they could turn her, the body gave a gurgle and a belch that had everybody puffing hard on their tobacco again. "There are a few minor, post-mortem injuries on the lady's back."

"Post-mortem?"

"Yes, Doctor, definitely post-mortem. Minor scratches, no doubt caused during the transportation of the body from the scene."

"I concur," said the professor.

"I see. And those wounds on the breast. There. Yes. Those. Those two holes there."

"Maggots," said the professor.

"Undoubtedly," said Dr Templeman. "The emergence of maggots. The all-conquering worm."

That gave me a shudder and then the Chief Constable leaned close and whispered in Dr Sturrock's ear and the good doctor muttered: "You're obsessed, man," but then he said: "Is there any indication as to whether the deceased was criminally assaulted?"

They leaned across her body, the two of them, in a way that was indecent even for a doctor, and the professor said: "There is not."

"There is not," said Dr Templeman. "But you might have known that by her limbs being tied together. Gentlemen, we can say conclusively that this lady was murdered by a number of blows to the head, any one of which might have been fatal, almost certainly using the poker found at the scene. She was attacked from behind, the blows falling here and here," he made chopping motions with the edge of his hand against his assistant's head, "and here. She made no attempt to defend herself, so, mercifully, the attack came as a surprise for which she was unprepared. The cause of death is shock, occasioned by haemorrhage brought on by a series of blows to the head. And now, the last kindness we can do for this poor soul is to get her in the ground as quickly as possible."

The great men got on with the business of dropping their rubberised gloves into buckets and dumping their aprons and scrubbing at their hands with great blocks of blood-red carbolic soap and the rest of us left Coullie to his work and went out into the clean and decent night, where the November wind scoured away at least something of the stink. Mr Mackintosh the Fiscal walked with Dr Sturrock and Chief Constable Sempill. Suttie and I stayed at an appropriately respectful distance, but I heard every word. Or almost every word.

Mr Mackintosh said: "You do understand the gravity." And he said: "Must be seen to."

The Chief Constable agreed, over and over, strongly and repeatedly.

Mr Mackintosh said: "I don't think you're equipped. I insist."

And, at that, Mr Sempill flew up in a temper. "No. Absolutely not. No. Impossible."

"I must insist."

They stopped walking, so Suttie and I stopped walking too, but Mr Sempill was no longer making any attempt to speak privately. "You can insist," he said, "but you cannot instruct, and I may tell you no Dundee detective will set foot in Broughty Ferry. The magistrates will not tolerate it and I will not tolerate it. I will telegraph to Glasgow in the morning, but I'm damned if I will let a Dundee man anywhere near my investigation."

Mr Mackintosh, standing on his dignity, said: "Then see that you do. I bid you goodnight," and he walked off through the cemetery gates.

8

IN THESE MODERN times, I may assure you, the police make use of the most modern methods. Do not imagine that the Broughty Ferry Constabulary has no resources to draw upon beyond the boundary of the burgh. Nothing could be further from the truth.

First thing on the Monday morning, the 4th of November 1912, our own Mr Sempill communicated with Chief Constable Stevenson of Glasgow by the police telegraph, asking him to let us have the services of a detective officer to assist in investigating the murder.

Later in the forenoon Mr Stevenson communicated by telephone to inform us that he was despatching Detective Lieutenant John Trench with the train from Glasgow. Mr Sempill was highly delighted by the news since John Trench was a figure in police circles after his great success when he hunted down the killer of poor Miss Marion Gilchrist, a wealthy woman beaten to death in her own home in what the papers called "The Oscar Slater Case".

"He has an enviable record," said Mr Sempill. "Wasn't he the very man who traced that vicious little Jew in just exactly the same circumstances? We must make every arrangement to welcome him."

But we were not idle in the meantime. No indeed, very far from that. Along with the photographs recording the scene, Mr Sempill collected a *carte de visite* from the studio of the photographer Mr Rodger, which Mr Rodger had earlier prepared for Miss Milne, and he took it, together with the negative glass, along to the offices of the *Broughty Ferry Guide and Gazette*, where they used it on a poster, produced at the expense of Burgh Police. I reproduce it faithfully below.

About 9.20 am on Sunday 3rd November, 1912, Miss JEAN MILNE was found murdered in the hall of her house at Elmgrove, a large mansion house standing in extensive grounds in this Burgh.

Miss Milne resided alone at the above address and was a lady of eccentric habits, having few friends or visitors. She frequently left home for long periods and went to London, sometimes without intimating her intention of doing so to any one. The last time she is believed to have visited London was on 9th April, 1912, when she remained away until 2nd August, 1912. On that occasion she stayed at the Palace Hotel, Strand. She was last seen alive on or about 21st October, 1912.

The murder appears to have been of a brutal nature, the deceased lady being badly battered about the head and arms with a poker which was found beside the body. Her feet were tied with a curtain cord and the wires of the telephone, which is situated in the hall where the body was found, were cut.

The whole affair is at present a mystery and, although a considerable quantity of valuable jewellery and money was found in the house and on the person of the deceased lady, nothing appears to have been disturbed.

Any information likely to lead to the elucidation of the murder will be gratefully received by the subscriber.

J. HOWARD SEMPILL
Chief Constable
Burgh Police Office
Broughty Ferry
4th November, 1912

Anybody looking at it might see for themselves that the picture of the late Miss Milne at the top of the handbill is worse than useless and may as well have been drawn in mud. I also disapproved, privately, of the terms in which it was written, for it was already obvious that Miss Milne had met her end long before October 21. There was the evidence of the *Evening Telegraph* lying, unread, on the table under a half-eaten mutton pie. Was it likely she would have left that to lie about for days? And, forebye all that, had the Chief Constable not had me go through her letters? The postbox had been untouched for three weeks until I broke it open with my own hand, and the earliest letter in it was stamped October 15, the morning after the newspaper. Why would Miss Milne ignore the letters piling up for a week? No, if anyone had asked me I would have told them confidently that she died long before Dr Sturrock or the reporter claimed to have seen her on the street, but my opinion was not sought and, in any event, the content of that advertisement mattered but little. The whole of the Ferry was already abuzz with talk of the murder, long before the typesetters of the *Guide and Gazette* had their handbills on the street, and Mr Sempill's efforts were, it must be said, far surpassed by the work of Norval Scrymgeour. His report, which in truth reported very little since there was very little to report, nonetheless filled up two full columns in the middle pages of that morning's *Courier*. Nothing so vulgar as news has ever been known to figure on the front page of the *Courier*. That is reserved for commercial advertisements.

But nobody in the Ferry was reading the advertisements that day. We had a constant stream of callers at the front counter and telephone calls which must have numbered well into double figures, each and all of them with something to say about Miss Milne. We were nearly overwhelmed. It was all we could do to note down their names and addresses and record them for future interview, so we were not short of work.

And then at the back of three o'clock, Mr Sempill instructed me to accompany him to Dundee, where we were to meet Detective Lieutenant Trench off the train.

We arrived at the West station with plenty of time in hand and so, rather than stand out on the platform in the biting wind, I followed Mr Sempill into the waiting room, where there was a good fire going, but before we even had our gloves off, the better to warm our hands, Mr Sempill gave out a groan. He was standing, looking out the window, and I followed his gaze and there on the platform was the reporter Scrymgeour and that same photographer trotting along behind with his camera on its long stand.

"How in God's name—"

"Dundee, sir," I said. "They are no respecters of confidences."

"Or the Fiscal. Between them they want to show us up any way they can, damn them."

"Do you want me to see them off, sir?"

"I'm sure their platform tickets are in order, Sergeant Fraser. Leave them be."

Mr Sempill got on with the business of looking deep into the coals, washing his hands over and over in the glow of them, while I kept an eye on the platform, and we had not long to wait before the Glasgow train arrived, trailing long bride's ribbons of steam and mourning bands of smoke, and in among the throng of folk there was one we took at once for Detective Lieutenant Trench.

He was a fine, tall, well-set-up man, but that's not unusual amongst the police, where a man is expected to be able to hold his own, and he could certainly grow a moustache. He carried an umbrella with a kind of military air and, well, he stood out. If you asked me to describe him in a phrase, the phrase I'd choose would be "beef-fed". We should have been on the platform to make ourselves known to him, but since we were as good as hiding in that waiting room, the reporter Scrymgeour had already buttonholed him by the time we were out the door.

And that was where we got the measure of Detective Lieutenant John Trench, for while meeting Norval Scrymgeour had left Mr Sempill at a loss for words, Mr Trench met him with a laugh and walked past him with never a second glance. He put down his suitcase a step or two away from the Chief Constable, held out his hand and said: "Detective Lieutenant Trench reporting, sir."

Mr Sempill shook his hand. "Glad to see you," he said. "This is Sergeant Fraser," and I shook his hand and knew him at once for a brother of the Craft.

But Scrymgeour was determined to intrude himself and he tried to draw attention, repeating "Chief Constable? Chief Constable? Detective Trench?" until Mr Sempill lost patience and snapped at him: "What do you want? You were told you'd be kept informed of developments."

"Yes, Mr Sempill. And are there developments?"

"You might very well see for yourself that there are, indeed, developments. The investigation is continuing apace and with the assistance of this gentleman, trained in the most modern and scientific methods of detection, you may be assured that the culprit responsible for this dreadful crime will very soon be brought to justice and held accountable for his vile actions, to the extent of the direst penalty open to the law."

It took Scrymgeour a moment or two to catch up with his scribblings, so, without even looking up from his notebook, he said: "You were responsible for the conviction of Oscar Slater for the murder of Miss Gilchrist, Mr Trench. The Glasgow tragedy has, in some respects, a great similarity to that now under review – an old lady of means cruelly done to death. Have you anything you would like to add, Mr Trench?"

"No." And that was all he said, which increased him greatly in my esteem.

Then without so much as a tip of the hat, we left. "The next train is not for half an hour," Mr Sempill said. "We'll take the car and I will brief you on the way."

There was a tram for Broughty Ferry waiting at the halt, and we sat outside, for the sake of privacy, Mr Sempill and John Trench in the very back seat while I sat two rows forward, discouraging anyone else from joining us.

When we were driving and as private and secluded on the top of that tram as if we had been locked in the back cell of Broughty Ferry police station, Mr Sempill said: "Your Chief Constable must have outlined to you the circumstances of the case already. Let me add a few things."

He handed over a large brown envelope, which Mr Trench carefully opened. He took out a photograph of the murder scene, printed on heavy card, which Mr Rodger had stamped with "Rodger Photographic Studios, Brook Street, Broughty Ferry" in flowing gold script across one corner, just as he would have done with a lady's portrait or a view of the castle. Mr Trench examined it intently for a few moments, paying especial attention to Miss Milne's head.

"Has the body been removed?"

"That was necessary, yes," said Mr Sempill.

"Nothing else?"

"No, it's all exactly as you see it there."

"Pardon me, sir. The carpet."

"What about the carpet, Sergeant Fraser?"

"You ordered it should be rolled up and removed, sir."

"But you've not done that already, man?"

"It was done last night, sir. While we were in Dundee for the post-mortem. On your order, sir."

"But I didn't mean there and then!" He turned to Mr Trench. "The Fiscal. It was the Fiscal who ordered it. He was there for the lifting of the body."

"Of course."

"I simply . . ."

"It doesn't matter. It's all recorded here. These things happen."

Mr Trench dipped back into the envelope and came out with a folded sheet of paper: Mr Roddan's plan of the murder scene, very neatly done in ink, with a proper scale marked down two sides.

Mr Trench said: "In the normal course of things, the first hours of an investigation are crucial, but since the lady has been dead for so long, that hardly applies. Your man is either long gone or so sure of himself that he has simply returned to the normal routine of his life. Either way, we'll winkle him out."

He folded the map again and laid it on the bench at his side with the photograph on top, the blank cardboard side uppermost to shield it from view, and then he took from the envelope the surgeons' report. "Excuse me," he said. "A moment, if you please."

Mr Trench was absorbed in the report for a few moments and, in truth, a few moments was all it took. I had seen the report that morning, indeed I placed it in the envelope, and, aside from the lengthy preamble setting out the two doctors' great number of qualifications, it said almost nothing beyond the fact that Miss Milne had died from a series of blows to the head.

"Is this all?" Mr Trench said.

The Chief Constable said: "Not at all. We have not been idle in Broughty Ferry. There is also this," and he produced from his pocket a folded copy of the handbill which he had prepared that day. I'm near certain I saw more than one of them blowing past us on the chill November wind as we drove.

Mr Trench added it to his little bundle, saying: "This will be very useful," in the indulgent tone of a disappointed father and then, with a little sigh, he added: "I see you've let it be known that the deceased lady was tied up."

"Yes. Well. I. Was I wrong to do so?"

Mr Trench carefully folded everything back into the brown envelope. "What can you tell me about her?" he asked.

"Oh, I'd say a respectable woman, well known in the community, devoted to church affairs," said Mr Sempill.

"Family?"

"No, a maiden lady."

"Yes, I gathered as much, but had she family living nearby?"

"No, completely alone."

"No staff."

"Not even a lassie, nor a woman coming in."

"That's odd."

"You might say that exactly," said Mr Sempill. "But she was odd." I think Mr Trench caught me giving the Chief Constable a look.

"But comfortably off?"

"Apparently so. As you may see from the report, we discovered quite a pile of cash in the house. So, yes, comfortably off, so far as we can tell. Thus far."

"You've made no inquiry of her bankers?"

"The body was discovered on a Sunday, Trench. The banks were shut."

Mr Trench took out his watch and consulted it. "And now it's past four o'clock and the banks are shut for another day."

"She certainly never gave any indication of being short of money. She liked to travel. She was always going away on trips here and there – wasn't she, Sergeant?"

"Yes, sir," I said.

"And she would alert your office before she left?"

"As a matter of routine. The house was regularly patrolled – several times every day. That's how we know she's been at home since August."

"But she was gone for months. Was she visiting somebody?"

Mr Sempill looked at me with a frown. "Sergeant?"

"I'm sorry, sir, I have no idea."

"Well, that's something to be looking into, I suppose," a remark which I thought remarkable for its generosity.

In the small number of minutes that it took for the car to reach the top of Fairfield Road, Mr Sempill and I explained all that we had discovered of the killing, the money found in the house, the great amount of correspondence which had first raised the alarm and which now must be gone through, all the tiny bits of circumstance which, together, amounted to almost nothing. And then, since ours was the next stop, we made our way downstairs with Mr Trench insisting on carrying his own bag. It was but a short step from Strathern Road to the gates of Elmgrove, where we saw Constable Suttie standing at his post with a fallen leaf stuck to his helmet.

Mr Sempill brushed past him, saying: "Smarten yourself up, man," and he led the way through the small gate.

"There are some things I'd like to show you," he said.

But Mr Trench said: "Please show me nothing. I'd prefer to look with fresh eyes." He went off down the path that led to the ruined garden, head up like an animal scenting the air, looking at everything, noting everything. Would you believe he went so far as to count the number of chimney cans? I saw him standing there, sinking into the mossy grass and picking them out against the western sky and noting them down in his notebook. He examined the fern house and the conservatory and the vinery, all of them dirty and dusty and broken down, their glass broken, the fine tiled floors strewn with broken pots and rubbish, piles of dried leaves whispering in the corners.

"We have made a thorough investigation of all the outbuildings and gardens," said Mr Sempill.

Mr Trench said: "I do not doubt you for a moment. But I would like to see with my own eyes."

He carried on round the house, looking, looking, looking, rattling at doors, pressing through neglected bushes that brushed their damp fingers against the dirty windows, down the stairs to the back court and the iron postbox with its broken lock and the shattered glass where Coullie had forced a way in.

Mr Trench found nothing. We had found nothing and he found nothing. When he returned at last to where he had begun, the Chief Constable was standing at the door, ready to lead the way, but Mr Trench said: "If you please. Fresh eyes."

I suppose Mr Sempill realised he had called for help because he had not the skills nor the wit to do the job for himself, so he simply turned the key in the lock, opened the door, stepped aside with a modest good grace and said no more than: "Of course."

When Mr Trench dropped his case on the floor of the vestibule, the whole house rang with that same sad, empty echo I had heard when first I tried the door, two nights before. His umbrella clattered on the tiles. The noise of it, like a gunshot going off, set the crows complaining from the trees that lined the garden and they whirled round the house in the gathering shadows and settled again in the branches, trailing a little more darkness in their wings when they came. It was a mischancy place.

We held back a little, as we had been bid, but I heard Mr Trench inside, the soles of his boots moving on the bare boards of the hall where the carpet had lain beneath her body, grit and dust grinding under his feet as he felt his way to the gas, the rattle of a matchbox in the darkness, the scratch and flare, the hiss of gas, the pop of its lighting, the glow of it flushing across the room like dawn – not like the electric lamps that are so commonplace now, that come on with a flash and fill the whole room in an instant with their cruel light.

Though it was not yet fully dark, Mr Trench went round the lobby, lighting every lamp as we stood together, the Chief Constable and I, watching from the vestibule doorway.

He had the envelope in his hand again and he had taken Mr Rodger's photograph from it. He stood near the corner of the room, in just the place where Mr Rodger had set up his tripod, and he held the photograph before his eyes until it matched the scene in front of him, up and down, the picture, the room, the picture, the room, matching and comparing, checking, looking with an artist's eye.

"And she lay exactly here." He pointed in a long line across the boards. "Just as you see in the picture. Was the gas lit?"

"Not when we found her," I said.

"Then, it happened in the daytime? But I suppose that signifies nothing. He could easily have turned it off when he left. Would he do that? Why would he do that? Where is her sitting room?"

But before either of us could answer, he set off at a trot and found it for himself. "Here. And the table. And the lamp." He picked it up and shook it gently. "Empty. Burned dry. So, if it happened at night, he could have left it burning and walked out the door."

"She has the gas in," said Mr Sempill. "Maybe she forgot to fill the lamp. She had no need of it. Maybe it's been dry for months."

"Maybe. Maybe. You could be right. I have no idea. I'm attempting to fill in the gaps. I'm inventing. I'm making up stories, that's all. One of them might fit."

"And this is your investigative technique? You might have done as well making up stories sitting on your lavvy back in Glasgow, man!"

"We've not begun yet," Mr Trench said. He was trying to be respectful.

The shadows were creeping closer round the old house. Mr Trench reached up and lit the gasolier that hung over Miss Milne's table and the glow of it shone back from the big, mirrored sideboard.

"These drawers were like this, half opened, when you found them?"

"Exactly as you see them, sir."

"And the carving set? Open and on view, just like this?"

"Nothing has been moved, sir."

He looked at the half-eaten pie on its plate and he looked at the newspaper it sat on. He turned his head to look at the date. "I see," he said. "In the fireplace. Why hasn't that been removed?"

"What, sir?"

"That cigar stub."

I looked and he was right. There was a cigar stub poking out of the ashes. The Chief Constable was gaping into the grate, half astonished, half embarrassed.

Mr Trench said: "To judge by the label, that's a Romeo y

Julieta. You might pay a shilling or more for a cigar like that. And it's still there, so the ashes were cold when it went into the fireplace. Did Miss Milne smoke a cigar?"

"Not as far as I've ever heard, sir."

"The notes you gave me suggest she was in the tobacco trade."

"Oh, that was long years ago," said Mr Sempill. "I think we can say this is not old stock left lying about the place."

Mr Trench said: "I see. Fire tongs, shovel, no poker. It's outside."

"Yes, sir. Broken in half."

And then he was on the move again. "The bedroom is . . . Here! Bed dishevelled, but she kept no maid. Wardrobe. Just as it was found?"

Mr Sempill said: "You may take it from me that everything is just as it was found. Everything. My men know their jobs, Trench."

"And you recovered the bag of coin from this drawer?"

"That very drawer. The Fiscal and I were making investigation."

"Was it well hidden? How long did it take to find it?"

"A matter of seconds, man. He opened the drawer, put his hand in and came out with the purse. It lay there," Mr Sempill pointed, "on top of her linen."

"So, not hidden at all. I see. Back to the hall." He was off again. He almost trotted out of the bedroom, stooping to examine the piles of dried twigs lying on the table and in the doorway, the poker, in its two parts, the broken rock at the cloakroom door, the garden secateurs, everything, minutely. And then, as if in answer to some far-off call that neither of us could hear, he broke off and bounded down the kitchen passage. Mr Trench had his Vesta case out again and he was lighting the kitchen lamps and then, with that done, he sat down at the table and began to disturb the piles of letters I had spent so long sorting.

"You were right about the great amount of correspondence. Is there anything of interest?"

"I've not had an opportunity to go through it all perfectly, sir," I said.

"Never mind. You've made a good start, Fraser. And now," as if he was stopping to draw breath, "I noted the blood spots on the carpet of the third tread of the stair."

"Yes, that has been noted," said Mr Sempill.

"And, close by, more blood on the railings – with hair attached and further spots of blood on the wall at the foot of the stair, together with the blood smears on the finger plate on the hall door – that will have to be removed for forensic examination."

"All noted," said Mr Sempill.

"And, from where I'm sitting now, I see a towel by the sink, clearly stained as if by blood."

"Already noted. I discovered that myself, Trench. The culprit obviously washed blood off his hands."

"And that bit of paper on the floor."

"It's a bit of paper, Trench. A bit of paper."

I got down on my knees and reached under the sink. "There's blood on it, sir."

"Blood?"

"Looks like finger marks, sir. Three finger marks." I carried the scrap of paper to the kitchen table and I laid it down in front of Mr Trench, like a dog bringing game to his master. We all looked at it for a while, none of us saying anything. He was in the room with us. These were marks that he had made. This was the shape of his fingers. These were the fingers that held the poker. This was the hand that beat Jean Milne to death, and he had come into this kitchen and put his hand down on that little bit of paper, without thinking, without even noticing, and he stood at that sink and washed the blood away. But he left the paper. It was proof that he was there.

"This could put a rope round somebody's neck," said Mr Sempill.

"It might at that." Mr Trench took a plain, greaseproof envelope from his pocket and very gently, with the tips of two fingers and being careful not to touch the blood, he tucked the scrap of paper inside. "We can have that down to Scotland Yard tomorrow, the day after at the latest. They have finger-print men there who can do miracles."

He looked up from his work, smiling: "We're making progress already, gents."

The Chief Constable was pleased too. "I promised them modern policing and modern, scientific method and, by God, that's what they're going to get."

"But we're not done yet," said Mr Trench. "The rooms upstairs."

"Entirely empty."

"Astonishing. A house this size would need at least three servants, gardens like that – with all that glass – a man and a boy, at least. And yet she lived in just these rooms, entirely alone. Let's take a look anyway."

"The rooms have all been swept, as Mr Sempill ordered," I said. "And the sweepings preserved for your examination."

"Did you discover anything?"

"Dust and mouse droppings, sir."

We came out of the kitchen corridor and back into the hall. The carpet, with its odd, black stains soaked through it, was standing rolled and tied with string in the far corner of the room. Everything else was just as it had been. There were marks on the floorboards and each of us in turn was careful to avoid them as we passed on our way to the stair. The gaslight glinted back from her false hair where it lay against the skirting board, the cut cables of the telephone prodded the air. There was the gluey lump of blood and hair on the bannister rail, there was the dark mark on the stair carpet, the landing, the turn up the stair, the second piece of curtain cord, left exactly where it was found, exactly where it featured on Mr Roddan's drawing, and then the upper landing and darkness.

But the rooms were not empty. Not entirely empty and the darkness was not complete. There at the end of the corridor, the silent dance of candlelight and, in the glow of the candles, Miss Milne lying in her coffin.

It was a scene I found greatly affecting: to think that she lay there now, on this last night, in the house where she had lived and died, where perhaps in that very room she had slept as a child, surrounded by the homely comforts of a loving family and where now she slept alone, as we all must do.

I am sorry to have to report that the Chief Constable again gave way to profanity and blamed the joiner Coullie for having done his work too well and without informing the police of his actions.

"She's to go to Barnhill in the morning," he told Mr Trench. "I'm afraid there was no possibility of delay."

"Then I should see her," Mr Trench said.

The Chief Constable looked at me and I looked at him and Mr Sempill said: "My best advice is not to bother. She's been dead for weeks. For God's sake, leave her alone. The doctors' report will tell you all you need to know."

But Mr Trench insisted. "I don't relish it, but it is my duty. I understand if you prefer to stand apart."

We did stand apart. Neither Mr Sempill nor I ventured over the threshold of that room, and if either of us had shown a shred of good sense, we would have waited out in the garden while Mr Trench got on with his work. But it did not seem right to abandon him entirely, so, instead, we stood in the shadows of the corridor, not talking, trying not to breath. We heard Mr Trench try to lift the coffin lid, but Coullie had already screwed it down.

The click of his pocketknife opening. The long business of turning the screws. His breathing as he lifted the lid, the wooden sound as he propped it against the wall and then the stench, everything that had been trapped inside that box for a night and a day coming pouring out. It seemed to seep from the room in a gasp that dipped the candles as it passed and Mr Trench, poor Mr Trench, was in the middle of it.

After a few moments we heard him replace the lid and begin to replace the screws and, before long, he came out of the room, wiping his fingers on his handkerchief. I was glad that we could not see his face in the shadows.

"We may be not much closer to catching the man who did this," he said, "but from all we have seen, from all you have told me and from all my experience, I can tell you this for a certainty: no sane Britisher did this. A murder of this cruelty and ferocity and brutality could have been committed only by a maniac or a foreigner."

9

I DOUBT THAT you can properly imagine Mr Sempill's relief and delight when he heard those words: "A maniac or a foreigner."

There were no maniacs in Broughty Ferry – or none that we knew of and, even if some poor soul had escaped from a shameful, private confinement, they would surely be held blameless on account of their madness. Better still, if they were blameless, then we of the Broughty Ferry Constabulary and, especially, its Chief Constable must be equally blameless.

But a foreigner! A foreigner was a Heaven-sent blessing. A foreigner was beyond the control of anybody. The magistrates and ratepayers of Broughty Ferry could never hold the force responsible for the actions of a foreigner, and, best of all, he must have left the burgh as quickly as he came, unseen and unnoticed, and we could, all of us, sleep soundly in our beds.

First thing in the morning, when I arrived at the police office, I found Constable Suttie sitting at the police telegraph with Mr Sempill standing over him dictating a warning that: "Following the murder of Miss Jean Milne of Elmgrove, Broughty Ferry, information is sought on any foreigner coming to the notice of the police."

I know these days, after Dr Crippen was hunted down in the middle of the ocean, after help was sent racing to those poor souls on the *Titanic*, such a thing is regarded as a commonplace, but I still think of it as a kind of miracle that communication can be achieved instantly from one end of the country to another in moments. From the extremes of these islands and, if needs be, across the breadth of the Empire, men could be put on their guard, thousands of pairs of eyes watching for our killer.

But beyond "a maniac or a foreigner" they had little enough to go on, so Mr Sempill set us to finding out.

"Fraser, from now on you are to consider yourself as Mr Trench's right-hand-man. Abandon all other duties. Make yourself useful to him. Sleep when he sleeps and obey him in all things."

Mr Trench said: "Glad to have you, Sergeant. Let us begin with the funeral." And so I found myself travelling one stop on the train from Broughty Ferry to Barnhill and then the step up the brae to the new burial grounds.

After two days of newspaper reports and the Chief Constable's handbills and a whole washing day of gossip, you may guess at the throng of folk who had come to gawk and gawp. The ladies, of course, did not approach the burial, as it would be both indelicate and unhealthy, especially in November. But the womenfolk of Broughty Ferry were well represented around the gates of the cemetery – not the fisher wives, you understand, for they were ordinary working women who could hardly take time away from baiting lines and caring for their children for a mere show – but ladies of quality who found themselves at a loose end on a Tuesday morning. I recognised several ladies prominent in the Anti-Suffragette League, of which Miss Milne had been a trenchant supporter. They had taken the trouble to find a bit of sombre black in their wardrobes, a mourning hat with perhaps a seemly veil to keep the chill wind off their complexions, and they were prepared to go out, see their friends and make sure that they were themselves seen. Our little murder had turned into quite the social event.

The men, of course, were a little different. They made up all types and conditions; some of the quality had strolled along with their ladies, and the magistrates and baillies of the burgh council were there, of course. They would not normally attend the funerals of any but the most prominent citizens, but, in this case, a show of concerned fellow feeling was very much required. The Chief Constable, naturally, had gone on ahead and I noticed him making determined effort to avoid the gaze of Norval Scrymgeour, who, though his notebook was in his hand, at least had the good grace to arrive without his photographer while Mr Mackintosh, the Fiscal, could hardly bear to look at either of them and, filling out the crowd, were the usual idle loafers who might have been turning their hand to an honest day's work but, instead, had chosen to come along for the fun.

While they all crowded round the cemetery gates, I stood a little way off, on the other side of the street, with my detective lieutenant. He perfectly understood that a man in the midst of the crowd could see nothing of the crowd and the only way to keep a proper watch was to maintain a distance.

There was a murmuring in the street until we heard the sound of horses' hooves on the road and the crowd began to notice the approach of Coullie's glass-panelled hearse.

Coullie himself was walking in front, swinging his cane, top hat in hand with its long ribbons of black fluttering in the wind. He had provided two black horses to draw the hearse – he hired them in as needed – and it was driven by his elderly father, who sat on the box with the ease of a man who had performed such a service for his neighbours these many decades.

Behind the hearse, with its grim cargo, there came the minister. Mr Trench asked who he was and I told him it was Mr Shaw, the minister of St Andrew's Kirk in Dundee, for Miss Milne, who as an incomer to Broughty Ferry had continued her connection with that congregation. At his side, walking bareheaded, another, younger man in a very suitable broadcloth coat, just newly bought, I took for the deceased Miss Milne's nephew.

"Frank Milne, " I told Mr Trench. "He lives in a place called Croydon, on the outskirts of London. We asked the local police to advise him of the circumstances. He must have come up by train overnight. The only living heir, so far as I know. The son of her late brother. I suppose he agreed the expenditure for Coullie's glass hearse with her man of business in Dundee."

The crowd parted to allow the coach to pass in silence, the men doffing their hats as it went by, and, once it was through the gates, they followed along towards the grave, as indeed we are all doing.

But Mr Trench remained leaning quietly on his umbrella, so I stood with him like his loyal hound. "We're not here for the funeral, Fraser. We are here to observe the funeral. Observe the faces. Is there someone here more interested in looking at us than looking at the coffin? Is there someone taking delight in the day's events when they ought to be shedding a tear? Is there someone excessively affected, someone perhaps with a guilty conscience and bloodstained heart? You are a man of the world, Fraser. You know well enough what is usual at a funeral. Look out for the unusual."

After a time Mr Trench judged it appropriate to follow the funeral party up to the grave and we watched the whole proceedings from afar, but we noticed nothing remarkable.

The Minister preached at the graveside most touchingly, taking as his text the eighth chapter of Romans: "For I am persuaded, that neither death, nor life, nor angels, nor principalities, nor powers, nor things present, nor things to come, nor height, nor depth, nor any other creature, shall be able to separate us from the love of God," which is most appropriate for a funeral service and offered great comfort, I am sure, to the poor lady's grieving friends and could not have failed to touch those who had come merely as sightseers. I know I found great solace in his remarks. But, as I say, we observed nothing out of the ordinary.

With matters concluded, the funeral procession broke up and made its way back to the cemetery gates. It was then that Mr Trench walked up, tipped his hat and made himself known to Miss Milne's nephew. "The police forces of Glasgow and Broughty Ferry join me in expressing sincere sympathy and sorrow," he said.

Young Mr Milne seemed as upset as any man could be who has just come into a large mansion and a considerable fortune. He shook hands and said: "Thank you for your kind interest," and he was making as if to walk on when Mr Trench put his hand on his elbow and, very gently, held him back.

"Were you very fond of your aunt?" he asked.

"We weren't all that close. We lived, well she lived here and I live in London."

"Did you have much to do with her? By that, I mean, can you tell us anything about her life or habits? Anything that might give us any insights. To help with the inquiry, you understand."

Young Mr Milne said: "I'm most eager to assist in any way I can," in that peculiar English accent of his.

He nodded towards a gentleman standing at his side and said: "Mr Kyd here, he's Auntie Jean's solicitor, and he tells me I can expect to come into quite a sum of money. I'd like to offer a reward of . . ." He looked at the lawyer, almost as if he needed permission to spend his own money as he chose. "A reward of one hundred pounds."

And then he seemed to understand the weight of what he had just said, although there was nothing we could do to hold him to it, and he said: "It's her money. Not my money, really. It should go to catching the man. Bait the hook. You know."

Mr Trench made a great show of thanking him for his generosity and assuring him that we would make the reward widely known through the papers and all along the police telegraph. "I feel certain that it will produce speedy results," he said. "Now, can you tell me when you last saw your aunt?"

"As I said, we were not close. She was a bit, well, eccentric, I suppose. When Father was alive we used to come up and visit, but she wouldn't allow us in the house. Wouldn't hear of it. She used to make us take lodgings and we would see her in tea shops and so on. It was strange. She bought me a motor car not too long ago. What do you think of that? But I'm afraid I've seen nothing of her since some time in July. It was during her last visit to London. She came up to town pretty frequently but the exact date I cannot say."

"Were you expecting her?"

"No, we never knew when to expect her. One day a postcard came . . ."

"A postcard?"

"Or maybe it was a letter. I don't recall, but it definitely said that she would be pleased to see me at the Palace Hotel, Strand, where she was staying. About a week after, I called at the Palace Hotel and saw her."

"What did you talk about?"

"Oh, you know, this and that."

"Did she mention why she was in London? Did she say anything about anyone she had met, anyone who had befriended her?"

"Oh, she was always making friends. That was what she liked most about travelling. She liked going about and meeting people."

"But did she mention anyone she had met on this trip? Did she mention a Mr Clarence Wray?"

I recognised the name. Clearly Mr Trench had spent the night wisely, reading through that pile of correspondence.

"If she spoke of him at all, I don't recall it."

"You're quite certain? Clarence Herberto Wray?"

Young Milne glanced at Mr Kyd as if seeking reassurance. The lawyer said: "I think Mr Milne has already explained that he does not recognise the name."

But Mr Trench ignored him. "Mr Milne, are you quite certain?"

"I'm not being unhelpful," he said.

And the lawyer said: "I would have thought that Mr Milne's generous offer of a reward would have been indication enough of that."

"No. No, I'm sure. But you do understand, every scrap of information is vital to us."

"I only wish I could tell you something more. I met her at the Palace on the Strand and we took tea and we chatted about this and that. That's all."

"And you never saw her again?"

"The last time I saw her was about a fortnight afterwards, when I again visited her at the hotel. She seemed in good health and quite cheerful."

"Then let that be a comfort to you," Mr Trench said, and he tipped his hat and stood aside to let the two men pass on their way.

When they were gone, he said: "I suppose there's no possibility he could have done it? The sole heir. Just got sick of waiting for the apple to fall from the tree? Maybe he tired of taking tea with his auntie and talking of this and that."

"The local police say there's no indication that he's been out of London for years, but the train will get you there and back in a day and a night," I said. "The proof is before your eyes."

10

MR TRENCH WENT stepping out, back down the hill to Barnhill railway station, long legs going like a windmill and his umbrella over his shoulder like a gun. He kept up a pretty pace, but I am a man of above the average height and I matched him stride for stride easily enough.

A number of the ladies we had seen at the cemetery gates were still waiting there on the wooden platform and they whispered to each other behind their gloves. Mr Trench might have gone as far as touching the brim of his brown bowler hat, but beyond that I don't think he gave them any acknowledgement whatever.

We rode together, without a ticket I may say, through Broughty Ferry station and on to the West Ferry station, where Mr Trench walked up the stair and past the ticket collector with hardly a glance, saying no more than "Police business." I gave the man thruppence for his trouble.

Once out of the carriage, he felt more free to talk, and though he spoke to me on the walk up the hill to Elmgrove, I had the firm feeling he was really talking only to himself.

"We've got this all wrong, you know."

I said nothing.

"I said: 'We've got this all wrong.'"

"How so, sir?" I said.

"The dates. The dates. The dates."

"The dates, sir?"

"The dates, Fraser. She couldn't possibly have been seen alive on the 16th, as Dr Sturrock says, far less the 21st."

"No, sir. That's obvious."

He stopped in his tracks. We were just at the place where Grove Road makes its sharp turn to the right and the brae flattens out. "Obvious? What do you mean, by that, Fraser?"

"Only that the evidence of the newspaper suggests she died much earlier, and her post, sir. Why would she have let the post lie unattended for days in that box in the back court? The earliest stamp on those letters is the 14th, the same day as the newspaper, and they continue to Saturday, the day Postie Slidders raised the alarm."

Mr Trench looked at me with such a look. "You've known this all along?"

"Yes, sir."

"And yet you allowed Mr Sempill to publish that damned stupid handbill."

"The Chief Constable did not seek my opinion, sir."

"So you did not offer it, I know. Fraser, from here on take it as a standing order that I am seeking your opinion. Anything that occurs to you, anything that you know, share it with me. I need all the brainpower I can muster on this case and it seems at least one officer of Broughty Ferry Constabulary has a brain."

That pleased me very much.

"But," he said, "it doesn't explain away what the doctor saw."

"Mrs McDougall, sir. Just up the road, at Caenlochan Villas on the other side of Strathern Road. And there's also Miss Jane Miller of 176 King Street. They are both somewhat like Miss Milne in appearance and style of dress. They dress, well . . ."

"They dress younger than their years."

"I suppose so, sir."

"Let's see if we might not introduce the doctor to these ladies. Get him to change his mind."

We were nearly at the gates of Elmgrove and I was just reaching into my pocket for the keys when he said: "Have you looked at the lady's letters?"

I told him I had.

"And what did you think?"

"I thought them odd, sir."

"Some of them are downright queer. I sat up with them last night. She seems to be endlessly hinting to her women friends that she has some kind of intrigue going on with a man – at least one man or maybe more. It would not be respectable in a woman half her age. It's half mad in an old lady."

I told Mr Trench that I had always found Miss Milne respectable, never mad, and that she had not struck me as elderly.

"What age do you think she was?"

"She was a lady in her fifties," I said.

"She admitted to sixty-five and I wouldn't wager my pension on that either. Did you read the letter from Clarence Herberto Wray?"

I told him that I had and that I was surprised by it.

"On violet paper. What man writes his letters on violet paper – even letters of that nature?"

I said that I had never written a letter of that nature, on violet paper or on paper of any other colour.

"It's not manly. We need to find this Wray character and account for his movements. And 'Herberto'. That's odd too. That's not a British name. Herbert is a British name, but there's something odd and foreign about 'Herberto', something Spanish or South American. Those are hot-blooded peoples, Fraser. They lack self-control."

We were standing at the small gate for foot passengers that

leads into Elmgrove and I was just about to turn the key in the lock when he said: "The house has nothing more to tell us. We need to talk to people. We need to find out more. And we need to find Wray."

"Will you go to London?" I asked him.

"No, I'm needed here. Mr Sempill can go to London and gather some more pieces of the jigsaw, but somebody has to fit them together. Now, who have you got on your list of witnesses? Who's handy?"

My notebook was almost full to bursting with lists of concerned citizens, gossips and busybodies, anybody who had the tiniest bit of information to offer and plenty of others who simply wanted the attention.

I said: "We might do worse than speak to Mrs Ritchie, up at Lindisfarne," and, I suppose because he had no better idea, that was what we did.

The Ritchies lived up at Lindisfarne, in Edward Street, which is the name they used to give to Grove Road after it has crossed Strathern Road, but Dundee already has an Edward Street so they took ours away and now the whole thing is Grove Road. It was to avoid confusion, they said. In my view they simply wanted to remind us who is the master now.

Lindisfarne is exactly the sort of fine house you would expect to go with a fanciful name like that. There were well-kept hedges with a fine gravel walk through an entirely ornamental garden, which, although it spoke of idleness and frivolity, no doubt kept a man hard at work. The brass bell sheltered under a broad porch, and when the maid answered, Mr Trench handed in his card.

We had not long to wait. We both of us took off our hats as the lassie showed us in. Mr Ritchie was a figure in the jute trade of Dundee, a broker marrying cargoes with customers and customers with cargoes. He had a fine, comfortable house and the wife to match.

Mrs Ritchie received us in her downstairs sitting room, where she was taking her morning tea. She was one of those women, the sort who never trouble too much to be right in the fashion because they know very well their own quality. The fashion that season was to be thin, but Mrs Ritchie tended to the old style of things.

She did not get up when we entered the room but she offered her hand, indicated where we were to sit, and told the girl: "Effie, bring some more cups on a tray for the gentlemen."

Mr Trench had not given up his umbrella at the door. It seemed to go everywhere with him and he sat now with it planted in front of him and his bowler hat dangling from the top of it. It made a comic picture and left him without any hands for taking notes, so that fell to me, as usual.

"I understand, Mrs Ritchie, that you might have some information about the terrible tragedy that happened over the road," he said.

Mrs Ritchie expressed her deep shock and distress as she poured out the tea and handed us our cups. The saucers sang and tinkled in her plump fingers. I left my tea sitting on the arm of the chair and began taking notes.

"It's a terrible thing," she said. "We've known – that's Mr Ritchie and I – have known Miss Milne seven years, since Mr Ritchie took this house, and we always spoke if we met in the street."

"Did you know her well?" Mr Trench said.

"I don't know that anybody could say that. For my own experience, I could not describe Miss Milne as anything but a hard, greedy woman."

Mr Trench's eyebrows rose a little.

"Yes, I know you think that harsh, but there's no point in anything but directness now. That won't do you any good at all. Cake?"

Mr Trench declined.

"She was absolutely money-obsessed. I recall once I was in a shop in the town and there was Miss Milne and she said to me, 'What would you like to buy?' and I said how many lovely things there were to choose from but one must consider the expense, and then she held up a shabby little purse and said: 'There's £90 in there.' Can you imagine? Look at that." She pointed at an advertisement on the front page of the paper. "A three-piece suit for ten shillings and a coat for ten shillings more. She was carrying clothing for a hundred and eighty men in that one little bag."

"What did you say to her?"

"I advised her to get to the bank as fast as she could."

"Very wise."

There was a lull in the conversation as Mr Trench cast his eye round the room. "You have a lovely home," Mr Trench said.

"Thank you." She sparkled a little at that. "A biscuit? They're awfully good. Well, we overlook Elmgrove from our . . . from the upper floor and I always had, well, I don't know what you'd call it, but, let's say a certain fear about Miss Milne staying all alone in there."

"Did you ever visit? Did you ever go into Elmgrove?"

"No. Oh no. It wasn't quite that kind of an acquaintance. Anyway, we, that is, my husband and I, we quite remonstrated with her for so doing – for living all by herself with not even a lassie. Miss Milne assuredly did not know what fear was, living alone in that big house without even a dog for company – that would have tried anyone with the best of nerves. I don't believe a maid would have stayed even one night there.

"I remember, oh, some time ago now, of Miss Milne telling me of an incident which showed how plucky she was. Mr Trench, for many years she had been in the habit of sitting alone, writing or reading. The blinds were never drawn and she sat in full view of anyone in the garden. On this particular evening, as she sat reading, she became conscious of being watched. She looked up and saw a man's face at the glass."

"My stars!" said Mr Trench.

"My stars indeed. But Miss Milne was in no way alarmed. She simply walked to the window and boldly ordered the man to 'Clear out!' I told her anything might happen and, well, see for yourself, it has. That poor soul lying in there dead for days – weeks even."

Mr Trench looked at me. "Any report?" he said.

"We never had any such report, sir."

Mr Trench put his cup down in his saucer. "How long is it since you last saw Miss Milne?"

"I only saw light in Miss Milne's house twice since she came home from London in the beginning of August last, and that was in the early part of September. I have always made it a point to look out of our . . . from the upper-floor window, each night before going to bed, to see if there was light in her house. I have done that for years. Faithfully."

"And is that what you wanted to tell us about, Mrs Ritchie? That you've not seen Miss Milne."

"Indeed not. You'd think me a very silly woman if that was all I had to say." She had a small bag beside her on the settee and she reached in and took out a little pocket diary. "It was this. On September the 20th during the forenoon I joined the tramcar at Grove Road, for Dundee, and Miss Milne joined the car at Ellieslea Road. Now she might easily have got on at

Grove Road and I can only think that she did not because it saves a penny on the fare.

"She got on and I said to Miss Milne: 'I have not seen you since you came home from London,' and at once she began to speak about a nice gentleman she had met while in London, and oh, but he was a very nice gentleman and that he had been travelling for months before that."

"Did she mention a name?"

"She did not. No names. Only that he was a charming man, that she had a letter from him a day or two before and that he was coming to see her at Elmgrove. She mentioned no names.

"She was then on her way to Glasgow that very day and thence to Inverness – on that day."

"I see." Mr Trench went back to sipping his tea, so it was left to me to say: "Is there anything else you can tell us?"

But Mrs Ritchie only snapped off a bit of biscuit in her saucer and said: "I would have thought that information of that nature, that she had some strange man, a world traveller, coming up from London to be entertained in her very home, would have been sufficient for anybody!"

We were out the door and back in the garden before Mrs Ritchie had finished her next mouthful of shortbread.

And that was what our life became. The whole of that day and every day after that for days and days we spent tramping the streets of Broughty Ferry or riding the cars up to Dundee, knocking on doors, ringing bells, talking to folk who knew Miss Milne well, folk who knew Miss Milne slightly and folk who didn't really know Miss Milne at all but who might once have seen her from afar.

From early in the morning until late in the evening, we made our house calls and everybody who knew nothing – or next to nothing – was mad keen to tell us about a neighbour who swore she knew something. From one to the other we trudged, Mr Trench stepping along with me on one side and his umbrella swinging on the other.

And little by little, slowly but surely, we began to see something of the picture, because wherever we went and whoever we spoke to, there was always one part of the story linking them all together. A man. There was a man. A man she had spoken of. A man she had boasted of. A man she was seen with. A man who was seen in the overgrown shadows of Elmgrove.

Look in my notebooks. I have them with me still. David Nicoll, merchant of 22 Panmure Street, Monifieth. "One day about five or six weeks before the news of her death broke out, I chanced to meet her in Dundee in front of D. M. Brown's department store. We stood chatting together a few minutes and I remarked that as I would be visiting some friends in West Ferry one day soon I might then pay her a visit.

"She made a reply to the effect that she did not receive gentleman visitors, but added that she had received a letter the other day and was expecting a gentleman visitor from the south. By way of a joke, I remarked that in that case there was no chance for me then."

A man.

Marjory Cassady, the wife of the dentist in Brook Street. "One day, shortly before 7th October 1912, I went up by a tramcar about noon to Dundee. When at Ellieslea Road in Strathern Road, Miss Milne and a gentleman joined the car. I was the only one sitting inside.

"Miss Milne and the gentleman were talking to each other. I paid little heed to the gentleman, who was about five foot six inches in height."

A short man.

Margaret Campbell, maidservant to Mrs Luke at Caenlochan Villas. "Our house overlooks the gardens of Elmgrove. In the mornings when I am making the beds I have often looked into the grounds and remarked to myself on their wild and neglected appearance.

"About 10.20 one morning either in the first or second week in October, I was looking out of the bedroom window and I was surprised to see a man walking about in the private grounds at the back of Miss Milne's house, walking up and down with his hands in his trouser pockets.

"He was a man between thirty and forty years of age, about six feet in height, well-made and well-set-up, a handsome-looking man. I should say definitely a gentleman from his appearance, wearing an evening dress suit with an expensive shirt front, and bareheaded."

A man. A handsome man in evening dress in the middle of the morning.

Margaret Sampson, a lady of independent means of 2 Blackness Crescent, Dundee, depones that she has known Miss Milne for many years. "In the spring of this year – I think April – my sister and I met her in Perth Road. We were going into town and she turned and walked with us.

"She told us that she had just returned from London, where she had made the acquaintance of the very nicest man she had ever met in her life, a cultured, scholarly man, neither English nor Scotch.

"She said that he wanted to come to Elmgrove to pay his respects to her. She said, however, that she was not prepared to receive his visit to Elmgrove in the meantime.

"We had now reached the High Street, and she left us to board the car for the Ferry, saying she was all packed and going back to London. I remember I said to her: 'He must be very attractive when you cannot stay away from London or from him.' And she replied: 'Oh, but he isn't in London just now.'

"She was tremendously excited, talking and giggling shrilly about the man so much so that people were turning round to look at her and we were relieved when she left us and we remarked to each other: 'She's insane.'

"Some short time after this meeting I received a letter from her from the Strand Palace Hotel, London. The next communication I received were three postcards, one from Portree dated September 1st and postmarked the 3rd, the next written on Saturday, at Oban, and postmarked September 21st, and the third written the following Monday, at Fort Augustus.

"On Monday, 14th of October 1912, my sister and I met Miss Milne in Nethergate, near Park Place. We stopped and spoke and she was showing a stone fixed at her neck. She said: 'I bought this cairngorm at Inverness. It is a very fine one,' and she also said: 'I've got a new ring I'd like to show you,' and she began to unfasten her glove and then she said: 'Oh you will see it another time.'

"I never saw her again."

A man, a man, a man. A short man. A charming man. A handsome man in evening dress. A foreigner. And a ring.

11

ALL THROUGH THAT week, the man haunted us. We pursued him through the Ferry. We saw the tail end of his coat disappearing round every street corner, we spotted the top of his hat just on the other side of the wall, but we could never quite grasp him.

And all that week we were hindered by reporters – and not just our own Norval Scrymgeour and his like. The *Courier* men were canny-enough lads who waited to be told, but the murder had brought floods of reporters to the burgh from Edinburgh and Glasgow, some from as far away as London, the Harmsworth papers, the *Daily Mail*, the *Daily Express*, the *Graphic*, the *Illustrated London News*, the *News of the World* and I don't dare say who else, all tripping over themselves looking for a story, racing each other up and down the street, fighting to be first with "the facts" and, if they couldn't get facts, any old rubbish would do. Every street corner had a photographer taking pictures or an artist making sketches for lurid engravings to titillate readers across the Empire, and more than once I had to chase a man with a notebook off a doorstep. It was wearing.

And then came the Saturday papers.

WHO TOOK LIFE OF RICH MISS MILNE

Whose Body, Wrapped in Sheet, is found in Broughty Ferry Mansion?

Assailant Cuts Telephone Wire to Prevent
Alarm Being Given

And, under that, they had gathered together what few facts we had given them and mingled them with a rich stream of drivel, gossip and wild imaginings to produce the most offensive rubbish it was possible to imagine.

She went her own way, lonely but happy . . .

How could they possibly pretend to know that?

. . . and that way has ended in death in one of its most chilling aspects. Miss Milne has been struck down by a ruthless slayer who has had a three weeks' start in the flight from justice and the authorities are busy trying to solve the greatest mystery in the history of crime in this country.

Happy in the belief that she was enjoying not only complete solitude but privacy, Miss Milne went her way, little dreaming that her movements were being watched by a ruthless killer bent on raiding her home . . .

There was not a shred of proof of that. Not a shred.

. . . who would not hesitate to crush the life out of her frail old body in order to accomplish his purpose. In the garden of Miss Milne's villa, Elmgrove, West Ferry, near Dundee, the man who was soon to bear the mark of Cain upon his brow crouched in the shadows and followed with wild, restless eyes the doings of the rich lady who sat in the dining room with none of the blinds drawn.

It was a simple matter to see that Mrs Ritchie had been as free with her anecdotes to the reporters as she was with us.

> What exactly he wanted in that house, no one knows but, whatever it was, he meant to have it at all costs. He chose his time, made his venture and found himself confronted by the solitary mistress of the house. The ruthless, cowardly assailant rained upon her blow after blow with a steel poker 15 inches long.

How could the length of the poker have any import in the matter? I almost threw the vile thing in the fire, but then I was shocked to read a smaller headline in the middle of the column.

Sovereigns in a Drawer

They knew of that! And, a little further down

Slayer Washes His Hands

That too!

> The slayer, it would appear, took every precaution to destroy any clues to assist the police in tracking him down. He actually went into the kitchen and washed his hands before leaving and the towel, which the police took possession of, is deeply stained with blood.
>
> The absence of any fingerprints would seem to show that the miscreant took every precaution to cover up clues which may lead to his identification. But, in their cleverness, often the cleverest rogues err at times and the possibility of still securing a fingerprint will no doubt be uppermost in the minds of detectives.

There was a good deal more of this stuff and then it descended into a torrent of the worst kind of vile, disrespectful, gutter filth.

Dressed Like Lady of Twenty-five

> Miss Milne was a woman of a romantic disposition and the periodical journey to London seems to have afforded ample scope for the gratification of her whims.

That. What could that possibly mean? What was that supposed to mean? "Ample scope for the gratification of her whims"? They might as well have come right out with it and accused her of whoredom and harlotry.

> Once away from home she despised convention . . .

Again. That, again. Speak Scotch or whistle. "Despised convention" indeed.

> . . . she had a great love for finery and attracted a good deal of attention by her gaudy attire. More like a young girl than a woman nearing the allotted span.

Gaudy!

> Indeed she did not mind being teased a little about having a sweetheart.

WHO WAS THE HANDSOME STRANGER WITH WHOM MISS MILNE MADE TRIP IN HIGHLANDS?

> Without a doubt Miss Milne led a double life. Two ladies who paid a visit to the house of mystery . . .

The house of mystery!

> . . . informed the *News* that they travelled with Miss
> Milne on the same steamer from Inverness to Fort
> Augustus, on board the Cavalier. When on the way
> Miss Milne and her male companion emerged from the
> cabin. Miss Milne and her male companion, a tall, good-
> looking man of about 35 years walked about the deck
> chatting. At Fort Augustus they left the boat together
> and were seen to proceed up the road into town.

A man again. That man. More groundless accusations of whoring. I could not bear to read more. I cast the paper from me and went to find Mr Trench, who was in the back office and reading through another pile of witness statements, but I could see he had a copy of the same paper on his desk.

I went up to where he sat and said: "It seems the newspapers know a great deal of our business. I am heartily sorry for that and I take the responsibility. I will have words with the men, find out which if them is responsible and take the matter further."

Mr Trench said: "You mustn't blame the men. It's nothing to do with them. I judged it useful to have a quiet word, here and there, with a few of the newsmen."

"You, sir?"

"Yes."

"But the things they said, sir. This is pure invention and they have blackened that poor lady's name."

"I can't help that and Jean Milne is far past caring. These are modern times, Sergeant Fraser, and this man has a head start on us. I want this on the front pages. I want the hue and cry to go up from one end of these islands to the other. Take a look at that." He jabbed his finger at the newspaper. "Latest certified circulation over 430,000 copies weekly. That's almost half a million households, each paper seen by four or five people. That's more than two million policemen looking out for this man and I want him to know it. Two million informants after his blood."

I make no secret of the fact: I did not believe that the ends justified the means. I still do not. However, I bit my tongue in front of Mr Trench. I said: "I have been informed, from a private source, that two days after the murder was committed, a telephone call came from London for Elmgrove – lY2 Broughty Ferry – but of course got no answer."

"'A private source'? What do you mean 'a private source'? You can't go about having 'private sources'. I need to be informed of everything. Who is this 'private source' of yours?"

"It's private," I said, "but it wouldn't take much working out."

"No. It wouldn't take much working out because it's an offence under the Telegraph Act to disclose any such information, and since the only person who would know about a telephone call that was never answered is the Post Office, I think we should take a stroll along there."

It is no distance at all from the Police Offices and the Burgh Chambers to the Post Office, which is a fine stone building just on the other side of the railway, a graceful addition to our little town with all the dignity you would expect from such an important institution. It has Roman pillars on either side of double doors and the royal cypher of the old King on the gable and, inside, a long counter where five attendants are constantly employed.

One of them was Annie Liddell. She was a poor, on-the-shelf sort of a woman, still unmarried at the age of thirty-one and sent out by her mother to work for her keep. She took fright when she saw me, thinking that I had betrayed her over the telephone call, but I tipped her the wink and shook my head to reassure her as I closed the door behind Mr Trench.

He took no notice of the queues of folk waiting to conduct their business but simply announced: "We'd like to see the postmaster."

"Mr Smeaton," I said, and Annie Liddell drew down the curtain over the front of her booth, shut her drawer and went hurrying off.

A minute or two later and she was back at her seat, counting pennies and handing out stamps, and the big green door into the sorting office opened quietly beside us.

Mr Smeaton was there in his dove-grey frock coat, looking at us over his half-moon spectacles and he didn't say a word, simply opened the door and waved us through. With the door closed again he said: "It'll be the murder," in a quiet voice.

Mr Trench said: "I understand a telephone call was placed to Elmgrove from London some two weeks ago and it went unanswered."

"I wouldn't know. We keep no record of unacknowledged calls."

"But a call like that, from London, it must require a number of connections. Don't they have to book? What would be the point of making such a call and going to all that effort if the person on the other end had stepped out for a moment?"

"I'm certain I cannot advise you," said Mr Smeaton. He raised his hand and snapped his fingers and called out: "James!"

A young man emerged from among the tall shelves of pigeonholes where the post was sorted and came trotting up as Mr Smeaton said: "Ask Miss Liddell to join us for a moment and we'll see if there is something which we can talk to these gentlemen about."

We waited awkwardly for a few moments until Annie Liddell returned with James and Mr Smeaton gave her permission to speak. "Tell these gentlemen what happened," he said.

The poor lassie. Looking at Mr Trench, it was all she could do not to bob a curtsy, and when she spoke it was little more than an embarrassed whisper that none of us could make out.

The postmaster said: "Speak up, Miss Liddell. You have no reason to fear the police. This is Britain. In this country the policeman is not your master but your servant, your protector and your friend. Simply tell the gentleman what happened."

"Well, sir, I . . ."

"It was just coming up for closing time on October 11," James said.

"And who are you?"

"James Delaney, sir. Telegraphist and sorting clerk. The way I remember is, I was off duty but I came in to see Mr Smeaton because he was going on his holidays and I was supposed to take over his duties while he was away and he wanted to sort out a few things."

Mr Smeaton nodded and said: "Quite true."

"I was standing right there, in that doorway, between the public counter and the back office here, and a man came in – didn't he, Annie?"

"A man came in," she said.

Mr Trench tried to be charming, but his moustache and his umbrella had quite overwhelmed the poor woman. "Did you see the man, Miss Liddell?"

"I saw the man, yes."

"And did he speak to you?"

"He spoke to me, yes."

"What did he say?"

"He asked me where Elmgrove was."

"And what did you tell him?"

James Delaney burst in. "She never told him anything. She's no more idea how to give directions to Elmgrove than fly to the moon."

Mr Smeaton said: "That'll do, James."

"Yes, sir. Miss Liddell came up to me and asked me where Elmgrove was and I told the man. I just hope to God that I didn't send the murderer to her door."

"It would be wise," Mr Trench said, "not to go about repeating things like that, not with all these reporters around the place. Describe this man to me."

"He was a queer-looking type. He was wearing a tile hat – what you might call a top hat, sir. But there was something about him. What was a man like that doing asking for Miss Milne at Elmgrove! That was what struck me, sir. That was what made me look at him."

"You're sure he asked for Miss Milne by name."

"Oh certainly, he asked for her at Elmgrove."

"He asked for her, sir," said poor Annie.

"And there he was, a man in a tile hat, badly needing a shave. He had the look of a broken-down cabman. He was about five foot ten and he had what you'd call an ordinary face – although I only saw him side-on – brown coat and either the collar of his coat was turned up or he had a muffler on and I think he had a small handbag. It's just that . . ." He seemed unwilling to say more, but Mr Trench encouraged him with a gesture. "It's just that it seemed strange for him to be asking for Miss Milne at Elmgrove after what the Postie Slidders said about her."

Slidders again. The man who had brought all this down on my head. "What did Slidders say about Miss Milne?"

"Only that she was a wee touch, well, that she had her eccentricities."

"And so have we all," I said. "You nor Slidders have any right to make remark on that good lady. Judge not that ye be not judged!"

I found Mr Trench looking at me with a queer look. "Right you are, Sergeant Fraser," he said. "Right you are."

He thanked Mr Smeaton and his staff, and asked them to come into the station at their convenience to make signed statements, and we went out again into the weather. Mr Trench turned his collar up against the wind and he said: "Had you some special fondness for Miss Milne?"

"She was well known to me," I said, "and to many folk in the Ferry."

"But had you some special fondness for her?"

"I like to think I have a special fondness for everybody who is entrusted to my care. I am a policeman, as Mr Smeaton said, a servant, a friend and a protector."

He said once more: "Right you are, Sergeant Fraser," and we left it at that, as I did not care to explain myself further.

But we had not gone more than a few yards before Mr Trench spoke again. "Is that one also in your special care?"

He looked me full in the face, but with his eyes he was indicating a rough and shabby old man on the far side of Queen Street with a large, square pack on his back.

"He is also of my flock," I said. "That's Andy Hay the pedlar."

"Well, he seems awful keen to get your attention."

And, true enough, though he was standing in the one place and making no attempt to cross the street, by a strange system of jerks and winks and twitches he was trying to attract my attention.

"I'll wait here," Mr Trench said, and as soon as Andy saw me coming towards him, he stopped his twitching and turned and looked deep into the hedge at his back.

"Dinna look at me, dinna speak," he said. "Ahm no here. Yiv no seen me."

I made an effort to look the other way.

"Ah canna be seen talkin wi you, Mister Fraser, but it's the lady. It's the lady. The lady that was murdered."

I stood quietly, not looking at him, listening to Andy's story, about how he walks the same route, regularly, never calling at any house more than once in three weeks, never wearing out his welcome. That was how he knew he was on Grove Road on Wednesday three weeks before. And he was fond of Miss Milne.

"She never bought a thing aff me, but she was very good at giving me a thrupenny piece. Ah was just goin in by the wee gate when Ah met a gentleman comin on his way oot. He didna speak.

"Ah went on up tae the hoose and rung the bell but got no answer. When Ah went back tae the gate – are yi lookin at me, Mr Fraser?"

"No, Andy, I'm not looking at you."

"Ah went back tae the gate and, when I was at the ootside o the gate the same man Ah met comin was ten or fifteen yards up Grove Read, comin doon towards me. Ah got oot his way an crossed the street, but the man went in by the gate.

"Ah went along Albany Road to the junction wi Ellieslea an I sat on mah pack tae hae a smoke, waitin so as to allow the servants at Miltonbank time tae get their dinner before Ah should go up tae them. While sittin smokin, the same man come back doon Albany Road again, tae whaur Ah wis an he says tae me: 'You are taking it very easy,' he says, 'You are taking it very easy.'

"Ah answert him sayin, 'The servants in the big hoose are aw at their dinners an they widnae look at me the noo.'

"The man stood at the roadside for twa, three minutes, but he didna speak again tae me. Then he went up Ellieslea Road towards the car route. He returned back again to whaur Ah wis, lookin backwards and forwards but he didna speak. Then he ran up tae the car route again. Ah heard the bell but Ah couldna say if he got on."

I said: "What like a man was he, Andy?"

"He was past thirty but he wisna forty, the ordinary height, a wee, thin fair moustache, stout wi a braw, heavy gold double Albert watch chain across his breast, wi a jewel hingin aff it."

"And you're quite certain of the date? That would be Wednesday the 16th."

"The very day Ah sold a comb tae the maid at Miltonbank."

And then a strange thing happened. Andy looked at me and he gripped me by the wrist. "Yir askin aa the wrang fowk," he said. "Yir askin aa the grand ladies and gentlemen. They never see us but we see them. Ask the wee fowk like masel."

12

I LOOK BACK on that time now as one of impossible strange-ness. We were not idle in Broughty Ferry, never idle, and the men always had enough to do. I made sure of that. But in those days after the murder was discovered, we learned what work was. We rose early and sometimes we left so late for our beds that we met ourselves coming in. There was no time to waste rising from our desks in the morning to turn down the gas in the lamps since we would still be there, working, when it was time to light them again. There was never a minute of peace. The reporters were constantly at the front counter, and even when we told them there was nothing to say, as we always did, they would linger at the door for an hour and then come back to ask again. The police telegraph was constantly chattering, the Fiscal telephoned for information morning, noon and night, there were all the usual duties of the Burgh Police, which never slackened, a lost dog, a broken window, a day's washing stolen from the line, drunkenness and wife beating, everything as much deserving of all our care and attention as before, but now suddenly silly and small and pointless. There was no rest, a shortness of sleep, we were stretched like fiddle strings and sometimes I recall those days through a cloudy, milky glass of exhaustion.

Mr Sempill very well knew, as did we all, that if the papers could not deliver a story of detection and arrest they would provide a story of baffled, clueless, incompetent police officers, and the pain and disgrace of that would only be sharpened by the ill-disguised delight of the City of Dundee Police.

The magistrates and councillors of the burgh were every bit as insistent as the press in their demands for some sign of progress and poor Mr Sempill had nothing to offer them. I know he felt the weight of that terribly, for the responsibility fell on his shoulders, but he was not alone, as we of lower rank lived among the ordinary folk of the burgh and every tradesman, every shopkeeper, every neighbour, if they did not dare to speak it aloud, looked at us with burning, questioning looks.

None of us was spared. The Chief Constable looked to Mr Trench for results, insight, clues, some definite line of inquiry which might be pursued, and every hour that passed, every hour when we had to tell the crowds of reporters that "You will be kept informed of developments," was another blow.

But, all unknown to us, the dreadful burden of the murder was bearing down on others too. Mr Trench and I had not long returned from our meeting at the Post Office when I heard the voice of Dr Sturrock at the front counter, asking for the Chief Constable, and Broon, as calm and quiet as an ox, as he always was, saying: "I'll just see if he's in, sir."

Broon had no sooner turned away from the bar to make his way to Mr Sempill's office than Dr Sturrock lifted the latch and came bustling through, saying: "Enough of your nonsense, man, you know very well he's in," and on he rushed to the Chief Constable's room, bursting in with barely a skim of his knuckles on the door.

Mr Trench rose to follow after and I, ever the loyal hound, came a step or two behind. "That'll be all, Broon," I said, "go about your duties."

Standing in the doorway, I could see Mr Sempill at his desk

looking startled and Dr Sturrock, grey in the face and his eyes all rimmed red like a man who has wasted his nights pursuing sleep. Mr Trench took him by the elbow and pressed him to a chair and the doctor spoke in a great sob.

"Sempill, I've been up for days. I cannot get sleep. I'm troubled in my conscience."

At that, Mr Trench looked at me and I looked at him, and for a moment he and I were thinking the same thing: that perhaps Dr Sturrock had come to confess to the killing. Trench was a stranger. I could not blame him for feeling that washing wave of relief and delight, as of a weight lifting, but I knew Dr Sturrock, I had known him for years, I knew his wife and his children, and the thought that he might soon hang revolted and terrified me.

The Chief Constable said: "Speak your mind, Doctor, speak your mind," and then, to me, "Close that door, Sergeant."

When we were all inside and quiet together, Dr Sturrock began to talk in a quiet, tired way. He said: "Have you removed the productions from Elmgrove?"

"Everything material has been brought down from the house. The men have been working on cataloguing every last item."

"And what about her clothes?"

"They are still at Elmgrove."

"The clothes she was murdered in? The clothes she was wearing? The ones they took off her at the post-mortem?"

"Oh, those. No, those are here."

"Then I need to see them. There's something I want to show you. I'm tormented with the most awful notion."

The Chief Constable looked at me with a raised eyebrow.

"Everything is secured in the cells, sir. In boxes."

"Then let's take a look, Fraser, let's take a look."

So we all trooped out of Mr Sempill's office and down the back corridor to the cells, every eye on us as we passed. "Get on with your work," I said and I was careful to close the door at our backs against prying eyes.

Dr Sturrock seemed more like himself now, a little restored, as if the fever had broken. "John Fraser, let me see your list of labels."

I handed him my ledger and he began running his finger down the long list of labels. "Where are her clothes?"

"Here, sir."

"Roll out that mattress."

The mattress in a police cell is none too thick and none too clean, but I did as I was bid and and spread it over the iron-framed bed, and the doctor started to lay out Miss Milne's bloodied clothing: her blue serge skirt, her linen blouse with its lace collar and then, on top of those, her corsets, her camisole, her linen chemise until there was the shape of a small woman lying there on that filthy bed.

When he was finished, Dr Sturrock said: "You remember the night of the post-mortem – you were there, Fraser."

Mr Sempill and I agreed.

"That was the night before you got here, Mr Trench. During the examination I drew attention to holes in the flesh of the deceased lady."

"Yes, I recall," said Mr Sempill. "Maggots."

"Maggots. Exactly. Maggots. Sergeant Fraser, would you be so good as to hand me Label 31?"

That was easily done. I gave the doctor the big, bone-handled fork from the carving set, the one that was lying on the floor of the hall by Miss Milne's body when we broke in. It had a paper luggage label tied round the handle with brown string and my signature and Broon's and a large "31" written in ink.

"This has been rattling round in my head for days, gentleman. Observe." Dr Sturrock took the fork and held it against two small holes in Miss Milne's blouse. The prongs of the fork matched exactly. "There," he said, "and there. And there. And there. And there."

I heard Mr Trench saying: "Dear God. Dear God," and Mr Sempill said nothing at all.

Suddenly we could see that her clothing was full of holes – riddled with holes. The more we looked, the more we found, holes in the shoulder, holes in the breast, holes in the back, through her blouse, through her underwear, through her corsets right through to her flesh. We counted twenty holes in the back of her clothing; on the right breast, eight punctured holes; on the right wrist, two more; and on the left breast, just over the heart, two more. Where they pierced her undergarments, the cloth was stained with blood and not one of the holes was placed over her corsets, which, as the villain well knew, would have resisted his blows.

"Maggots," said Dr Sturrock. "There's your maggots. Thirty-four separate wounds. He stabbed her with this fork seventeen times. Seventeen times front and back. Seventeen times! And to think I bowed down and worshipped in front of the professor and his damned maggots."

The doctor flung open the cell door and went staggering out with Mr Trench and the Chief Constable on his coat-tails and so it was left to me to pack everything away.

Afterwards I washed my hands under the tap in the back yard.

And when I came into the building again, bolting the door at my back, Dr Sturrock and Lieutenant Trench were once more gathered in the Chief Constable's office, where Mr Sempill had opened a restorative bottle of sherry.

Dr Sturrock was sipping from a glass held in trembling fingers and the Chief was talking to Dundee on the telephone, demanding "an urgent meeting with Mr Procurator Fiscal Mackintosh, most urgent. In fact, immediate."

They made an odd picture sitting there together: the doctor who was well known to us all as one who cared for the weak and the infirm of our community, himself being tenderly cared for, and Mr Trench, with his great hedge of a moustache, a hand on the doctor's shoulder, playing the nursemaid.

Like an eavesdropper I found myself lingering aimlessly on the threshold of Mr Sempill's office, where I had no business to be and, certainly, I had work of my own to be going on with, but the gentlemen were taken up with their own matters, and if they noticed me at all they made no sign.

They seemed somehow set apart there together, the Chief Constable, the respected professional man and the lieutenant of detectives, and although I had handled all her clothing, although I had unpacked it from its boxes, although I packed everything away again, I was not offered a glass from the Chief Constable's bottle.

In very truth, I suppose I remained there only a moment and I was about to return to sit down at my own desk when Constable Suttie came hurrying up with a message from the police telegraph. He wanted to take it in to Mr Sempill, but I prevented him. "Give it to me," I said.

Suttie handed me the slip of paper. It was a message for the Chief Constable from the detective branch of Scotland Yard reporting that one Clarence Herberto Wray was in residence at the Bonnington Hotel, London.

"They are busy with important matters," I said. "I will hand it over in a moment. When they are free."

13

A NUMBER OF events then transpired of which I have no direct knowledge and of which I learned only later, at second hand by way of conversation or through police reports which I have read with very close attention.

Mr Sempill and Mr Trench were somehow flung together of a sudden and came to rely on one another in a friendly and familiar way, which, I suppose, was only right and proper for two gentlemen in that position.

I was not required to accompany them when they went to Dundee for the interview arranged with Mr Fiscal Mackintosh, but I was informed that Dr Templeman, the police surgeon of Dundee, was also in attendance. Professor Sutherland was detained by his duties at the Royal Infirmary and unable to attend.

I have no desire to attribute petty or ungenerous attitudes of mind to the Chief Constable, but it would have taken a man of more than ordinary flesh and blood not to gloat. After all that he had suffered at the hands of Mr Fiscal Mackintosh, after the days of ceaseless demands and, above all, the clear imputation that we of the Broughty Ferry Burgh Police were not up to our jobs, he must have relished the moment when he was able to produce unanswerable reasoning from our own Dr Sturrock proving that important evidence had been blithely overlooked. But, as I say, I was not present at that interview.

However, I do know that the telegram message from the

Metropolitan Police was discussed at the meeting and it was agreed that Mr Sempill should proceed at once to London to meet Mr Clarence Herberto Wray and carry out further inquiries.

We also managed to confirm, by simple, straightforward routine policing methods, the date of Miss Milne's death, almost to a certainty.

We traced – that is to say I traced – the van driver of the Dundee Steam Laundry Company who made a regular weekly call at Elmgrove. His name was James Macrae, and he called at the house every Thursday without fail.

On October 10th he brought a parcel of clean laundry and took a parcel of washing away to be done. He tarried long enough to help Miss Milne clear some leaves from the gutter of the back kitchen, and, no doubt, he benefitted from a generous tip, but he made no mention of that in his statement to me.

"On Thursday, 17th October 1912, about 1.15 p.m., I called at Elmgrove with a parcel from the laundry," he said.

"The small entrance gate was open, and on going to the front door I rang the bell twice, but got no answer. Miss Milne had previously arranged with me that, should I be later than 1 p.m. in calling, she would leave the kitchen window unsnibbed and the parcel inside, so that I would open the window, and take the one and leave the other.

"On going to the window I found it snibbed. I looked all round the house and saw all the windows shut except one upstairs, the centre one, looking south. I then noticed that the flap of the Chubb lock on the front door was up, and thinking Miss Milne had gone out for the afternoon, I took the parcel back with me.

"On Thursday, 24th October, about 12.45 I again called at Elmgrove and rang the front doorbell twice but got no answer.

Then I noticed the flap of the Chubb lock exactly the same as it was when I called the previous week. I then thought Miss Milne had left on holiday and had forgotten to inform the laundry. But she wasn't on her holidays, was she? She was lying dead at the back of that door."

I regarded that as an excellent piece of police work, but when Mr Sempill returned from the town he was far too busy to take any notice of the van man's evidence and nearly mad with excitement over his coming visit to London. He ran about the office, snatching up notebooks and arranging pocketfuls of business cards and babbling about his "mission" to the capital. Broon and Suttie were out on the beat, so they were spared it. I stuck close to my work and tried not to look up.

"Would it be wrong," he wondered, "to take a few small presents for senior officers in the Metropolitan Police? I favour those tins of shortbread they sell at Goodfellow's along in Gray Street, the ones with the view of the castle at sunset printed on them. It would be something definitely of Broughty Ferry."

Poor Mr Sempill was greatly torn between the possibilities of arriving empty-handed in front of his hosts and running the risk of appearing mean-spirited and tight-fisted or, on the other hand, looking like a country bumpkin, bedazzled by the capital.

"I think it's important to remember," he told Mr Trench, "that I am a Chief Constable in my own right. Yes, admittedly, Chief Constable of a small force – when considered alongside the Metropolitan Police – but a Chief Constable nonetheless. My responsibilities to this small burgh are not less than those faced by the Commissioner in the largest city of the Empire."

Mr Trench said: "Indeed."

"I think I'm right in saying, Trench, that the Commissioner himself may be the only officer of the Met who can officially outrank me."

"I could not say."

"Well I can. I can say it with confidence. So, the shortbread. What's your view?"

"I would say not," Mr Trench said gently. "Best to keep things on a purely professional footing."

"Professional. Damn it, Trench, you're right."

"Friendly, but not familiar."

"No. No. Familiarity breeds contempt. Don't want that."

"You are, after all, the Chief Constable of Broughty Ferry."

"Indeed, and if the plain, unvarnished Chief Constable of Broughty Ferry is not to their liking, then damn the lot of them."

Mr Sempill hurried into his office and came out again a moment later with his dress uniform on a hanger over his arm. "How will I find Scotland Yard?"

"Take a cab, sir. From the railway station."

"Yes. A cab."

All Mr Sempill's self-doubt was rolled up in those two words. He was flabbergasted by the possibility of getting in a cab, not knowing where it might go or how much it might cost. The extravagance of the notion appalled him – which was entirely to his credit since he knew he would have to be accountable to the burgh treasurer for every penny and, through him, to the ratepayers of Broughty Ferry themselves.

"It's the best thing," said Mr Trench. "You are the Chief Constable."

Mr Sempill was persuaded, and after not much more fussing he was ready to quit the office for his turreted house amongst the Scots pines of Orchar Park and finish filling a bag for the journey that evening.

"I want to make it quite clear," he said, as I held the door for him, "that Lieutenant Trench takes on full responsibility for the Elmgrove inquiry in my absence – at least as far as it pertains to Broughty Ferry. Obey him in all things as you would me."

"Yes, sir. Are you sure you won't be requiring assistance with your bags?"

"Thank you, Fraser, I can manage. I will be in touch daily. At least daily." And away he went, with a long thread of reporters trailing after him, all shouting questions. "Lieutenant Trench will assist you, gentlemen. Speak to Lieutenant Trench!" So they all came in to the front counter, waiting for a word from the lieutenant like dogs waiting for a biscuit, and it fell to him to explain that, in light of recent developments which he was not at liberty to disclose, our Chief Constable was away to London, following up definite lines of inquiry regarding the murder and working hand in glove – that's what he said, "hand in glove" – with Scotland Yard. He made no mention whatever of the business with the meat fork and said nothing at all about shortbread, which I regarded as very wise.

When the reporters had gone and the office was filled again by nothing more than the sharp ticking of the clock on the wall, Mr Trench went off towards the Chief Constable's office, where he had set up a table and which he could now count as his own for a few days.

"Will you be needing me this afternoon?" I asked him.

"I don't think so, John. Is there something you need to do? The murder inquiry must take the first importance in everything, you know."

"A few private inquiries of my own, sir."

"I don't think I quite approve of private inquiries. This is not a private inquiry agency. This is a police force."

"Oh I understand that, sir, but, with respect, you are a stranger here and some of these people, well, they might . . ."

"You think they'd be more willing to talk to one of their own, like the pedlar?"

"Aye, sir. Something like that."

"You might be right, John." And then, as if to underline his newfound authority, he said: "But I expect a full report. You must keep nothing from me."

He went into the Chief Constable's office and, from behind the door, he called out. "And be sure to wait until Suttie comes back. We can't leave the office unmanned."

Luckily that wasn't long.

I was lying. I had no reasons of my own for wanting to leave. At least none that were connected to the inquiry. Or perhaps all my reasons were connected to the murder. I was simply sick of the sight of the place and tired of listening to people who had no idea what to do or how to begin to do it. I wanted to walk and feel the wind chill me and have the cold rain wash my face, someplace away from the hiss and glare of gas lamps. I tramped the beach, eastwards, away from the police office and away from Elmgrove, along Beach Crescent, with its fine ornamental lamp posts, all cast-iron curls and twists, past the old Provost's house, under the shadow of the castle on its rock, sharp and black against the rolling, marbled blackness of the clouds, past the stalls and the beach huts, shut up now for the winter, away to where the fine houses of the Esplanade ran out and then on, through the dunes to the mouth of the Dighty Water, which marks the boundary of our little burgh, where I stopped to look at a flotilla of swans, appearing and disappearing like ghosts among the waves. The wind carried sprays of fine sand along with it. I could feel it gently rattling against the cloth of my trousers in tiny, harmless volleys as I stood there, little pieces of rock that might once have been mountains, ground as fine as dust by water and wind and time. How long must it have taken?

How many millions of years? And yet, if some cataclysm saw it all pounded together again into rock and worn again into dust, even that would not be an eternity. I thought on poor, dead Jean Milne and I thought on myself, who must soon follow her. I was put in mind of the 139th Psalm: "If I take the wings of the morning, and dwell in the uttermost parts of the sea; Even there shall thy hand lead me, and thy right hand shall hold me. If I say, Surely the darkness shall cover me; even the night shall be light about me. Yea, the darkness hideth not from thee; but the night shineth as the day: the darkness and the light are both alike to thee." But the darkness had covered me and I thought again on poor Jean Milne and I turned my back to the weather and went away, grateful.

Andy Hay the packman was right. The great and the good had shown themselves to know nothing. It was the little people I had to ask. I had to find out what they knew.

14

Finger Print Department
New Scotland Yard
London, S.W.

Sir,

Re. Finger Marks

In reply to your communication dated 19th inst, I have to
inform you that the finger marks do not possess any clearly
defined characteristic detail. Consequently they are useless
for the purposes of comparison with the fingerprints of any
person.

I am,

Sir,

Your obedient servant
(Signed) M L Macnaghten

The Chief Constable
Burgh Police
Broughty Ferry

15

I WASTED THE rest of that day warming myself at the fire and dozing in a chair. I seem to recall waking suddenly as the book fell from between my fingers. I seem to recall stooping to retrieve it and beginning again. I seem to recall filling the kettle and making a pot of tea, but the exhaustion was seeping from my bones and before long I gave in to sleep.

But part of my mind watched and waited, and when the bells of St Aidan's Kirk struck three, I rose from my chair, took a little tea and polished my boots. The rain had eased and the wind turned to the south, which brought the mist rolling in off the river so it lay in beads and cobwebs on my coat as I walked, westwards this time, towards Elmgrove.

By four o'clock I was there. Quietly, so as not to disturb the family, I opened the gate of Westlea and stood in the shelter of its deep shadows. The gaslights down the hill were blurred and softened by the mist, and the wind rising from the river brought gentle wave sighs with it. Sleep had almost caught me again when I heard the slow sound of hoof beats and wheels on the road, coming from the top of the hill, and a cart rolled to a stop on the other side of the street, under Elmgrove's dripping boughs.

"James," I whispered. "James Don."

The carter looked about himself in terror.

"Here. Over here, James."

He was a big man and not one to be easily frightened, but he seemed relieved to see me step out of the gate.

"You know me," he said, "but who the Hell are you?" He

wore a heavy coat, with a sack tied across his shoulders and a fisherman's oilskin sou'wester that flopped down over his eyes and hung in a tail over his neck.

"John Fraser, Burgh Constabulary."

"I've done nothing wrong."

"Now, we both know that's a lie."

"No since the last time. Whatever they're sayin it's a damned lie."

"Nobody's accusing you. I need your help."

James Don nodded towards the locked gate. "The business in there."

"That. What do you know?"

"I saw him, sure as daith."

A cold shiver ran down my neck. No more than a dribble of mist. "Tell me what you saw."

"It was the Monday, three, four weeks ago."

"When, James? The dates are important."

"Och, Ah dinnae ken. Ask at the depot, they keep aa the books. But I'm sure and certain it was a Monday, just this day and just this time, half past four of the clock. I was working in Albany Road and working alang this way towards Grove Road, lifting ashes and soil and ribbish from fowk's bins as usual."

"Aye, James, but what did you see?"

"Ah was jist past the wee gate intae thon big hoose, Netherby, in Albany Road, not more than a matter o yairds in this direction, when I saw a man by the light o the lamp, this verra lamp, at the gates o Elmgrove.

"The man came out by the wee gate," James pointed with his whip, "and he cam forrit twa three steps and stood there, in the middle o the path like he'd been cock o the midden. He lookit tae the sooth," he pointed with his whip down the hill towards the river, "an he lookit tae the north," a flick of his whip over his shoulder to Strathern Road. "Then he took a step backwards, back tae the Elmgrove gates. Then he stood there for a good half minute, gave a wee cough and off he went doon the hill at a smart pace."

"What sort of a cough?"

"What sort of a cough? A cough. He coughed, that was all. Like as if he had the cauld."

"Was there anybody else about?"

"At that hour?"

"Would you know him again?"

"Ah couldna say. It was a queer thing what wi Miss Milne being a wumman on her ain an he was undoubtedly a stranger. There's damned few folk in the Ferry Ah dinnae ken."

"Can you not even tell me his age?"

"Verra few men in Broughty Ferry that ah dinnae ken. Verra few. Aa mah days Ah've bin here. Ah'd say he wis atween thirty and forty, no tall, five foot eight or nine, slight, awfy white in the face, a wee thin moustache, dressed like a gentleman wi a dark coat doon past his knees."

"Hat?"

"Oh aye, he had a hat. What like a hat Ah couldnae say."

"Cane?"

"Naw."

"Umbrella?"

"Naw, naw, nithin at all like that."

"And what then?"

"He went his ways." Another flick of the whip down the hill.

I took a note of his details and we parted, the cart rolling gently down the hill and James Don grunting as he got down to do his work. But there was nothing there for me, so I turned north, up to the car route, and waited. The street was silent, as it should be at that hour, when honest folk are still in their beds, but before long I heard the ringing of the rails and the great yellow lamp of the tramcar appeared through the mist, glowing like a monstrous eye, blue-white sparks spitting from the overhead lines as it turned the last corner.

It is a great credit to the management of the Dundee, Broughty Ferry and District Tramways that their service is available to members of the public even at that early hour, for, by that means, working men can easily and cheaply reach their employment, even though it be at a great distance. Persons of quality are by no means too proud to use the cars, but if I wanted to find Andy's little people they would be here, riding to another day of hard labour to earn their daily bread.

The car clanged and juddered to a halt beside me and the conductor rattled the sliding doors back. Inside it was bright with electric light while the windows shone back, black and blank and gleaming with a chill silvering of November mist.

The car was almost empty – just a handful of hunched figures under worn-out work clothes, bowed down with tiredness and the awful thought of another day of labour. They barely had the energy to look up when I came in, but I stood up to as much of my height as the wooden ceiling would allow and I called out: "I am Sergeant John Fraser of the Broughty Ferry Burgh Police. Is there anybody on this car who has any information about Miss Jean Milne?"

I had no plan for what I might do if no one answered – get off and wait for the next car, I suppose – and there were no signs of stirring from all those grey, exhausted heaps of clothes, but, from up the stairs, a voice cried out: "Aye. Up here."

I climbed the stair and there, with his back to the wind, was a strongly built man smoking a pipe.

"Are you not freezing up here?" I said.

"I'll be out all day in it. There's no escaping it and I like my pipe." He held out his hand. "James Urquhart."

"John Fraser. I know your face. Is it St Vincent Street you bide?"

"The same. It's a great tragedy about Miss Milne."

"Did you know her?"

"Must be getting on for thirty years."

"When did you see her last?"

"I'll tell you to an exactitude." He reached into his jacket and brought out a battered notebook in a paper cover. "It was the 14th of October – the Monday. The way I know is I got a position working at the Eastern Wharf, unloading a cargo of jute. Now, that was the first day I was working there and I have my National Insurance card stamped and I make a note in this wee book of all the hours I work. So I can tell you we got done just shortly before the stroke of six o'clock."

"And then?"

"Then I walked up from the harbour to the Stannergate and I took the car from the burgh boundary home to Fort Street. When we got to Ellieslea Road, there was Miss Milne, running back and forth along the pavement alongside the car and peering in the windows as if she was looking for somebody. She was trying to keep up with the car as we moved off and shading her eyes to look through the glass, searching among the passengers."

"And that's the last you saw of her?"

"The very last."

"Did you ever see a strange man about Elmgrove?"

"About Elmgrove? I never had cause to be at Elmgrove, but –" he stopped for a second and pulled on his pipe, "– there was a man. It was a couple of days later – the day that cargo got finished. The Wednesday. We were later getting started that day and I went up to my work at the jute by the 7.30 car from Gray Street. I was sitting on the top on the back seat, much as we are now. There was one other man up top with me, sitting on the front seat. Then at Ellieslea Road a man came up on to the top and sat with his back towards Dundee just about there, about the third seat from the back. He dropped down in the seat like he was completely worn out and done and he threw his feet up on the next bench. I thought to myself: 'Aye, you've been out on the randan. You've been a night in the tiles.'"

"Did he speak?"

"He did not. He neither looked nor spoke. But I had a good look at him and he looked queer – he seemed scared, excited and nervous-like; his eyes never halted, but he was constantly looking down to the floor of the car or at the trees at the side of the road. He minded me of a man with the horrors – have you ever seen that?"

"Oh, I've seen that more than once or twice."

"Well that's what he was like, but he was quite sober. And I said to myself: 'The house you have come out of, the servant has not been very particular with your shoes.' They looked as though they had been blackened but not polished. He kept his right hand in his overcoat pocket."

"He wore an overcoat?"

"Oh aye, he wore an overcoat."

"And what like a coat was it?"

"A dark, slate-coloured waterproof coat, down to his knees and buttoned to his throat. And he kept his right hand in his pocket all the way up the road and sat with his head laid on his left hand."

"Was he dirty or bloodied?"

"Never a bit. Clean and tidy, well washed but awful flushed about the face, like a man blushing, as if he had been working hard. I mind that because he had this thin, fair moustache and it quite stood out against his face."

"What happened then?"

"Nothing. I got off at the burgh boundary as usual and walked to my work. So far as I know, he sat there all the way to Dundee."

"Would you know him again?"

He took a couple of puffs on his pipe. "I wouldn't want to swear. I saw him for as long as we've been speaking now, but I can say this, he was a stranger to the burgh. It was a face I had never seen before – and nor have I seen it again. He was just an ordinary-looking chap. About thirty I should say, ordinary height, ordinary size, what you'd call a common face, but he was every inch the dapper gentleman, fine shoes and, man, he even had a wee white stripe down the sides of his socks! Would you credit that?"

All this information I carefully recorded, typed up into statements and had duly sworn and signed by the witnesses. I even checked with the foreman of the Cleansing Department and had him swear a statement that James Don was working on Monday the 14th and his duties would have taken him to be in Albany Road and Grove Road about 4.30 a.m. All these things I presented to Detective Lieutenant Trench.

There was one other thing. James Don the rubbish picker told me that about twenty minutes after his meeting with the handsome young gentleman under the lamp post, he was working in Edward Street – that bit of road north of Grove Road they have renamed now – do you remember?

He told me he was lifting ashes at Mr Bulloch's house in Edward Street when he looked back to Strathern Road and saw the figure of a man passing, walking towards the Ferry. The man was about a hundred yards off, so they did not speak, but one thing was clear: he was a police officer.

16

IT WAS REMARKABLE to me how the advice of Andy Hay had proved itself to be both wise and good. Nobody sees a servant. It is a necessity to believe that they do not exist. How could a man who called himself a man lie abed until eight while some wee scrap of a lassie carried coals up and down the stairs to get his fires going at five o'clock in the morning? How could any mother see another mother's lassie work herself grey and ragged so her own daughters might keep their hands soft and smooth for nothing more than embroidery and piano playing? Only by pretending that it was not so.

Respectable people had learned to blind themselves to the very presence of their servants. A mountain of washing would transform itself into crisp, clean laundry, starched and ironed and snowy white every Monday, but nobody knew how that happened, because the mistress was eating cake and taking tea up in Dundee.

Every morning shoes were standing at the bedroom door, gleaming black and polished, but nobody knew how that happened because they had all been asleep in their beds.

Breakfast, dinner and tea, plates of hot food arrived on the table, but nobody had any idea how that happened – although the mistress was awful unhappy that the butcher's bill had gone up by nearly two shillings this week and something would have to be done.

In every room of the house, fires were lit, fires were fed,

ashes were emptied and grates were swept, but nobody ever saw it done. An invisible army swarmed amongst the grand houses of Broughty Ferry unseen and all unheard, unnoticed, unregarded and ignored. But they had ears to hear and eyes to see. And some of the things they told me made my heart sink.

Jean Milne would never have noticed Ina McIntosh. She lived along the road from me at Links Cottages and she worked in the bleachfield alongside the Dighty Water, lifting great heavy loads of newly spun, wet, stinking linen cloth on her back and spreading them out on the grass to whiten. Jean Milne never worked like that a day in her life.

That was Ina, a lassie of seventeen years, and there's her sister Jessie, a full three years older, who rises at God knows what hour to labour in a mill in Dundee for a pittance of pay, day and daily. These places are a kind of Hell with the noise and the dust so a body can neither breathe nor hear – far less speak or think.

And yet they had love, those two lassies, love enough to walk a good mile and a half up to Caenlochan Villas on a Monday night and take a cup of tea with their sister in service in Mr Potter's big house. Not tea of their own, you understand. Oh no. If a lassie takes tea with her sister, she makes a brew with the leaves she has saved from the mistress's pot.

And then, when those two girls came out again into the night, ready for the walk home, cooried in together against the October winds, walking home to bed and a few hours of fitful sleep before rising again to another day of work, what should they see but a man with a yellow moustache. Poor Ina.

"We keeked through the gate into the grounds of Elmgrove and, just then, a man came out of the grounds and opened the small gate and stepped out on to the footway as if he owned the place. He was sweating and flushed in the face and he gave us a stare as we passed and walked down Grove Road – a right gentlemanly-looking sort, with a fair moustache and a long dark overcoat.

"Jessie thought he was after us. He stood staring after us, but he never followed us, though I had my hatpin ready."

John Wood the gardener, who lives in Chapel Lane, he saw the man with the thin moustache too. In fact, he opened the door to him.

I found John along at St Aidan's churchyard, tending the ground around a tiny block of marble no more than a foot square. It had "Mother" written on it in letters of lead. There was no name and no dates.

"All we could afford," he said. "She used to say we were her monument. Damned shame. She should have had more." He gathered up his tools and rubbed each in turn on a rough bit of oiled cloth. They gleamed. There was no spot of earth or mud on any of them, not the slightest trace of rust anywhere. "I'm surprised you've taken so long to find me," he said, "since I did her garden for years – or as much of it as she would let me do."

"Most of it is away to rack and ruin," I said.

"Aye. It would break your heart to look at it."

"But if you did her garden for years, why did you not come forward?"

"Because I did her garden for years – that's why. I have no wish to say anything about poor Miss Milne, but, if you ask me, I'll speak."

"Tell me what you can," I said.

"The poor soul was man daft. She was an unmarried woman of a certain age. Those things should all have been past with her, and if they were not, she had no business speaking about them with me. The way she carried on, it would not have been respectable in a lassie, and in a woman of her age and position it was just – well, it wasn't right.

"She was never done talking about meeting nice gentlemen; that was always her particular theme, about getting acquainted with French and German gentlemen. That was all her conversation. It was a daily occurrence every afternoon I was working at Elmgrove and she was at home and, ach, she would spend hours in frivolous talk about the nice gentleman or gentlemen she had made acquaintance of.

"After she came home in August she said she had had a good lot of travelling with a German gentleman who was living in a hotel in the Strand – a tea planter. She said he was to come and visit her at Elmgrove. She had a letter from him while I was working there and she was always talking about this gentleman in particular or about other nice gentlemen she had met."

I leaned back on one of the larger gravestones, an enormous lump of red granite sacred to the memory of a long-gone minister, "a faithful servant of Christ and beloved of this congregation", though not, perhaps, as well beloved as John Wood's mother. "Did you ever see any of them at the house?" I said.

"It grieves me sorely, but I have to tell you that I did. The day before Miss Milne left for her last holiday – now that was the 19th of September; I have it in my account book, I was working there. It was getting near finishing time, about half five, and she came out. I thought we were going to get more of this silly chatter about her gentlemen friends and, I'm telling you, I was sick of it, but, no, out she came and asked me back into the house to help her lock the different doors of rooms and shut the windows, and she said she was going away the following day. Near all the windows is painted shut or screwed down, but I closed the dining room window and her bedroom window and I took the keys to her in the hall.

"I was in the hall when the front door bell rang, and for

some reason she asked me to go to the door. I went and found a gentleman there, a proper toff, in a claw-hammer coat, a man I'd say getting on for forty, with a thin, yellow moustache.

"He asked if Miss Milne was in. I said she was and I went back to the kitchen and told her: 'Miss Milne, there is a gentleman at the door.' Well, she fairly skipped to the door to meet him, skipped like a lassie, and they took each other by the hands – both hands – very affectionately and Miss Milne said: 'I am so glad to see you here,' and asked him in. They both came in the vestibule and they passed me at the foot of the stair, where I was standing, without a glance. I might just as well not have been there.

"After they passed me, I made to go out, but she called me back and she put two shillings in my hand."

"What was that for?"

"She said it was 'for my trouble'. But we both knew fine it was to shut me up. She planned to stop my mouth with silver."

"But you don't feel bound to that?"

"I agreed to nothing. My duty is to tell the truth. I did not seek you out, Sergeant Fraser, you came to me."

He was hurt and humiliated. He was only the gardener, only a servant. He was meant to see nothing, and if by chance he should find a respectable single woman admitting a strange man to her home at the close of the day, then it would take no more than twenty-four bright little pennies to shut him up. We both of us looked down at the grass for a minute or two, John Wood sucking hard on his pipe while I counted daisies until the moment had passed.

"What happened then?" I said.

"The man in the claw-hammer coat walked right into the dining room as if he was no stranger to the place and I left the house. You may know where the gentleman passed the night, but I do not."

I did not know where the gentleman with the thin yellow moustache passed the night, but I knew this much: there was no more than one bed in Elmgrove.

"I bitterly regret I let him in," said poor John Wood. "I have chided myself that I opened the door to the man that killed her. Pity me now when the only service I can do for her is to ruin her reputation."

I tried to comfort him. "It may be that no one need know. We have our ways. We are not without delicacy."

John Wood shook his head, laid his tools on his shoulder and began to walk. "It's too late for that. You know."

But I knew already.

It seemed half the Ferry knew.

James Urquhart the docker knew. He told me he sat on the tram one Wednesday afternoon in October while Jean Milne disported herself with "a stout gentleman aged about sixty with an English accent."

"I was surprised at the way Miss Milne was carrying on with the gentleman, by her talk to him. I could not make out all their talk, but Miss Milne was always addressing the gentleman: 'Yes, dear' and 'Yes, pet.' It was that, those endearments over and over, oft repeated, that was what drew my attention. Miss Milne was always looking at him." He said that. A man who sat there on that tramcar, his face black with dirt and stinking of sweat after a day of hauling jute bales about with his bare hands. A rough working man, and he was horror-struck at what he saw of that woman.

She rubbed it in their faces. She didn't care who saw. But they were only little people. What could it matter what they thought? It was disgusting. Disgusting!

17

THERE IS NO secret to the success of the Bonnington Hotel. Discretion, that's all. Nothing flashy. Nothing grand. Nothing pretentious. The Bonnington is not the Ritz. The Bonnington is not the Savoy. At the Bonnington Hotel, they invariably offer a poached egg for breakfast, never *une oeuf poché*.

At the heart of fashionable Bloomsbury, a stone's throw from the British Museum, the Bonnington is the last word in modernity: an elegant, fashionable hotel offering every facility expected by ladies and gentlemen of quality but all of it set within the facade of a much older building. The Bonnington offers everything to be expected in these first years of a new Georgian era, when flying machines now dart almost daily across the Channel and communications encircle the globe, quite literally, with lightning speed. The Bonnington is a jewel of modern design and convenience, but all within the setting of the elegance of a bygone age. Quality and service are the watchwords but with a proper restraint. Nothing Frenchified or foreign. Modesty. Discretion.

But there is nothing discreet about a policeman. Still less about two policemen, one of them all frogged and belted and braided, with his little pillbox kepi and his patent shoes, and the other a bull of a man in a dark-blue coat with silver buttons, a chain across his chest for his whistle and a tread that shook the china in the breakfast room.

The one with the frogging down his tunic walked up to the

front counter and rang the brass bell, which was totally needless since Miss Minnie Gibbons was in her usual place at the desk dealing with a guest. The guest gave the police officer a look. Miss Minnie Gibbons felt she could spare him no more than an arched eyebrow. She moved the brass bell to one side. The police officer was suitably abashed.

When the guest had been satisfactorily dealt with, Miss Minnie Gibbons turned her gaze on the police officer with the frogging and the braid. "Good morning," she said. "How may I help you?"

He cleared his throat. "Good morning. I am Chief Constable Sempill of Broughty Ferry Burgh Police. Here to see Mr Clarence Wray. He is expecting us."

"Of course. Have you a card?"

He took one from his pocket and handed it over. Miss Minnie Gibbons considered it briefly, moved the brass bell back to the middle of the counter and gave it a sharp 'ping ping'. "The dreadful business with Miss Milne, of course. Dreadful. Simply dreadful. She was quite a favourite at the Bonnington."

A boy came running up in answer to the bell and Miss Minnie Gibbons said: "Jack, show these gentlemen into the large parlour and take this card," she handed it to him by the corner, "to Mr Wray in 209."

The boy, who was also wearing a kepi, though his was red and he kept it on his head at all times, said: "Yes, Miss Gibbons," and "This way, please, gentlemen," and he set off at a quick-smart pace down a brown corridor with a thick blue carpet.

By the time the two policemen had caught up, the boy was standing, holding open the door of the large parlour. "If you'd care to wait here a moment, sirs, I'll just run up and enquire after our Mr 209."

The two policemen, Chief Constable Sempill and the large

sergeant whom Scotland Yard had assigned as a courtesy to be his guide and assistant, went into the room and waited. It was the hour when ladies and gentlemen went to attend to their letters, so, though the writing room was no doubt very busy, the large parlour was deserted.

There were two chairs together in a window looking down onto Southampton Row. It seemed to Mr Sempill that there were more people in that one street than in the whole of Broughty Ferry.

"Don't sit down," he told the sergeant. "Leave that place for Wray. Bring another chair when he comes and sit close enough to make a note and corroborate his statement."

The sergeant said: "Sir."

"Are you Scottish?"

"Sir."

"I hadn't realised. Not until you spoke. Just then."

"Sir."

Mr Sempill moved the net curtain aside with the tip of a finger and looked out into the street again.

"That way to the British Museum, is it?"

"The other way, sir."

"The other way. I must pay a visit before I leave."

"Sir."

They seemed to have exhausted their conversation. The clock ticked. The coals settled in the hearth. And then the door handle gave a sharp click and a man came in.

He was pale and nervous-looking, thin with dark circles under his eyes, and Mr Sempill was pained to notice that he had no moustache. Still, he thought, that would be the work of a moment. On the other hand, Clarence Herberto Wray was quite obviously not a man in his thirties.

He held out his hand. "Mr Sempill. How do you do?"

Mr Sempill said: "How do you do?" and indicated the second chair in the window. "This is Sergeant . . . my sergeant. He will assist us in taking notes."

"Of course." They nodded at each other, in a not-unfriendly way.

Mr Sempill was the sort of man who believed in the pleasantries, but there seemed nothing to say. "I trust you are well," he said.

Mr Wray gave a thin smile.

"Yes, well, we know why we are here. I should like to hear, from your own lips, how it was you came to know Miss Jean Milne."

"She was a guest at this hotel. We were guests here together. There's no secret. But so were many people. Why are you questioning me about this?"

Mr Sempill reached into his frogged and braided uniform jacket and came out with a lilac-coloured envelope. "You corresponded with Miss Milne."

"I don't think that's any of your business."

"In the circumstances."

"The circumstances? The circumstances hardly alter the case for a gentleman."

Mr Sempill took that hard. "Is this the letter of a gentleman? Written on lilac paper? As you very well know, this is not your only correspondence with Miss Milne. Indeed, you even stoop to poetry – of a sort. Am I right in thinking you are a foreign gentleman?"

"I was educated in America, yes."

"And your mother?"

"She was a lady of Uruguay." He made it sound like a confession.

"Make a note of that," Mr Sempill told the sergeant. "Now,

if you don't mind, please set out – exactly – how you knew Miss Milne."

He gave a little braying laugh then, as if it was all silliness and nothing could have mattered less. "The little Scotch canary." And he tittered again. "That's what we used to call her. She was always darting about the place like a little bird – packing up the fires and arranging the furniture. I thought that she was a shareholder in the hotel. It's run by a Scotch syndicate, you know. She was just like a little bird."

"And you took her under your wing," said Mr Sempill.

"My wing is broken, Chief Constable. I came back to England for the sake of my health. I suffered a complete nervous breakdown when I was in Africa."

"Mental troubles. I see. Note that also, Sergeant."

"I am quite well now. I was never out of my wits. I came back here for the rest. Then, back in January I came upon poor Jean Milne weeping quietly to herself in the writing room. Well, naturally I tried to comfort her."

"Naturally. The action of a gentleman. Do you know why she was weeping?"

"She had had a letter from the minister of her church back home offering her some advice and she was deeply touched. She said: 'I had not known there was anyone in the world who had so much concern for me.'"

"And what was the substance of this advice?"

"Spiritualism. It's all the fashion these days – table tapping and so on. He was advising her to have nothing to do with it. Apparently she had been trying to reach her dear departed brother 'beyond the veil' and she had informed her minister, who told her to have nothing to do with it."

"And it was then that you began your flirtation."

"I resent that! There was no flirtation. I am a married man.

130

I must have bored her witless talking of my wife. Miss Milne interested me very much. She appeared to be a real good character, innocent and did a lot of philanthropic work. Her conversation was always of the highest possible order, and perfectly clean. We all liked her and thought she was a good little woman – well read, high-minded and in every respect a little lady. One of the happy faculties I have is in making friends; I get their confidence and I hold it. This is one of my most fortunate possessions."

Mr Sempill gave him a look as he tucked the lilac envelope back into his jacket, but he said nothing. He waited for the thin man to speak again.

"She went to start loading the fire again and so I offered to put some coals on for her. She allowed me to do so, thanked me, and asked what I was reading. I told her I was reading Omar Khayyám in Edward Fitzgerald's translation, and that lead up to other conversation. I was convalescent at the time . . . as I said. My nerves. As I said."

"And the acquaintance continued."

"Well, I suppose it did. I was almost always here in the evening and had a good many conversations with her. I recall, one evening, attending a lecture held in the hotel by a phreno-logical society. I think Miss Milne knew the speaker and she was good enough to invite me. After the meeting she began a discussion on phrenology, but as I had never read up on the subject I could not discuss the matter with her. We rubbed along together here for a month or so, and then in the last week of February I went to Cornwall on business. From there I travelled back to work in northern Nigeria. Six months."

"So you were back in England in October."

"A few days only. I stayed here until the 16th, then I went to Sardinia on business, and I have only just returned."

"These things can all be checked, you know," Mr Sempill said.

The thin man smiled again. "You mean the dates don't fit with the murder. I'm sorry to disappoint you, Chief Constable. Feel free to check to your heart's content."

Mr Sempill was disappointed. There was no disguising it. A half-breed Latin, brought up in America, a man with self-confessed mental problems – Clarence Wray fitted the description exactly. A maniac or a foreigner, that was what Trench had said, and here was a man who was both. But, no, the dates would not fit. A man could not be running a mine in Sardinia and, at the same time, beating a woman's brains out in Broughty Ferry.

He pressed on. "Did Miss Milne ever discuss her financial affairs with you?"

"She told me she had some shares in Broken Hill – those are silver and lead mines in New South Wales, the greatest in the world. She told me that she had paid £5 for £1 shares. That's all I know. But I did try to advise her.

"While we were here at the Bonnington, some adventurer came from Canada and tried to get her to invest some money in his mines. In British Columbia, I believe. I advised her to have nothing to do with it. I told her to beware and that I did not think much of any man who would induce a woman to invest money in a mining operation that she could not see."

"Did she mention a name?"

"I don't think so. If she did, I can't recall it. I did not speak to the man at all; in fact, I avoided him. I did not like the look of him one little bit and any time he was in conversation with Miss Milne, showing her the prospectus of his mines and the plans he had or something like that, then I went away to the little parlour to avoid an argument. My nerves, you see."

"I see. And can you describe this man?"

"I'd say young. Younger than I am, under forty, I should say. Perhaps forty. Very well dressed. Excellent clothes. The look of a gentleman. Round face. Well fed and a slight, fair moustache."

18

Superintendent Neaves,
Kent Count Constabulary,
Tonbridge,

We have a man in custody here on false pretences who will be
before the Court tomorrow at 11-30 a.m.

He gives the name of Charles Warner, 210 Wilton Avenue,
Toronto, Canada. His description is: Age 38, 5 feet 9 inches,
hair dark brown, turning slightly grey, eyes grey, complexion
pale or sallow, round feature clean shaven, tattooed Masonic
and Oddfellows signs left forearm, gold stopping front teeth;
dressed grey lounge suit, dark overcoat, cap, gentlemanly
appearance. This man is a mystery to us, and we thought
perhaps he might be connected with the Dundee murder. Will
you interview him?

Chief Constable J. Howard Sempill
Broughty Ferry Burgh Police
C/o Scotland Yard

19

IT WAS IMPORTANT to remember, thought Miss Ann Myfanwy Jones, that Father was very disappointed too. Miss Ann Myfanwy tried to remember that every time she took her book and sat on one of the iron benches of the promenade and looked east across the great river estuary to Liverpool, pretending that she was looking west to Wales.

If she had been at the other side of the peninsula, she might have looked to Wales and seen its silent, far mountains. Instead, she had to look at Liverpool, with its docks and all the ships going back and forth in the river, where it was not silent, not green, not Wales. That was disappointing.

Miss Ann Myfanwy comforted herself with the thought that the river rushing by her feet was mingled with the sea, the same sea that washed the edge of Wales where the mountains came down to bathe their feet. But she could not see Wales. It was just a little way behind her, beyond the pleasant streets of New Brighton, but, no, she could not see Wales and that was disappointing.

Still, Miss Ann Myfanwy made the daily effort not to blame Father. As much as she was disappointed, Father was disappointed too. Father was not to be blamed. Disappointment was what came to those who set too much store by things. She realised that. She understood it and it would not do to be disappointed. There were many others far worse off than themselves, many others who would gladly change places and think themselves blessed.

Nobody could be disappointed to live in a house like No. 102 Magazine Lane, New Brighton.

No. 102 Magazine Lane was a very fine house indeed, a tall red-brick house or, at any rate, half of a tall red-brick house – what the estate agent had described as "a most prestigious, semi-detached villa" – but it was, really, only half a house and that was a little disappointing. Just a little.

Standing together, Nos. 100 and 102 had the look of a fairy-tale tower, soaring up on either side to half-timbered pent-houses that overhung the entrances. They were like something from a child's picture book, a suburban version of the Castle of Chillon, which was appropriate, because while Miss Ann Myfanwy had a fervent wish to be the Lady of Shallot, when she was inside No. 102 Magazine Lane she did feel rather more like the Prisoner of Chillon. Still, there was a kind of romance about the place, as if Magazine Lane would be forever incom-plete without an armoured knight on a rearing black stallion, pawing at the pavement by the front gate and striking sparks with its hooves. From up there, Miss Ann Myfanwy could let down her hair and allow the knight to climb up to her on a long, silken rope or she might launch a hail of darts or a cascade of boiling oil on the heads of any who dared assault No. 102 Magazine Lane. But nobody ever did and, though she often looked from her window as she combed her hair in the evening, the knight never came.

Still, nobody could be disappointed by a house like No. 102 Magazine Lane. It was just across the street from the lovely public park – just across the street – and Father had been very generous and given her the topmost room so she could look out across the trees and down to the river. It was lovely. Anybody would have to agree that it was lovely, although her tower included the bathroom and the bathroom was back to back with the bathroom of No. 100 and the walls were, well, perhaps a little thin. All the same, the park was lovely. It was absolutely lovely. But it was public and it was across the street. It was not the park of No. 102 Magazine Lane as the park of Bodyngharad was the park of Bodyngharad House. It did not roll right up to the door, as did the parks of Bodyngharad. There was nothing but wild country at the door of Bodyngharad, but there was a street right outside the gate of No. 102 Magazine Row, which was disappointing.

The important thing, as Miss Ann Myfanwy always said, was to remember that Father had been greatly disappointed. Greatly disappointed in many ways. He had, after all, worked so hard in the business all his life. He had achieved so much. He had provided so liberally for the family, succeeded so brilliantly and then, by careful husbandry, at the close of his life, he had made sufficient provision to allow them to retire to the country – to Wales. How happy they had all been to turn their backs on Liverpool and to return to Wales and the beautiful estates of Bodyngharad. It was a new beginning, which was important for an unmarried woman of thirty-two.

"This is a new beginning," said Miss Ann Myfanwy Jones, who was still a young woman in Bodyngharad and by no means regarded as an old maid or on the shelf. Father bought her a horse called Boxer and she wore a top hat set over at an angle with a spotted veil over her face for the sake of the mud and she had a gold pin in her scarf, with a pearl in the top of it, and she carried a crop with a horn handle and she caught the eye of Mr Pryce the corn merchant, who was a widower and almost fifty – but what of that?

Mr Pryce the corn merchant could be very tender, though he was a widower and almost fifty. He said: "Miss Ann Myfanwy, you are most lovely," and they came to an understanding as they sat together on the terrace one evening, under a lead urn spilling with nasturtiums. No definite word was said. But they had an understanding.

That was three days before Father's awful disappointment, when the shutters went up at Bodyngharad and Father went back to work in the rubber business and they all moved to No. 102 Magazine Lane to begin again. Not all of them, of course. Poor brother Arthur had no choice but to strike out alone for America and make his way in the Burroughs Advertising Company of Detroit, Michigan. Miss Ann Myfanwy missed him horribly, but, in truth, she missed Boxer rather more, and Arthur would always be her brother but Boxer was somebody else's horse.

All of that was seven years ago and, the last she heard, Mr Pryce the corn merchant had married the headmistress of Bodyngharad school and had two ginger-headed daughters although he must be not far short of sixty now, which was rather ridiculous, so when she looked back on what might have been, she was not disappointed in the least.

Miss Ann Myfanwy Jones was always reassuring people that she wasn't disappointed. Many a time she had sat down with a book on an iron bench on the promenade, and before long a nice lady would sit down beside her and they would strike up a conversation, which, it seemed almost invariably, would turn to the story of these past seven years, although Miss Ann Myfanwy disliked talking of herself and her troubles. Boxer would always feature in these conversations and sometimes Arthur too, although rather less so, and she always made a point of explaining that she was not at all disappointed at the way things had turned out.

Miss Ann Myfanwy never engaged gentlemen in conversation. She made a point of that too, but one morning in September a strange thing happened.

She had gone out after breakfast as usual, not through the park but towards the red sandstone turrets of the old artillery magazine and then down the lane to the water's edge. It was a crisp, bright morning and summer's last throw. She disliked the coming of autumn. It was a reminder of the passage of time. Seven years since she lost Boxer. Soon it would be eight.

She had her book in her coat pocket and she read for a while as usual, on her usual bench at the usual place on the esplanade when a man went past, coming from the direction of the Egremont Promenade. He stopped at the next bench, turned and looked at her, and she looked back at him – for only a moment and then looked back at her book. When she looked up again, the man was gone.

And then, after a while, because the clouds began to threaten, she put her book away and buttoned her coat and took a stroll up to Victoria Street, just to look in the shop windows, and there was the man again – that same man who had stopped to look at her on the promenade – and he was looking at her again. He was quite a handsome devil, very well dressed, with dark hair showing from under his cap and a pleasing tinge of silver at the temples.

He was coming towards her, looking her full in the face, and Miss Ann Myfanwy – it must be admitted – was the tiniest bit alarmed. What if he were a maniac or a garrotter? One heard such stories, but, no, the man stopped and raised his hat in the most courteous manner and said: "Pardon me for addressing you when we have not been introduced, but are you not Miss Nancy Jones?"

Only those of Miss Ann Myfanwy's most intimate circle ever addressed her as 'Nancy'. Mr Pryce the corn merchant had never dared, despite their understanding, and she could not think of the last time anybody had called her by that name.

She forgot completely that her father had called to her from the front door only that morning to warn her that it looked like rain. Miss Ann Myfanwy was astonished to hear a stranger enquire after her as "Nancy", but he did have a very beautiful coat and the silver in his hair showed him to be a mature and trustworthy individual. "What a lovely coat," thought Miss Ann Myfanwy. "I do like your hair." But she said: "I'm sorry, sir, you have the advantage of me."

The stranger was politely apologetic: "Forgive me. You have a brother, Arthur, in America in the advertising line in Detroit, I believe. You are Miss Nancy Jones, are you not? I'm not mistaken, surely."

"You know my brother?"

"I was sure I was right! I knew it. Permit me to introduce myself. My name is Charles Walker, of Detroit, Michigan."

Miss Ann Myfanwy slipped off her glove – naturally she was never without gloves – and offered her hand. "How do you do, Mr Walker?"

He took hold of her fingers gently and said: "How do you do," with a not unpleasant American twang.

"But how do you come to recognise me?" she said.

"Why, Miss Jones, your brother keeps your picture in a silver frame on the piano in his home – the one with . . ." He let his hand tumble down in an uncertain, cascading motion from his face to his chest.

"Oh the picture with the fur stole! That silly thing."

"I don't think it's silly at all. I think it rather beautiful. I know Arthur is very fond of it and you may judge how closely I have made a study of it, Miss Jones, if I am able to recognise you by sight and 'in the flesh' as it were, weeks later and thousands of miles away. But, if I might say something . . ." He waited.

"Please, yes, go on."

"That portrait does not do you justice, Miss Jones."

She noticed he was still holding her hand and, a little reluctantly, she took it back.

"You know Arthur?"

"Why, of course, Miss Jones. We run across each other frequently. In fact, I saw him only a few weeks ago, just before I left the States."

"Are you in the advertising business too?"

"No." He gave a kind of throaty chuckle and she noticed, for the first time, he had three gold teeth at the front of his mouth. "No, I'm a horse trader. I couldn't do Arthur's job, stuck behind a desk in the city all day. I need to be out in the open air in all weathers, with my horses and . . ."

She was staring at him.

"Oh. You noticed my teeth."

"I'm so sorry. I didn't mean to stare."

"I understand. It's peculiar, I know. The glue in the seat of my pants failed me one fine day, Miss Jones, and I came out of the saddle and broke my fall with my face."

"Oh, you poor man. Poor, poor man." She put a hand on his arm.

"It's nothing to grieve over, Miss Jones. I came away with no real hurt and an extra-shiny smile, that's all. You've got to expect something like that when you're in my line, working with horses every day . . ." Horses. Horses every day. The thought of horses beguiled her. " . . . although I like to pretend it has something to do with my lack of success with the fair sex."

"Oh, come now, Mr Walker. I find that hard to believe."

"Well, believe it or not, Miss Jones, it's true."

"You're not married?"

"No. I regret to say I'm not."

He wasn't married.

"It would mean a great deal to me to have someone to care for, Miss Jones, and it would mean a great deal to have someone who could care for me. I regard the married state as one of the most noble institutions of mankind and, speaking as a religious man . . ." Oh, a religious man. He was religious and he traded in horses and he was unmarried. ". . . one of Heaven's most gentle blessings and an intimation of the bliss to come. But perhaps it is not meant for all of us." He gave another of his little chuckles. "Anyway, I don't think it's very likely I could find a little lady who would put up with my feeling for horses, Miss Jones. No, I don't think that's likely at all."

"Mr Walker, you'd be astonished. I for one have a perfect passion for horses."

"No! You do? Well, don't that beat all?"

"Arthur must have told you . . ."

"Yes, of course. You know, come to think of it, he did!"

". . . about my dear old chum Boxer."

"Boxer, yes of course. How could I have forgotten?"

"Well, as you know, we had to say 'farewell', we two, Boxer and I."

"Yes, of course, after, after . . . You need say no more, Miss Jones."

"I can see you are too delicate to mention Father's business disappointment, Mr Walker, but I'm sure Arthur has spared you nothing of his opinions on the matter."

"I wouldn't go so far as that."

"You are being very kind, but we both know that Arthur took it hard. I am only a woman. I was protected from the worst of it, but poor Arthur had to fly the nest and make his way in the world."

"Miss Jones, I know very well that you suffered too." And then he said just one word, softly and sadly. "Boxer."

"Yes. Poor, dear Boxer." She looked down at the pavement and noticed the first splash of a raindrop. "The weather is taking a turn for the worse, Mr Walker."

"Indeed, Miss Jones. Indeed, it is. I wonder. I hardly dare to ask, but would you do me the great honour of joining me at the Royal Ferry Hotel? I believe it is a respectable establishment and suitable for ladies. I would be delighted if we might continue our conversation over a cup of tea."

"Mr Walker, I should be delighted too." So he offered her his arm and she took it and they walked off together.

20

IT SEEMED THAT time simply flew by while they were together in the parlour of the Royal Ferry Hotel. It was the very finest hotel in New Brighton, right at the pier head, so it was almost the first thing anyone saw as they left the boat from Liverpool, but the parlour was burdened with a rather untrustworthy fireplace, which gave occasional coughs of smoke and not a great deal of heat. Still, it had a certain charm.

They chatted happily, and when the waiter came Mr Walker ordered tea for two with cakes and scones: "Let's have a treat while we enjoy our chat," he said. But no sooner had the waiter left with their order than he leaned across the table and interrupted Miss Ann Myfanwy in the middle of a story about a hat she had seen and said: "I'm sorry, could you excuse me for just one moment?" and hurried out.

He returned again a moment later and everything was as happy as before and he had her laughing behind her hand when he told her about the dreadful stormy crossing "over the pond", but when the waiter returned there was only one sandwich, one cake, one scone. She noticed, but she did not remark.

"Won't you, please, have a sandwich? That ham looks delicious." He handed her a tiny plate. "Please, do."

She was unsure, but when he insisted she slid half a sandwich, a little thing the size of a calling card, onto her plate.

"No, no, please. You must take all of it. I invited you for a proper tea, but I find I'm not in the slightest hungry. I had an enormous breakfast – as is my habit when I'm working with the horses – but I haven't done half the work I'm used to."

"Are you sure?"

"Quite sure. Please. Milk?"

She nodded and he poured tea for them both and he seemed so happy and easy that she forgot all about the business with the sandwich. "Tell me more about your horses," she said.

"Well, I run a small ranch a day or so outside Detroit. My grandfather set the place up getting on for eighty years ago . . ."

"Did he have to battle the redskins over it?" she said.

"I'm sure he had some stories to tell. Things were pretty wild in those days, you bet!"

She liked that. "You bet!" It was all so young and daring and so American.

"But I reckon some of Granpaw's stories got bigger with the telling."

He told her about the time of the big drought when the bull-frogs latched on to the old milch cow and sucked and sucked and when Granpaw came out in the morning they were bigger than the cow.

"He had a lot of stories like that. Like the time it froze so hard he couldn't hear the cattle until the thaw came and all their moos unfroze."

She laughed over that one too. "Do you still run cattle?"

"No, my dad thought it was an awful lot of work for not much wages, so he decided to go into horses instead. People are always going to need horses, that's what my old dad said, and he was right."

"Then you're not a believer in the motor car, Mr Walker?"

"It's a flash in the pan. It's a confidence trick perpetrated on the public – the wealthy public with more money than sense. A fool and his money are soon parted, that's what they say, and if you're looking for a fool parted from his money, you will find him behind the wheel of an automobile!"

"Why, Mr Walker, you are very fervent!"

"Then I beg your pardon, but this is a matter I feel strongly about. I believe in honest dealing and I call it a downright swindle to sell a man a noisy, stinky automobile that can rattle along at upwards of twenty miles an hour when there is no road that can take him at more than five miles an hour! And I will go further, Nancy – no man alive could ever make friends with an automobile or feel for that mountain of nuts and bolts as you felt for your dear Boxer!"

She was impressed. He was hot-blooded. He was passionate. He believed in honest dealing. He understood what it was to love, truly love a horse, he was of a religious turn of mind, he was unmarried – and he had called her Nancy.

Miss Ann Myfanwy regarded him over the rim of her teacup for a moment, watching him push fingers through his thick, dark hair in an agitated fashion.

"Cake?" he barked.

"You called me Nancy."

His hand flew to his mouth. "Why, Miss Jones, a thousand pardons. Please accept my apologies. Here I am, an absolute stranger to you, I intrude myself upon your acquaintance and now I force you into a familiarity I have no right to demand. Please, forgive me, Miss Jones. It's only that all I've ever known of you is that dear photograph on Arthur's piano and it has always been to me simply 'Nancy'. I offer you my most sincere and humble apologies, Miss Jones."

She laughed out loud at him then and said: "I do not object in the slightest, Mr Walker. Cake?"

After that, of course they were – "Call me Charlie, won't

you?" – the very best of friends and she forced him to share the one, solitary cake and she cut the scone in half and spread a tiny knob of butter very thinly across both sides and doled out the damson jam as if they had been sharing rations under siege.

He left his place on the other side of the table and he went to sit beside her and they watched the rain drumming up the pier to fling itself against the windows.

"Call me Nancy again."

"Nancy." He brushed his fingers over hers. "Nancy."

And then she called him "Boxer".

She said. "Why did you make the waiter bring cakes for one?"

"I told you. I'm not hungry."

"Is that all? Really?"

"Really, that's all."

He told her about his life raising horses and how he had brought the best of them all the way across the Atlantic, sleeping alongside them in the hold of the ship so they might have at least a familiar voice to listen to in the dark, and how he had crossed all the way to Ostend to sell them and how, in a few days, just a few days, he would join his ship at Liverpool and sail back to America.

"This time I plan on making use of my cabin. It's going to be a good deal more comfortable but a whole lot lonelier."

"Where are you staying?" she asked.

"Oh, I've rented two rooms from a fine old lady, Mrs Graham, along in Riversdale Road. No. 10. You will always reach me there."

The waiter came in to tend to the fire, and when he was finished he made a point of noisily clearing away their tea things.

"The rain has stopped," Walker said. "I suppose we should go."

"Yes . . . Boxer."

"Unless you want a fresh pot of tea."

"No . . . Boxer."

"Nancy!"

"Yes . . . Boxer."

"Why do you call me by that silly name?"

"It's not a silly name. And you remind me of him. Your mane is not so long and it is rather more silver, but otherwise there is quite a resemblance."

"Did he have a mouthful of gold teeth too?"

"Don't be silly . . . Boxer."

By the time they had their coats on and he had paid and left a few pennies in the saucer for the waiter, by the time they were back out on the street, his new name seemed perfectly familiar and commonplace.

They walked slowly together down to the pier head and then back along the shore to the promenade where they had first seen one another, talking, talking, talking all the way mostly about how lonely they each were and how disappointed they had been but mostly about how lonely they were and how happy they had been for these few hours, all the way back up the hill to the gates of the old magazine.

"Father will be home from the business soon," she said. "I must go in and see to his dinner."

"Of course. Of course. I understand. Of course. Nancy, do I dare to hope that we might meet again tomorrow?"

"I should like nothing better. I long for it. When? When shall we meet?"

"As soon as we can. Let's meet as soon as we can. When can you be free?"

"I can be here at nine o'clock."

"And we can have the whole day together. The whole day." He folded his huge hands around her tiny hands and kissed her fingers. "Oh, Nancy. My Nancy. Until tomorrow."

"Until tomorrow, my dear, sweet Boxer."

He stood at the corner of the lane and watched until she went through the gate of No. 102 Magazine Lane. She turned, waved to him and opened the door. His arm was still raised in farewell when she went inside.

"Stupid bitch," he said.

21

THE RAIN WAS unceasing all through the night. Miss Ann Myfanwy Jones lay in her narrow bed in the tower of No. 102 Magazine Lane, listening as it hammered on the windows. Far away, downstairs, she heard the clock strike one. She watched the tiny pile of coals in her grate cool to a single stuttering flame and go out. The room was suddenly darker. The wind howled in the chimney. She heard it screaming among the trees across the street and imagined them reeling and bounding and dancing out there in the night. Miss Ann Myfanwy Jones was afraid that he might not return, that the weather would keep him away. How could it be, how could it be that now, after all these years of waiting and watching when, at last, the knight had arrived on his horse to save her, the weather might part them? Her pillow was a lump of rock. She beat it with her fists. The bedclothes tangled round her frozen feet. As the clock struck two, she rose and remade the bed, stopping to look out her streaming window. If the storm kept up, the ferry might be cancelled and Father would not be able to go into the business. He would expect her to spend the day with him. He would expect her to entertain him. He would expect her to smile at snatches of articles he read from the paper – little snippets he thought suitable for ladies. She would have no excuse for going out. Hope sank in her chest and the familiar sense of disappointment returned. "It doesn't matter," she said. "It doesn't matter. It doesn't," and lay down again.

She did not hear the clock strike three, but at seven o'clock she was awakened by a violent and repeated flushing of the water closet and the sound of Father running his bath. When it was her turn, she found a scattering of whisker shavings in a tidemark round the sink and a dribble of tooth powder where he had spat it out. He always did that. She always meant to talk to him about it, just to mention how, little by little it was driving her mad, just to ask if he might not simply wash round the sink, only for a moment, after he had used it, just to tell him how damned annoying it was. But she never did. It was so important to remember that Father had his share of disappointments too and she had no wish to add to them by appearing bitter or complaining or ungrateful.

"I expect the ferry has been cancelled for the sake of this storm," he said at breakfast.

"Yes, Father, I suppose it has." The threat of the day ahead loomed over her.

"So, I shall have to hurry up. If I leave promptly I can catch the train from New Brighton station, but I don't suppose I shall be the only one thinking that this morning. There's bound to be a crush and the train takes that bit longer, and if I want to be at my desk for the start of business, I'd best get a shift on. You know what they say about the rubber trade, m'dear."

"Yes, Father, we always bounce back."

"We always bounce back, and don't you forget it, Nancy my girl. I should have had that carved over the gates of Bodyngharad as a family motto – and I might yet. We always bounce back, that's what I say!" He stopped by her chair and bent to kiss the top of her head. "Don't you touch those dishes, m'dear. Leave them for Tetty when she comes in. She might as well work for her pay. What will you do today?"

"Oh, I don't know. I had planned to go up to the library

and change my book, but the weather is so awful, I just don't know."

"You'll find something," he said and he left her. Then there was the sound of him struggling with his coat and hat, a brief call of "I'll try to be back at the usual time," a blast of damp air as the door opened and the noise of it banging shut behind him.

Miss Ann Myfanwy looked up at the wall. It was barely eight o'clock. There was still an hour – at least an hour – before Boxer was due at the old magazine gates. Was that a long time, too long a time or not long enough? There was time to dress, time to undress and get dressed again. The dress she wore yesterday, when they met? A different hat? This hat? That hat? She longed to see him, she feared to disappoint him, but why would it matter? How could it matter after a scant day of acquaintance on a day of rain when she would be covered, top to toe, in that dreadful raincoat?

She changed her hat for the third time and glared at herself in the mirror. "He liked me well enough this way, yesterday," she said. "Maybe he will like me well enough again today." She hurried down the stairs to the front door, but the clock said it was not yet half past eight. She could not go out and stand in the rain for half an hour in the hope that he might come. She could not. She would not. It was beneath her dignity. So she cleared away the greasy breakfast dishes and took her coat off and rolled her sleeves up and washed them all, plates and pans and cutlery, in the kitchen sink – despite what Father had told her. Miss Ann Myfanwy was careful to wash the soda off her hands and she hoped they would not go rough and red and she wondered if Mrs Corn Merchant Pryce ever had to wash her own breakfast things a single day of her life.

Even boiling a kettle had done very little to eat up the empty time of waiting. She remembered how, long ago in a different life, she had learned French because it was regarded as an accomplishment suitable for young ladies, like playing the piano or embroidery or watercolours. Each and all of them made a girl more marriageable, and Miss Ann Myfanwy was highly accomplished in each and all. But she was stubbornly unmarried. The French for 'waiting room' was '*salle des pas perdues*' – the room of lost steps. It was a lovely thought. She stood in front of the hall stand, where the umbrellas and the walking sticks were kept, where the coats and the hats hung, and she looked at herself in the big round mirror and at the backwards clock behind her. "*Il est neuf heures moins cinq,*" she said. There were bruised shadows under her eyes. A night of broken sleep – that was all. She leaned forward and looked close in the mirror. Two or three red threads of broken veins across her cheekbones. That was what came of spending so much time on the promenade. Soon she would be as weather-beaten as a sailor. She pointed her chin to the ceiling and rubbed at her throat. The flesh was still quite firm. It was. Truly. But Mother had developed a dreadful turkey wattle in her last years. She dreaded that. "*Tu n'est pas jeune mais tu est vraiment de rigolade.*"

She resolved not to waste a single lost step. She would stand there in one spot, never moving, watching the clock moving backwards until it reached the hour. She stood waiting, watching, breathing calmly, but then the glass in the door darkened, the sound of a key in the lock, the doorknob rattled, and Tetty came in, scattering raindrops everywhere.

"Miss Nancy! You near gave me a heart attack standing there!"

"Tetty! Oh." She felt she had been caught out in something wicked and her only thought was to flee. "I was just going out," she said. "Must dash. Goodbye."

She was already beyond the gate when Tetty said: "Will you be home for dinner?" She was already at the corner when the clock in the hall struck nine, and he was already waiting under the turrets of the old gate.

She stopped running. It was unseemly that he should see her running like a girl and unbecoming that he might think she was running to him, but when he saw her, he ran to her so she stopped stopping running and started again and they met in the middle of the street. In the middle of the street, in the rain.

"Nancy!"

"Hello, Boxer. You're all wet."

"I had to walk a mile along the shore to get here and I've been waiting half an hour at least."

"I've been waiting too, but I was indoors, afraid to come out."

"I was afraid too. Horribly afraid. Nancy, I've wrangled some mighty big animals, but none of them ever gave me the terrors like you."

"I'm not terrifying."

"No, but not seeing you is."

She took his arm and folded herself close to him and turned her face up to be kissed, but he did not kiss her, which was disappointing.

"Do you think we might find somewhere out of this weather?" he said.

No. 102 Magazine Lane was just around the corner. She could see the top of it from where she stood, but it was impossible. "Yes," she said. "I know exactly the place. Let's run!"

So they ran off together through the rain, Miss Ann Myfanwy kicking along in half a dozen short steps to each of his long-legged strides, her long coat and the wet hem of her dress binding round her ankles as she went, and then, when they reached Seabank Road, they could see the tram coming. They hurried to jump on board, shaking raindrops off their clothes in glittering circles like spaniels emerging from a ditch, and they sat down together in the privacy of the rearmost bench.

"It's a circular route," she said. "We can pay our fares and then, so long as we don't get off, we never have to pay again. We can stay here all day for tuppence each."

When the conductor had left again and gone back to standing at the front of the car with the driver, he said: "That's a strange thing to say, Nancy. What made you think of that?"

She looked at his face, at his eyes and his nose and his mouth, and settled her gaze on his chin. "I was thinking – I was up half the night with thinking . . ."

"Oh so was I, Nancy my dear, so was I." He gave her hand a squeeze and she hurried to pull off her damp glove and squeeze his hand in return.

"Yes, but I was thinking about when you took me to tea and there was no cake for you, only for me."

"I told you. I simply wasn't hungry."

"Is that all? You're not the tiniest bit strapped for cash?"

"Oh, Nancy. You mustn't say such things." He lit a cigarette from a silver case – he asked her permission first, of course – and drew deeply on it, but when she dared to look up into his eyes, when she kept her gaze fixed on his, at last he crumbled. "Oh, there's no point lying to you. I may as well try to deceive myself."

"So you are in difficulties?" She was delighted, not because of his troubles but because she was right and, more than anything, because she had forced it out of him.

"It's all so stupid. Simple bureaucratic nonsense." He took another long drag on his cigarette, and when he lifted it from his lips, she reached up and took it from his fingers. He had never kissed her, but now her mouth was on the cigarette, still a little damp from where his mouth had been. He watched as she puffed on it, almost shocked.

"You are very daring, Miss Nancy Jones."

"My brother taught me."

"Arthur? Well, I'll be! He turned his back on the evil weed. Gives me the most awful rollicking if he ever sees me smoke."

"Never mind that. Tell me about the money."

"Oh, I hate to talk of it."

"Please, dear Boxer. Aren't we friends? Friends share their troubles."

The tramcar rattled and jolted its way round a long bend. "You mustn't give it a thought," he said. "I'm sure things will sort themselves out tomorrow. Or in a day or two at most."

"What things? Please tell me."

"It's just a mix-up with the banks, that's all. I have three and a half thousand pounds coming to me, more or less. The profits from that cargo of horses I sold over in Flanders, but there's some hold-up with the bank. They are quick enough to take the money out of my customers' accounts, but they are taking their own sweet time about transferring the funds to me."

"How long has it been?"

"Nearly two weeks. I write them every day, but I can't get any sense out of them."

"You don't think you might have been swindled out of your horses?"

"Nancy!" He was offended. "I've known Anton for years. This is not the first time we've done business. No, I don't believe that of him for two reasons: he's an honest man, and he knows I'd come back and kill him where he stood."

She looked at his gold teeth glinting and she believed it.

"Then I'm sure you are right. Just another day and it will be sorted out."

"Yes. Just another day."

They spoke of other things. Life in America, horses, horses, horses, the endless rolling fields of fine grass, the sweet, floral smell of hay in a stable, what it feels like to run a brush over a horse's back, Arthur, only half a day away from the horse farm, what the house was like, square and low and sheltered by trees with a dusty road running by it but lonely and empty and, above all, lonely. She told him about Bodyngharad and she told him about Boxer again, but she did not tell him about Mr Pryce the corn merchant or their understanding. She told him about her tower and its view across the park to the river and the Lady of Shallot and the Prisoner of Chillon and how her room in the tower was like his house on the stud farm: lonely and empty and, above all, lonely.

"You have your father," he said.

"Or he has me."

"Nancy, I have no one at all."

They had returned again to Seabank Road and the thought of the money came back to her. "How much do you need? Just to see you right?"

"Nancy, please don't."

"Stop being so stubborn. Let me help you. Wouldn't Arthur want me to help?"

"If needs be, I can cable for money. I'm just grateful I paid old Mrs Graham in advance. Ten shillings for two rooms and a shilling a day for breakfast, so I won't starve."

"But you need more than that."

"That's the worst of it. I do need more than that and I haven't a bean. Not one red cent. And if my bankers don't come through, well, I don't know what I will do."

"Yes you do. You'll let me help you."

He said nothing.

"Let me help you."

He lit another cigarette.

"I can put my hands on twenty pounds."

"Twenty pounds?"

"Isn't it enough?"

"It's an enormous amount of money."

"Good, then it's settled."

"I cannot. My pride would not allow it. I cannot take money from a lady I have known for only a day."

"Boxer! Please."

"No. It's impossible. But, on the other hand, I would be proud to accept assistance from one whose life and fortune were forever linked to my own, from my fiancée. Marry me, Nancy." That was the first time he kissed her.

22

MISS ANN MYFANWY JONES astonished herself by her own composure. She was completely calm. Utterly dry-eyed. Perhaps a little disappointed, but that was only to be expected. She had never seen a police station before – not on the inside. This one was as bad as she had feared. It was so bad it made her long for her room in No. 102 Magazine Lane, where, though the walls were thin, it did not stink.

There were two policemen. An inspector and a constable. The constable read aloud to her from a piece of paper which the inspector said she would have to sign.

The constable said: "In September this year – I cannot say the exact date – I was walking along Victoria Street when a man, resembling very much the photograph you show me, approached me and said: 'Excuse me; are you not Miss Nancy Jones?' I said: 'I am afraid you have the advantage of me.' He then said: 'You have a brother Arthur in Detroit, America.' I asked him how he knew me, and he said: 'Oh, I've seen your photo at your brother's in Detroit.' I asked him when he had seen my brother, and he said: 'Only a few weeks ago.' I was quite satisfied in myself that he really knew my brother. He explained to me he was over here on business, that he had brought some horses over from the States to Holland, and that he had come to Liverpool from Antwerp. He said he was being delayed here owing to a cheque which he had been expecting going astray."

It was so strange to hear her own words coming from beneath the constable's huge moustache. They were all quite true of course. Absolutely true. But not the whole truth. So many things had been left out.

"We had this conversation in the Royal Ferry Hotel, New Brighton, where we had adjourned, as it was raining."

That was all true. Perfectly true.

"We took the car to Wallasey Village. We simply talked about Detroit and my brother and different parts of America. Nothing of importance occurred."

Oh, what a dreadful, black lie. He asked for her hand. That was a matter of great importance. He asked for her hand and he insisted it must be as quickly as possible. They were not young, he said, yes, yes, she would forever be his girl, even when they were old and bent and silver, but they had no time to waste and Father would not wish to give her up. He would forbid her. He would try to prevent her and keep her for himself. She must be strong, she must be his brave girl, his Nancy. If only she would come away, they could be married on the ship – the captain had the power to do it – and they could send for Father at once. The very day and hour they landed at New York, they would send a cable and summon him to a place of honour on the ranch, where they would love him and comfort him for the rest of his days and he would live and die with both his children at his side.

The constable kept reading: " 'Before we parted we arranged for me to meet him for lunch at 1.30 the following day at the hotel in question. The following day I reached the hotel about 2.30 and found him waiting.' "

No word of a lie. She could swear to all of that with her hand on the Bible. But it said nothing to explain why she was late and nothing at all to explain why he had waited. Why would he have waited for an hour?

It was the money, of course. She did not have enough money. She had the twenty pounds she had promised and: "Yes, of course, my dear, we will manage with that. It's only to see us through. Just to tide us over although, my own one, I will have to pay extra to book a passage for you or perhaps they would allow me to change my cabin for two steerage places – but we would be separated, my dear. What? Another ten pounds? That would be ample – more than ample. I will wait here at the hotel until you come."

And he did wait. He waited while she took the ferry to Liverpool and rode the car into town and closed her account entirely, all twenty pounds, four shillings and thruppence farthing. What would be the point of leaving four shillings and thruppence farthing gathering interest in a bank in Liverpool when she was raising horses on the other side of the wild Atlantic? So she took it all and signed the forms and came back to No. 102 Magazine Lane because there was money there. She knew where there was a little knitted purse of gold sovereigns in Father's desk. She knew the exact drawer. She knew exactly where the secret knobs were and how to pull them so the hidden compartment would fly open. Hadn't Father shown her often enough? Hadn't she delighted in it? Hadn't he warned her, over and over, that she must never sell his desk when he was gone – not at least until she had looked in the secret place? Of course taking Father's money was wrong – of course it was – but it had to be done. She was making a better life for him in America, where he could rest at last, where he could see Arthur and not work himself to death in the business. It was for his sake. He wouldn't have to go on until he dropped. He would see that and forgive. Boxer had explained all that and she could see – anyone could see – he was right. But Tetty was there, fussing about the place with her mop and duster, looking over her shoulder, snooping, and it wasn't her house, it was none of her business, why couldn't she just go? She had mislaid her spectacles. She found her spectacles. She had to adjust her hat. Now, where were her keys?

At last she was gone and Miss Ann Myfanwy turned the lock behind her and went into Father's study. It only took a moment, only a moment, and then it was done and she put everything back, exactly as it had been, and comforted herself with the notion that he may not even notice the money was gone before the cable came to invite him to America.

She hurried along the street, terrified that she might have missed him, so terribly afraid that he may have given up hope. What if he thought her courage had failed her? What if he doubted her love? Oh, the pain he would feel. She could not bear it.

But he was still there, still waiting by the fire in the hotel parlour, hunched over at the fireside, worried and tense, but he looked up when he saw her at the door and bounded to her and embraced her. And he took the money.

The constable read on: " 'It was arranged that I should meet him early in the afternoon or evening at the top of our road the following day. He seemed very anxious that I should meet him the following day.' "

Yes, he had seemed anxious. He was frantic. How he pleaded with her to be strong. Pack a bag. Only enough for the voyage. Just a few things. Everything else that she wanted could come on by ship with Father. And she mustn't be silly and worry about clothes; he would dress her in silks and furs as soon as they arrived in New York.

The policeman read on. His moustache bobbed as he spoke the words. " 'That was the last time I saw him, and I have not heard from him since.' "

No, she had not heard from him since. The last time. The very last time.

The policeman. What an accent he had. Coarse. Saying her words. " 'The next morning I wrote a letter to him at 10 Riversdale Road, Seacombe, the address he had given me, saying I was afraid I would not be able to keep the appointment in the afternoon, but I would be sure to be there in the evening.' "

She could not keep the appointment in the afternoon. How could she? Not after that morning, when she had wiped Father's whiskers from the sink and rubbed away his trail of tooth-powder spit. She could not leave without seeing him again. But in the evening, there would be time for a proper goodbye, one last kiss before she left. He might not know what it meant – not until later – but she would know. She packed her bag and laid it in the coal shed, on a copy of the *Daily Telegraph*, to save it from the dust, and she sent her letter by the first post. She poured out her love in that letter. So much wasted time, so much loneliness and sorrow, but now she could see that it was all worth it, that Heaven had placed those obstacles in her way only that she might now enjoy true, deep, lasting love and happiness with the man she had been destined for from the day the stars were made. She licked down the envelope, kissed it and marked it with an X.

The policeman mumbled on: " 'I kept the appointment in the evening, and after waiting about a quarter of an hour and he not putting in an appearance, and being afraid he had not obtained my letter, I went to 10 Riversdale Road and inquired for Mr Walker.' "

That poor old lady. Poor Mrs Graham. She hardly knew what to say. Yes, Mr Walker had been staying there, but he was gone. He left, my dear. The day before. Quite suddenly. About four o'clock in the afternoon. No, not an American gentleman, a Canadian gentleman. No, not a horse trader, a manager with the Cunard line, transferred suddenly and unexpectedly to Antwerp. Yes, dear, a letter had come for him. Yes, about noon. Why, yes, dear, it was in a blue envelope. Yes, with an X on the back. From you, dear? Well, you may as well. If you're sure.

Miss Ann Myfanwy opened the letter and showed the signature, no more than the signature, just so Mrs Graham might reassure herself. She read the letter again. Suddenly it seemed almost funny. She threw it in the fire.

The constable said: "He never made any reference to Scotland."

It was almost over. Like the agony of a tooth being pulled. One last wrench and then the agony would be past.

The inspector said: "And this statement is all truth? Sign here, Miss. Thank you, Miss. You've been most helpful. You can go."

She stood up. The constable opened the door for her and she walked down the corridor, alone, to where Father was waiting. He gave her his arm. He knew all about the money and he forgave her completely. He said: "I think you've had a lucky escape, Nancy. And I'm not angry. Not angry in the slightest. Perhaps a little disappointed, but not at all angry."

One last wrench and then nothing there. The gap of a missing tooth forever and ever.

23

AS A CONSEQUENCE of the message from Superintendent Neaves, Mr Sempill placed another reckless charge upon the ratepayers of Broughty Ferry and hailed a cab for the castellated glories of St Pancras station, where he caught a train which took him – by second-class carriage – to Tonbridge, in Kent. He was careful to keep the ticket stub as a proof of his expenditure, to be reclaimed at later date.

It was November 12th, fully nine days after poor Miss Milne had been discovered dead, and, to judge by the newspapers, not far short of a month after her murder. Still, Mr Sempill entertained the fond hope that close examination of the villain brought to his notice at Tonbridge Court might yet provide the evidence required.

Accompanied by Mr Neaves, he sat down in the public benches. He stood up again and moved to another spot. He wanted the best possible view of the man when he came up from the cells to take his place in the dock.

An elderly gentleman, a worthy of the town now given a position of respect and a little income in his old age, stepped onto the dais with heavy tread and announced the arrival of the magistrates with a long, wavering cry of "Court!"

Everyone stood. The three magistrates took their places and bowed solemnly. Everyone sat down. The business began.

Mr Sempill was cheered to find that crime in Tonbridge was not so very different from crime at home in Broughty Ferry.

It gave him a homely feeling. There was the usual tragic mix of drink, stupidity, nuisance and desperation but very little of genuine evil about it. And then, they reached Charles Warner.

He was led upstairs from the cells by a mountainous policeman. Following on behind, Warner was a tall, slim figure with a springing step, elegant and gentlemanly and, somehow, strangely cat-like.

Mr Sempill said: "A night or two in the cells seems to have done him no harm."

"My guess is he's quite at home there," said Mr Neaves. "It's not the first time he's seen the inside of a jail, I'll wager. And he's fit, I'll say that for him. So far he has totally refused to give any account of himself, beyond the fact that he walked from London overnight, with the intention of making his way to Dover and getting a boat across to the Continent."

The clerk stood up and read from a sheet of paper. "Are you Charles Warner, 210 Wilton Avenue, Toronto, Canada?"

"Yes, I am."

"You are charged that on November 5th, nineteen hundred and twelve, you obtained board and lodgings at Ye Olde Chequers Inn, High Street, Tonbridge, in the county of Kent, without paying or intending to pay and that you did so by fraud. How do you plead?"

"Not guilty, sir."

He was, well, Mr Sempill couldn't quite decide what he was. Calm, certainly. Composed. Arrogant? Cocky? No, that's not the way of the confidence trickster. He had to be cleverer than his victim, he had to be smart, but he couldn't afford to be sneering. You can't win confidence by sneering. You must be friendly: "Hail, fellow, well met." Warner had that all right: approachability, affability and something else too – authority. He seemed a little frail, with his jacket buttoned high at his throat, but he had the look of a man born to command. Officer class. Chief Constable Sempill recognised it at once. He had striven after it for years.

"There's no doubt at all in my mind that that man is a foreigner," Mr Sempill whispered, "even if he is a Canadian subject."

"Definitely foreign," said Mr Neaves.

The trial was a simple and routine affair, although it began in the unfamiliar English manner with the prosecutor setting out the circumstances of the case in a long series of unproven accusations instead of the civilised Scottish custom of moving directly to evidence.

"We will show," he told the magistrates, "that the accused Warner mercilessly preyed upon the good nature and trusting manner of Mrs Strange, the proprietrix of Ye Olde Chequers Inn, to obtain board and lodging to the value of ten shillings and nine pence, that he deceived Mrs Strange by means of a crude stratagem and that he personally benefitted by fraud."

The chairman of magistrates looked down from his bench. "Is there anything you would like to add, Mr Warner?"

"Your Honour, it's all a simple misunderstanding and I'm very glad to have this opportunity to clear matters up."

"Please, no speeches from the dock, Mr Warner. As you are representing yourself – which is of course your right – I will endeavour to give you every possible assistance, but there are certain forms which must be observed." The chairman dipped his pen in a large bottle of black ink and drew an inexplicable heavy line across his blotter. "Call your first witness."

And so it went on for an hour. The landlady, Mrs Strange, was called to give evidence that she was, in very fact, the owner of Ye Olde Chequers Inn and that the accused Warner had arrived and requested two nights' board and lodging.

The poor woman was downright apologetic about the whole business, as if it had been the proudest moment of her life to be defrauded by such a fine gentleman. "I should like to tell Your Honours that Mr Warner was a gentleman in all his dealings with me and with my staff," she said.

"Even when it came to paying his bill?" the chairman of the bench asked.

"Well, p'raps not that."

The chairman dipped his pen and drew another thick black line.

"But in every other respect, Your Honours, a perfect gent, and I'm heartily sorry it has come to this, Mr Warner, truly I am, on my life."

Warner made a soothing gesture from the dock as if to say: "There, there, dear lady. Please do not distress yourself."

Mrs Strange told a story that Mr Sempill had heard a hundred times before. An unknown gentleman arrives at the hotel carrying a large, heavy bag. He engages a room for two nights. He dines very well, from soup to nuts, and he selects a good bottle to wash the whole thing down. The gentleman is charming, generous and open-handed. Indeed, he insists on buying a drink for the girl behind the bar, much to the annoyance of the cellarman, who is secretly in love with the girl behind the bar, and "Just put it all on my bill," says the gentleman.

In the morning, the gentleman rises early and enjoys a hearty breakfast, conversing merrily with the landlady all the while. "Would it be possible," he wonders, "if it's not too much of an imposition, dear lady, would it be possible for me to leave something in your safe?

"I am en route to the Continent," he says. You will please notice the "en route", never "on my way" but always "en route". "I am en route to the Continent and I have a number of letters of introduction and a considerable number of cheques drawn on the American Express. I don't wish to carry them with me. Might I leave them in the hotel safe, until I leave?"

And, of course, he might. Of course it would be no trouble at all. The gentleman takes a thick envelope from his pocket. It is carefully placed in the safe. The gentleman is extravagantly grateful and now he must conduct some business in the town, but he hopes there will be some more of that excellent beef and porter again in the evening. The gentleman leaves and in all likelihood the gentleman will never be seen again.

But the girl behind the bar is also the girl who cleans the rooms and she gives the most awful cry when she drops the gentleman's case and two house bricks fall out on her toe and that brings the cellarman, who runs upstairs and takes in the whole scene with a glance.

Then he runs downstairs and opens the safe and finds that the gentleman's envelope contains nothing more than a torn newspaper, and then the cellarman – who never liked the gentleman – runs out into the street and find a constable, who apprehends the gentleman on the coast road to Dover.

"What identifies that bundle of paper as my property?" Warner asked the cellarman.

"You gave it to Mrs Strange."

"That is a matter of contention. Was a receipt issued? Was it signed for? Is there anything on that bundle of worthless papers to suggest that it has anything to do with me?"

"Well, I . . . We both know . . ."

"Did you have a lawful warrant?"

"A warrant?"

"A search warrant, entitling you to break and enter the property?"

"What property?"

"The envelope."

"Of course not."

Warner rocked back on his heels and addressed the bench. "I would ask Your Honours to discount the envelope entirely. Not only is there no connection to me, but it has been unlawfully obtained."

The clerk of the court stood up. The chairman of the bench leaned down. The clerk of the court whispered in the chairman's ear. The chairman sat down in his seat with a thump, dipped his pen and scored another black line. "Continue," he said.

"I have no further questions."

After that, there was nothing left to deal with but the closing statements when Mr Prosecutor was able to show the court overwhelming evidence of guilt and a clear and deliberate attempt to defraud. "I invite Your Honours to convict," he said, in a voice that scraped like a coffin lid closing.

The chairman of the bench seemed eager to do just that, but a tug on the sleeve reminded him that the accused had yet to speak.

Warner, of course, had not given evidence. He asked the bench to note that and to recall that they could make "not the slightest implication of guilt or innocence as a result".

"So noted," said the chief magistrate. "We also note that your closing statement is not open to cross-examination."

"And you are right to do so, Your Honours. In which case I ask you to consider what has been shown against me. I concede that I asked for two nights' board and lodgings. The reason that I did not avail myself of two nights' board and lodgings at Ye Old Chequers is that Kent Constabulary insisted, rather vehemently I might add, on providing board and lodgings of their own. It is claimed my luggage contained two bricks. Is it an offence in Kent, in England or anywhere in the British Empire for a man to carry a brick? Your Honours, many an honest builder would find himself where I stand today if that were so.

"The matter of the envelope has already been dealt with, and in short, all that has been shown against me is that I went for a morning walk, during which I was arrested. That dear Mrs Strange has been bilked of her payment is a fault which lies entirely at the door of the police."

With a flourish of the hand and a deep bow, he said: "I throw myself on the mercy of the court, secure in the knowledge that the fine tradition of English justice means I must soon walk free from this place, an innocent man with no stain on my character."

The three magistrates conferred together for a moment, nodded at one another, and the chairman scored another black line across the paper, banged his gavel and announced: "Guilty!"

With an icy smile, he said: "You wanted board and lodgings, Warner and you have already had a week's worth, courtesy of the ratepayers of Kent. You may now look forward to fourteen nights' more, with their best wishes. Take him down."

The mountainous policeman began the process of herding him down the stair, but before he gave way before the avalanche, Warner managed another courteous bow and he raised his finger to the brim of the hat he was not wearing in an insolent salute as he vanished into the pit.

Mr Sempill wasted no time. "The longer I observed him," he told Superintendent Neaves, "the more convinced I became that this man answers the description of the suspect seen at Broughty Ferry."

"I agree, wholeheartedly."

"Quite clearly this is an educated man with considerable pretensions of being a gentleman, and from the able manner in which he cross-examined the witness, I was inclined to think he had had a legal training. Neaves, would you oblige by instructing one of your men to have the prisoner's clothing examined?"

"Certainly. But, after all this time, you can't expect to find any evidence."

"It's no time at all, man. He's been in jug for a week, locked away from his own clothing and forced into prison uniform. From what you told me, he walked down here from London the day before – the day the body was discovered. I think he was flushed out of hiding by the news and making his way to the coast to flee to the Continent. If he had any money he would have gone by train, and a man who has no money might very well not have a change of shirt either. And I want him photographed too. If that's possible."

"Of course, that's easily done."

"Excellent. I look forward to inviting you to a hanging!"

24

FEELING HIGHLY SATISFIED with the outcome of the trial and justified in his own powers and abilities as a police officer, having employed the most thorough methods of modern policing to pursue the evil-doer almost from one end of the country to another, Mr Sempill decided that a damned good lunch was in order.

Superintendent Neaves knew of the very place, an old-fashioned inn with low, beamed ceilings and a roaring fire where they served excellent beer and quite a passable meat pie. The two men were sitting together in the back parlour, finishing off a handsome lump of Cheddar cheese when they heard a man calling out "Mr Neaves? Mr Neaves?"

"Through here, Bowles. In the back."

Bowles arrived, a young man, lanky, with the eager look of a new recruit. He had taken his helmet off and carried it folded against his ribs, to stop it scraping on the smoky ceiling of the parlour.

He stood at attention and said: "Begging your pardons, gentlemen."

"Stand easy, Bowles. Have you news for us?"

"Yes, sir. I beg to report that I have but lately returned from Maidstone jail, where I was escorting the prisoner Warner."

"And?"

"May I consult my notebook, sir?"

"No, you may not, Bowles. Tell the Chief Constable what happened."

"Well, sir, when we got to the prison gates I noticed he had not a shirt on. He had his jacket buttoned up high and a muffler at his neck, but he loosened it on the train and I said to him: 'Where is your shirt?' Just exactly in that tone, sir: 'Where is your shirt,' I said, and he said: 'I have made off with it because it was dirty. I have wrote for some money to come, and it will be here next week.'"

"For God's sake, man, was that all he said?"

"No, sir."

"What else, then?"

Bowles seemed to be struggling to recall. There was a long, silent period of effort, as if he had been doing long division in his head, until Mr Neaves said: "By all means, consult your notebook."

Constable Bowles opened his front pocket and began to read: "Sirs, whilst we were in the train going to jail the prisoner said in a conversation that I had with him about different things and what he said was 'I shall not come back to England again, as I have had enough trouble since I have been here. I landed on the 2nd August, 1912 at Liverpool and went to London, and then back to Scotland—"

"Scotland? Where in Scotland"

"I don't know, sir. He only said 'Scotland'." Bowles went back to reading aloud. "'. . . to Scotland and then back again to London. That is where I made off with my money, stopping at different hotels. I did not mean to stop in England long because I came over for a change. I pawned my ring, watch and chain to get money, until I had some come from Canada. I have wrote for some, but it has not arrived yet. I have cabled for money before and got it all right. I can't make it out why it did not come, and that is the reason I pawned my stuff to get the money.'"

Mr Sempill gave way to swearing again, as was his habit and, with many exclamations of profanity, mixed with cries of "The villain! The rogue!" and "Scotland!" he hurriedly paid the bill.

"We must telephone at once to Maidstone jail," he said. "Get me the head warder. By God, the day is coming and it is not long off when I will see this vicious, murdering blighter dangle at a rope's end. His judgement cometh and that right soon!"

They hurried back to the police station, running up the steps, banging the doors open, rushing through to the back office, everything fuss and bother and flurry. Mr Neaves was no philosopher, merely an ordinary policeman following an honest calling, but he was warm and sanguine after two pints of beer and a good meat pie with plenty of potatoes. Sitting at his desk while Mr Sempill roared into the telephone, he found himself musing on the many inconveniences of modern life: how, in times past, a letter might have been dispatched to Maidstone jail and it might have taken all the day to get there and all the next day for a reply to come back. In a matter of great urgency he might have signed for a railway warrant, but now there was the telephone and instantaneous communication across distances of miles was a mere matter of routine, but the moments that it took to bring the warder to the instrument became infuriating agonies of nervous expectation. The telephone, the railway, the telegraph, they all made life faster and yet, despite them all, there were no more hours in the day. Mr Neaves let out a gentle belch and paid no attention to Chief Constable Sempill's roaring.

"Yes, man, for God's sake speak up!"

A quiet pause.

"Yes, I'll wait. I am waiting!"

And then. "Hello? Can you hear me? Listen. Carefully. It. Must. Be. Preserved. Secure. Everything. Until. We. Arrive.

"Thank you. Yes. Yes. Goodbye."

Chief Constable Sempill was red in the face when he replaced the earpiece. He undid the top button of his Prussian collar and wiped his neck with his handkerchief. "The blighter took his chance," he said. "The warder tells me Warner was returned to jail in the usual way and given his prison garb. His shirt had disappeared, as Bowles said, but it's been found in the room where the prisoners get changed."

"And is there any sign of evidence? Any bloodstains?"

"Oh, better than that. They found it rolled up and jammed in a corner, under the bench, torn to shreds. The cuffs, the neckband and the shirt front – all gone. The first chance he got, the very minute he was allowed to get his hands on it, he destroyed the incriminating evidence."

"Then we have no proof," said Mr Neaves.

"It may not be proof, but it's still evidence! It shrieks of his guilt."

"Could you put it before a jury? When a man stands in fear of his life?"

"Yes! By God, I could and I would. I will have him."

Mr Neaves was a little shocked, so he waited a moment until the passion had passed off. "What would you like to do now?" he asked.

"We must get to Maidstone. I have to talk to him. Is it far?"

"Perhaps fifteen miles or so. We regularly send prisoners on the train and I will send a telegram from the station to have them meet us."

Mr Sempill was obliged to restore his top button before striding out, side by side with Mr Neaves, to the railway station. He was downright florid by the time they reached the platform and his buttons strained with every moment they had to wait for the train. Profanity would have helped, but he was a police officer, the Chief Constable of Broughty Ferry no less, and such indulgence was forbidden to him while he was in public. Even the comfort of a cigarette was out of the question, so he had to content himself with chewing furiously on his whiskers while Mr Neaves rocked gently back and fore on his thick-soled shoes, humming snatches of *H.M.S. Pinafore*.

"Is he reliable, the warder?"

"Perfectly, in my experience."

Mr Neaves returned to singing softly under his breath: "Many years ago, when I was young and charming, as some of you may know, I practised baby-farming."

The train arrived trailing hot smuts of soot and spitting hot steam, and the two men climbed into the front carriage, since it would leave first and be the first to arrive and speed was essential. A man in a brown coat tried to follow, but Mr Sempill put his hand on the door and pulled it firmly shut. "Terribly sorry, sir. This coach is taken. Required for confidential police business, I'm afraid."

In the opposite seat, Mr Neaves gave him a long look.

"I'm sorry, Neaves. I couldn't be bothered. My nerves are tight as fiddle strings. I have to admit this business is weighing on my mind. Murders are a rarity in Broughty Ferry and the burgh magistrates are keen to see a resolution. Most keen."

Mr Sempill had the embarrassed look of a man who has said too much. He smoked a frantic cigarette in three long draws, ground the stub under his toe and went back to the business of chewing his whiskers. To spare him, Mr Neaves looked out the window and sang softly to himself "and so do his sisters and his cousins and his aunts, and so do his sisters and his cousins and his aunts" in time with the clacking of the tracks as he watched the passing clouds.

25

MAIDSTONE JAIL WAS as grim a place as Chief Constable Sempill could have hoped for. One rough stone laid on another, piled four storeys high and left to soak in misery and fear for a hundred years until it was as lonely and grey and chill as the moon. If he could not have Warner standing on a trapdoor with his head in a noose, then Mr Sempill would be content to have him in Maidstone jail, inside these walls, behind that great, fortress-like gatehouse, watched over by those cruel towers – for now. But only for now.

They were expected, of course. Mr Neaves hammered on the huge, wooden gate with a gloved fist and a tiny part of it opened, like a door into the magic mountain. They stepped through the gate and out of the world into another place, where the clocks stopped.

The prison governor was waiting on the path circling a lawn which the prisoners were permitted to look at but forbidden to touch. He shook hands and welcomed them. "Warner is being brought up from his cell at this moment," he said. "He has not been told why, or where he is going. He has no idea that you are even on the premises."

The prison had taken root in Maidstone like a fungus in a fallen tree. Little by little, in the course of a century, it had spread out and up, away from its original design, with bits added on here and altered there so doors that had once led into corridors now opened on empty air and once-solid walls had been pierced. The warder led them by strange routes inside the building. It was a kind of drowning. The deeper they sank, the less light there was, and their ears were assailed by a heavy, distorted silence. Normal, human sounds were displaced by a weight of quietness and, far away and echoing, the sound of sadness and lonely misery, mad howls, shrieking laughter, hidden weeping, the sounds of shipwreck, as if the prison and everybody in it had suddenly been dropped in the middle of a cold ocean and the dark waves had closed over the roofs and poured into every cell and muffled every conversation and filled all their mouths with a choking brine which robbed them of speech and thought and left nothing in exchange but a moan of frightened pain and ceaseless, ceaseless boredom.

"In here, gentlemen." The governor turned a brass knob and flung open a door onto a bare room where Warner was waiting, standing under the high window between two warders. For a second he looked startled by the sudden opening of the door, but he recovered himself when he saw the two policemen. His chin was high. He actually dared to look down his nose at them and, damn him, he was smiling. Chief Constable Sempill hated him fiercely.

The governor said: "Warner, these gentlemen have come to ask you some questions. This is Superintendent Neaves of Kent Constabulary and this other gentleman is Chief Constable Sempill of Broughty Ferry Burgh Police."

"We meet again," said Warner, and he dared to extend his hand.

"We have not met," said Mr Sempill.

"We have not been properly introduced, that's true, but I saw both you gentlemen earlier today, for my big performance."

"It was certainly that," said Mr Sempill. "Sit down, please."

Warner put his hand away and pulled out a chair. He sat on one side of the table between the two guards; Sempill and Neaves sat opposite with their backs to the door.

Mr Sempill took out his notebook and spread it on the table. He took out a pencil and laid it across the open pages. Warner watched him intently all the while.

"I'm not going to beat about the bush," he said. "You are a person of great interest to me, Warner. The fact is I believe you are connected with the murder of an elderly lady in Broughty Ferry."

Warner's jaw dropped. "That's ridiculous. I couldn't find this Broughty Ferry place on a map. I've never heard of it – not until you showed up."

"So you've never been to Scotland."

"I've never been to Scotland."

"That's not what you told Constable . . ."

Mr Neaves leaned closer and said: "Bowles."

"Constable Bowles."

"I've never heard of Constable Bowles either."

"He was the police officer who accompanied you on your return from court."

Warner snorted. "That slack-jawed halfwit? So, you put him up to saying that I told him I went to Scotland and murdered some old lady, is that the game you're playing here?"

"Nobody put him up to anything. And nobody is saying that you confessed. He volunteered the testimony that you told him you had been to Scotland. You landed at Liverpool on August 2 and you went to Scotland."

"Well, it's a damned lie. I've never been to Scotland in my life."

Chief Constable Sempill took a deep breath and started to count to ten. He got to five and said: "Warner, you need to understand the seriousness of your situation. I want to talk to you in connection with the murder of Jean Milne—"

"Nice name. Jean Milne," Warner tested it out in his mouth. "Jean Milne, Jean Milne."

Mr Sempill brought his fist down on the table so his pencil flew about. "Murder, Warner. We are talking about murder. You could hang."

"Seems like you've got me hanged anyway."

"But if you care to give me an account of your movements, I can have them verified."

"That's mighty white of you, Chief Constable, and I'm grateful. I do not care to."

"May I ask why not?"

"Two reasons. Firstly, I come of good family and it would distress them immeasurably if they were to hear of my misfortunes. Secondly, I do not see why I should do your job for you. If you want to investigate me, go ahead and investigate, and if you think I killed some old lady, go ahead and prove it – but I won't help you."

"Listen to me. Jean Milne died between October 14 and the third of this month. I won't deny, I want to see a man hang for what happened to that lady, but I want it to be the right man, and I swear to you, if you can show me you are the wrong man, you will not hang."

Warner said nothing. He folded his arms across his chest and looked up at the ceiling, counting cobwebs.

"I am trying to help you."

Warner said nothing.

"Let's start at the beginning. Your name is Charles Warner."

"You know that already."

"Age?"

"Thirty-eight."

Mr Neaves stifled a laugh. "Have you been thirty-eight for long?"

"I'm thirty-eight," he insisted.

"Very well, we'll put thirty-eight. Address 210 Wilton Avenue, Toronto, Canada."

"You won't find anything of me there. That was my address at one time, but not now and not for some time."

"Then tell me your correct address."

"I prefer not to give my Canadian address."

"Why?"

"I told you that. I don't want you snooping round my folks."

"Very well. You're obviously an educated man. A college man. Where did you go to university?"

Warner looked down from the ceiling for the first time. "Chief Constable, give a guy some credit. I won't give you my address, so you think you can track me down through college? Oh, you're correct, I was educated at college. Which college I decline to say."

"Very good. Will you at least explain how you came to be in Scotland?"

"I already said. I have never been to Scotland." Warner gave a bored sigh. "Are you trying to catch me out, Chief Constable? You won't catch me out. I am a salesman in business. This past year I did myself a favour in mining stocks in Canada and the States."

"Mining stocks?" said Mr Sempill. "That's interesting."

"I don't know why you should be so interested. I made a heap and I decided to take a trip."

"What for?"

"Entirely for pleasure. I left Montreal on Friday, 2nd August, and went first of all to Philadelphia and, from there, on to New York. I sailed from New York on 10th August."

"What was the name of the boat?"

"You find out."

"Where did you land?"

"Find that out too. But I'll tell you this, I wasn't even in England when the old lady was killed."

"Scotland," said Sempill quietly. "She was killed in Scotland."

"I wasn't any place on your tiny, foggy little island. I left Antwerp on 16th October and I landed at Harwich the following day."

"The boat?"

"I don't know. But it's a downright lie that I ever told your man that I landed at Liverpool in August and went to Scotland. I have never been in Scotland in my life. When I landed at Harwich I took a train direct for London. Liverpool Street station."

Sempill asked: "Was this your first visit to London?"

"You work it out. I'm not helping you. First visit, last visit, it doesn't matter. The point is I was no place near your old lady. No place near."

"Where did you stay in London?"

"Here and there."

"The Palace? The Bonnington?"

Warner leaned across the table. "You're not listening. Here. And. There."

Mr Sempill remained calm. "What is your explanation for your shirt?"

"You may as well ask me to explain my shoes, or my coat."

"I think we can all agree that you are far, far cleverer than I, Mr Warner. Can't we, Mr Neaves?"

"Oh, he's too clever for both of us. No doubt about it."

"But, if it wouldn't be too much trouble, could you see your way to explaining how it was you arrived with a shirt, your shirt was returned to you, and yet you departed for court without a shirt? And how was it that your shirt was torn to ribbons and hidden in the prison changing rooms?"

"It was dirty."

"That's all?"

"It was dirty."

"Not bloodstained? Not covered in the blood of the woman you beat to death in Broughty Ferry?"

"It was dirty."

"Very good," said Mr Sempill. "I will record that as your reply and have you sign my notebook." He held out his pencil. "A college man like you won't have any trouble signing his name."

He scrawled "Charles Warner" across two open pages.

"Very good. Thank you." Mr Sempill turned to the prison governor. "Is your man here?"

"He's waiting next door."

"Excellent. Mr Warner, please go with these gentlemen and have your photograph taken."

The two warders jostled Warner out the door as Mr Neaves whispered: "Though a mystic tone you borrow, he shall learn the truth with sorrow, here today and gone tomorrow."

"Get his picture," said Mr Sempill. "Then we'll see how bloody clever he is."

26

BY GREAT EFFORT on his part, Chief Constable Sempill was able to return to St Pancras station that evening in plenty of time for the last post. He had with him a little packet containing a note for Detective Lieutenant Trench, advising him on recent developments in the inquiry and giving instructions for the enclosed photograph to be shown to such witnesses and informants as he thought useful and appropriate. This he dropped into the pillar box at the station with "POLICE BUSINESS MOST URGENT" written in the corner, trusting the Royal Mail to do its duty.

You may well imagine the interest with which we examined the contents of that little packet when it arrived in Broughty Ferry the following day. Sitting at the Chief Constable's desk, Mr Trench slit the envelope and withdrew the sheets of folded notepaper in that same two-fingered pinching grip I recalled from our first meeting on top of the tram, and read from Mr Sempill's letter with all the tenderness of a mother to her children.

"Mr Sempill says he has tracked down Clarence Wray, who admits his connection with Jean Milne but strongly denies any flirtation. According to Wray, our young man with the yellow moustache was sniffing around, trying to get her to invest in a Canadian mining interest."

We were all most taken with these snippets, Broon and Suttie above all, and I had to recall them to their right behaviours.

"However, Mr Sempill reports that he has uncovered another most promising lead, a Canadian confidence trickster now imprisoned in Kent—"

"A foreigner," said Suttie.

"Well, a colonial at any rate," said Mr Trench, "and he declines to give an account of himself, although he has admitted to an interest in mining shares."

"The very man! The man himself!" said Suttie with a kind of welcoming glee, as if he had suddenly stumbled upon Constable Broon in the bar of the Ship at just the very moment when he put his hand in his pocket.

Mr Trench waited until order and calm had restored itself. "Mr Sempill says he is enclosing a newly taken photograph of the suspect, which he urges us to exhibit to the witnesses in the hopes that they may assist the inquiry by providing an identification."

But the photograph was still inside its envelope and the envelope still lay, where Mr Trench had placed it, in the middle of Mr Sempill's desk. It was not for any of us to touch the envelope and we waited in silence until Mr Trench picked it up and removed the picture.

He examined it for a moment, blew through his teeth and tossed it on the table. "Mr Charles Warner of Toronto. There's our suspect, lads."

"That's him to the life, right enough," said Suttie, who was daily sinking in my estimation.

But, though Suttie had never seen the killer in all his days, there was no denying that picture was the living image of a murderer. He was in his grey prison uniform: a rough woollen jacket, a shirt without a collar. They had pushed him into a corner, with a mirror angled behind his head so both sides of his face were on view. His hands were crossed in front of his chest, like a coffined corpse, to record any distinguishing marks. There were none.

Mr Trench said: "No moustache, you'll notice. I want to see all the witnesses who claim to have seen the man, anybody who saw him near the house or on the cars or with Miss Milne. Pay them a visit and have them call in to see us. We need to let them have a look at this photograph. Come along, gentlemen, no time for slacking, I want to send my report to Mr Sempill by tonight, so let's get knocking."

So we went out and found them all, everybody who said they saw the young man with the thin blond moustache: John Wood the gardener, who said he let the man into Elmgrove; James Don the rubbish man, who saw him come out and stand under the street lamp; Margaret Campbell, maidservant to Mrs Luke at Caenlochan Villa, who looked out the window and across the street and saw a man strolling between the bushes; the McIntosh lassies, who ran away from him, frightened out of their wits; Andy Hay the pedlar, who growled at him as he sat smoking on his pack. We found them all – and others I have not troubled you with, like the young boys who fled from him when he disturbed them at play – and we brought them all to the police office and we showed them all a photograph of a middle-aged man without a moustache to see what they might say.

We had not the slightest difficulty in finding the witnesses. If we found any one of them at home, that person would put on their hat and coat and come running out of the house to help, and those who were not at home turned up immediately they found our cards at the back of the door. Not one of them had to be asked twice. In a little place, the force of gossip and scandal does as much to prevent wrongdoing as a hundred policemen, and the chance to be at the centre of approving public remark, to come face to face with a brutal murderer and have that witnessed and borne out by the police, the opportunity to be the heroes of their own little stories, made these good folk eager to assist.

To be fair to Detective Lieutenant Trench – and I take my hat off to him for this – he did his utmost to make it all as fair as possible by selecting pictures from our own files and hiding Warner's picture amongst them. He was trying his best, but Broughty Ferry is not a large burgh and our local stock of wrongdoers is small. Some of them might well have been known to the witnesses by sight – after all, James Don boasted to me that there wasn't a man in the burgh that he did not know – and the cards Mr Trench had found were all alike and each of them unlike the new photograph sent up from England.

In spite of it all, Mr Trench tried to do his duty. One by one, each of the witnesses was taken into the Chief Constable's office and gently lectured on the importance of the evidence they were about to give.

He impressed upon them that he, himself, did not know any of the men whose photographs he was about to show them and they must not think for a moment of trying to please him by selecting one picture over another. They must remember the dreadful responsibility that might attend upon their choice, he said, and consider before speaking that a man's life hung in the balance on the strength of their word. If they were unsure, it would be far, far better for justice and the sake of their conscience simply to say that they recognised none of the photographs, and nobody would think the less of them.

Then Mr Trench would take all his photographs out of the envelope, lay them on the table and invite the witness to make a choice. After they had finished he would thank them kindly for their efforts, bind them to silence in regard to their choice, send them out to make their statements in front of me or Suttie or Broon, shuffle his cards and begin again.

We typed furiously and to great purpose, but when evening came and the work was done, Mr Trench seemed strangely unsatisfied and he sat down in the hard chair beside Suttie at the police telegraph with a great, heavy sigh.

"Make to Chief Constable Sempill, Broughty Ferry Burgh Police, care of Scotland Yard, Whitehall, London. Message begins: Witnesses Wood, Don, girl Campbell, two girls McIntosh all say photograph strongly resembles man seen by them, but cannot say definitely. Wood, Don and Campbell think he is the man, but would like to see him before being positive. Malcolm and Urquhart say he is like the man seen by them in car. Boys Duncan, Bannerman and Potter say he resembles man in general appearance. Witness Hay says he is very like man met leaving Elmgrove on 15th October."

All those people and none of them certain. Mr Trench understood that more would have to be done to make them certain. Poor Mr Trench.

27

IT WAS NOT very long after receiving that telegram that Mr Sempill announced his intention of returning home to Broughty Ferry for the purposes of holding a discussion with Detective Lieutenant Trench in regard to the course of the investigation as a whole and the business of the identification in particular.

And it was the day after he informed us of his decision that he was back in his familiar place in the station, happy to be shaking the dust and soot and stink of the city out of his clothes in the sharp clean winds of Broughty Ferry once again.

Not that I judge he was entirely happy to be away from London, but, on the other hand, I think his conscience pricked him a little that he had – even in the course of duty – been able to enjoy a visit to the great Imperial capital, which had been denied to the rest of us.

Perhaps to ensure that we did not feel left out, he was careful and generous enough to return with small, souvenir knick-knacks for each of us, little bits of china showing the famous Tower Bridge (which, as you may know, opens in the centre and rises and falls to admit the passage of shipping) and suchlike articles. He also had a whole series of picture postcards, hinged together like an accordion, which he exhibited to our general interest and delight and showed scenes such as "Buckingham Palace, where the King lives," and "The Houses of Parliament with Big Ben, although, as I learned, that is a fallacy and Big

Ben is neither the name of the famous clock, nor the enormous tower which houses it, but only of the great bell inside, which is, of course, invisible," and, naturally enough, "Scotland Yard itself, the headquarters of the largest and greatest police force in the Empire and, you may as well say, the world. If you could see just round the corner of that tower, you would be able to see the window of the very office where I had a share of a desk during my stay."

But, very soon, the time came to return to business. Mr Sempill was quick to praise us for all our labours, the many interviews we had carried out in his absence, the witness statements that had been gathered. "You've done sterling work, men, employing the most modern and methodical techniques of policing. I may tell you that, having been in the very beating heart of Scotland Yard, they have very little – if anything at all – to teach the men of Broughty Ferry Burgh Police."

We were all gratified to hear these remarks.

"However," said Mr Sempill, "it now seems clear that further avenues of inquiry have opened up furth of the burgh. These are pressing matters which I must discuss with Mr Trench and so . . ." And so we all left.

Naturally, since I was not present, and Mr Sempill never discussed the interview with me, I have had to rely on what Mr Trench reported, but, by his account, it was a tense and, some might say, an unfriendly affair.

"Thank you for seeing those witnesses," said Mr Sempill.

"Delighted to be of assistance," said Mr Trench. "We're all of us doing what we can."

"The thing is, Trench, I'd like to have a another chat with them."

"Of course, if you wish. I'm sure they would be willing. They've all been keen to help."

"Yes. See if we can't get some of them to firm up their notions a bit, solidify their opinions. Yes. That's the ticket."

"I don't think I understand," said Mr Trench.

"Come along, I think you understand fine and well. These witness statements you've taken – they're a bit wishy-washy. Look at this." He took out Mr Trench's telegram and began to read from it. "Wood, Don, girl Campbell, two girls McIntosh all say photograph strongly resembles man seen by them, but cannot say definitely. Cannot say definitely? What bloody good is that? Malcolm and Urquhart say he is like the man seen by them in car. Not that he *is* the man they saw, only *like* the man they saw. Boys Duncan, Bannerman and Potter say he *resembles* the man in *general appearance*. In general appearance? In general appearance? And Hay – Andy Hay the packman says he is *very like* the man he met leaving Elmgrove. Well, I can tell you this, Trench, whoever met Andy Hay coming out of Elmgrove would have been careful to stand down wind of him and probably a good way off at that."

"Do you think these good folk are lying?"

"Of course I don't."

"Then what? What are you accusing them of? Wee boys who were playing in the dark and got a fright when they saw a strange man, two young lassies who fled from a man thinking he was about to chase them, a maidservant who peered out through the branches of a tree into the garden across the road, exhausted workmen on a tramcar, one of them just out of his bed, one of them struggling home at the end of the day. The only one who got anything like a look at the man is the gardener, but none of them were taking notes. None of them had a camera."

"You make my point for me."

"And what is your point, sir?"

"My point is, Trench, that if you are able, so easily, to demolish the evidence of identification offered by these witnesses, how much more easily would an able advocate shoot it to pieces when it came to court? I'm on your side. Aren't we both on the same side? But the fact of the matter is, I'd be astonished if the Fiscal was even willing to issue an indictment based on evidence of this nature."

"I see, sir. So what do you have in mind?"

"I only hope – you may be present if you wish or I'm happy to do it alone – I only hope to re-interview the witnesses and perhaps to press them a little more firmly, just to see if their recollections might not be rather more . . ." He paused to think of the right word. "Rather more concentrated. I have arranged for a further photograph of Warner to be taken."

"To what purpose, may I ask?"

"I'd like to have it shown to the witnesses."

"But they have already seen his photograph."

"This is a different photograph."

"Does this one have horns? Will it show his bloodstained hands?"

"Trench! Mind your tone. Are you accusing me of trying to influence witnesses?"

Mr Trench said nothing. He told me that later that evening, as he looked deep into a pint pot in the Ship, "I said nothing. I should have said something, but I said nothing. It's poor Oscar Slater all over again."

28

I WOULD ASK you to consider what a figure Chief Constable Sempill was in our small burgh.

This was a man of position, a man of standing, a figure of influence in Broughty Ferry. If he went about in his street clothes, sharp eyes shining out from under his hat, whiskers that proclaimed his manly bearing, straight of back, heavy of tread, mighty of fist, he would command respect. In uniform, he was a very terror.

There was nobody in the burgh, from the Dighty Burn in the east to the Stannergate in the west, from Claypotts Castle in the north to the silvery Tay in the south, nobody who did not well know Chief Constable J. Howard Sempill, nobody who did not aspire to his acquaintance or dread coming to his professional notice.

Imagine, then, how Margaret Campbell must have felt to be told that she might, at any moment, expect a visit from no less a figure than Chief Constable J. Howard Sempill on a matter of grave importance. Imagine wee Maggie answering the door for Mrs Luke at Caenlochan Villas, as she must have done times without number before, and finding Mr Sempill standing on the step. Imagine how warmly he greeted her and how he chuckled when she bobbed a curtsey and said she would get her mistress.

"But it's you I've come to come to see, Miss Campbell."

Can you conceive of it? The Chief Constable of Broughty Ferry addressing a maidservant in those terms?

"You've come to see me? But I'm not allowed callers at this hour. I have one Sunday a month off and I'd be most happy to receive you then."

"But this is police business, Miss Campbell. If you ask your mistress, I'm sure she won't mind – if she is at home, of course."

"I will find out, sir."

Now, of course, Miss Maggie Campbell very well knew that her mistress was at home since she had taken her tea in the sitting room not half an hour earlier. And Chief Constable Sempill also knew that it was highly likely that Mrs Luke would have been at home at that hour. When Maggie told a caller that she would "find out" as to whether her mistress was "at home" that meant only that she would ascertain whether her mistress wished to receive a call.

And, of course, Mrs Luke very much did wish to receive a call from the Chief Constable of Broughty Ferry, not only because he was the Chief Constable, but also because it put her within touching distance of the distressing events at Elmgrove. Oh, it was one thing to live just across the street from "the house of mystery" with a maidservant who may, perhaps, quite possibly, probably did see the killer himself, brazenly taking the air, smoking a cigar in the very act of planning his ghastly deed, but quite another to entertain the man heading the inquiry beneath her own roof. Mrs Luke knew that a visit from the Chief Constable – though it lasted but a moment – would provide hours of breathless conversation at her Thursday bridge night.

"Send him in, Maggie," she said.

"You're to please come in," said Maggie.

"Thank you, Miss Campbell," said the Chief Constable.

And Maggie, standing at the door of the sitting room, announced: "Chief Constable Sempill, Ma'am."

"Chief Constable," said Mrs Luke.

"Mrs Luke," said Chief Constable Sempill. Oh, it was all very warm and polite.

"Thank you, Maggie," said Mrs Luke.

Maggie, knowing her place, said nothing at all and withdrew.

It was only when she was gone that Mr Sempill, observing all the proprieties, enquiring after Mrs Luke's health, remarking on the unseasonable mildness of the weather, hoping that it might hold and that perhaps a few of Mrs Luke's charming roses would be allowed to linger on a week or two longer, it was only then that he introduced the awkward and difficult reason for his visit.

"I wonder," he said, "if you might permit a few moments of conversation with your maid? For the purposes of the inquiry, you understand."

"Oh, the inquiry, Mr Sempill. Well, if it's a matter of the inquiry." Mrs Luke cranked the handle of the bell pull by the fire and some way off, across the hall, behind a heavy door and down a corridor, a brass bell, placed high on the kitchen wall, jangled on the end of a wire.

There was a moment or two of awkward waiting: "It really is very mild."

"Yes, isn't it?"

"For the time of year, I mean."

"Yes, for the time of year."

Before Maggie knocked gently on the door.

"Come in."

And came in.

"Yes, Ma'am?"

"Maggie, Chief Constable Sempill would like a word with you about the murder."

"Yes, Ma'am."

Maggie turned to face Mr Sempill. She held her hands clasped in front of her, in the middle of her white apron.

"Miss Campbell, would you come and sit here beside me – you don't mind, Mrs Luke?"

Maggie? The maid? Sitting here? On these chairs? On her chairs? "No, of course, I don't mind, Mr Sempill. Come away in, Maggie. Come away in."

Maggie came in and sat on Mrs Luke's sofa beside Mr Sempill, not quite beside him and not quite on Mrs Luke's sofa, just perched on the very edge of Mrs Luke's sofa, just barely enough of it under her backside to stop from sliding onto the floor. She looked at Mrs Luke and gave a thin smile. Mrs Luke snapped a biscuit.

"Now, Miss Campbell, I think it's the case that you have looked at this photograph." He took the picture of Warner out of his wallet and showed it to her.

"Yes, Mr Sempill. Your Lieutenant Trench showed it to me."

"That's right. Just the other day."

"Might I?" said Mrs Luke.

"Well . . ." Mr Sempill hesitated, but only for a second. "So long as it's in the strictest confidence, Mrs Luke." He showed her the picture and her hand flew to her mouth in shock.

"Oh, the villain! Oh, the brute! Oh, Maggie, you poor wee soul, is this the man you saw from the window?" She was thoroughly delighted.

Mr Sempill waited for a moment. "Well, Miss Campbell, is this the man you saw from the window? The man you saw in evening dress in the middle of the day, boldly walking about in Miss Milne's garden and smoking on a cigar?"

Maggie said nothing and chewed on her lip. She had an awful terror that she was about to slide off the sofa and land on the hearth rug.

"Miss Campbell, I think it's the case that you told Trench the photograph 'strongly resembles' the man you saw but you cannot say for sure."

"That's right, sir. That's what I said."

"Well, you see, Miss Campbell, the law demands a higher standard of proof than that. The law demands that a jury must be convinced 'beyond a reasonable doubt' and, you must understand, the fact that you cannot say for sure means that the man will get off. "

Mrs Luke was outraged: "Oh Maggie, surely you can't let the man who killed poor Miss Milne get off? You must be sure."

"But I'm not sure, Ma'am."

"And that's exactly why I wanted to have this talk with you, Miss Campbell. You see, I was wondering if – just take another look at the photograph again, if you would – I was wondering if you might be a little more certain, if there is anything I could do to help you reach a rather firmer conclusion."

"Well, I don't know. It's awful important."

"Yes, Maggie, it's terribly important."

"You see, Miss Campbell, I was wondering if you were, perhaps, to see the man in person, if you might not feel more confident in your identification."

"Well . . ."

"It's a dreadful imposition, I know. It would mean travelling to London – yes, all the way to London – at the expense of the Broughty Ferry Burgh Police, of course, and it would mean having to stay in a hotel in London. It would take you away from your work for two or three days."

"Two or three days?"

"Well, if Mrs Luke could spare you. Do you think you could spare Miss Campbell for two or three days, Mrs Luke?"

Mrs Luke thought she could, although the place would be in a dreadful state by the time Maggie got back, but, on the other hand, there was Thursday bridge to consider.

"So there you are, Miss Campbell. Mrs Luke thinks she could spare you and it would be perfectly safe. You would be accompanied at all times, I'd ensure that, and you would have a room of your own in the hotel, with all your meals found. Of course you would have to confront the man directly, in an identification parade, but I can promise you it would be perfectly safe. Officers would be constantly on hand to ensure your safety. He wouldn't dare say 'Boo' to you and it would only take a moment. There would be plenty of time for taking in the sights of our great Imperial capital, Buckingham Palace, the Tower of London, the Houses of Parliament, maybe even visit to a music hall."

"That sounds nice, doesn't it, Maggie?"

"Yes, Ma'am."

"But, you see, Miss Campbell, there would be very little point in taking you to London and very little point in burdening the ratepayers of Broughty Ferry with the costs of your journey, the railway tickets, your hotel bills, all your keep, unless," Mr Sempill tapped the photograph with his finger, "unless you feel, in your heart of hearts, that seeing this man, face to face, might somehow clear your recollection."

Maggie sat for a moment, balanced on the very edge of Mrs Luke's sofa, looking hard at Warner's picture, his face reflected in the angled mirrors, his hands, those terrible hands, and tried to imagine him in evening dress, walking amongst the shrubbery, a cigar between his lips.

"It could be the man," she said.

"Are you sure, Maggie? Bear always in mind the ninth commandment."

"Nearly sure, Ma'am. I think, if I saw him face to face, I could be certain sure."

"Of course you could, Miss Campbell. Of course you could. I will make all the necessary arrangements."

"Thank you, sir." And then, remembering her place and the two or three days she would be away, she said: "Ma'am."

"That's all settled then, ladies," said the Chief Constable. "Thank you so much." He made his polite farewells and went to leave, and a moment later Maggie was closing the door behind him. But she did not return to her place in the kitchen, for the bell from the sitting room was ringing again.

"Yes, Ma'am?"

"More coal on the fire, Maggie. I think it's growing a little chilly."

29

WHO COULD SAY a harsh word against poor Maggie Campbell? Perched there on the edge of her employer's sofa, under the very gaze of Mr Sempill, with her mistress willing her on to come to a decision and the offer of a jaunt to London dangled like a jewel before her eyes, is it any wonder she wavered? Which of us would have stayed strong in such a circumstance?

And if Mr Sempill could bend a fine young lassie like Maggie Campbell to his will, how much more easily could he impose himself upon the others?

James Don the bin man boasted that there was not a man in the Ferry he did not know at least by sight, which was not surprising since he had hardly been furth of the burgh in all his days.

Imagine the temptation to a man like that, a man who regarded a trip on the cars to Dundee as high adventure and a crossing on the Tay ferries as something akin to uncovering the source of the Nile. Mr Sempill judged that there could be but one response when he was offered the chance to travel to the greatest city on earth, completely free of charge. He was not even asked to lie but only that he should be rather more firm in the opinions he already held. Mr Sempill was right.

And then there were the McIntosh sisters, Ina and Jessie, in their little cottage along the beach. They were like any other working lassies with barely two pennies to rub together at the end of each week. If they ever hoped to marry they would do it on the last day of the year, because New Year's Day was the only holiday they could expect. Just imagine what they must have thought when Mr Sempill offered them three days away from the screaming noise and dust of the mill, three whole days away from the stink of the bleachfields. A three days' holiday in the capital, at no charge and no loss of wages, with the manager's permission and their jobs held open for them when they returned – what an adventure – and the understanding was clear: they would not be asked to lie. Of course they agreed at once that a good look at the man in the picture might help them towards a more definite decision.

John Wood the gardener, the man who opened the door to the strange caller, was as unwilling to be bought and sold for Mr Sempill's visit to London as he had been for Miss Milne's two-shilling tip. But he was so consumed with guilt that he required no further persuasion. The thought that he might in some small way atone for his part in Miss Milne's death, and, worse, the destruction of her reputation, was sufficient inducement.

Some of the others, the working men who offered their evidence from the tramcar, were marked down in the Chief Constable's notebook as "not required on the voyage", and the pedlar Andy Hay was regarded by Mr Sempill as too fragrant for the journey unless the ratepayers went to the expense of getting him a carriage of his own, preferably one with an open top and at the very back of the train. But even without Andy Hay, the Chief Constable had a jolly party ready for his new London trip and he looked forward to it eagerly, as a visit to the capital now held no terrors for him and he regarded himself as a highly experienced traveller – the sort who could hail a cab in Trafalgar Square without a second thought, and if he could do that, what could he not do? Why, shooting tigers from the back of an elephant would be small beer to our Mr Sempill from now on; indeed he would probably think nothing of shooting

202

elephants from the back of a tiger if the circumstances called for it.

He was delighted with his efforts and, I am sure, still more delighted when, to my vexation, the Saturday papers were full of our business once again, just as I expected.

IS MISS MILNE'S ASSAILANT UNDER LOCK AND KEY?

Witnesses See Photograph of Man Sentenced for Minor Offence,

Who Answers Description of Suspect Seen Haunting Elmgrove.

MISS MILNE'S OPEN HYMN-BOOK ON ORGAN AT ELMGROVE

Beneath that there was a photographic illustration of the drawing room at Elmgrove, where there was a substantial pipe organ in a corner next to the fireplace. Miss Milne's velvet curtains, her patterned wallpaper, the elegant gas lamps, her pictures, her chairs, a tall vase of dried grasses on a shelf on the front of the organ – all displayed to every gawker who cared to look. Even the contents of her music stand were exposed to public view.

> O to awake from death's short sleep
> Like the flowers from a wintry grave
> Thy name, Lord be adored:
> And to rise, all glorious in the day
> When Christ shall come to save!
> Glory to the Lord.

> O to dwell in that happy land
> Where the heart cannot choose but sing
> Thy name, Lord, be adored:
> And where the life of the blessed ones
> Is a beautiful, endless spring!
> Glory to the Lord.

Far from regarding this intrusion almost as a blasphemy, the journalists of the *Weekly News* appeared to think they had uncovered a valuable insight.

> These verses, the concluding two verses from a beautiful hymn in the Scottish Church Hymnary, were observed by detectives who made a search of Elmgrove, the mansion house where Miss Jean Milne was mysteriously murdered. The hymn book was open at Hymn No. 490 which was a favourite hymn with Miss Milne, who was frequently heard singing it to her own accompaniment on the organ in her drawing room. The photograph shows a corner of the drawing room with the organ and hymn book open as they were left by the lady on the day she met her death.

It seemed the readers of the *Weekly News* were intended to take some solace from these circumstances, as if the dreadful hammer blows raining down upon Jean Milne's head until her skull split and her brains poured out were somehow softened by the fact that she had been singing of the life to come only a short while before.

Quite obviously, that photograph could not have been obtained without the permission of the police. You will not be surprised to learn that this infuriated me, but I was astonished to discover that, in ways I had not expected, it saddened Mr Trench. After all, it was Mr Trench who had cooperated so fully with the papers only the week before, because he believed it his duty as an essential part of modern policing. Now, it seemed, he regretted ever beginning.

"Look at this," he said. "How many men are there in Dundee – householders who might be called to sit on a jury? Now every single one of them has been advised that our suspect has something less than an unblemished record. That taints their judgement. That turns them against him before we even begin. And they have been told he resembles the wanted man. That is a matter of evidence. That's a matter for a witness to stand up in the box and swear to before God. That's a matter for cross-examination. It's a matter for the jury to decide, and they have already been told their opinion by the *News*."

Mr Trench sat at one side of the police office, reading the paper, and I sat at the other doing the same, and I surmised from his many huffs and groans when he had reached some particularly annoying section of the article.

"Have you seen this, Fraser? Have you seen this? Damn them." Mr Trench began to read aloud.

> It is not unknown that a person after committing such a serious offence as murder has, in order to throw suspicion off himself, committed a minor offence in a different district in the belief that prison is the last place the police would look for a wanted man.

"So, now he's not only a petty criminal, but he is so sly and cunning that he has committed his petty crime for the sole purpose of hiding his guilt as a murderer. This is an outrage! If we ever bring this man back to Broughty Ferry we may as well string him up from a lamp post at the railway station. Why bother with the formalities, let's just get it done."

There was a good deal more muttering and then: "They know all about the business with his shirt. Every damned detail!"

And then:

> Chief Constable Sempill applied for and obtained permission to have the man officially photographed.

"Hurrah for Chief Constable Sempill."

> It is probable that the witnesses may proceed to London to confront the original of the photograph.

"Oh it's probable, is it? I'd say it was highly bloody likely. Well, that's just grand. If there's anybody who has not been corrupted by the newspaper, a trip to London should do the job." And then, with a great sigh, he said: "It's come to this."

"What will you do?" I said.

"What'll I do? I'm damned well going with them."

30

BROON AND SUTTIE were at the station to see the party off and ensure there were no unpleasant intrusions by over-enthusiastic reporters. I was not there, but they must have seen me as they left on the train, even if they never knew it. I suppose I must have seen them. I saw their train, at least. Standing out at the end of the Pilot's Pier I could see the whole world.

I like the Pilot's Pier. It has a charm about it. Certainly the lamp posts bear the stamp of Dundee Harbour Trust, but that is forgivable. It is they who bear the costs of the Tay Pilot and the upkeep of the pier. We in Broughty Ferry choose to regard the pier as a small territorial concession for the greater good, an embassy, if you will, from the great city state of Dundee to our own little burgh. Ships from all over the world come to our river, and if, for the price of that small concession, the first man they meet is a Ferry man, then that is all to the good. Also it gives the laddies a place to fish.

I often go there and drink deep of the clean sea winds, pondering where they came from, what wonders they have seen. It is a good place to stand. When a man wants to feel the stars turning through the heavens and have the dust of old age blown out of his trouser cuffs, he might find a worse place to do it than the Pilot's Pier.

If I look to my left, to the east, there is the castle and a sky full of boiling, racing clouds, the sound of chattering, clattering, yammering gulls calling and calling to each other, the waves, as blue black as my uniform, all the way to the edge of the world, the very edge of the world, where they break in a standing line of foam across the bar, and a distant lighthouse looking out still further, beyond the edge of the world to a new horizon I cannot see, a great broad, blue sweep of forever bounded on the south by forest and hills and then a few houses and then a few more, growing denser as my gaze turns west, more and more of them, the closer they get to the railway bridge.

That bridge has been a way of escape for many of Dundee's more prosperous citizens – those not fortunate enough to find a refuge in Broughty Ferry. The bridge leads all the way from the black, stinking, smoking heart of Dundee, far across the river until it comes out clean on the other side, away from the dirt, away from the smells, away from poverty and disease and drunkenness and poor souls piled one on top of another as if packed away in the filing cabinets of Hell.

I was there on the Pilot's Pier that day when Mr Sempill and Mr Trench and their little party left for London. I saw their train puffing across the bridge, its ragged scarf of smoke blown to lace through the grey steel girders. I watched it all the way, not quite able to see it, so far off was it, but knowing it was there, and if they had cared to look down the river, they might have seen me too, a tiny dot in the landscape, unrecognisable as a man, but there anyway.

The day the old bridge fell, the one that blew down in a gale when I was a boy and carried a train and all its passengers to their doom, that was the last time we saw such a plague of reporters in the burgh, scribbling down their notes and making their sketches as we picked over the broken flotsam on the beach. Poor, mad McGonagall, who thought himself a poet and went door to door selling his ballads, was moved to write of the disaster. "The stronger that we our houses do build, the less chance we have of being killed." That was what he said, and whatever your view of his writing style, you could not fault him in his philosophy.

The new bridge has stayed up. It is, they say, the longest railway bridge over tidal waters anywhere in the world, an outward and visible sign of mankind's dominion over the forces of nature – but they said that about the last one. They said it about the *Titanic*. We have no dominion. We live our whole lives on the edge of a cliff. Did Jean Milne not prove that?

And I knew those on board the train with Mr Sempill would not be watching to see Sergeant John Fraser waving them off. Instead they would be peering from their windows for the peculiar thrill of seeing the stumps of the old bridge and laughing and giggling and wondering if they would make it over, laughing and dancing on the edge of the cliff, like the rest of us.

I wonder how long it was, after the train vanished into the southern hills, before the terrible truth of their situation began to dawn on them and they realised they were captives in a railway carriage and their three days' holiday would be spent – for the most part – trapped inside a rattling, jolting box. After an hour, perhaps, when they reached the Forth Bridge, still mightier and grander than our own? Or half an hour later when they passed under the feet of Edinburgh Castle, high up on its rock above the city, so much larger and stronger than our little castle dabbling its toes in the harbour? Or when they had to gather up all their traps and baggage and get off and race across the platform to change trains and wait, because the train was not there? Then they might begin to think how long they had travelled, how far they had come from their quiet homes and yet they had barely even begun.

And what did they speak of all through the endless hours to

London? The McIntosh girls had each other, of course. That would have made the journey easier. They had spent their lives sharing a bed, so they could at least stretch out their limbs in the cramped carriage without fear of intruding upon a stranger, but sometimes a constant intimacy can rob us of conversation. There is nothing new to be said. It must be as true for sisters as it is for married couples.

Maggie Campbell would befriend them and Mr Trench knew how to be charming, but Broughty Ferry burgh cleansing department is not known to engage its bin men and street sweepers for their conversational skills, Wood the gardener was gloomy and unbending, and Mr Sempill, well, Mr Sempill was Mr Sempill. He might play the part of jovial uncle for a while, but he had a heart of teak and all the dignity you would expect of the Chief Constable of Broughty Ferry. He would be no company at all for young lassies.

There would be refreshments on the way, no doubt. Smart girls like that – raised without servants to wipe their noses – would have thought to take something with them, and no doubt James Don had a bottle of beer in his pocket. Both pockets. Mr Sempill may even have treated them to a cup of tea and a bun during the long stop at York while they changed engines – being careful, of course, to obtain a receipt. But York was only halfway there and the newspapers and the magazines they bought would be squeezed dry ten minutes after they left the station. Oh, but it would be a long and weary journey, and the darkness would come down by the middle of the afternoon, so even the passing scenery would cease to provide any diversion.

Maybe they came to regret their bargain. They must have wondered if a day skivvying for Mrs Luke or tending a loom in the mill or manhandling bales of soaking linen might not have been better than sitting on those hard seats for the best part of a day. The hours must have dragged all the way into London, and by the time they arrived it would be too dark to see anything but the inside of their hotel and their beds.

But the McIntosh sisters did not sleep well. They had never passed a night alone in their own bed and now they were severed completely, sent to separate rooms, each with its own fireplace, each its own washstand, its own rug on the floor, pictures on the walls, a vast wardrobe filled with nothing but coat hangers that rattled in every draught.

People moved up and down the corridor – it seemed all night long – there were the clicks and creaks of a sleeping building that were not the sleeping sounds of their own cottage, and shadows moving on the wall that were not their shadows, while outside, even in the dead of night, there came the incessant sounds of a city, never really ceasing, and then gradually growing louder and more insistent with the dawn.

Two doors along, Maggie Campbell slept until five and then came spark awake as usual, as she had trained herself to do from the day she entered service at the age of twelve. But there were no fires to make up, no kettles to boil. Poor Maggie was bereft. She arranged the pillows at her back and sat up in bed with a copy of the *People's Friend* she had rolled in her coat pocket, looking into the cold black fireplace. There was an awful good serial in the paper about a schoolteacher who suddenly found herself heir to a Highland estate and Maggie felt sure that in this week's episode the village doctor would declare himself at last. But she could barely follow the print on the page. Halfway along every line her eye would fly to the dead grate, and she had not read a page of it before she was forced to get out of bed and make up the fire.

Mr Don the bin man was also schooled to rise early, but he overcame himself with the assistance of several large glasses of whisky, which he had appended to Mr Sempill's account in the middle of the night. They would, no doubt, come as a profound shock to the ratepayers of Broughty Ferry.

Chief Constable Sempill burrowed deep into his blankets, dreaming himself into the death cell, standing on a platform of wooden boards, waiting in breathless silence until the door opened and Charles Warner entered, wrists at his back, to stand on the trapdoor beneath the dangling noose. "Not so bloody clever now," he muttered.

And, while Mr Wood the gardener awoke refreshed from the sleep of the just, Mr Trench was returning to the hotel, silver beads of river mist webbed over his coat, eyes red-rimmed and burning, and his soul unquiet.

31

THEY ALL MET in the hotel dining room at 7.30, as arranged, and Mr Sempill, cheeks bright from the razor, whiskers combed silky, advised them to: "Help yourselves from the sideboard. Please eat all you like. We have a busy day ahead."

They sat down together over bacon and eggs as the Chief Constable explained the business of the day. "In a short while we will proceed to the railway station, where we will meet Mr Clarence Wray and Miss Minnie Gibbons. They knew the deceased Miss Milne during her stays in London and they may have seen the man. This will be their opportunity to view the suspect face to face.

"Please don't think me rude, but I will be in the company of Mr Wray and Miss Gibbons in a separate carriage during our journey to Tonbridge. It is most important that you are kept apart and not given any opportunity to influence one another in your testimony."

Mr Trench poured out a cup of strong tea as disapprovingly as it is possible to pour any cup of tea. "I'd be happy to ride with them," he said.

"There's no need."

And except for when Maggie Campbell said: "I don't think I like coffee," and the McIntosh sisters said: "Neither do I," they finished their breakfasts in silence.

Even for Jessie McIntosh, who was used to the noise of the mill, their first sight of London in daylight came as a shock. So many people, such a crush of traffic, the cabs, the omnibuses, the people jammed on the underground trains and pushed along through a hole under the ground, the pavements crowded like a net of herring, the smoke, the stink, the clamour, the madness of it all.

Jessie and Ina linked in together for fear of becoming separated again, and Maggie Campbell, now the firmest of friends, took Jessie's free arm, but they had to progress along crabwise for fear of blocking the pavement.

"Oh, but what if we are parted?" said Ina. "What if we got lost? How would I ever find my way back to the Ferry from here? I'd be left to starve amongst strangers."

"Don't be afraid," said Mr Trench, which was easy enough for him to say, pushing along the street as broad as a door and head and shoulders above the rest of them. "We will not be separated. I will not permit it, but, if we should be, you need only walk up to any policeman and announce yourself as Miss Ina McIntosh of Broughty Ferry, on official police business, and he will be compelled to see you safely on your way." They all laughed at that and the girls were comforted.

Before long they were in the very shadow of St Pancras station, with all its towers and battlements, vaster than any castle, clocked and towered like the Houses of Parliament, swirling with the smoke of engines and echoing with their furious breathing.

"We must wait here at the barrier," said Mr Sempill, handing out their tickets, "until the London witnesses join us." But they soon came. There was a certain awkwardness with the introductions. Nothing anybody could put their finger on. Mr Wood the gardener and Mr Don the bin man would never have noticed, but Maggie Campbell spent all her days among the better sort of folk and watched them being polite to each other, so she spotted it. There was contempt when Mr Sempill introduced: "Mr

Clarence Wray," contempt for a man who would write a woman bad poetry – and do it on lilac paper – and a difficult, chilly embarrassment for "Miss Minnie Gibbons", the receptionist at the Bonnington who had bested him. She had a wonderful amount of hair piled under a daring hat and a tiny waist and a coat with a green velvet trim. Maggie wondered if, one day, she might not like to be a receptionist at a fancy London hotel too.

"Trench, be so good as to accompany the Broughty Ferry witnesses."

"Sir."

"I will travel with Miss Gibbons and Mr Wray. For the reasons I have described."

There was no discussion. They simply went through the barriers, each of them showing their ticket to the inspector on the gate, and then there was the rattling journey to Kent with Mr Trench wondering every minute if Mr Sempill had a photograph of Warner with him, if it might not have been easily slipped into the pocket of his jacket, if it might not easily be slipped out again and displayed, if the two witnesses now kept secure and separate in another carriage might not be shown that picture and asked, merely for interest, for the sake of conversation, if they recognised that man and then, just as easily, if that picture might not be put away.

Mr Trench retreated into the corner of the railway carriage, tipped his hat down over his broad face and pretended to sleep for the rest of the way. But it was a lie.

At Maidstone there was more herding and nursemaiding as the party was gathered and collected into three cabs and driven off to the prison. "Here's fun," said Don the bin man. "A three days' holiday they promised me and we're to pass it in the jail. I've been on better Sunday School picnics." He gave a belch. "Always take a kipper for breakfast if ye can. Ye'll enjoy it all the day."

Miss Gibbons was a little uneasy and she sat with her head tilted and her hat shading her face. "What if someone were to see us and form the unfortunate impression that we are visiting persons of our acquaintance? I have a professional reputation to consider – not to mention the reputation of the Bonnington."

"Do not distress yourself," said Mr Sempill. "We are expected and the gates will be opened for us. You can get down away from prying eyes."

She seemed reassured. The cabs halted in line. There was the sound of voices, locks turning, great bolts moving, hinges groaning. The cabs rumbled over the cobbles and the gates shut again with an echo.

The Chief Constable gallantly offered his hand to guide Miss Gibbons down, and she took it, but with no indication that she had forgotten or forgiven the incident with the bell.

When they were all gathered together again and the tired grey cab horses stood, gently jingling their harnesses, each with one hoof raised and rested on its tip, as tired horses will, Mr Sempill addressed them all as a company. "I'm sure none of you has ever been inside a prison before and I can imagine you may find it a distressing experience. Prisons are not intended to be welcoming places. They are designed to be somewhat overwhelming and intimidating and, as you know, this place is home to some unpleasant people. Please do not distress yourselves. You are perfectly safe. No harm can possibly come to you.

"While we are here, your safety and the conduct of the identification is not my responsibility. It is the responsibility of this gentleman," he indicated the prison governor, "Mr Hill, who is Chief Warder of this establishment. I will now hand you over to him."

Mr Hill said: "Good morning," with a slight bow and

selected a large key from an iron ring he was carrying. "If you ladies and gentlemen will be pleased to follow me."

He led the way inside the building to a small room packed with chairs and tables. At one side there was a counter and beyond that a kitchen hard at work. There was a long row of windows along the far wall, but, like all the windows in that place, although they let in light, they were too high to look from. "The officers' mess room," Mr Hill explained. "In a moment, you will be asked to go into the yard outside, one at a time. I will accompany you. There you will find ten men. I would ask you to look at all of them, each in turn, and decide if there is any one of them you recognise. Miss none of them out. You may take as long as you wish. You may go up and down the line as often as you wish. There will be officers in the yard to guarantee your safety and one of them will be standing by the door on the other side of the yard. I would ask you to leave by that door. If you recognise a man, you may indicate that by placing a hand on his shoulder, but it is not necessary to do so. The officer standing by the door will record your answer, whether you recognise a man or not, and you may simply tell him where in the line the man you recognise is standing. Is that clear?"

They all nodded and mumbled.

"Then we'll begin. If you would all please line up against this wall, then there will be no possibility of accidentally looking into the yard while someone else is making their choice. In that way there can be no suggestion of signalling between you or anything of that kind. If we might do this alphabetically? Miss Campbell?" Maggie raised her hand. "Thank you. If you would please stand here. Mr Don?"

While the governor got on with arranging the witnesses into a queue, Mr Sempill spoke up. He said: "I would like to add a few words, if I may. I would urge you not to think of the photograph you have seen. Put all thoughts of the photograph you saw earlier out of your heads completely. Do not give it another thought. Forget about it completely."

Mr Trench ground the tip of his umbrella into the floor and twisted it furiously.

"Is that perfectly clear?" said Mr Sempill. "You have come all this way to look for the man you saw previously in the flesh and not, by any means, the man you saw in the photograph." He nodded to Mr Hill, who opened the door into the yard and beckoned Maggie Campbell forward. When she passed through, he went with her and closed the door again.

The others were left alone, with nothing to look at but each other. The clock on the wall ticked. Miss Gibbons sensed that a hair had come loose and deftly tucked it back into place with gloved fingers.

Mr Trench stood imagining Maggie Campbell walking across the prison yard, counting her steps, slowing down a little fearfully as she reached the first man in the line, standing in front of him, looking up at him, taking a step backwards to ease the crick in her neck. Mr Trench imagined her searching the man's face, carefully doing her duty. He let the clock tick five times and then, in his mind's eye, Maggie moved on. A step to the side. Another count of five. She moved again. Ten men, five seconds each, a little time to walk out into the yard, a little time to walk out the other side. A minute and a half should be plenty of time. Mr Hill the governor must be returning for the next witness now.

Three minutes passed.

The Chief Constable said: "This is taking a Hell of a time."

"I imagine," said Mr Trench, "the time passes even slower if you're standing on a trapdoor."

32

SITTING IN FRONT of the fire in the hotel parlour, a third of the way through another large brandy, Mr Trench read from the typed sheet of paper which Mr Sempill handed him. The prison governor, Mr Hill, prepared his report dutifully and carefully. He recorded that Wood, Don and the McIntosh sisters "identified Warner without any hesitation, although I made the men take off their coats and so on, but Miss Campbell was doubtful. She said no at first, but afterwards said she was not sure. Miss Minnie Gibbons and Clarence Wray were more certain in their opinion. They both agreed they had never seen Warner before."

"I suppose I need not ask your opinion," said Mr Sempill.

"I think you already know my opinion." He was glad they had the room to themselves.

"In my view it is misguided."

"Really? We know a man was trying to ingratiate himself with Jean Milne when she last stayed at the Bonnington Hotel. A young man with a moustache. Clarence Wray and Miss Gibbons saw the man several times – many times – in relaxed conditions, in good light, over a period of days. It would suit Wray very well to name Warner as the guilty man, if only because it would get you off his neck, and yet they both say quite the opposite. They recognised nobody in the identity parade. Warner is not the man they knew from the hotel."

"The others were perfectly clear."

"Nonsense. Maggie Campbell is anything but clear. It's in the report. She first said no and then changed her mind to maybe. A fleeting glimpse of a man is not evidence. What's the evidence? A man seen under a lamp post for a moment by two frightened lassies? A man seen under a lamp post in the early morning? A rough old pedlar who passes the time of day with a man who was running for a tramcar? A man seen on a tramcar?

"Sempill, do you not see everything that was ordinary yesterday becomes extraordinary tomorrow if, in the interval, some crime has been discovered? Somebody sees a man under a lamp post and it means nothing. In the normal course of things they would have forgotten about it entirely the day after tomorrow. But then they hear that a neighbour has been murdered. Imagination runs riot and the man that 'wee Jeanie saw' or 'our Jimmy spoke about' at once becomes the evil-doer. If a man's actions are themselves suspicious, if he's hanging about on a certain street at a certain time or looking at a certain building and then that building is burgled, then identification is immensely valuable. It is prized. That's why it is provided.

"Take any dozen individuals, men, women, any age, any character, any station in life, it doesn't matter, and have somebody walk past them unannounced, as slowly as you like. Have them write down what they saw – believe me, I've tried. You can't get one out of the twelve to give you anything like a description. Most of them are well wide of the mark and some are just ludicrous. Time and again I've seen it, time and again, a stream of conflicting, contradictory, nonsensical drivel. 'How was he dressed?' I'd say. 'Oh, a light suit and a dark cap. Or maybe the cap was not so dark. I'm not sure. But he was definitely wearing light-coloured trousers.'

"Then the neighbour breaks in and says the suit was brown,

but by the time I've finished with her the suit's black and he's wearing a felt hat.

"They are ready to swear a man's life away. You'll have a man murdered if you can just get enough good-natured fools to name him. But it won't wash, Sempill. It won't wash. Didn't you say it yourself before we left Broughty Ferry? If I can rubbish their testimony, how much more easily would an able advocate do it in court? There is nothing – nothing, I tell you – linking Warner to Miss Milne."

Mr Sempill was growing increasingly short. "What are you backtracking for, Trench? You yourself told me that Miss Milne was murdered by a maniac or a foreigner."

"I didn't say it was this foreigner. There are many foreigners – millions of foreigners. The Tsar of all the Russias is a foreigner; the German Kaiser is foreigner. The great bulk of the world is made up of foreigners and half of them are living right now in London."

"Wood. There's Wood. Wood is unimpeachable. Absolutely beyond reproach. He unhesitatingly identified Warner and he was the man who opened the door to him. It was Wood who let the killer in."

Mr Trench was astonished. "Are you now reduced to Wood alone? How long does it take to open a door? How long to walk across the hall of Elmgrove? Seconds. Seconds, Sempill, mere seconds."

"It's good enough for me."

"Oh I know that. I understand that very well. You have fixed on Warner and no power on earth will be enough to make you change your mind."

"Go carefully, Lieutenant Trench. Go very carefully."

Mr Trench drained his brandy glass. "Didn't you tell me that we are on the same side, Chief Constable? I'm trying to help you. I understand the demands that are being made of you, truly I do. The same demands have been made of me, believe me. A dreadful crime has been committed and people are demanding action, they want answers, somebody must be made to pay. But what's the point in making the wrong man pay? You'll end up with two victims, Sempill, one with her head bashed in on the floor of Elmgrove and one dangling from a rope with a broken neck. Stop now, man. Stop before this goes any further. I'm begging you."

"You are making yourself ridiculous, Trench. I know my duty and I do not need you to remind me of it."

"Do you not see your soul is in danger?"

"My soul? My soul? This is the brandy talking, Trench."

"I think I need a little more." Mr Trench had nothing left to say and no more brandy left to drink. He sank back into his chair as he had on the train to Maidstone, almost cowered in it, as if to hide himself in it, with his two broad hands over his face.

"No more, man. Stop. Get a grip of yourself and go to your bed. Tomorrow I expect you to make application to the Procurator Fiscal at Dundee and obtain a warrant for the arrest of a Charles Warner, currently a prisoner of His Majesty at Maidstone. Get it done, Trench, and we'll say no more about it. We'll go on as before and no more said. I bid you goodnight."

Mr Trench waited until he heard the electric whirr of the lift motors taking the Chief up to his room and then he rang for another drink.

33

The North British Railway Company
General Enquiry Office
Waverley Station
Edinburgh

Broughty Ferry Murder Case

I am in charge of the Enquiry Office here, and having read the statement made by scavenger Don I think you should know the following and judge for yourself whether it is worth your attention. On Tuesday or Wednesday, 15th or 16th October (I cannot be sure of the exact date) about 9-50 a.m., a man answering the description given hurriedly entered my office and asked which was the quickest way in which he could reach the Continent.

I gave him the times via Harwich and Hook of Holland, also Antwerp and, latterly via London and Dover but, apparently he favoured the Queensboro' and Flushing route and, although he did not tell me his destination, I had the impression that he wished to get to either Rotterdam or Amsterdam.

I told him to get away by the 10-0 a.m. train to King's Cross, and he seemingly left to do so. He was labouring under a great deal of excitement, and had a nervous haunted expression. About 30 minutes later I was very much surprised to receive another visit from him, and without giving any explanation as to his sudden change of mind, he made enquiries about the night trains to London and the morning service from there to the Continent. On his first appearance he had the haggard look of a man who had not slept, but he had washed before returning, and his manner was much calmer. He had a decided foreign accent. It is possible that he came off the train due here at 9-45 a.m. from Dundee, and should that be the case the circumstances are certainly suspicious.

Yours faithfully.
(Signed) Andrew Brown.

Officer in charge
Criminal Investigation Department
Central Police Office
Edinburgh

34

PRISON IS A shaming thing for everybody involved. It is embarrassing for a man to be sent to prison.

To be a prisoner, to have nothing to think about and nothing to do, to be helpless, at the mercy of others, with no control over your life, where you go, what you do, when you eat, when you sleep, when you keep silent, when you may speak, all of that diminishes a man. He may try to carry it off with swagger and braggadocio, but in his soul, he shrivels a little. And it is only a little less terrible for his jailers. They know they have done this awful thing to a man and a brother. They know that, like him, they are prisoners too. They spend their lives behind those walls. They serve longer sentences than most, willingly passing their lives away inside a jail and, most galling of all, they count themselves as volunteers. They are not, of course. They have wives to keep and children to feed and rents to pay and shoes to buy. Circumstance forces the jailers into jail as much as it does the prisoners, merely circumstance. Such knowledge is embarrassing and never more so than on the day of a prisoner's release, when he stands at the gate in his own clothes and the warders are in their uniforms, still in character, still playing their parts, still not set free. They try to make light of it, of course, as if by recollecting some little kindness they might be excused for this great cruelty, as if the whole business has been no more than a little social awkwardness, like using the wrong fork at dinner. That is why prisoners are released very early in the morning. It's so that nobody sees.

But when Charles Warner came out of the prison gate, Mr Sempill was there to see it and so was Mr Trench, standing a little apart and a little behind, his coat open, leaning on his umbrella as he always did, whatever the weather.

When Mr Sempill stepped forward, despite his best efforts there was a look of grey shock on Warner's face. He had expected to walk away a free man, a shilling or two in his pocket, a breakfast in his belly, ready to start again, but when he saw Mr Sempill, he understood. He stood still. There was no point in running.

The Chief Constable put a hand on his shoulder – it was a purely formal gesture – and he said: "Charles Warner, you are under arrest . . ."

"What for? What's the charge?"

". . . for the murder of Miss Jean Milne in the house known as Elmgrove, Grove Road, Broughty Ferry, in the county of Angus, at a time and a date unknown between October 14, 1912 and November 4, 1912. Come along with me."

Two large constables, supplied by Superintendent Neaves – Warner had not noticed them when he came through the gate – appeared at his sides and took his arms. Together they marched him to the horse van on the other side of the road, forced him up the steps and inside, onto a hard wooden bench. Warner was furious. His gold teeth showed as he pulled his mouth into a snarl. "You're bloody mad! You're all mad! I've never been to Scotland in my life. I couldn't find your shitty little town with a troop of Indian guides to help me." The door of the van banged shut and the driver whipped up his horses.

Mr Neaves shook the Chief Constable by the hand. "Well done," he said warmly. "Well done."

Mr Sempill said: "Thank you. Thank you for all your kind

assistance. But for your vigilance, we would never have caught him. Thank you."

Mr Neaves offered his hand to Mr Trench also. "Well done," he said again.

"I can't take the credit," said Trench. "The Chief Constable is the driving force behind this inquiry."

Mr Sempill offered his hand too and Trench shook it. "Congratulations," he said flatly.

"Thank you, Trench. That means a great deal."

The police van went on to the railway station, where Warner was made to stand on the platform, wrists chained together in front of him, until the train came. Mr Neaves' two constables stood at his side. They waited there like statues. Mr Trench went and stood in front of Warner, right in front of him, and yet the prisoner somehow contrived not to see him. He was standing looking across the tracks to where the low hills far away were appearing through the dawn in the colours of a Chinese scroll. The morning sky had faded to an ashy grey, the hills were standing out, a little darker grey against them with a low cloud, white and blushed pink, just kissing their tops and the morning mist running up like a river between them, folding over on itself and vanishing.

"You're in my way," Warner said. "I haven't seen much sky recently and you're spoiling it for me. A bit of sky is good for the soul."

"You believe in the soul?"

"I believe in mine. I don't make any claims for yours."

Mr Trench felt a terrible need to apologise, but he could not bring himself to do it. He said: "Is there anything I can do for you? Something you need?"

Warner made no reply. He simply held up his two hands, chained together.

"You know I can't do that."

Warner put down his hands again and went back to looking at the clouds. They were vanishing more quickly now as the sun grew a little stronger.

"Nothing?" Mr Trench waited for an answer, perhaps a heartbeat longer than was dignified, and then the Chief Constable called from the other end of the platform, where he was standing with Superintendent Neaves. "Trench, a word please."

He obeyed and the Chief Constable said: "Best to avoid familiarity or fraternisation. In my experience."

"Yes, sir."

"It would be like naming the pig," said Mr Neaves. "We always had a pig in the back yard, but Father never let us name it. Mustn't get fond, you know."

Mr Trench did some hard smoking until the train came and then Warner was loaded into the guard's van with the milk churns and the parcels and his two policemen, and there was more handshaking with Mr Neaves, who was thanked profusely for all his efforts and his vigilance and assured that if ever there was anything that he needed from Broughty Ferry Burgh Police, he had only to ask.

"And you won't forget my invitation to the hanging?"

"We certainly won't forget that! Will we, Trench?"

"Sir."

Trench was relieved to find that the train was packed and their carriage for the journey to London was full all the way to St Pancras. If they had been alone, or even if the train had been a little less crowded, conversation would have been expected, but, jammed in between two well-fed citizens, with the luggage racks full to bursting and the whole place a tangle of elbows and open newspapers, he was at least spared that. He passed the journey looking over his neighbour's shoulder and spotting mistakes the man had made in the crossword, but he was, of course, far too polite to put him right.

Mr Neaves had called ahead to Scotland Yard, and at the railway station another enclosed black horse van was waiting to take them on. Trench and the Chief Constable collected Warner from the two police constables and loaded him into the van.

"No fuss now," Mr Sempill cautioned. "Easier all round if there's no fuss."

Warner curled his lip and gave a disgusted little laugh, but he sat down quietly and made no comment.

The van rolled on through the streets of London, carts and cabs and tramcars jostling by on every side.

"I always say that a ride in one if these vehicles is a kind of commentary on life," said Mr Sempill.

Lieutenant Trench had no wish to hear Mr Sempill's commentary on life, so he said nothing.

"Don't you want to know why?"

Before he could answer, Warner winked at him from the bench on the opposite side of the van and said: "I know I do."

"I wasn't asking you, Warner, although, I must say, it's an observation from which you might benefit." Mr Sempill took a deep breath as if to steady himself before delivering his party piece recitation at one of Mrs Sempill's soirées. "I always say that a ride in one of these vehicles is like a commentary on life because our destination is a mystery out of our own control. We none of us know where we are going, or how we are to get there, but, while the future is a mystery to us, the view behind – as it were to the past – is perfectly clear, although closed off behind iron bars, unreachable, untouchable and unalterable."

"That really is remarkable," said Warner.

"Thank you."

"Did you never think of going into the Church, Chief? Talking horseshit like that they'd make you Archbishop of Canterbury inside a month."

"You impertinent oaf! How dare you? Do you not realise the peril in which you stand?"

"I'm sitting, Chiefy."

"You'll be hanging soon enough."

"So you say – and you're to be my judge, jury and executioner. This is your famed British justice, is it? Every man innocent until proved guilty. I could laugh until I throw up."

Warner turned his head away and looked through the barred window in the van door, back the way they had come, back towards the past. Nobody knew what he saw there. Nobody but him. And, since there was nothing else inside the van for anybody to look at, soon all three of them were gazing backwards out of the bars in silence, two of them watching the mad jostling jumble of the London streets, one of them looking up into the gaps between the great, tangled buildings, looking for a glimpse of sky.

35

THEY LEFT CANNING Street police station in the windy dark of a late November evening, making for the overnight train to Scotland. Mr Sempill had arranged with the railway company that they should have the carriage to themselves. In the circumstances, they were very accommodating.

Standing on the platform, Mr Trench read the *Weekly News*. There was a photograph taking up more than half the page inside, a studio portrait of the witnesses, taken on their return to Dundee, with Mr Wood the gardener and Don the bin man standing at the back and the two McIntosh sisters sitting at a velvet-draped table in front. The girls looked exhausted, as if they had just been jolted up and down the country on a train with nothing to look forward to but rising early for another day of hard work, but they were trying to look their best. No doubt the reporter who met them at the Tay Bridge station had wheedled and ingratiated and begged. No doubt he had promised them each copies of the picture. No doubt the girls had been tempted by such unaffordable luxury, and if those two old men with their walrus moustaches had to be in the picture, a pair of scissors and a frame could take care of that. But there was no Maggie Campbell. Where was Maggie?

> The fifth witness, Miss Margaret Campbell, declined to be photographed, saying: "There's been far too much of that kind of nonsense."

Trench laughed out loud at that. He could picture her saying it, scowling at the reporter, seeing through him and the great favour he was offering. He could see her picking up her bag and striding up the station steps for the tram stop. "If you're that keen on getting your pictures in the paper, help yourselves. I'm away to my bed!" Good for Maggie. But he felt for her. She must be troubled in her conscience. A girl like Maggie would feel that sorely.

"Must I be handcuffed all night long?" Warner said, as the train pulled out of the station.

Mr Trench stood up and took his bag from the luggage rack. He brought from it another set of handcuffs and about four feet of chain. "I came prepared," he said. He fixed one of the manacles through the chain and the other to the steel leg of the bench where Warner was sitting. Then he unlocked one of Warner's cuffs and attached it to the chain. "It's the best I can do," he said.

"You should be grateful," said Mr Sempill.

Warner looked at him with scorn. "Oh I'm so grateful. More grateful than you can imagine. Deeply, deeply grateful." He turned to Mr Trench and said: "Thank you."

Mr Sempill began to fill his pipe. "You may smoke if you wish," he said.

"I seem to have left my cigarette case in my other jacket."

"Take one of mine," Trench said.

"I can't return the favour. I seem to be temporarily strapped for cash, as you Britishers say."

"It's all right. A money order came for you. I cashed it at Maidstone."

"You don't say! How much for?"

Trench looked over at the Chief Constable. "I think it was ten pounds one and fourpence."

Mr Sempill nodded agreement.

"Hellfire and damnation. Don't that beat all? I knew my folks wouldn't let me down. If that had arrived a couple of days earlier, none of this would ever have happened."

Mr Sempill was quick. "Warner, I have to remind you that you have been properly charged and cautioned. That's why there are two of us here, to corroborate anything you may choose to say, and anything you do say may be taken down and used in evidence."

"Oh, don't get your bloomers in a knot. I was only going to say . . . Oh forget it. I'm not going to confess to anything. I told you before, I didn't do it and you can give me the third degree all you like, you won't make me say it."

"The third degree?"

Trench said: "It's American interrogation techniques, sir."

"It sure is. They know what they're doing there. That's a modern country, with some modern ideas. Not like this old place. The jolly old Empire is dying flat on its ass. All your best and your brightest have crossed the pond. All your young men, the ones with some get-up-and-go. They've all got up and gone and what's left? Small-town cops like you, that's what."

"And you," Mr Sempill said.

"Me? I'm just passing through. I'm making my way back to the New World the long way round."

"You're just a remittance man. You ruined some girl or, more likely, dipped the till somewhere. You brought disgrace upon your people and they paid you to get out of town and they pay you to stay away."

"I'm an adventurer. I've been and seen and done."

"Well," said Mr Sempill, "it's going to be a long night. Why not tell us? Keep us entertained? Where have you been, what have you seen?"

Warner gave a sneering laugh. "You boys have never seen

past the ends of your own noses. Now, me, I was with Roosevelt on the charge up San Juan Hill. I was right there beside him with the Rough Riders – damnation, do I dare to say 'with' the rough riders? I was a Rough Rider. Just about the roughest of all of them. Not that we did much riding. We went on foot all the way up the hill with Colonel Roosevelt leading the way on his horse. That's where I got this here bee-yoo-tee-ful smile," he opened his lips in a shark grin to show off his golden teeth, "from a Spanish gun butt in the hand-to-hand stuff at the top of the hill. That's living, boys, let me tell you. A drop of rum, a señorita, a hammock in the shade and, the very next day, the bullets popping all around as hot as Hell. Yee-haw."

"Fascinating," Mr Sempill said, though he sounded less than fascinated.

"I liked the war in Cuba so much I joined up for your little tea party in South Africa. That's the kind of war you British are good at – herding a lot of terrified women and kids behind barbed wire and watching them starve. That's the British way. You ever been in a war, Trench?"

Mr Trench retreated a little further into the corner of the carriage and tipped his hat over his eyes. "It's a long way to Dundee. I'd like to get some sleep."

"The way you gents are going about things, I'm going to have plenty of time for sleep. Once you get that rope round my neck and . . ." The train gave a jolt as they crossed over some points so they were almost shaken from their seats. Warner laughed "Yes, sir, just like that. I just about broke my neck right there."

"If you want to avoid it, the remedy is in your own hands," Trench said. "You say you didn't do it. You say you've never been any place near Broughty Ferry in your life. Then help us. Give us an account of your movements."

"What for? So you can pick holes in it and trip me up? No, sir. I know how these things go. I make one tiny mistake and you'll pass a noose through it. I know I didn't kill the old coot and that means you can't prove I did it. Not that I want to teach my grandmother how to suck eggs, but that's still how it works, I presume. Innocent until proven guilty under the laws of jolly old England."

"Scotland," said Mr Sempill. "You'll be tried under Scots law."

Warner flicked a mocking salute. "As you say, Chiefy. Just as you say."

"And neither Mr Trench nor I has any wish to put you on trial for a crime you did not commit."

"Well, let me say I take that as right neighbourly of you both and, for the record, let me also state that I believe that – of one of you."

"Go to sleep," Trench said.

"So what do you want to talk about? The ladies? I could tell you a few tales to put a smile on your face." And he went on, jabbering that way about where he had been and what he had seen, everything he'd done and who he'd done it to.

Mr Trench folded his arms across his chest and pretended to sleep. He hoped that, as with a difficult child, indifference might be the best response, but Warner yammered on through the night for mile after mile and Trench found himself lulled into a doze, but as he dozed, he listened, and as he listened, he took notes. "No. Not a stupid man. In fact, I'd say he is a man of considerable intelligence and well educated but, at the same time, a man who can be very, very coarse and vulgar. Evidently travelled a lot. Claims to be a great Freemason. Never done with talking about the Lodge. Sneers at everything British. Says he's forty-one years of age. We bargained him up from thirty-eight, anyway, but he looks at least sixty. Repulsive face. Repulsive. That's the soul shining through. Good knowledge of prison life and discipline – particularly French and American. I'd bet my pension he's seen the inside of a few jail cells. Claims he was once a wealthy man. He has that way about him. The entitlement that goes with money."

Warner must have feared he was losing his audience when neither Mr Trench nor Chief Constable Sempill made him any reply. So he commenced to singing.

> Who were you with last night,
> Out in the pale moonlight?
> It wasn't yerr sister
> It wasn't yerr maa
> Aaaa Aa Aha Aha
> Who were you with last night,
> Out in the pale moonlight?
> Are yah gonna tell your missus
> When you get home
> Who you were with last night?

"Shut up, Warner, for God's sake."

"Come on, come on, let's have a sing-song. They loved this one in the halls back in London. It's absolutely the latest thing."

"That's true, actually," said Mr Sempill. "It was all the go when I took the witnesses on their night out."

Warner was suddenly furious. "Sonsabitches. So that was all it took was it? That buncha rubes and hicks and you paid them off with a night in a hotel and a trip to the music hall. That was all it took to buy them, the stinking bastards. Lousy, stinking bastards. You'd think a man like me would be worth more than a pint of warm beer and a plate of pie and mash. Bastards.

Every one of you. Do you know – can you begin to think what it's been like for me? I'm accused of murder. You're out to kill me and you celebrate with a night at the music hall. Bastards."

"Then talk to us," said Trench. "Help us."

"We've been through that!" Warner was almost screaming at them. "Go piss up a rope."

Nobody said anything. They were embarrassed. The train rattled on in the dark. They heard the sound of rain, like gravel flung at a lover's window. They waited for Warner's anger to fizzle out.

"Did I ever tell you," he said at last, "about Eddy Guerin?" The storm had passed. "Eddy Guerin the Devil's Isle prisoner. Yes sir, he's a friend of mine. A good friend. And the Frenchies took him off to that Hellhole. Eddy's no more than a jewel thief."

"A notorious hotel jewel thief," said Mr Sempill.

"He's only notorious because he got caught. When he wasn't caught, nobody knew his name, which is considered as something of a qualification for a jewel thief. Not to get noticed, that's the thing. Come and go."

"If you know him, then you must know he is responsible for thefts worth many millions of francs."

"Then I tip my hat to him, Chiefy. I tip my hat and I say with good ole Teddy Roosevelt 'Bully for you!' Yes, indeed, bully for you, Eddy Guerin, wherever you are!"

"He should be ashamed," said Mr Sempill. "And you should be ashamed to know him. He is justly punished."

"Oh get the burr out of your ass, Chiefy! What harm did Eddy ever do you or anybody else? He helped himself to a lot of old ladies' rocks, that's all. And how did they get them? Come on, Chiefy, we're both men of the world here. They got them by whoring themselves to wealthy men, that's all."

"Ridiculous."

"And how did their husbands get the money to pay for it all? Why, by grinding the faces of the poor, that's how."

"Absolute nonsense."

"It's the goddamn truth. Nobody lost out by what Eddy did. All those rocks were insured. They got their money back and the insurance companies stole it all back again with a penny on every policy."

"Those pennies add up."

"And they sent poor Eddy off to Devil's Island for stealing a penny. Now that's the real crime."

Mr Sempill sat fuming like an outraged Sunday School teacher as Warner – "Lemme have another one of those cigarettes, Mr Trench" – boasted of the great men he had known. "The very best thieves and crooks and conmen," Swenney and May Churchill and others Mr Trench knew only from the papers and Scotland Yard bulletins, and when his stream of raucous anecdotes dried up, he would go back to singing his song: "Who were you with last night, out in the pale moonlight?" The words of it seemed to rattle round in all their brains so that even when Warner wasn't singing it or whistling it out between his gold teeth, the train clattered it out on the tracks: "It wasn't yerr sister, it wasn't yerr ma, it wasn't yerr sister, it wasn't yerr ma, it wasn't yerr sister, it wasn't yerr ma."

"I know what you think," Warner said. "You think a man like me, a man living by his wits, has to be a great talker. Well, as usual, boys, you could not be more wrong. It's not fast talking that gets a man like me his scores, no, sir. It's listening. If you want to get on, be a patient listener – and I mean really listen. You'll pick things up. Information. Information is the key to the door. And don't look bored. Never look bored. Listen with interest to what the other fella's saying – especially if the other fella is a lady.

"Politics – stay off it. Wait for the other person to reveal any political opinions, then agree with them. Agree and agree and agree. Same with religion. If he's a red-hot Bible-thumping Baptist, out-thump him. If he's an atheist who wants every priest hanging from a lamp post, that's fine too.

"And stay off sex. You can hint at it, but don't follow it up unless the other person – man or woman – shows a strong interest. Same with illness. People don't care about your ailments and they don't like to be reminded of their own. But these are all just general rules. In general, stay off illness, unless some special concern is shown.

"Go slowly, that's the thing. Never pry into a person's personal circumstances. Believe me, they are bursting to tell you everything if you just give them time. Never boast. There's no need for that. I'm a seriously important person. You're damned lucky to have the chance to be in my company, so I don't have to tell you that. It should be obvious. Keep clean and tidy – and I'm downright fastidious about that, boys – and stay off the drink. Stay sober at all times."

"Are you downright fastidious about that too?" Mr Sempill said.

"When I'm working, yes."

"Working!" Mr Sempill was a quiver of outraged whiskers.

"What I do is as much work as what you do. Persecuting world travellers and scraping old drunks off the road doesn't count as work in my book."

"Listen to me, you blackguard . . ."

But Mr Trench decided to intervene. "Just go to sleep, Warner. Go to sleep. I've done my best to make things comfortable for you, but, if you prefer, I can just as easily cuff your hands behind your back."

Warner showed his golden shark grin again, but he said

nothing in reply. And that was how they passed the night: saying nothing more. The guard came in some time after ten and asked permission to turn down the gas. Mr Trench agreed. It left them with no more than a glow of blue round the edge of the blinds onto the corridor, faint and milky like those worn bits of sea glass you find tumbled on the beach, and, at the other side, sometimes suddenly wiped away by the startling lightning-flash clatter of a passing train, only a rain-streamed sheet of black where the orange tip of Warner's cigarette reflected back at them.

Trench sprawled on his chair like a saloon bar bully, his legs stretched out to block the door, just in case Warner moved in the night. It was far from silent. The rain. The steam whistle howling like a lost beast in the darkness calling to its kin. All the shaking, rattling, thumping, creaking, squeaking noises of a moving train. The clickety-clack sound of the wheels moving over the tracks. Mr Trench had schooled himself to sleep whenever he got the chance and he might have slept through all of that, but there was something else too, very quiet and almost imperceptible so that sometimes he had to struggle to listen, as if to reassure himself that it was still there on the other side of the railway carriage and not right there on the seat beside him. It was Warner sucking and blowing through his golden teeth, not quite a whistle but more than a breath, and that tune: "Who were you with last night, out in the pale moonlight?" over and over again.

36

THE RAILWAY LINE passes through broad farmlands on its way north and then, briefly, into a tight cutting that contains and magnifies all the noise of the engine and then out again into open air along the edge of the Tay before launching itself onto the bridge. It was early in the morning – barely five o'clock – in late November and still as black as midnight with a heavy mist swirling about the train and clinging to the windows, but Mr Sempill could tell at once that they were almost home. The sound of the train changed and softened when they left the shore and went out onto the high bridge; everything became fainter, almost gauzy, as the roaring of the furnace, the screaming of great metal wheels turning on iron rails, the rattle of chains, the thump and bump and crash of carriages was carried up, out and down, warning them that they were now suddenly hanging over nothing with only the surge of black water waiting to swallow them if they fell.

The sound of the train changed again as it slowed on its approach to the other side, then on the long curving bend that was still, officially, "bridge" but now, at least, safely over land. Looking through the window they could see almost nothing – a few uncertain lights along the streets and, here and there, a lamp in the windows of a town waking to another day of misery and hard labour that only drunkenness could soften.

"Up," said Mr Sempill.

They went through the tiresome business of disconnecting

Warner's chain, locking and unlocking, unfixing and refixing his handcuffs, and when it was done and his wrists were once again manacled together, Mr Trench stood, holding the chain that linked them in a fist the size of a ham.

"Don't try to run," he said.

Warner looked at him with cool contempt.

"I mean it. Believe me, you won't get far with the cuffs on. It's surprising how tying a man's hands interferes with his legs, and you'll have the whole city after you. You will be caught and it would look worse for you."

"I'm not running," Warner said. "I've got nothing to fear."

The train stopped, so gradually and so slowly that, for a moment, they were unsure if it had actually happened. Trench got down first. Warner was waiting on the step of the railway carriage, Mr Sempill's restraining hand on his shoulder. Trench turned and gripped the handcuff chain again, urged him forward, and put his free hand on Warner's elbow to help him down. It was a kind gesture and Warner, who was unused to kindness, looked down and smiled.

On the platform, everything smelled of smoke and hot machine oil. There was the sound of heavy wooden doors banging shut along the length of the train. The engine released a gigantic fart of steam as they passed. It curled up and backwards from the concrete lip of the platform and was lost in the fog, disappearing among the billion drops of water already hanging in the air. Mr Sempill led the way, carrying his cane like a club, ready to bring it down on Warner's head if he tried to break away. Behind him came Mr Trench, one hand gripping Warner's chains, the other carrying his overnight bag with his umbrella – always his umbrella – securely buckled to the side of it with leather straps.

They went past the little wooden book stall with its bales of newspapers dumped by the door, up the stairs, through the abandoned turnstiles and out into the street. It was like walking into the midst of a cloud or seeing what the divers see when they are screwed into their huge, heavy brass helmets and dropped off the side of a ship. Everything was softened by the mix of darkness and mist and weary gaslights that made blobs of yellow in the air and shone no further than their own shadowed feet. Behind them there was the workaday brick of Tay Bridge station. Off to their right, the pier for the ferries that went back and forth across the Tay. To the left, the mad, baronial, Italianate fantasy of the West station, and across the road, silent but for an early coal cart, the Parisian grandeur of Mather's Temperance Hotel with, beyond that, the lights of the ships tied up along Victoria Dock.

"I see they have failed to provide a police van," said Mr Sempill. He made no complaint. It was as if he were pleased to be disappointed and let down by the City of Dundee Police. "They insist on us keeping him here, though God knows what's wrong with our own cells. The very least they could have done was send the van on time."

"They knew we were coming?" said Mr Trench.

"I sent the telegram myself." He fished in his coat pocket. "Look, there's the receipt. Every penny properly accounted for."

Warner gave a throaty laugh. He held up a stub of cigarette in two cuffed hands for Mr Trench to light. He had a look in his eye that said: "Oh, you can just bet every penny is properly accounted for."

"I could have the stationmaster call, if you like, sir."

"We'll give them a moment." Mr Sempill knew the pleasure of calling Dundee Police headquarters would be all the sweeter if he could complain he had been forced to wait in soaking, freezing fog for a time.

But Warner's cigarette had not burned down before they saw the lamps of a horse van approaching down Union Street, and not very long after that, it was rolling and clattering over the worn and broken cobbles in front of the station.

The man in front knuckled his hat and said: "Chief Constable Sempill?"

"You're late," he said, although it was clear he wished the man had been later.

The driver got down from his seat and unbolted the door at the back of the cab.

"Good God, man, what is that stench?" Mr Sempill was horror-struck and he clamped a handkerchief to his face.

"Last customer, sir. Boaked in the back. There wisnae time fer tae tak a bucket tae't. But ah can pit a blanket ower it."

"Please don't trouble yourself," said Mr Sempill. He slammed the door shut. "We'll walk."

"Gee whizz," Warner said. "It's mighty generous of you, Chiefy. I will say that. Real white of you, but please don't trouble on my account. I've been in places that stunk worse, believe me. Last night, for example."

Mr Trench said: "Shut up." He took a key from his pocket, then released Warner's left handcuff and fixed it round his own right wrist. "Now walk."

They made an odd sight, the three of them, trudging through the waking town: Mr Sempill, quietly satisfied to have been so spectacularly let down, Mr Trench with his case and his umbrella in one hand, and Warner balancing the other side while the stinking police van rolled along beside them, back up Union Street, up Tally Street, through the Overgate with its tiny shopfronts and its verminous closes and its tenements piled high to the dark and dripping sky, up Lindsay Street and then to the Police Chambers, just across the lane from the new burial ground with its mortuary, where Miss Milne had lain for a little while.

It was, without a doubt, considerably more impressive than the modest little station of Broughty Ferry. There were magnificent gates that led through to a courtyard and, beyond that, a great stone building fitting for a body of the power and majesty of Dundee City Police, with much in the way of polished brass work, gleaming mahogany and carved folderols. The police offices formed one wing of a massive monument to justice. In the centre there was the court, with its pillared entrance portico under the royal arms. Here were the offices of Mr Procurator Fiscal Mackintosh – no friend of Broughty Ferry Burgh Police – and the Sheriff Clerk. Here were several magnificent and terrifying court rooms, in one of which, Mr Sempill devoutly hoped, Warner would shortly be condemned to death, and, at the far side of the building, in a wing which mirrored the police station with a perfect Grecian simplicity, the city jail. It was a matter of deep regret to Mr Sempill that hangings were no longer permitted in Dundee prison. The authorities, in their great wisdom, had ruled that, for reasons of decency and dignity, His Majesty's Prison at Perth was more fitting for such events. Still, as he signed the necessary papers consigning his prisoner to Dundee, Mr Sempill decided that a trip to Perth was not too severe an imposition. It would take no more than half an hour on the early train. He could arrive in plenty of time for an eight o'clock appointment. Or might it be wiser to stay overnight? The George? An ideal spot for a celebratory lunch. You could get an excellent steak pie at the George and a bottle of Guinness to wash it down. Mr Neaves would like that. It would make the whole thing into a jaunt and well worth the trouble of the visit. You couldn't ask a man to come all the way from Kent for a hanging and not give him a bit of a feed too. Mr Sempill signed his name with a flourish.

"Thank you, sir," said the desk sergeant. "Now, if you'd care to bring the gentleman along, sir, we'll get him tucked up with a nice bit of breakfast."

Mr Trench left his case and his umbrella on the front counter and walked along the white-tiled corridor, leading Warner to the first cell with an open door. It was clean and tidy and, all things considered, it hardly stank at all. He led Warner inside and unlocked the cuffs.

"Maid's day off?" Warner said.

"You've had worse," Trench said. "You told me yourself."

"Indeed I have. Like last night." But the joke was as stale as the air in the cell.

Warner sat down on the bed, but the desk sergeant said: "Up!" as if he meant it. "Get up. You go to your bed after lights out and you don't get back in your bed until lights out. In the daytime, you sit there." He motioned to a hard wooden chair beside the table in the corner.

"I sit there?" Warner got off the bed and sat down where he was told. "All day?"

"Not if you don't want to," said the sergeant. "If you don't want to sit—"

"No, don't spoil it. Let me guess. If I don't want to sit, I can stand."

"I can see you and me are going to get along like a house on fire." The sergeant turned to Mr Trench. "Anything else, sir?"

"He needs his breakfast."

"Coming along shortly, sir. We never stint on a breakfast here, sir. Take a pride in that, so we do."

"Very good. I have some cash I want to sign in to the prisoner's account. Ten pound one and fourpence."

The sergeant raised his eyebrows. "A handy sum. I'll make out a receipt."

"Thank you."

Mr Trench turned to go, but Warner said: "Wait a minute. What am I supposed to do?"

"Sit on that chair and have your breakfast."

"And then what? You can't just throw me in this lousy hole and keep me here."

"You're going into another identity parade. The witnesses who did not travel to Kent."

"You mean the ones you couldn't buy with a trip to the Hippodrome!"

"There are more than a dozen witnesses who saw a man answering your description, either in company with the dead woman or lurking around her house or both. Over a dozen, Warner. We will hear what they have to say. Then their testimony will be put before the Sheriff. He will decide if there is a case for you to answer. If he agrees that there is, you may be committed. If you are committed, you will be held in prison until your trial."

"And how long will that be?"

"Not more than one hundred and ten days."

"So you say, copper."

"It's the law."

For the first time, Warner seemed concerned about his predicament. "I think I need a lawyer."

"I think you do."

"Will you help me? Please?"

Mr Trench looked up at the roof for a moment and huffed out a big breath from under his moustache. "I'll do what I can. It's a good job you got that money order."

"A tenner won't get me through a murder trial."

"Let's cross that bridge when we come to it." Mr Trench started for the door again.

"Could you spare me another cigarette?"

Trench tossed him the broken pack. "It's half full. All right for matches?"

Warner nodded and the cell door clanged shut with an echo. As Mr Trench went back down the corridor he heard the sound of a man singing – singing in a nervous, shaky voice, singing to keep his courage up – "Who were you with last night, out in the pale moonlight? It wasn't yer sister, it wasn't yer ma – ahh ah ah ah aha aha."

37

MR TRENCH KNEW almost nothing about lawyers, but he understood policemen very well. When he took his breakfast in the station canteen – Mr Sempill had long ago left for the dining room of the Queen's Hotel – he found a chair next to two of the local plain-clothes men and, between mouthfuls of ham and eggs, asked for their advice.

"I'm looking for an honest lawyer," he said – and they all laughed.

"Would you settle for a virgin hoor?"

Mr Trench said: "Well, as honest as you can think of."

They looked at each other and thought for a minute. One said to the other: "Blackadder?"

"Not as bad as some."

They agreed. "Try Blackadder. He's got a good name and he's not one of those that tries to make us look like fools in the witness box – you know the way some of them are."

"Oh, I know," said Mr Trench. "I know. Where will I find him?"

"He'll be next door, at the Sheriff Court early on. More than likely he'll be queuing up waiting for the doors to open."

But when Mr Trench finished his breakfast and walked round the corner to the court, the pavement ringing under his heavy tread, the doors were already flung open. He was not challenged when he walked in, nobody asked what he wanted, what he was doing there, if he knew where he was going, what his business was, nobody even asked: "Can I help you, sir?" People looked at John Trench and they knew he was a policeman.

The courts were not yet in session. The corridors alongside, where solicitors would linger between cases bantering with their colleagues and with policemen waiting to give their statements, were empty, so Mr Trench followed a sign that pointed towards the library, knocked as gently as he could and went in.

As he entered, a man in a tweed suit looked up from the big desk in the middle of the room. He had the spectacles of a man who has spent too long looking at books and the physique to match, but he smiled when Trench came in and said: "Hello," kindly.

"Are you Mr Blackadder?"

The man took off his spectacles and laid them on the open book in front of him. "Yes, Mr Trench."

"Have we met?"

"No, but I read the papers. What can I do for you?"

Trench pulled out a chair and sat down. "Nothing," he said. "Nothing for me. But you have been recommended to me as an honest man."

"High praise indeed. But if you have no need of an honest man, why have you sought me out?"

"If you read the papers, then you know why I'm here."

"Of course. The Elmgrove business."

"We've just brought a man from London – well, from Kent actually – a suspect in the case. He's going into an identity parade shortly and then he appears before the Sheriff accused of murder. He needs a lawyer."

Mr Blackadder picked up his spectacles, put them back on his nose and opened his notebook. "You'd better tell me everything."

"Don't you want to talk about money?"

He put down his pencil. "Mr Trench, you've gone to a great deal of trouble to arrest this man. You've hunted him from one end of the country to the other and dragged him back here in chains to hang him and yet you," he jabbed a skinny finger into Trench's chest, "you, sir, tell me he needs a lawyer. That tells me two things: first, you think he's innocent and second, he really needs a lawyer. Some things are more important than money, Mr Trench."

A quarter of an hour later, Mr Blackadder was sitting in Warner's cell, and at three o'clock that afternoon he was standing in the courtyard of Dundee town jail overseeing the identity parade.

Mr Robertson, the head warder, had no difficulty in assembling the necessary number of men – in fact he excelled himself. When Mr Blackadder came through the gate and into the courtyard, there were fourteen men already lined up and waiting. To the trained eye, a couple of them were quite obviously policemen, with the look of policemen, but for the most part they were just ordinary-looking men, none of them remarkably short or stout, none extravagantly tall.

"Where should I stand?" Warner said.

"It doesn't matter. They will let you pick your own spot and you can change it between witnesses, as often as you like, or remain where you are. It's your right and I am here to ensure your rights."

"But I was wondering if you might not have some advice. You know, about a good place to stand."

"One is as good as another," said Mr Blackadder, "if you are innocent." He waited until Warner had taken his place in the line, third from the left, and then he went back into the building to see the first of the witnesses.

There were fifteen in all: respectable matrons from Broughty Ferry, neighbours of Miss Milne and their maids, workmen who had seen a man on a tram, businessmen who had had an unexpected and suspicious caller, the staff of Broughty Ferry Post Office, taxi drivers, a barber, waitresses, men and women who rode the tramcars along Strathern Road and, of course, the three little boys who had been "playing at Boy Scouts" one evening in the leafy shadows around Elmgrove. They were all gathered in the warders' mess hall waiting their turn, including the Boy Scouts, who had come with their mothers, hair brushed, faces rubbed – "Spit on this hankie" – necks washed. Mrs Potter had even dressed her laddie in his Sunday kilt, so he could be nicely turned out for meeting a murderer in the flesh.

Mr Blackadder followed the first of them out into the yard: James Delaney, the telegraph clerk from the Post Office who saw the strange tramp in the tile hat come in and ask for directions. Delaney went up and down the row.

He called out: "I think I might know him if I saw him in profile."

"All right, you men," Mr Robertson said, "face to your left."

The men shuffled round, complaining.

Delaney went to have another look. He stopped twice, once in the middle of the line and once at the right-hand side, but he stepped past Warner with never a second glance.

"Do you see the man?" said Mr Robertson, the warder.

"No. I do not."

"Very well, you can go. Thank you for your trouble."

"What about," he dropped his voice to a whisper and leaned in close, "Miss Liddell and Mr Smeaton?"

"Wait on the other side of that door. They will be along presently."

A policeman opened a door on the other side of the court-yard and Delaney hurried out.

"Do you wish to change your position?" Mr Robertson said.

"No."

"Mr Blackadder?"

"If he is content, I am content."

"Then let's get on before we lose the light."

Mr Robertson knocked on the door behind him and Annie Liddell came out. She put her toe down on the courtyard as if she had been walking to a firing squad, but she steeled herself to look every man in the parade right in the face and she recognised nobody. Mr Blackadder made some notes in his pocketbook.

And that was how it went on for almost the next half-hour, witness after witness coming into the courtyard, walking up the line, walking down the line, examining faces, leaving without a word. Warner changed his position in the line twice, but, for the most part, he stood his ground. He was winning. It would be foolish to break his luck.

But then Alexander Potter came in.

"Now then, young chap," Mr Robertson was making an effort at being friendly and reassuring, "you're no to be feart at these men."

"I'm not, sir."

"They cannot touch you."

"No, sir."

"And if any dares say 'peep' at you, these officers will fall on him like a ton of bricks."

"Yes, sir."

Up and down the line he went, head up, shoulders back, kilt swinging just as his mother had told him. He made a show of looking at every face, but it was clear from the moment he came through the door that his mind was made up.

On his second pass down the line, he stopped in front of Warner and put his hand on his shoulder.

"This is the man I saw," he said.

"You never saw me in your life. When did you see me?"

"I saw you one night in Grove Road," and then his courage failed him and he ran for the door.

"Not that way, laddie," said Mr Robertson. "Other side."

The boy hurried away, skirting round two sides of the court-yard to reach the far door rather than dare the line of men again.

"Will you change your position?" Mr Robertson asked.

"Damned right I will." Warner walked three places along the line and took up a new spot. He had schooled himself to stand idly and easily. He made his living by making an impression and striking a pose, so he was doing his utmost to take on the role of a man who just happened to be standing in an identity parade. He fought every impulse. A man was coming toward him down the line. Should he look that man in the eye? Should he stare straight ahead no matter what, even when that man was standing looking right at his chin or minutely examining the pores of his nose? It was dignified, sure, but was it normal? Was it what was expected from a man in that position or should he crack a smile, comment on the weather? He wanted to be outstandingly ordinary, so when those women came down the line, he looked straight ahead. He did not lean forward to watch them come, and when they passed he did not lean forward to watch them go. He took enormous trouble to breathe normally.

And he was breathing normally when the next witness came down the line. It was James Urquhart, who saw the man with badly polished shoes on the early morning tramcar. He walked by without a word, he examined every face without a word and he left without a word. Warner relaxed and let his breath come as it pleased.

John Malcolm was the next through the door, a foundry labourer who looked like a foundry labourer, a man who, every morning, walked into the heat and fire and clamour of Hell and sweated there all day, a man who said he saw the killer carrying a doctor's bag on the same early morning car, two days later. Malcolm did not walk the line. He stepped boldly up to Warner and touched his shoulder. "That's the man," he said. "Him."

"That's a damned lie. Where did you ever see me before?"

"I saw you on the car coming from Broughty Ferry at half past five a.m. on Wednesday the 16th of October."

Warner clamped his golden teeth shut at that. There was plenty he could have said and plenty he wanted to say, but none of it fitted with the role he was playing. He stayed silent.

"That's the last of them," said Mr Robertson. "Escort the prisoner back to his cell."

When everyone had dispersed and Mr Robertson took the lawyer Blackadder back into the building, they found Mr Trench was waiting in the corridor with Chief Constable Sempill and Fiscal Mackintosh. "I will submit my report in writing," said Mr Robertson.

But the Chief Constable could not wait. "Never mind that! Was he identified?"

Mr Robertson pretended to consult his notes. "He was, yes. He was conclusively identified by two of the witnesses, the boy Potter and witness Malcolm."

Mr Sempill clapped his hands in glee. "That'll do me!" he said. "Mr Fiscal, are you prepared to issue the indictment?"

"Indeed I am. We have our man. It is, formally, a matter for the Crown Office in Edinburgh, but, all other things being equal, I am confident we can bring this villain to trial."

Trench said nothing, but there was a look of fear in his eyes as he glanced at Mr Blackadder.

"You're not serious," the lawyer said.

"Do you accuse me of being flippant? In a capital trial? A trial for murder? When a man will hang? Mr Blackadder, this is a matter of utmost gravity. Of course I am serious. We have our man. He has been identified."

"Identified by two witnesses and utterly disregarded by thirteen others."

"You forget the witnesses who travelled to London – five of them."

"Four of them. Only four. One of them has withdrawn her testimony. And you ignore the others, the hotel clerkess and the man," he consulted his notes, "the witness Wray. They also failed to identify."

"There are at least six people willing to go into the box and swear that man was seen by them acting suspiciously in or around Elmgrove at the time of the killing. That's what counts. The thirteen who failed to identify in Dundee and the two who failed to identify in London have simply failed to identify, that is all. Their testimony neither condemns nor exonerates. You're a lawyer, Blackadder, you don't need me to tell you this."

"But their testimony contradicts. Young Alexander Potter – alone of the three playmates – identifies Warner as being the man he saw, a man wearing a top hat, a man whose face he says he did not see but which he now recognises. How can he identify a face he did not see? The man Malcolm says my client is the same man he saw on the tram carrying a doctor's bag and wearing a bowler hat. So where's your top hat, Mr Fiscal? It's not in the house and it won't fit in a doctor's bag."

"Pray do not address me in these terms, sir. Save your speeches for the jury. The fact is that your client has been conclusively identified. He was, undoubtedly, in the area at the time of the offence and he refuses to give an account of himself."

"That is not sufficient, sir!"

"I am content to leave that to a jury of the electors of this burgh. Good day."

The Fiscal and Mr Sempill pushed their way past and swept down the corridor. Mr Robertson the warder was not far behind, but Trench lingered with the lawyer, heads together, whispering like conspirators for a moment until: "Mr Robertson." Blackadder went hurrying down the passage. "Mr Robertson, I'm sorry to trouble you. I'd like a word with my client, if you please."

"Of course. This man will assist you." He indicated one of the turnkeys, who led the way back to Warner's cell, opened the door and stood aside to let the lawyer in.

"Close it, please," said Mr Blackadder, "and stand well back from the door. Confidential matters."

Inside the cell he leaned close over the scrubbed table and explained the situation to Warner in hushed whispers. "They intend to hang you," he said.

Warner put his hands flat on the worn wood of the tabletop, pale and grey with the grain all raised and polished by constant rubbing and the slow friction of passing time. He folded his fingers together and peaked them into a steeple. "Can you bring me some more cigarettes?" he said.

"Of course."

"And something to read? A newspaper or maybe a book?"

"Yes, if that's what you want."

"What about Trench?"

"I'm convinced he is on your side. He's an honest man, but, if we are to save you, we need you to help us."

For the space of three breaths, Warner said nothing. He was deciding on his next role. He was choosing which part to play. "Write this down." He shook the last of Mr Trench's cigarettes from its packet and lit it, smoked half of it in one breath, blew the sweet smoke out again through his nostrils, and then he said: "My name is Charles S. Walker. I was born in Guelph, Ontario, Canada, on April 24th, 1871. I left New York on Saturday, August 10th, on S.S. *Rochambeau* of the French line and landed at Le Havre, France, on Monday, August 19th."

38

UPSTAIRS IN THE office of Mr Procurator Fiscal Mackintosh the pile of typed pages lay on the desk, leaking disappointment into the polished mahogany.

"And this is exactly the statement he made, Trench?"

"Exactly, sir. I noted it, read it back to him, he corrected me and made changes where I had gone wrong in my notes, and it was signed and witnessed. It's all in order."

"And the map of Antwerp?"

"He drew it all out there and then, sir, apparently from his own recollection."

Mr Mackintosh prodded the papers around on the desk with the end of his pencil, as if he feared contamination. "Well, it proves nothing. He could have learned it all from a Baedeker's Guide. It doesn't mean he was ever in Antwerp and it certainly doesn't prove when he was there. That's the crucial thing."

"Well, at least we got him to admit to being forty-one, but even that is horse feathers," said Mr Sempill. "It's all horse feathers. It's balderdash from beginning to end. Nobody could possibly produce this stuff from memory – dates, times, names, places, it's incredible, literally incredible. It is beyond being believed."

"I must admit," said the Fiscal, "if somebody asked me to give an account of my movements from last week it would tax the memory, but this stuff," he picked up the bundled of papers from off his desk and let it drop again, "this stuff goes back months."

"It is quite obviously a fabrication," said Mr Sempill. "He has invented this grand tour of Europe to account for his movements and convince us that he could not have been in Broughty Ferry at the crucial period. That's the only possible explanation."

"He's a liar, sir," Trench said.

"My sentiments exactly."

"No, I mean he is a professional liar, sir. Lying is how he makes his living. For all we know that's how he has made his living for years, and the thing about lying is you have to keep your story straight. Maybe this astonishing feat of memory is merely a professional accomplishment."

"Or nothing more than a worthless fairy tale!"

Mr Mackintosh said: "There's a simple way to find out."

"You can't be serious. You can't possibly intend to take this seriously."

"And if I don't, what then? You may be assured, Chief Constable, that Blackadder will take it very seriously. I am the investigating authority in this affair. I direct the investigation, and if I chose to ignore a matter of this weight, he would not. My position is utterly untenable with this hanging over us. However, I agree with you: it is an obvious lie. Warner, or Warne or Ware or Walker or whatever his right name may be, is clearly lying, and when we expose him in those lies it will only serve to tie the noose all the tighter round his neck. This statement is quite clearly designed to put off the evil day of retribution, but it has only served to make it more certain and swift. Trench," the Fiscal turned his gaze across the desk, "wire to London, tell them you want to speak to the officers involved in this statement. Examine them carefully. Impress upon them the nature of your errand. Make no error. And you, Mr Sempill, find the quickest way to Antwerp."

"Antwerp? But I have no French."

"Do not distress yourself, Sempill, they probably speak very little French either. Antwerp is a Dutch town."

Mr Sempill gaped like a landed fish.

"Be calm, Sempill, be calm. Think of your standing. Scotland Yard keeps a man in Rotterdam. Go through the channels. Make arrangements. He will be your guide and assistant."

And so there was another difficult train journey to London, in the morning this time, without either the excuse of sleep or the cloak of darkness to hide their ill-tempered silences, with Mr Trench sitting in one corner of the carriage, Mr Sempill as far away as possible on the other side, hiding himself in wreaths of pipe smoke. They stopped for refreshments at York and Mr Trench wondered if he might not somehow contrive to be left behind on the platform or find himself in the wrong carriage. He would willingly have abandoned his suitcase, but he feared to be parted from his treasured umbrella and even the long hours of sullen, bitter silence were preferable to that, so he did his duty, mounted the train again and buried his nose in a file of typed notes.

Although the carriage had filled up at York and there was no room to spread his arms, Mr Sempill did the same, the plain cardboard folder placed on a briefcase across his knees like a desk, each sheet of paper taken out individually, one at a time and read as guardedly as if there were a French novel hidden inside, lest any of the other passengers in the crowded carriage might catch a glimpse of his official police business. Still, despite the show of secrecy, Mr Sempill found himself unable to control the occasional, involuntary outburst: "Incredible!" or "Ridiculous!" or "The scoundrel!" Mr Sempill was secretly delighted when his exclamations drew the attention of his fellow passengers. He feigned not to notice, waiting until they had looked back to their newspapers before he looked up to enjoy the expressions on their faces, holding back, holding back until a moment of calm before releasing his next "Poppycock" in a fusillade of disgust. Trench saw it all. He felt the seat hard on his aching back as he wiped the steam off the window with a gloved fist and looked in the other direction.

At Peterborough the carriage emptied again for a moment and Mr Sempill folded the last of his papers away. He glanced briefly across at Trench and then up into the luggage rack. "What do you intend to do about this?" he said.

"Sir?"

"About the story. These improbable claims."

"No more than my duty, sir."

"What do you mean by that remark? Are you suggesting that I don't know mine?"

"When have I ever said any such thing? You asked me what I intend to do. I'm a detective: I will detect, sir. That's all. We are police officers. We investigate. We investigate the evidence. The evidence doesn't play favourites. It will tell us what it tells us. It will tell us, in a few short days, whether we have got our man."

"You still think I want an innocent man to hang."

Trench leaned forward in his seat, suddenly huge and bull-shouldered. "I'll tell you what I don't think," he said. "I don't think you will lie about what you find. I don't think you will go there and distort the evidence. As much as you want Warner – or whatever his name is – to pay for this crime, if you see with your own eyes that he is telling the truth, I do not believe you would lie about that. If you come back from Antwerp and tell me to my face that what's in these files is all lies, then I will shake your hand and drag him to the gallows myself."

The door of the railway carriage opened again and a man

came in with two little boys. Trench and Sempill had nothing more to say to one another until they reached King's Cross and there was that awkward moment of parting again, the gathering of their cases, opening the door, standing aside for the father and his boys, finding themselves together on the platform.

At the ticket barrier, Mr Sempill said: "Well, I go this way. Heading for the boat train."

"Yes. I'm the other way for town."

There was another difficult pause until Mr Sempill put down his case, pulled off his glove and held out his hand. "Well, good luck, Trench."

"And to you, sir." They shook hands, briefly, and went their separate ways.

39

MR TRENCH NEVER ceased to be amazed by the kindness of policemen. They are rough men, not gentlemen in any sense, and they work in a rough trade with other rough men. They are never welcome visitors. They only ever come in moments of disaster. People want to hurt them and they hurt people and yet, time after time, they do something strange and soft and kind, even if it's only a cup of tea for some poor tart down on her luck.

There were two of those men waiting for him when he pushed his way down a lane almost under the shadow of Tower Bridge and into the Anchor Tap. Mr Trench had rarely been to London and, certainly, never into the Anchor Tap, but the elderly barman nodded to him as soon as he opened the door and jerked his thumb over his shoulder towards a distant back room. Why should he have done that? Why should he have noticed Mr Trench coming into his shop? Why did their eyes meet? Why did Mr Trench notice his gesture? Training, that's why. Habit. A long lifetime of watching and looking and seeing and noticing. That and the strange Masonic brotherhood of policing. They meet on the level and they part on the square and they recognise one another by their bearing whether they walk into a bar or work behind it or stand beside it. That was how Mr Trench recognised the two men waiting together, each standing with an elbow on the bar of the back room of the Anchor, each nursing a jug of ale, each waiting to give all possible assistance to Detective Lieutenant John Trench because their inspector told them to.

"Bill Amer?" he asked.

The man held out his hand. "And I don't have to ask who you are. The famous John Trench. Say 'Howdyadoo', Charlie Clark."

They shook hands as the barman arrived carrying three more jugs and put them down on the bar. "Well done, Tom," said Bill. "Mr Trench is paying."

Tom waited while Trench fished in his pocket for a coin, took it, counted it in the palm of his hand and left, saying nothing.

"Good luck to you boys," said Mr Trench, picking up one of the tankards, and he gulped down a mouthful with a satisfied gasp. "First of the day," he said.

"And it won't be your last," said Bill, "not if the ratepayers are picking up the bill."

"Don't you worry about that. Consider yourselves guests of Broughty Ferry Burgh Council – but you have to sing for your supper." He took a picture out of his pocket. "I'm inquiring after this bloke and, according to his statement, he claims to know you. Charles Stanley Walker, which he says is his proper name, also trading as Tommy Walker, or C. J. Ware, sometimes Warner or Warne or A. Hart. Might be a salesman in the drapery line, but he evidently passed himself off as of numerous professions, such as company promoter, for one."

Bill looked at the picture. He flipped it round and showed it to Charlie Clark.

Mr Trench said: "It would have been about three months ago. End of August."

"That would be exactly right." Bill Amer took out his notebook and began to flick through the pages. "Me and Charlie-Boy here did him a favour – remember, Charlie-Boy?"

Charlie-Boy grinned into his pint and nodded.

"Here you go," said Bill, "August 28. He got himself nicked down in Soho, at the Falcon in Wardour Street. Drunk as a lord and pissed as a fart, trying to get served, spent the night in Vine Street cells, went in front of Bow Street magistrates the following day."

"And why does any of that concern you and Charlie?"

"Well, here's the story."

"Here's the story," said Charlie, who preferred not to talk too much if it meant breaking off from his beer.

"We found him sitting outside the court waiting for the cart to jail. Oh, great was the weeping and the wailing and the gnashing of teeth."

"So he had a hard-luck story?"

"Did he ever have a hard-luck story," said Bill.

"Did he ever," said Charlie.

Bill took another sup, and when it was down he said: "He told us his name was," he looked in his notebook, "Charles Stanley Walker."

"Seems to be his real name," said Mr Trench.

"Aged forty-one."

"Well, we won't quibble about that."

"Said he was a Canadian. Said he'd been on a spree and he ended up with a ten-bob fine."

"Ten-bob fine," Charlie echoed.

"With the alternative of seven days indoors."

"Seven days indoors," Charlie said.

"Now then, Charlie. Now then. One singer, one song."

"On you go, mate." Charlie went back to his beer.

"Well, the prisoner was in a very distressed state, as he had no money to pay his fine, and he begged us to see him right in his hour of trouble with the result that Charlie-Boy—"

"Yours truly."

"—went down to No. 30 Waterloo Road to acquaint the landlord of the prisoner's position, when he ascertained that the prisoner was not known at that address."

Mr Trench banged a shilling on the edge of the bar and ordered three more pints. "So that was the end of it? You let him go hang?"

"Well, maybe we're just too soft but, no, we didn't. He swore blind he would pay us back if we could just keep him out of clink, so between us we scraped up his ten bob."

"That was rash."

"Anything to help out a Brother in distress. But he weren't going nowhere. We walked him down the Waterloo Road, arm in arm like long-lost pals, and he took us to No. 20 – not 30 after all. So we went inside—"

"Inside," Charlie said.

"—and he went in his bag and he came out with – you'll never guess, Mr Trench."

"Oh, I think I can."

"Never in a month of Sundays."

"Was it a Colt revolver?" said Mr Trench.

Bill nearly choked on his pint. "Damn me, how did you know that?"

"Because it's exactly what he told me in his statement. Exactly. And you took it to a gunsmith and he sold the revolver and he paid you back the money you lent him."

"No. 5 Waterloo Road," said Bill.

"Twenty-five shillings," said Charlie.

"So, he paid you back and had money left over. Anything else?"

"A rail ticket. Bet you never knew that. The return half of a ticket to Southampton."

But Trench knew that too. It was all there, everything, every dot and comma in Warner's statement.

I left my luggage – two bags – in the left-luggage office in Cannon Street railway station, and after being a few hours in London I left London for Liverpool.

I slept in Liverpool on Thursday and Friday, the 22nd and 23rd August, in a Temperance Hotel near North Western station. Next day, Saturday 24th, I returned to London and went to No. 20 or 30 Waterloo Bridge Road. I remained there till the following Friday morning, 29th August (I remained there till morning of 30th August, 1912). I then went to the American Express, where I had been having my cheques cashed, and purchased a 1st class ticket for Southampton. I did not have much money, and went to Southampton so that I could write to my brother in Detroit, Mr E. R. Walker, of Craig, Wright and Walker, 629–631 Majestic Building, Detroit, Michigan. I took a cheap lodge, 4/6 a week, at No. 2 Fitzhugh Street, Southampton West. I immediately communicated with my brother by mail and he cabled funds to the American Express, No. 25 Oxford Street, Southampton. I only received about £10.

It was as if Warner or Walker – or whatever his name was – had decided at last that nothing could save him except the truth, but even then he could hardly bring himself to break the habit of a lifetime and stop his lies for even a single day. Standing on the steps of the gallows he still insisted that he was no more than forty-one years of age and he was lying about his reasons for travelling to Southampton. "I went to Southampton so that I could write to my brother in Detroit." Rubbish. An obvious and transparent lie when there was pen and paper in every house in the country, a post office in every village and a pillar box on every street corner. And why go to Southampton to pick up money from the American Express when there was a branch in London? And why buy a first-class ticket if he was as hard up as he said? More front? More keeping up appearances? Or was it because a man with a first-class ticket was more likely to be trusted with a loan if he suddenly found himself strapped for cash?

And why was Warner's statement wrong – just a little bit wrong? Why did he get his London address wrong? He could remember everything, names and dates and places, but the statement was a little bit wrong. Why? Was that a mistake? Was Warner gilding the lily? Was he trying to make things a little bit less than perfect and a little bit more believable?

I found it impossible to secure a passage, as all reservations were booked up till the 18th of September. The American Express at Southampton can verify this. I did not have sufficient funds to sail by the Olympic on 18th September, so concluded to go to Liverpool to see if I could secure a cheap passage. I left Southampton on the 12th September for Liverpool. I slept the night of the 12th and 13th September at a small Temperance Hotel near the Station. I then secured a lodge in Seacombe with Mrs Graham, No. 10 Riversdale Road, Seacombe. I remained there six days, till the following Thursday morning. I had found out it was impossible to secure a cheap passage. I had been told by seamen that there were lots of cattle-ships leaving Antwerp, Belgium, for Montreal, and easy to secure a passage. I determined to go there before my funds became exhausted. On 19th September (Thursday) I went to Cook's Ticket Agency, in Liverpool and purchased a second-class rail and boat to Antwerp. I think it was exactly

30 shillings. I left the Central Midland Railway Station at 2-30 on Thursday, 19th September, and arrived in Antwerp on Friday, 20th September.

The gunsmith at No. 5 Waterloo Road kept perfect records. He had everything written down in his ledgers, signed and dated. A Colt revolver, serial number 59830, purchased for twenty-five shillings from a Canadian, Charles Walker of 20 Waterloo Road on August 29. It was still in the shop and, yes, that was his picture. It all hung together. Arrested drunk on August 28, a night in the cells, sentenced on August 29, borrowed his fine from two kind policemen, sold his revolver to repay them.

None of that proved his innocence of course, but it wasn't Warner's job to prove himself innocent, it was up to Mr Procurator Fiscal Mackintosh to prove him guilty, and every time that Warner or Walker or Ware told the truth about something, the stronger his alibi got.

Standing on the pavement outside the door of 20 Waterloo Road, Mr Trench saw the thick layer of sooty street dust gathered in the corners of the window frames, the strand of fern thrusting from the wall where the cracked gutter pipe dripped rainwater kisses and soaked the bricks behind, the broken paint peeling from the door frame, and the only thing drowning out the noise of the cabs and the dray wagons and the omnibuses rolling towards the Waterloo Bridge was the screaming of the children behind the door.

Mr Trench knocked.

The screaming continued.

Mr Trench knocked again and he heard the sound of movement inside, a thumping about, a heavy tread and the sound of a child's screaming growing closer, the lock turning, a bolt shot, the door opening. There was a young woman standing there, half her hair unpinned, sleeves rolled up, red-armed, red-faced. There was a basket of washing on her hip and a child in her arm, chewing at a strand of loose hair, another peeking from behind her skirts and a long line of shirts hanging from a rope strung along the ceiling.

"No veganzee," she said and she went to close the door again, but Mr Trench put his hand against it and said: "A moment, please."

He showed her his warrant card: "Police," and he watched the colour drain away from her face. "Don't be frightened. You're not in trouble. Nobody has died. I only want to ask a few questions." Mr Trench was used to being an unwelcome visitor, but this girl was not afraid of him because she had done anything wrong. She was afraid because she had fled to London from someplace where it was always wise to be afraid of the police.

The traffic went rumbling past. He had almost to shout to make himself heard. "May I come inside?"

She hesitated, fearfully.

"You are allowed to say 'No.'" Without taking his weight off the door, Mr Trench reached awkwardly into an inside pocket with his left hand and brought out the photograph. "I only want to ask you about this man."

The woman's eyes flamed. "Comm in plizz," she said.

Mr Trench walked into the lobby, pushing wet laundry out of the way with the handle of his umbrella as he went.

"In kitchen plizz."

There was more washing in the way, but Mr Trench found his way to the kitchen table and opened his notebook. The woman poured some very black tea from a huge pot stewing on the stove and handed it to him. "Plizz," she said again.

Mr Trench put the cup down on the table and held out his two hands to her. The woman was still burdened with a child on her hip. Mr Trench nodded at the baby. "Let me. I'll take him."

She hesitated for a moment and then, in a moment of relief, she handed the child over and sank into the chair at the head of the table.

He smiled at her. She smiled back.

"Now then," he said. "Looking at the directory, I think I'm right in saying you are Mrs Florence Ohlendorf."

She nodded.

He laid the picture on the table. "And you know this man?"

"I know him, yes."

"He stayed here."

She nodded again.

"Can you say when?"

"I do not keep record of boarders. But I well remember about the end of August I had this man in my house."

"For how long?"

"A week. Nearly."

"Could it have been the 24th to the 29th?"

She shrugged and looked embarrassed. "Maybe. They come. They give money. They go."

"Was he an Englishman?"

"No. Not English man. He was," she searched for the word, "Canada man."

The baby was gnawing on the handle of Mr Trench's umbrella. "Can you remember anything about him?"

"I believe his name is Walker. He was addicted to drink. I must take all sorts in my house. When he is here about a week, he goes out for a night. When he returns about noon, he says he is charged with being drunk. He into his bedroom goes, and almost at once he again leaves and goes to the guns shop opposite. After this he stays about one night only more in my house then he says he is off. And then, about six weeks ago . . ."

"Can you tell me the date?"

"I don't know dates. I don't know. All I know is he comes back to my door and he says he is just then come from Amsterdam, and he would come again to stay here but he needs first a little money and borrowed half a crown from me. I have not seen him since. I remember it was on a Friday when he called."

Mr Trench took half a crown from his pocket and laid it on the table. "Mr Walker wants you to have this," he said.

40

H. M. Prison Dundee
December 1, 1912

Friend Aubrey,

Pay particular attention to this letter as I am in
Scotland charged with murder. You spoke of going
South but I sincerely hope you are still in Antwerp.
You remember you told me you walked from London
to Dover in two days. Well, I stole an overcoat in
London and started to walk to Dover but was
arrested at Tonbridge. I had lodging and breakfast
and could not pay so was sent to Maidstone Prison
for 14 days under the name of Charles Warner.
On my discharge I was arrested and charged with
murder in Scotland. I was never in Scotland and
have given Police full account of my movements
since landing at Havre, 19th. Go and see Mr Cox
Vice Consul and tell him everything you know about
me and dates and also name I lived under at your
hotel. Tell him exact date, how you got my parcel

at Station and put me in small room over night. Tell him about my putting my name in Book next day. And also about writing to Turkish Consul. Be careful about dates. Tell about maid locking my room on me and then letting me in. Your Boss can prove everything. Don't forget about young American that you took to ship. When the Officers come, tell them everything – I mean the Boy I borrowed 5F from Browning I think. Mention about Mr Thomas, 'The Cowboy'. He came to Antwerp on same train as I did from Rotterdam. Get the date he registered at your hotel. Try also and find out exact date I first spoke to you, and you told me about a cheap Hotel in Brussels. Take young Boy from Terminal Hotel to Mr Cox and tell about Raincoat with German. In case this letter is forwarded to you write the Police here or Mr Cox in Antwerp. Be sure and speak about the Warrant you told me Boss took out. Bad pen.

Truly yours
    C. S. Walker

Also tell about Transvaal Hotel and Rhinelander Hotel

41

CHIEF CONSTABLE SEMPILL was not a traveller. "Go out on deck, dear. So long as you can see the horizon, you'll be fine," that's what Mrs Sempill said, but the fog had closed around the ferry the moment it left the quayside and he saw nothing but the heaving deck and a widow's veil of grey mist all the way across.

The passage was agony, but the final moments, when the lights of Antwerp drew close and yet never drew closer, when they left the sea and rolled into the Scheldt and the rhythm of the engines changed and the ship slowed as it approached the dock and rose and rolled over the wash of its own bow wave, bouncing back from the harbour walls until, at last, the sailors shot their ropes and the ship was tied up and the ferry lay there, rolling greasily but hardly at all, and the smells of hot engine oil and funnel smoke hung in the air with no breath of wind to carry them off, and securing the gangplank took an age and queuing for it took even longer and those last steps onto dry land sprung and bounced under his feet – those were torment.

When he finally stood again on solid ground, Mr Sempill was chilled to the bone and flooded with nausea. He stood against a lamp post with his bag between his feet, his two boots planted on the granite cobbles, his back braced against that iron pillar, and he battled to control his heaving stomach. The torture of it went on, the terror of shaming himself by vomiting right there on the pavement, the sudden flush of icy sweat he could feel soaking his hatband, so he failed to notice the large man standing just a little way off to his left.

Sergeant Cosgrove was a caricature policeman: large brown boots sticking out from brown trouser cuffs, a rubberised raincoat that gave him the look of a mushroom and, above it, an enormous brown moustache under a brown bowler hat. "Rough crossing, sir?" he said, holding out a silver-topped flask.

"Not really. But I'm no sailor."

"Brandy, sir. That's the ticket. Just a drop, mind, a tiny drop to swill round the gums and take away the taste. Spit it out. Don't worry, sir, nobody's looking."

Mr Sempill did as he was bid and tasted the brandy, just a sip – he barely tipped the flask – but it was enough to let the fumes flood his head, and the moment he tasted the brandy he felt his gorge begin to rise. He was helpless to prevent it and he doubled over, vomiting up a stream of yellow bile.

"That's the way, sir. Better out than in. There's a good gentleman." Sergeant Cosgrove was as tender as a mother. "You'll feel better now."

"I've been sick," said Mr Sempill.

"Yes, sir."

"On dry land. They'll imagine I'm drunk. I'm not drunk."

"No, sir. Don't give it a thought, sir."

"I take it you're Cosgrove?"

"Yes, sir. Rodney, sir."

"Sergeant Rodney?"

"No, sir, Sergeant Rodney Cosgrove. Try another little drop. You'll feel better, sir. See if you can swallow this time, sir. Try and hold it down this time, sir."

Mr Sempill obeyed meekly. The brandy filled his nose and burned its way down his throat. He managed to raise himself against the friendly lamp post and he wiped his face with the handkerchief he habitually carried, took off his hat and dabbed it inside. "Right," he said. "Better now. Thank you, Cosgrove."

"Let me take your bag, sir."

They walked off together, slowly, a little unsteadily, the mist glowing around the street lamps and forming in tiny cobweb beads on Sergeant Cosgrove's rubberised overcoat and meeting and joining and trickling down to his ankles and falling away as he walked along.

"Another drop, sir?"

"No thank you."

A wind came up from the pier head and began to shift the fog away. There was a tired orange sun trying to break through, just above the horizon, like one of those fashionable Impressionist paintings Mr Sempill hated so much. Mr Sempill hoped he was not a philistine. Mr Sempill was sure he was not a boor, but he believed in accuracy and he was convinced it was every bit as important in art as in police work. Just because the sun might sometimes, very rarely shine that way, in a way that meant it was almost unrecognisable as the sun, that did not mean it should be painted that way. Such things were needlessly confusing.

"We could stop for breakfast, sir. I knows of a nice hotel."

"Thank you, but I don't think I could face it. If you don't mind, I'd prefer to get straight to business with Mr Cox in town."

"As you like, sir."

They stopped on the station platform for a cup of coffee and took the next train with nothing much to say and Sergeant Cosgrove quietly mourning over his breakfast.

"Do you know Mr Cox?"

"Oh yes, sir."

"What sort of a man would you say he was?"

"Oh, the middling sort, I'd say, sir."

"Yes, but what does he do?"

"Do, sir?" The train went slowly round a queasy curve and they found themselves, quite suddenly, in the heart of the town. "He's the Vice Consul, sir. He does much as I do, sir. He keeps one ear to the ground and both his eyes peeled and represents 'is Majesty amongst the 'eathens."

They left the station, still with Sergeant Cosgrove carrying the bag, as he led the way to an ordinary-looking building in a street of ordinary-looking buildings. Beside the door leading onto the stairwell there was a board with a column of brass nameplates screwed on, including the name of Mr Cox and his designation as "His Brittanic Majesty's Vice Consul". The two hooks where the flagpole was meant to hang, proudly displaying the Union Jack, were standing empty.

"Is he in?" said Mr Sempill.

"They tend to keep bankers' hours, sir. Never open too early, never shut too late. But Mr Cox is always in, sir. I've never known the man to sleep."

They climbed the gloomy staircase, gas lamps burning faintly on every landing, until they reached the fourth floor, where Mr Sempill felt the worn wooden boards turn to linoleum under his feet.

The outer door stood open, and from inside, a bright oblong of yellow light fell onto the landing through etched glass bearing the Royal Arms of England.

"In we go, sir," said Sergeant Cosgrove and he opened the door without so much as a knock. "Mr Cox? Mr Cox? Sergeant Cosgrove, here."

"This way, Sergeant. Back room. I'm making a cup of tea."

A man in morning dress, a black claw-hammer coat and

dove-grey trousers emerged from the back room carrying a tray. "You must be Sempill. Welcome to Antwerp, Chief Constable." Mr Cox nodded towards the tray he was carrying. "Forgive my not shaking hands. One feels so silly." Mr Sempill admired his snowy-white spats.

"I'm first to arrive – again – I'm afraid, so I must fend for myself. This way, gentlemen."

Sergeant Cosgrove opened the door into the private office and stood aside as the Vice Consul carried his tea tray across a thick Persian carpet and laid it on his enormous desk in the bow window looking out over a square.

"I can't get through the day without tea," said Mr Cox. "May I offer you some, Chief Constable?"

"Thank you." Sempill was awkwardly eager to get in with the business of disproving Warner's alibi, but good manners dictated that everything must wait for tea.

Mr Cox handed him a cup and saucer. "A pleasant crossing, I hope, Chief Constable."

"Yes. Thank you. Very pleasant."

"Yes? Good show. I've never enjoyed the Channel, I'm afraid. Always sick as a dog. The great thing is to try to forget that one has the return journey to look forward to."

Mr Sempill sniggered thinly. "Indeed," he said. "How true."

They sipped tea for a moment and then, putting down his saucer, Mr Cox said: "Now then, I understand from Sergeant Cosgrove that we are caught up in a murder inquiry."

Mr Sempill took out his wallet and produced the photograph he had ordered from Maidstone jail. He leaned forward in his chair and slid it across the desk.

"That's the very chap," said Mr Cox. "No doubt about it. I've definitely met that scoundrel before." He rose from the desk, crossed the room to a large filing cabinet and returned with a ledger. He found a space next to the tea tray and began to leaf through the pages. "The man in that picture," he said, "came to this office October 17."

"The 17th? Are you absolutely sure, sir? It's just that we have him in Broughty Ferry very close to that date."

"No doubt about it. He represented himself to me as," Mr Cox consulted the ledger, "as Charles S. Ware, born at Guelph, Ontario, Canada, and previously of 16 Palmer Street, Royal City. He stated he was destitute and anxious to get back to Canada. Claimed he had tried to get a passage by one of the regular lines leaving Antwerp for the United States or Canada but had been unsuccessful. I'm afraid I was completely taken in. I believed he was a British subject in distress and we issued him a pass to London at the expense of the British Poor Fund."

"You mustn't blame yourself, sir. He's an extremely plausible villain. We've had exactly the same story from what you might call your 'colleagues' in the Canadian High Commission back in London. He walked in there, bold as brass, and swindled them out of nearly £2 for a ticket to Liverpool and some money for his pocket – a loan, mind you, all to be repaid upon his honour – and all on the strength of being a Mason back home in Canada."

"Really?" said Mr Cox. "How extraordinary. And I take it you are not, yourself, a member of the Craft, Chief Constable? Well, that's all I can tell you, I'm afraid, unless perhaps Sergeant Cosgrove has something more to say."

The sergeant opened his notebook and he began to address the court. "I have the honour to report," Mr Cox rolled his eyes and drank some more tea, "that inquiries have been made in Rotterdam regarding the porter John Starfield mentioned in the prisoner's statement. He no longer works at the Hotel Victoria. It seems there was some difficulty over money. He borrowed several small sums from colleagues and then there was the matter of a minor theft and he has moved on, possibly to Antwerp.

"Inquiries were also made with Mrs Schmidt at 2 Stationsplien, where Starfield lodged until about a month ago. Money problems again. Couldn't pay the rent. But it seems there is absolutely no doubt that the prisoner Warner was with him for a week at the end of September. They shared a room with a curtain down the middle and Starfield seems to have acted like a brother towards him. Paid for breakfasts for himself and Warner. He sold Warner's razor and strop for him," Sergeant Cosgrove went back to his notebook, "to a Mr Vreds, the hall porter of the Victoria, for the price of a ticket to Antwerp.

"Mrs Schmidt believes the man went to live with her on September 24. She won't make a formal statement, but she's told me he stayed for seven days and once afterwards he wrote to Mr Stanfield from Antwerp."

Mr Cox settled his teacup in its saucer with barely a rattle. "Seems quite an irregular type."

"That's the least you could say about him, sir. But I wonder if I could trouble you to take a look at this." Mr Sempill unfolded the two pages of sketch maps which Warner had drawn out. "He claims this indicates the location of various hotels and drinking dens where he is known."

Mr Cox glanced at the papers. "Yes, this is perfectly correct so far as I can see. A more or less accurate depiction."

"Then that's where I must continue my inquiries."

"Do you speak the language at all, Chief Constable? French is usually acceptable, but they prefer Dutch – or something like it – in these parts."

"No. But I'm sure, if I speak slowly, I can make my meaning known."

"Yes. I'm sure," said Mr Cox. He fiddled with his saucer. "That almost always works for me and, indeed, for most of the Diplomatic Corps, but in the event that it should not, I'm sure you'll find Sergeant Cosgrove a great help."

"You speak French?" Mr Sempill was astonished.

"Yes, sir. And a bit of Dutch. Some German. My Italian isn't what it might be."

"So you're in good hands," said Mr Cox. "And now, gentlemen, if there's nothing else I can do for you . . ." He stood up from behind the desk and, this time, graciously offered his long, slim hand for shaking. "And, Cosgrove, old man," he pointed to the flagpole standing propped in the corner by the door, "if you wouldn't mind hanging that up on your way out, I'd be obliged."

42

ON THE 1st, 2nd and 3rd of October I stopped at the Hotel Transvaal in Antwerp, paying one franc, 50 centimes per night. I stayed there three nights. On 4th and 5th October 1912 I was in Brussels, returning to Antwerp on 6th October. I slept at the Hotel Transvaal, Antwerp, again on October 6th, which was Sunday. On Monday, the 7th October 1912, I met Bert Aubrey, porter of the Hotel d'Alsace, 13 Rue Loos, right close to the Central Station. Aubrey is a French Canadian.

He took me to the Hotel d'Alsace and I remained there till Tuesday, 15th October 1912. I was unable to pay my bill, and the proprietor told me I could not stay there longer. On the 16th October I again returned to the Hotel Transvaal and slept there Wednesday night, 16th October. Next day, Thursday, 17th October, I met my friend Aubrey, and he advised me to go to the British Consulate and get to an English-speaking country. I told him I did not care for any report or that kind to get to Canada, but he told me to do so under an assumed name. I went to the British Consulate and met Mr Cox, Vice Consul, and told him my circumstances under the name of C. S. Ware. He issued transportation to London so that I could call the Commissioner of Canada. I arrived at Liverpool Street Station, Friday 18th October 1912. I remained at the docks all day and took a night's lodging at a small house near Canning Station, the exact address I do not know.

43

WHEN MR SEMPILL was sitting opposite Mr Cox, on the other side of his desk, with a tea tray between them, he had recognised, upside down of course, but quite distinct, the signature of C. S. Ware. Had he asked to do so, he might have examined the signature in more detail. Mr Cox would undoubtedly have consented and the Chief Constable might easily have compared that signature with the two specimens: C. S. Ware, C. S. Ware, neatly, clearly, casually, one above the other, which the prisoner Warner had so thoughtfully provided in the bottom corner of his sketch map. For reasons he could not explain, least of all to himself, Mr Sempill chose not to do that, but when he arrived, after a short walk, side by side with Sergeant Cosgrove, at Place Verte, he knew there was no need. Hope shrivelled in Mr Sempill's breast and he felt the broad flagstones of the square shift under his feet like the greasy deck of that vile ferry. "The great thing is to try to forget that one has the return journey to look forward to," Mr Cox had said. Mr Sempill could not forget.

Here was Place Verte exactly as Warner suggested in his drawing; here the cathedral with its strange little onion dome and its lopsided towers, one short and square, the other rising in jagged pinnacles which Mr Sempill found reminiscent of Edinburgh's own magnificent Scott Monument – except for the rather gaudy clock, of course – all the trees in their two-by-two avenues, the statue of Petro Paulo Rubens behind his iron railings.

Mr Sempill held the map open between his two hands and turned on the spot. The Europa Hotel, the San Antonio Hotel, both exactly where Warner said they should be. In the opposite corner of the square, beyond the flower stalls, the Flanders Hotel and, between there and the cathedral, the street which, according to Warner's map, would lead to Hotel Reuters and the proof that he was in Antwerp when Miss Milne died.

Mr Sempill turned his back and walked away.

"Through the square and just down the road to the left, sir," Sergeant Cosgrove said cheerily.

"Thank you, no, Cosgrove. This way, I think. The Hotel Rheinland. Warner claims he stayed there. Let's see."

Mr Sempill began to walk. "Plaine Falcon? Down here, I think? I'm right, am I not?" and he kept walking, no longer at Cosgrove's side but leading the way, stepping out in long, loping strides with his coat flapping behind like crow wings as Cosgrove struggled to keep up, winding away from the flower stalls and the tourist postcards towards a place where the streets grew narrower and darker and filled with shadows.

"Have a care, sir," said Cosgrove.

"I'm a police officer, man. I have nothing to fear."

But when the street opened out again into a great, fish-shaped marketplace with high tenements on either side and women standing, waiting on the corners, and men standing, watching in the doorways, and it felt that, suddenly, all eyes turned to look at him, then Mr Sempill slowed his pace and waited for Cosgrove to catch up.

"Hotel Rheinland, sir. No. 23 is just there."

There were three dirty steps going up to a double door where nobody had bothered to polish the handles for a long, long time and, inside, surrounded by the smell of stale carpets, an old man dozing in a booth, with his elbow on the desk and his chin in his hand. He had a thick sandwich wrapped in newspaper sitting on the desk beside him.

Cosgrove said: "*Veut voir le patron*," and the man went away slowly, saying nothing. They heard him shuffling down the corridor and, when he was out of sight, the sound of a door creaking.

"That was French, I take it," said Mr Sempill.

"Yes, sir."

"Is it completely necessary? "

Cosgrove said nothing.

"I think a little less of that kind of thing might be in order."

"Sir, they speak French."

"Surely not all of them."

"French and Dutch, sir."

"I understand that. I'm not talking about them. I'm talking about you. Is there any need for that damnable accent? It's as if you were encouraging it. I realise you must talk to them, but try to be a little less enthusiastic about it, if you would."

Cosgrove said nothing and chewed on his moustache.

"Is that clear?"

"Sir."

They waited awkwardly for a few moments until they heard the sound of the creaking door again and a quick step approaching down the corridor, and a short man in a checked waistcoat appeared in the lobby. "*Politie?*" he said.

Sergeant Cosgrove said: "Yes."

"English?"

"Yes."

The man laughed and said something in Dutch. He pointed to the door with his cigarette and said it again.

Mr Sempill said: "He wants us out."

"He says your writ doesn't run here, sir."

"Or words to that effect. Tell him we're not going." Mr Sempill took out the photograph and held it up. The man stopped laughing. He reached out and took the picture.

"You know him?" said Mr Sempill.

"This bastard? You should have said." He held out his hand. "Leon Mirbach. I am the proprietor, Hotel Rheinland. Please come." Mirbach leaned over the counter to where the old man had been sitting. His watch chain rattled against the counter as he stretched to pick up the hotel ledger. "What has he done? A very bad thing I hope."

"Murder."

"Good. He runs away from me without to pay. Now you will, I hope, hang him."

"He stayed here?"

"Two times." Mirbach looked in his ledger. "More than one year. Last September. He one week stays. See. Look here."

He pointed with a broken fingernail to an entry bearing the name of C. S. Walker. "See? Look. You see."

Mr Sempill took the book and examined the entry. C. S. Walker, age forty, occupation promoter, born St Louis, America. Domicile, Jefferson Hotel.

"Look at that, Sergeant. Last year he was forty, this year he was thirty-eight."

Mirbach said: "He was very well dressed and rich. Every day he eats breakfast and goes. Every night he comes back. After one week he pays and goes on SS *Menominee* and to Boston goes."

"But you said he left without paying."

"The next time. The next time I saw this man – look again in the book – one year later, this year 20th September, when he again came to my hotel. This time he left without paying. Twenty-eight francs. I have not seen him again." He smiled. "But I have his good leather bag."

Mr Sempill smiled under his walrus whiskers. It seemed like the first time he had smiled since the day Sergeant Fraser brought the news from Elmgrove. "That old trick?" he said. "What was in the bag?"

"The bag is locked. I never inside it have looked."

"Get the bag, man! For God's sake, get the bag. Cosgrove, tell him! Tell him to get the bag."

Sergeant Cosgrove said something that sounded like a man loudly clearing his throat and Mirbach went hurrying away into some dark place beyond the porter's booth. He was gone only moments before returning, dragging a long leather kit bag, closed at one end with brass fittings and shut with a padlock. Mr Sempill thought he had never been so happy. It was all he could do to stop himself from laughing out loud. "Break it. Break it," he said.

Sergeant Cosgrove produced a clasp knife – he was the kind of man who could be relied upon to carry such a thing – and he wrestled with the bag, right there on the floor of the hotel lobby. But the lock would not give until, at last, the elderly porter came shuffling up with a dancing, hopping step, carrying a hammer. It took six blows to burst the lock. Sergeant Cosgrove pushed his hat back on his head. "There you go, sir," he said.

The Chief Constable knelt down on the filthy carpet and opened the bag. "Make a note," he said. "One white shirt, one striped shirt, shirt collars," he counted, "two, four, six, one dozen collars marked C. S. Warren, one brown bowler hat, one pair blue trousers, and one undervest. And there's this. A telegram form. Unused. Addressed Miss Nancy Myfanwy Jones, 102 Magazine Lane, New Brighton."

44

HENRY BRUST. "40". Proprietor of Hotel Rubens. Pearl Street. Antwerp says: I recognise the photograph shown me as that of a man who first came to my hotel two years ago. He stayed at my hotel at that time one night. I cannot remember the name he was under.

He said he was a dealer in jewellery. I next saw him in 1911, when he came into my cafe for coffee on two occasions. He next came to my hotel about the beginning of October 1912. I was working in the kitchen when he called. He asked to see me personally, and he was shown through to the kitchen. He asked me to loan him some money for a few days, as he was very hard up and waiting for money from America. I suggested that he should pawn his watch or ring, but he said he did not care to do this. Ultimately, he persuaded me to loan him F.15 on his rainproof, which he left with me. He returned about 10 days afterwards - 16th October, about 3 p.m., when he came to settle about the overcoat. I arranged to give him F.2.50 more, on the understanding that the rainproof would become my property. I asked him to make out a receipt for the coat (produced), which he signed. I am positive it was the 16th October 1912 because, when he handed me the receipt, I compared the date on it with the date on the calendar. My waiter, Ormond, who has since left my service, was present when the receipt was made out, and can speak to the date.

45

ANTWERP, 4th DECEMBER, 1912

ARMEND DEDERICH, "35", Waiter, Rue de l'Aquidue 7, Antwerp, says:– I entered the service of the proprietor of Hotel Rubens here about 9 months ago and left on 29th November 1912. I remember the man whose photograph you show me, coming to the hotel some time in September. He came as a customer, and seemed to be friendly with the proprieter. I know the proprietor advanced him some money on a waterproof coat. I was present on 16th October 1912 – I think between 5 and 6 p.m. – when he made out a receipt making over the overcoat to my master. I am positive it was the 16th October, because one of my duties in the hotel every morning was to adjust the calendar in the bar to date, and I distinctly remember the date put on the receipt corresponded with that on the calendar.

46

WALKING HURRIEDLY, BENT over, through the Place Verte, his coat buttoned up this time, one hand on his hat, one hand pinching his collar shut against the cold, Mr Sempill looked up from the pavement just at the very moment the chill December wind stripped the last three leaves from the trees of the square and sent them whirling into Petro Paulo's stiff bronze beard with a lover's outraged slap.

He was on his way to the Central station, pretending he knew how to get there, turning left and right – "Down here, sir" – as Sergeant Cosgrove – "I think this way, sir" – offered directions.

"Why the station, sir? If you don't mind my asking."

"Because it's where we will find him."

"Who, sir?"

"Who, sir? Aubrey, sir! That's who, sir. Warner's little French Canadian friend."

"Can't we just go to the hotel, sir?"

But Mr Sempill did not even trouble to reply. He simply strode out, knowing the way now, recognising the signs, the converging tramlines, the thickening crowds, the hurrying travellers with their suitcases banging against their knees, the cabs jostling for business and there, up ahead, a great broad arch, a cast-iron rainbow spread across the horizon, a half a sky of glass to let the light shine through and all of it blackened and dimmed with soot and dust and dirty raindrops and chilly disappointment.

Despite the gale blowing at his back, Mr Sempill felt his heart beating warm in his chest. He was happy still. Happy for the first time in weeks, and he carried in his coat, folded into his pocket book, that telegram form with the name of Miss Nancy Jones, clearly, unmistakably, in Warner's hand.

What would Miss Nancy Jones have thought if someone had told her that, far across the sea from No. 102 Magazine Lane, New Brighton, in a foreign country, on a piece of paper in Warner's bag, her name was waiting? Perhaps she would have taken it for a sign that she had not been entirely deceived, that, after all, he cared, he had repented, he was on the verge of summoning her to his side if some other, entirely understandable, wholly excusable circumstance had not intervened. Again. Perhaps it would have been a comfort to her. She would have understood.

Certainly that little note was a comfort to Mr Sempill. He held it close to his heart like a glowing cinder. Miss Nancy Myfanwy Jones was a clue – a veritable clue – and he had uncovered her, not Trench, not the bloody Procurator Fiscal, but J. Howard Sempill, Chief Constable of Broughty Ferry. Mr Sempill was unable to contain his delight. This would prove that he was a policeman in the truest sense of the word. "They'll know. They will see," he muttered.

"Yes, sir?"

"Oh, shut up, Cosgrove."

He ran up the station steps, crossed the booking hall in half a dozen strides and came out in front of the ticket barrier a full four seconds before Cosgrove joined him. "Go away," he said.

"Sir?"

"You look like a policeman. Go and buy a paper. Join me over there."

Mr Sempill went to sit on a bench at the back of the platform and he took out his pipe, watching the crowds.

He ignored the people hurrying towards the trains. He discounted anybody leaving the station. In a few seconds, he had found his man.

"That one," he said when Cosgrove returned with the newspaper. Mr Sempill pointed quietly with the stem of his pipe at a young man patrolling the ticket barriers like a lost puppy. "The pretty one."

"What makes you think that's Aubrey, sir?"

"Because he's so pretty."

"Pretty? You mean you think Warner is an invert? But the victim was a woman, sir."

"I don't know if Warner is an invert or not. Nothing would surprise me. Such types have an infinite capacity for deception, in my experience. They wheedle and ingratiate and that's exactly Warner's method. For my money, I'd say, no, there is nothing unnatural about Warner, but he undoubtedly preys on men of that type at least as much as he does on women. Look at what you discovered in Rotterdam. He meets a man in the port and that man takes him back to his room, feeds him and shelters him for a week from his own pocket. Why? Why would he do that?"

"There was a curtain down the room, sir."

"Oh, well, since you put it that way, that makes all the difference. There could be no opportunity for impropriety in a room with a curtain down the middle!"

Mr Sempill took a couple of slow draws on his pipe and let the smoke out through his nose. "Our Mr Warner has an uncommon gift for making friends and I'm willing to bet that waiter you discovered in Rotterdam – what was his name, again?"

"Stanfield, sir."

"Stanfield, yes. I'm betting he was pretty too. Was he?"

Sergeant Cosgrove looked at his boots. "I'm not much of a judge in matters of that nature, sir."

"Well I am, Sergeant. I am. I can smell them, and that pretty boy over there stinks of it. Go and get him for me."

Mr Sempill watched as Sergeant Cosgrove rose from the bench and approached the young man through the crowd. He jumped like a kitten when Sergeant Cosgrove put a hand on his shoulder and his face turned grey when he heard the word "police". He might have tried to run for it except Sergeant Cosgrove pointed over to the bench by the entrance, perhaps to tell him where to go, perhaps to tell him there was no chance of escape. Mr Sempill raised his hand in a fatherly greeting and sucked on his pipe. That young man had met the police before.

Mr Sempill did not rise when the young man approached across the platform, with Sergeant Cosgrove just half a pace behind. He did not offer his hand. He barely even looked up. He simply slid across the bench a little and said: "Have a seat, son."

The young man sat down. He kept his two hands on the knees of his polished trousers, rubbing away nervously, as if he had been ready to spring up and dash away but there was no chance of that. Sergeant Cosgrove was standing over him like the Rock of Gibraltar with its hands in its coat pockets.

"Name?" Mr Sempill said.

"Bert Aubrey."

"Age?"

"I am twenty-seven."

"So young," said Mr Sempill. "And so pretty." He took the photograph from his jacket pocket and showed it. "Do you know this man?"

Aubrey said nothing for a moment, chewing his lip as he

looked frantically from the picture to Sergeant Cosgrove, to the side of Mr Sempill's head, calculating the distance to the gates on the far side of the platform.

"Do you know this man? Come on, it's a simple-enough question."

Aubrey's two hands fluttered up from his knees to his mouth as he stifled a squeal, and Mr Sempill turned to Cosgrove with a knowing look. "What did I say?"

"So you do know him."

Aubrey nodded. His eyes were brimming with tears and he squirmed on the bench.

"Read this."

Mr Sempill handed him a folded sheet of paper, a copy of the letter Warner had written from his cell, pleading for help.

It was too much for Aubrey, who began dabbing at his eyes and, at last, hid his face in his handkerchief and wailed, rocking back and forward in his seat with many cries of *"Mon Dieu! Mon Dieu!"*

"Make a note of that, Cosgrove," said the Chief Constable. "Now then, Aubrey, is any of this true?"

The young man was snivelling like a child and choked with sobs. *"Non! Non! Non!* Not true," he said. "No word is true. Charles is a kind man. A gentle man. He is not a murderer. This is all lies. I think you are a very bad man and a very bad policeman."

"I have no concern for your opinion, sonny. Now get a grip of yourself and think. Is there anything in Warner's statement that is true? Is he telling the truth about you and when he met you? Think, boy, this is important."

Aubrey rubbed at his eyes again and blew his nose with a fanfare. He was composed. He set his lips and jutted his chin with a martyr's grimness.

"Never will I condemn him," he said. It would have made a cat laugh, but Sergeant Cosgrove was patient with him.

He said: "Nobody's asking you to condemn him. Just tell us the truth. He says you're a French Canadian. Is that true?"

"Yes."

"Now, that wasn't so hard. What about the rest of it?"

Aubrey looked down at the letter again. "It is so. We met here, right here. I was meeting the trains."

"When?" said Cosgrove. "The date. Dates are important."

"I don't know. I can check in the hotel register. Near the beginning of October. A Tuesday. He came forward to me and asked me if I could recommend a cheap hotel to him. I recommended my own hotel, Hotel d'Alsace, and told him that if he stayed a week it would cost him five francs per day.

"We went to the hotel and he entered his name in the register as Charles Warren. He told me he had no money but expected a remittance from America every day."

Mr Sempill almost spat his pipe out. "He told you he had no money and yet you allowed your master to take him in? For God's sake, why?"

"I liked him. Has that ever happened to you, sir? Somebody likes you?"

Sergeant Cosgrove stepped in. "Get on with it," he said.

"He was always in good spirits. He told me he was an American from Detroit. He did not say what his occupation was, but it was clear he was a man used to command money. Always very well dressed. I lent him money on different occasions—"

"You lent him money? Cosgrove, what did I tell you? What did I tell you? Why in God's name is a hotel porter like you lending money to a guest? Why would a guest even ask?"

Aubrey took out his handkerchief and began dabbing at

his eyes again. "I told you! I liked him. We were friends. See, here, look on this letter, he writes 'Friend Aubrey'. I see, Mr Policeman, nobody likes you and you have never had a friend. Charles was my friend. He borrowed money from me while he was here, and I know he borrowed money from different visitors staying in the hotel. But, after a few days had passed and his remittance did not come, I suggested he should look out for a job, and if he liked I would see to one for him. He said, no, he did not want to work. Then one day – yes, the date! October 16, I remember. October 16, you can check the book, but I know I am right because it was Gustave's birthday—"

"Who is Gustave?"

"Another friend, Mr Policeman. You have no friends, but I have many. That morning he simply walked out of the hotel and did not come back again. The following day in the after-noon he came to me here at the Central Railway station and showed me an order from the British Consul for his passage to England. I was afraid he would sell it and try to remain on in Antwerp, so I told him a lie. I said the boss at the hotel had a warrant for his arrest over his unpaid bill. There and then I took him down to the Harwich boat and saw him onto it. I paid his tram fare to the boat, and I bought him some sandwiches for the journey and I gave him all the money in my pocket."

"You gave him all the money in your pocket." Mr Sempill shook his head in disgust. "What did I tell you, Cosgrove? Am I right?"

Sergeant Cosgrove stood aside to let Aubrey leave. "We found you once, we can find you again if we need you. Don't try to run." And then, because he was kind, he took two francs from his pocket and pressed them on Aubrey. "No. There. Take it. And, for God's sake, stop crying. Be on your way."

Aubrey left, shoulders heaving but trying not to cry, and Mr

Sempill, who was not kind, looked after him, not knowing what to say. Sergeant Cosgrove sat down on the bench and waited in silence. A train left and a porter went by rolling a leather trunk on a trolley.

Mr Sempill said: "I'm going home."

"Yes, sir."

"My work here is done. I will have to report that Warner appears to be telling the truth."

"Yes, sir."

"Still, my time has not been entirely wasted. I can tell you this for sure and certain: that Nancy Jones is either his accomplice or his mistress. That may explain why, amongst all those pages telling us where he passed his time, he completely neglected to make any mention of her. There's undoubtedly some reason he was carrying her address round with him and making preparations to wire her."

"Quite obviously, sir," said Sergeant Cosgrove. "Unless . . ."

"Undoubtedly. A criminal harlot. A co-conspirator. She has probably acted to ingratiate herself with his victims and paved the way for him to step in. Either that or he is not, after all, an invert and they are lovers."

"There's another possibility, sir, if I may."

"Damnation, man, you're right. She may actually be his employer. We would be mad to rule it out simply because she is a woman. Warner may be her pawn – a helpless dupe caught in her web."

"Or she could be another victim. That might explain why he has failed to mention her, sir. You are – we are – assuming this Jones woman is, well, what I'm saying is she may be as old as Miss Milne. For all we know she may be as dead as Miss Milne."

"Why would he keep her address? Why incriminate himself

when he has been so careful to cover his tracks at Elmgrove? Still, I suppose I should look into it. On my way home. I suppose."

He knocked his pipe out on the edge of the bench. "Who is this Petro Paulo chap, anyway?"

"Sir?"

"The statue in the square?"

"Oh, him, sir. That's Rubens, sir. Peter Paul Rubens. Famous artist, sir, of years gone by, as you might tell by his outlandish dress. Famous for his ladies, sir. Liked 'em meaty."

"Rubens? Well, of course I know who Rubens was. It was the name that confused me. They all talk of 'Petro Paulo' when that wasn't his name at all. Why would they do that, Cosgrove? What possible pleasure can it give them?"

"I told you, sir – 'eathens. Every one of 'em. 'Eathen savages. It's no explanation at all, but it's all the explanation that makes any sense and it explains everything, sir."

47

OUR MR SEMPILL took quite some days to return to Broughty Ferry, stopping off, as he did, on the way to interview Warner's landlady in Seacombe and an unfortunate young woman Warner appeared to have cruelly deceived in a place called New Brighton. Both of these places are near Liverpool, I believe, and the people living there probably know as little of our lives in the Ferry as we do of theirs.

However, while Mr Sempill was away there was an interesting event, in the form of an unusual envelope of very good quality which arrived for his notice, bearing striking stamps from the colony of Bermuda and with the postmark of Hamilton. I consulted the almanac and learned that Hamilton is the capital of Bermuda.

Almost all the mail was opened and dealt with in the usual way, but this was marked as "strictly private and personal. If undelivered, return to Chief Constable and Provost Marshal General, Hamilton, Bermuda." Naturally I did not open the letter, but when I went into Mr Sempill's office – which Mr Trench was still using as his own – I made a great show of laying the envelope down in the middle of Mr Sempill's desk and I gave it a meaningful tap with my finger before I left again.

It was not long after that before Mr Trench came into the main office and made a telephone call. Naturally, I overheard nothing, but it was not many minutes later before the telephone rang again. Mr Trench hurried to answer it, and when he had finished his conversation he beckoned me over.

He leaned in close and muttered: "It's right enough. They are looking for a Chief of Police in Bermuda. Bermuda! That's quite a step up for the old boy."

I took the view – and it is a view I maintain – that Broughty Ferry could hold its head up with any part of His Majesty's dominions and that Bermuda would be more like an exile than a promotion, but I did not disagree with Mr Trench, although something of my opinion must have shown in my face.

He said: "Well, what I mean is you might have thought he would have tried his wings in someplace a little less exotic. Edinburgh, maybe, rather than taking on an entire colony. It is a very small colony."

We speculated together throughout the day as to why Mr Sempill should have carried out his correspondence with Bermuda through the police office and not from his home address in the park. There were only two possible reasons: either he did not wish Mrs Sempill to know of his plans for some reason, or it was because he wished the letter to be seen so that we would all realise what an important individual he was and how much in demand from police forces throughout the Empire. We decided it was the latter.

The envelope gathered dust on Mr Sempill's desk for another day and a half before the Chief Constable finally returned to Broughty Ferry.

This time he did not bring souvenirs for us because, as he explained, Antwerp has no places of interest and, in any event, it is foreign. I think the truth is that Mr Sempill had become a little jaded by travel.

He was very jolly when he arrived, praising himself for his detective work on the Continent and full of stories about "that daft old maid in New Brighton" and how completely Warner had taken her in. "Were I not a respectable and upstanding member of society, that would be my hobby – whispering sweet nothings to on-the-shelf spinsters and picking their pockets as I went. Still, life has taken me down another path," and he rubbed his hands together and went off, laughing. "See me when you have a moment, please, Trench. We need to prepare for our visit from the Fiscal."

I have to say, I am strongly of the view that Mr Sempill would have made a better policeman if he had been blessed with a little more kindness. He gave no thought at all to what that lady had suffered and it is a source of amazement to me that men who have no understanding of human failings and care nothing for mortal weakness, the loves and hates and fears and hopes that drive us all, can make a career in the police, where such things are the mainspring of every crime. How much more easily might crime be detected by men with a little more kindness and a broader understanding of human nature?

Still, I must acknowledge that when Mr Procurator Fiscal Mackintosh arrived for his appointment that afternoon, the Chief Constable was good enough to invite me to join the meeting.

Such was the success of his mission to Flanders that he, no doubt, wished as many as possible to see it and applaud, and it was, undoubtedly, a thorough piece of work. He did not read through every witness statement, but even to rehearse the burden of their evidence took the better part of half an hour, and when he turned the last page in the file, Mr Sempill looked up in expectation of well-deserved congratulations. "I think that proves it," he said. "I need hardly point out that the prisoner's second statement differs very materially from the statement made at Maidstone jail. It will also be noted that in this second statement Warner gave us a very comprehensive narrative of his movements," Mr Sempill looked at his notes, "dating from 10th August till 4th November. Very comprehensive. Almost encyclopaedic.

"It will be noted too, that he was able to give the exact day of the month, with the corresponding day of that week, on which he said he was at all the different places he said he visited. He dictated all this from memory, and it is an impossible feat for any man to do unless he had purposely, with the object in view, mentally noted the different dates in his mind on which he was at all the different places he mentions.

"On his own account and on that of the witnesses which I took in Antwerp, Brussels and London, he was living a most irregular life, at times drinking heavily and living by his wits, flitting between Antwerp and London, London and Liverpool, Liverpool and London, London and Southampton, Liverpool and Seacombe, Seacombe and Antwerp, Antwerp and Rotterdam, Rotterdam and Antwerp, Antwerp and Brussels, Brussels and Antwerp, and Antwerp back to London."

Mr Mackintosh the Fiscal clasped his hands carefully over his waistcoat together before he spoke. "Oh yes, you've proved it all right. You've followed him all round Europe, back and fore, England to Holland, across to Belgium, back to England, and every place you went you found things exactly as Warner described, met people exactly as he said and they all testify to the truth of what he says. So, congratulations, Chief Constable, you have proven beyond all shadow of a doubt that he could not have been even in the same country when Miss Milne was murdered, far less the same street."

"No, no, no, you don't understand." Mr Sempill was licking his thumb and rifling through his piles of papers. "You see there's a gap. Here, look, here."

I looked to Mr Trench, but he was looking down at the floor.

"Look, we know that Warner obtained a travel warrant from the authorities in Antwerp on October 17 and by his own account – out of his own mouth, mind you – he says he got to London on, here, here it is, on the 18th, when he wasted the day hanging round the docks. The next day, he obtained money under false pretences at the Canadian High Commission and they told him to come back again on the 21st. The 21st. Don't you see, that's a two-day gap. That's more than enough time to get to Broughty Ferry, do the deed and return to London, where he could be seen by a respectable figure like the Canadian High Commissioner."

"But how could he pay for the ticket? He was strapped. That's why he asked the Canadians for money."

"I've already through of that," said Mr Sempill. "That was part of his plan. If he could establish that he had no money for the rail fare, that would rule him out as a suspect. But he *did* have money. Or perhaps he swindled somebody out of the fare, or begged assistance. He has very strong Masonic connections."

"That's true," said Mr Trench. "A couple of constables in London helped him out on the strength of it." He was trying to be helpful.

Mr Mackintosh flicked through Warner's statement. "According to this he stayed in cheap lodgings for those two nights."

Mr Trench said: "Nobody remembers him and there are no records. We did look."

"So, according to you, he swindled the Canadian High Commission out of cash he did not require, or stole some money, or begged some money, and came to the Ferry to murder a woman he had never met and fled again. In the name of God, why?"

Mr Sempill was becoming exasperated, and he spoke to the Fiscal as he would to a stupid child struggling over his multiplication tables. "Because it's the perfect crime of course. If I murder somebody I know, I will be caught because there's a connection – there's a reason. If I murder somebody at random, somebody totally unconnected, there's no reason to trace the killing back to me."

"But why? You still haven't told me why."

"Miss Milne was well known in London, splashing her money about the place like a drunken sailor. Obviously he heard of her or met her – at the Bonnington Hotel, for example—"

"Nobody there recognised him."

"There was some dubiety, but set that aside. He knew she had money, he got on the train, dashed her brains out, ransacked the place, got back on the train and sealed his alibi with a visit to the Canadian High Commission. The perfect crime."

The Fiscal went back to his notes again. "And you say that he murdered her on the night of the 19th or the 20th?"

"Precisely!" Mr Sempill was triumphant.

"But the evening paper lying on the table tells us she died on . . ." Another flurry of notes.

Mr Trench cleared his throat and said: "The 14th, sir."

"Well that's obviously wrong. Clearly. We've got that wrong. The paper was left lying about for a few days. Maybe she set it aside to light the fire. Maybe he sat down to read it, after the killing. Maybe he ate that pie. We don't know. But we do know this: he's a foreigner. He is definitely a foreigner. Trench will bear me out on this, won't you, Trench? Foreign, isn't he?"

"Yes, sir." That was all Mr Trench said.

But Mr Mackintosh would not bend. "I know the law, Sempill, believe me. There is no part of Scots law which makes it an offence to be foreign. Nothing. Anyway, I've had that journalist in my office today, that Norval Scrymgeour, demanding to make a statement insisting that he saw Miss Milne alive and well in Dundee on the 21st."

"Surely you don't believe him?"

"Of course I don't believe him. She was dead on the 14th, that's why I don't believe him. He is confused. But he has offered himself as a witness for the defence. Sempill, I want this wrapped up. You've made a mess of it. Just get it finished with. I'm signing the papers to have Warner released in the morning."

I thought Mr Sempill was going to have a stroke. He turned grey where he sat, then he stood up from his chair and his face turned purple and he bellowed across the desk like a bull. "No! You won't land me with this midden! I have a name and a reputation. My name is in print across the Empire because of this case. Do you think you're going to ruin me and keep me here in Broughty bloody Ferry for the rest of my days? I'll have you know I have considerably bigger fish to fry. I'll have you know—"

"Bermuda," said Mr Mackintosh, calmly. "Everybody knows. Everybody in Dundee, anyway. Everybody who is anybody. We all know. We all know how you've worked your way into the papers. We all know you've been leaking information, making yourself out to be a dogged detective, hounding your man across the globe. Sempill, all you've done is piss God knows how much of the ratepayers' money up the wall to prove beyond a shadow of a doubt that you've got the wrong man and your only suspect is as innocent as a babe. But don't worry, you can expect a glowing reference from me. You can write it yourself, if you like, and I'll sign it. Anything. Whatever it takes to get you out of town."

The Fiscal turned to Mr Trench. "I expect you to clean this up," he said. "You are not blameless in this."

"No, Trench. Not blameless at all." Mr Sempill's voice had risen to a squeak. "It was him. He told me it was a foreigner." And then the Chief Constable collapsed in his chair with his head in his hands.

There was a moment of embarrassed silence before the Fiscal continued. "We need a version. I'm relying on you to come up with some sort of explanation for this disaster. Something that will let us get out of this with a bit of dignity. Do it."

"Yes, sir."

Mr Fiscal Mackintosh stood up and took his hat from the hook on the wall, so we all stood up, except for Mr Sempill, who sat where he was with the look of a felled ox. Mr Mackintosh straightened his hat in the mirror. "Well, have a good trip, Sempill. I think you'll like Hamilton. Barely three thousand souls in the whole town and not half of them white men. You'll look back on Broughty Ferry as the very pinnacle of your policing career."

We left Mr Sempill then and he never emerged from his room for the rest of the day. Not that it mattered, for Mr Trench had me sit with him at a desk in the front office and I typed while he dictated his story. It took quite a time and he smoked a remarkable number of cigarettes, but we got it done.

"I am inclined to believe," said Mr Trench, "that robbery was the motive of the crime and that the person who committed the crime probably got a considerable sum of money in the deceased lady's handbag.

"I have investigated numerous clues; an enormous mass of correspondence has been received from all over the country from all sorts and conditions of people; letters containing ideas, suggestions and theories have all had close attention, but all have come to nothing. I have personally interviewed the numerous witnesses who speak to having seen various men in the grounds or leaving the grounds surrounding Elmgrove and whose statements have been supplied to the Procurator Fiscal. In conjunction with Deputy Chief Constable Davidson of the Dundee Police, I have made many inquiries in Dundee, but all without definite result."

Here Mr Trench rehearsed the long catalogue of injuries inflicted upon Miss Milne's body, paying particular attention to the discovery of the wounds caused by the carving fork and the many times and different locations where she was stabbed. I prefer not to record that here, as it is too distressing.

"Keeping an open mind on the murder, I incline strongly to the theory that robbery was the motive of the crime, and that probably the person who committed it had slipped into the house by the front door while Miss Milne was in the grounds collecting roses and pieces of holly to decorate the dining room table, as numerous dishes on the table contained roses and other flowers, and that probably Miss Milne, on coming into the house, discovered the person in the dining room and threatened to telephone for the police, when her assailant seized the carving fork, which may have been lying or the drawer may have been open a little, showing the weapon. He drove it repeatedly into her back and as she spun round drove it into her body, as shown by the various punctures in her clothing, finishing his ghastly work by battering her head with the poker.

"The two curtain cords with which the deceased lady's legs were tied undoubtedly came from the curtains hanging in the lobby leading to the hall. I examined the whole of the house but could find nothing like them in any of the various apartments.

"The explanation: One of the curtain cords being found halfway up the stairs may be explained by assuming that the deceased had run partly up the stairs, pursued by her assailant, whose intention may have been to tie her up, and that, in the struggle with her assailant, he may have dropped one of the cords where it was found on the stair. There is no doubt that the deceased lady had made a desperate fight with her assailant, and that her murder was of a particularly brutal nature, such as might have been committed by a maniac or a foreigner."

I never in my life heard anything so courageous as that. Mr Trench must have known that his story was ridiculous and, what was worse, that it would make him ridiculous. All the reputation he had made as the hero of the Oscar Slater case would be destroyed in a moment by the writing of such nonsense, but he chose to do that rather than take any part in putting the life of an innocent in danger again. I was genuinely pained when we said goodbye on the platform of Broughty Ferry station.

I suppose that Mr Trench wanted to take a share of responsibility for the whole sorry affair on himself because he knew there was some truth in what Chief Constable Sempill had to say. If he had never put the blame for the murder on a foreigner, we would not have wasted so much time chasing Warner across half of Europe while the real killer got clean away.

And I knew, of course, that I let Mr Trench down. I was no more than a sergeant of Broughty Ferry Burgh Police, but he ordered me to speak my mind with no thought for rank and to share my thoughts with him, almost as an equal. I should have done that. If I had, then things might have been very different.

You must have raged, as I did, when so many people at the Bonnington Hotel saw Miss Milne in company with the young man with the yellow moustache, the young man who made such efforts to persuade her to invest in his Canadian mine, and yet nothing was done to trace him. Look through the records. There is no mention of a search of the hotel register. No effort at all to find who that young man might have been. Mr Sempill had his eye on poor, stupid Clarence Wray with his ghastly poems on purple paper and his hot, panting love letters that always hinted but never said just quite what it was he had in mind. And when Wray turned out to be a dead end, then Mr Sempill went darting off to Maidstone jail, racing across the country like a cat chasing a feather on a string. He had Warner safely locked away, so he was not interested in finding the young man with the yellow moustache. I should have spoken up. I should have insisted.

It was the same when we learned of Miss Milne's entirely improper trip through the Highlands on board the *Cavalier*. More than one saw her emerge from the cabin with that young man, the same young man with the thin yellow moustache. More than one saw them go off together and return together. They are all listed there in our records, passengers and ship's officers, all telling the same story about the same young man. Will you find a single word from the company listing the names of those who booked passage on the *Cavalier*? You will not. Is there a complete list of passengers, with their names and addresses? There is not. Was any attempt made to match the passenger list against the registers of the Bonnington Hotel? There was not. Once again, I have no one to blame but myself. I should have spoken.

The young man with the yellow moustache was seen in his fancy dinner jacket, strolling amongst the overgrown gardens of Elmgrove, taking the air, puffing on his fancy cigar – a cigar not unlike the one recovered from the fireplace, a cigar the likes of which Warner had never put to his lips. He was seen again in the street, emerging from the house both late and early. He was seen on the tramcar early in the morning, done up in a rainproof coat on the very day that Warner was selling his own coat for pennies hundreds of miles away and across the German Ocean in Antwerp. The young man with the yellow moustache, it was the young man with the yellow moustache. He was responsible for Jean Milne's death and not Warner. Not Warner. It was never Warner.

And yet, have you not seen, have you not noted how carefully we worked, how every piece of evidence is piled one upon another? Every single witness statement is recorded, down to the smallest detail, even when the witness has nothing more to say than that they have nothing to say. Look at them. All of them in the file. Have you not seen how, in the proud tradition of Scots law, every statement is corroborated, because without corroboration it is worthless gossip? It is not enough for Mr Vice Consul Cox to say that he paid out so much cash on such and such a day. The word of Mr Vice Consul Cox is not enough. But here is his ledger duly signed and noted and corroborating every word. It is not enough for a hotelkeeper in far-off Antwerp to say that he bought a coat from a starving scoundrel for two francs and fifty centimes – but here is his waiter, who says as much. And it is not enough for James Don to say that he was sweeping streets and lifting rubbish in this street or at that time, no, we must also have the word of his foreman, who can point to his daily records and say that it is so.

So when James Don said that he saw a policeman going about alone in Strathern Road, all unaccompanied, at that uncommon hour of the morning, surely there could be nothing easier or more fitting than to investigate who that might have been. Surely there could be nothing simpler than to check the duty logs and establish which of the officers of Broughty Ferry

Burgh Police were on duty that night, which of them would have been patrolling in Strathern Road, near its junction with Grove Road about that time, or to check the reports to see who might have been called from his usual patrols to an incident in that area at that hour. Surely nobody would be better acquainted with the daily duties of the force than its sergeant. That would be me. And yet it was not done.

48

THE PIERROTS AND the showmen have returned to our beach again, like swallows finding their way back for the summer. The songs are old and worn out, the jokes stale but somehow welcome for their familiarity; the sideshows are moth-eaten swindles; fortune tellers in spotted headscarves who will prophesy "a journey over water"; a man in a top hat who claims to be a professor of phrenology; hoopla stalls where no hoop could ever fit; coconut shies where the coconuts are nailed down; roll-the-penny boards where the pennies roll straight into the showman's bucket; and an endless stream of white mice and goldfish to give away. We get only the third-rate showmen here, passing through on their way to someplace where the pickings are richer. But this year they are trying a little harder. One or two of them have invested in fancy new machinery – hand-me-downs from their better-off cousins, no doubt – meant to take a few coppers away from the donkey drivers on the beach. There is one who has installed a couple of "What the Butler Saw" machines in his shed, great metal beasts with brass goggles to look through and a handle to crank. He has repainted them in good red enamel and picked out their cast-iron details, the roaring lions and swirling foliage, in gold, and for a penny you can watch a flickering image of a girl dancing in her drawers – if you dare.

In the hut next door, somebody has installed an electric-shock machine, the "Improved Patent Magneto-Electric Machine for Nervous Diseases". It is an oak box, like a cupboard standing against the wall, decorated with painted pictures of eagles carrying jagged lightning bolts in their claws and there are two copper handles standing up from a shelf at the front. According to the framed notice written on the side in golden script, that machine is an effective cure for everything from rheumatism to gout, "including but not exclusively, nervousness, lameness, women's troubles, deafness, hysteria, constipation and other bowel troubles, skin inflammation, dandruff, boils, impetigo, masculine deficiency, flat feet . . ." and ending with "hypochondria".

When I went past in the afternoon there were no invalids waiting to be cured, but some of the local boys were there, daring each other, taking turns to drop a ha'penny in the slot, crank up the machine and hold on to the copper handles. Idiots, all of them. But something drew me to them and I watched in a kind of fascination. One after another, afraid, not daring to show their fear, overcoming their fear, the pain, the contortion, the bravery that comes from being terrified of shame, the pain, the pain. It made me think of our boys as they queued to throw themselves into the war. They had to be killed because they could not face the shame of not being killed.

I happened to be passing again that evening, out of uniform this time. It was very still. The oil lamps round the tents were flaring straight up in the air, children were laughing, young lassies with their best hats on, hanging on the arms of their chaps, there were snatched kisses in the gaps between the tents, the showmen barking out for custom. I went to that machine and I dropped my ha'penny in the slot and it fell with a thud like a hammer blow and I turned the crank and I gripped the copper handles and I felt it then, the power of life running through me, the same terrifying shock I felt in that summer of my fourteenth birthday when Miss Milne pressed me against a mossy wall in her father's glasshouse and slid her hand down the front of my trousers and kissed me hard on the mouth.

Everything about that moment came back to me then as if it had been stored up in the mechanism of the machine and only now was it free to pour out along the wires and into my skin, into my flesh, into my soul, but I knew, even then, in that instant, that was all untrue. All those things were waiting inside me, not lost at all, simply waiting to be revived by the electric jolt that made everything come alive in me again.

I felt it all. The heat of that great glasshouse, the thickness of the air, the damp, the ferns, the palms, the moss growing over the bricks, the pond, raised up like a wishing well glistening and shining and moving with fish, the music of the water, all of it. I was just a boy. I was a boy. You know what a boy is at that age. Not a boy, not a man, just a boiling cauldron of anger and heat and lust.

I had hopes that, one day, I might be a gardener, but then it was my job to wipe the windows of the glasshouse, keep the dust off the outside and sponge away the green growth on the inside. Such a care I took of everything. The paths were weeded clean, the lawns were edged sharp and those windows gleamed – how they gleamed – because it was only when the windows were clean that I could see Jean Milne passing.

Jean Milne saw me watch. I thought she was all unawares, but, no, I know now she saw me watch. She knew I saw her when she was in the garden all alone and she would stop and put the toe of her boot on a bench – a bench I had painted – and lift her skirts away far more than was needful and tie her laces. That was for my benefit.

When she sat in the shade of the big cedar, pretending to

read her book, the top button on her blouse undone, or maybe one button more so the lace of her corsets was peeking out, fanning herself, she well knew that I was watching from the other side of her father's rose bed.

And when she came upon me in the palm house and touched me in that way and put her finger on her lips to shush me and pulled my hair and kissed me and let her tongue wander inside my mouth, Jean Milne knew I would make no complaint.

"A word, John Fraser, one word and you will lose your position," she said. "I will destroy your character. You will never find employment for the rest of your days. Nobody would ever believe you – you, just a laddie of fourteen—"

"I'm fifteen!"

"Not yet awhile. A laddie of fifteen – let's say – and a respectable lady of twenty-five. Who would believe that?"

Twenty-five. She was nearer forty, but I had not the sense to see it. I believed her. I believed everything. I loved her. I believed she loved me. I was in a paradise. Any lad in the Ferry would have given his right arm to be in my place. A kiss up a lane with a fisher lassie who smelled of bait was beyond their most heated imaginings, but I was a man who had tasted love with a grown woman, a lady, whose hands were soft, whose dainty underpinnings would fall away at my touch, leaving trails of lavender in the air.

And she need have had no fears that I would betray her confidence. It was clear enough that if we were discovered it would end, and why would I want that? Why would any laddie? I was deep in love, but I was wise enough to know which side my bread was buttered. And so I worked away quietly all the summer, climbing ladders to clean the mud and dead leaves from the gutters, bringing vegetables from the kitchen garden to the house, dragging the cast-iron roller over Elmgrove's endless lawns and always, every day, wiping the windows of the glasshouses to keep them clean.

All those weeks I watched and waited for any chance she might want me. Every minute of waiting was agony. Every moment spent wiping those windows I was reliving in my mind the moments before when we had been together, everything over and over, every kiss, every touch, the parting of her flesh, the soft cries and – I remember once coming unexpectedly on a pair of doves pecking at the bare earth under the shade of a tree and they rose up together, suddenly, in terror – that, that feeling like a hurried rush of feathers, over and over in my mind, again and again until, with no notice at all, she would find me in the palm house or crook her finger from the other side of the garden and I would go running, like a puppy with my tail in the air and wagging.

"You mustn't tell, John Fraser. Promise you won't tell. Say it and then you can kiss me. Say it."

"I won't. I'll never tell. I promise."

I never told a soul. When old Mr Milne died I would have comforted her. It was my duty as her beau, but she put on black and walked behind the hearse and shot me such looks as I doffed my cap when she passed. I knew enough to stay away until I was bid.

And then, some days later, after a fit period of mourning, when the tobacconist's shop had opened again and young Mr Milne was running the business up in Dundee, and Miss Milne was alone in the house, she found me scrubbing flowerpots under the outside tap.

I looked up from my work – my fingers were frozen around that rough scrubbing brush – and saw her standing there. There was a stream of water curling along the brick floor and forming itself into a silver question mark around the toe of her boot. "I can't open the window in my bedroom. It's stuck. I need you to go and open it. Now." And she turned on her heel and left me there. I heard the grit crunch under her boot as she went. The tap squeaked, the water hissed and bubbled in the pipe as I turned it off, oh, how suddenly sharp everything had become. I wiped my hands on my trousers. I followed her to the house. She was standing on the stairs.

"Take your filthy boots off at the door."

I did as she said. I was wearing the thick green socks my mother had knitted for me. There was no sound as I went up the stairs. Nothing. Only a clock ticking somewhere deep in the house. Upstairs, every door on the corridor was shut except for the room at the end, the room she lay in on that last night. I stopped at the top of the stairs, breathless.

"Come along. Hurry."

I looked round the door and she was standing at the window. It was open.

"Get on the bed, John. Lie down."

She was unbuttoning her dress where she stood. She wouldn't let me do it. "Never a word, John Fraser, or I'll say you forced yourself on me."

I said: "Yes, Miss Milne."

"Yes, Miss Milne," she said, mocking me. "Oh, yes, Miss Milne."

"I love you, Miss Milne."

"That's what I want, John. Love me."

I said: "Miss Milne, would you do me the honour of becoming my wife?" But she only laughed.

"My father is dead," she said. "Who would give me away?"

49

JEAN MADE FUN of me for loving an old crone in her twenties. "You should be chasing lassies down at the beach, not wasting your time on the likes of me," but I never gave it a thought. She and I were as we were. There was no purpose in wishing it otherwise. The sun rose in the east and Jean Milne was ten years older than me and it would have been as foolish to repine that accident of birth as it would any other, the colour of her eyes or the size of her feet.

I have noticed that men, both when they are very old and when they are very young, have no skill in judging the age of a woman. An old man nearing seventy will look at a matron in her forties or fifties and think her no more than a lassie. A young lad might look at some prim school ma'am in her twenties and think her a dried-out old maid of forty. So I forgive myself for believing Jean Milne, though she harped constantly on her great age. I remember one day she read to me from a book, something written by Benjamin Franklin. It was no more than a long list of reasons why a young man should choose to consort with an older woman and I remember nothing of it now but for the end, which was: "They are so grateful." Jean told me that Franklin had been a figure in the American Revolution and the inventor of the rocking chair. That made a great impression on me, as I had never before considered that someone must have first contrived a rocking chair, any more than there must have been an inventor of the table. But I believed her. Jean Milne was my teacher in so many things.

I believed everything she told me. I believed her when she said I would be ruined if we were discovered. When I longed to run through the Ferry screaming her name and boasting of all that we had done together, when I longed to tell the world, or as much as fitted in my tiny corner of it, that I had discovered love as Livingstone discovered the Victoria Falls, that I knew things nobody else had ever known, that I had seen things and done things that nobody else could ever comprehend, fear of exposure was all that held me in check. I was convinced I would face imprisonment and ruin when a fool might have seen that the catastrophe would be all on her head and not on mine. I was a fool.

I was fool enough to ask her to marry me again.

One day in the garden at the corner of the palm house I asked her again to be my wife. "You're just a boy," she said.

I told her that would pass. She laughed.

I told her that the work of a husband was to guard and look after, and that by marrying me our love would be recognised as pure, her honour would be restored and nobody in the Ferry would dare to mock her when she was my wife.

She only laughed again, all the harder. "Come with me," she said. I followed her across the lawns to the big cedar, a little apart and a little behind, respectfully and decently so that anyone looking over the walls of Elmgrove would see only the mistress of the house about to set a laddie to some task, and then, when we stood under its branches in that great, arching, tented cathedral, standing on a soft, silken carpet of needles with the scent rising up like perfume, with the branches swooping down like roof timbers – "Kiss me, John."

That was how she would order me about, even when we

were hidden away together, even though I was already half a head taller than her with a lot of growing still to do, and while I stood there, kissing her, she began unbuckling the belt on my trousers and tugging away at my shirt tails.

"You like this, don't you, John? Don't you?"

"Yes, Miss Milne."

"Yes, Miss Milne. Do you want me to stop? You only have to say." She took her hands away just for a second and it was all I could do not to cry out. "Do you?"

"No, Miss Milne. No."

"Then I won't stop. We will go on just as we are, with no more silly talk of marriage. I can't marry you, John. You must see that. I'm a lady. I have a position. And you are a gardener's laddie. But we will always have this."

"I love you, Miss Milne."

"I know. I know."

Afterwards, when I was weeding the big flower bed at the side of the house, I heard the window of the drawing room go up and she sat down at the organ and played "Rock of Ages". She had a lovely singing voice.

50

WHEN I WAS a child, I understood as a child, but when I became a man I put aside childish things and understood as a man. I understood why Jean and I could never marry. There was a time, after her brother died, when I entertained those same childish hopes, but that quickly ended. Our stations were too distant. She was too wealthy. Jean Milne could not leave Elmgrove and live in a policeman's cottage. A lowly policeman could not spend his days and his nights doing what policemen do and then come home to Elmgrove to eat cake with the neighbour ladies of Caenlochan Villas. Even the Chief Constable would have been abashed. Jean was right. We could not marry.

She was right about the other thing too. "We will always have this," she said, and we did. If I passed on my night patrols and the gate was standing open, well, naturally I would have to investigate and sometimes those investigations might take half an hour or more before I was able to resume my beat.

But Jean changed over the years. She became strange. She withered like the gardens of Elmgrove. It was as if they were a mirror of one another, the lady and her grand old house, slowly collapsing into shadows and neglect together. Little by little, Jean withdrew from life. She no longer saw visitors. Her mother's elaborate tea sets gathered dust in the cupboards, the pictures were hung with sheets and she retreated into those one or two rooms on the ground floor, like an animal preparing for the long sleep of winter. One day, after one of those terrifying summer storms when the sky suddenly turns boiling black and towering clouds throw down rain and thunder, after all the rain had passed and the wind had died to nothing, I was walking down Grove Road with a warm mist rising from the wet pavements – rainbows on their way to being born – and I looked through the gates of Elmgrove and the roof of the palm house had fallen in. The place where Jean first touched me. It was collapsed utterly, like a shipwreck. I took it for a sign.

You remember what I said about young men and old men and how they cannot tell a woman's age? I am a man in his middle years, the prime of life, and yet Jean remained ten years older than me because Jean had always been ten years older than me. "A lady in her fifties." That's what I told Mr Trench. Love makes us blind. But it cannot protect us from suffering.

Jean was, as the papers said, "a woman of a romantic disposition". My attentions were not enough. They were never enough. That was why she made those "periodical journeys" to London for "the gratification of her whims".

Think what I felt every time she arrived in the police office to hand over her keys. Every time she left the Ferry, I knew why she was going. She was going to London to whore herself, and I knew it and she knew that I knew it. It was in her eyes. I felt it in the tips of her gloved fingers when she laid the keys in my hands. "Now, you will take good care, Sergeant Fraser, won't you?" and she stood there waiting, her hand resting in mine like a little leather bird, waiting until I said it. Waiting.

"Yes, Miss Milne," I said. There was something less than a smile, a dark little curl of triumph in the corners of her mouth.

I bore it. I had no choice. Love is like that.

I knew about the young man with the yellow moustache, with all his money and his fancy plans. Of course I knew. How could I not know when she whispered to me about him in the night, how young he was, how handsome, such a man of the world, what a success he was, how different things might have been if only I had been more like him, goading me, belittling me, boasting of her whoredoms.

I put my trousers on in the dark. I sat on the edge of the bed and tied my boots. She trailed her fingers up my spine, little electric shocks of pleasure at every touch. "How you've grown, John. How you've grown."

I made no reply. I tied a double knot in my bootlace and tugged it tight.

"I said!" she repeated. "How you've grown, John. If a young lady makes a remark, it is considered polite to reply."

The bed squeaked in its familiar way as I stood up. "Yes, Miss Milne."

She rolled over in the bed and said: "Goodnight, John."

I bore it all because I loved her and because we all have our little ways. None of us is perfect. I bore it when he came to stay. I bore it when the smell of his cigars lingered long after he was gone.

"I like the smell of a cigar," she said. "It's manly. It puts me in mind of my father."

I bore it when she went off with him cruising in the Highlands. I bore it even when she made no mention of the trip to me. Not a word. She loved to boast of "the gratification of her whims". She spared me no detail. She revelled in it. But she said nothing of the cruise on the *Cavalier*. Could she have thought to keep it a secret from me? I am the sergeant of Broughty Ferry Burgh Police – of course I knew. Did she think, when Postie Slidders delivered the tickets, he would not gossip about an envelope from the Caledonian Steam Packet Company? Did she think the laundry man would keep it a secret that he had been told not to call? And yet she said not one word to me, and the keys for Elmgrove never arrived at the police office. Then I knew this was more than a whim and I began to fear, but it was only when she returned – a ring on her finger and showing it off to anybody who wanted to look – that my fears turned to a black, burning fury that raged in my chest. I waited and I watched.

51

OF COURSE THE Chief Constable was right: it is well nigh impossible to hunt down a random killer. It's always the connection that betrays them. Murder is a weighty business. We do not kill those who mean nothing to us – there's no reason to do it. But those we love, there might be a thousand reasons to kill them. The connection, that's the thing.

That was why I listened to the pedlar Andy Hay when he said I had to seek out the people of no account, the maidservants and street sweepers, those that go unnoticed. I had to find out what they had seen. As it turned out, they had seen nothing. They go about unseen because they count for nothing and they do not see their own kind. They are invisible, even to themselves. Their eyes were on the fine young gentleman with the yellow moustache, and his fine coat and his fine suit and his fine boots, not quite properly polished.

A fine young gentleman might easily beguile Miss Milne, but a grand lady like that would never take any interest in a lowly police sergeant. No, there could be no possible connection between one so high and one so low, and if the sergeant were to call in, once a week at least, whenever Miss Milne was at home, that could only be to hand back her house keys or to offer some word of comfort to the poor old soul and surely not to bend her over the kitchen table, fling her skirts over her head, unbutton his police trousers and set about her withered old haunches while she grunted and shuddered like an old sow, singing out the old refrain: "Not a word, John Fraser! Not a word or I'll say you forced me."

"Yes! Miss! Milne!"

I think I must have known that the young man with the yellow moustache had arrived in the Ferry only minutes after he got off the train from Dundee. He went into the paper shop across the street and tried to pay for a box of matches with a gold sovereign. They were still talking about it when I went in for my tobacco not half an hour later and, foolishly, they had let him have the matches for nothing, trusting him to return the money because, after all, he was a gentleman.

In very truth, I knew he was here before that. Something sang in my blood. There was a feeling in the air, that crackling heaviness that comes before lightning. Still, I should have done nothing. Love cannot protect us from hurt, but that's no reason to seek out more misery. I might have sat at my own fireside, imagining the two of them together and that would have been misery enough but, no, nothing would do but that I went there to see for myself. Sometimes the only thing that can take the pain away is more pain.

That night as I stood in the darkness of the old, familiar trees that had once been my friends, I had no idea who might have seen me come but, the truth is, I cared little. I stood well back amongst the tangled branches, my uniform as black as the shadows that wrapped me, and I looked into the one lit room, there on the ground floor at the other side of the lawn.

It was like watching a play, or maybe more like a picture show, for there were no words. Still, the scene was clear to anyone who cared to watch: the lovers. Domestic bliss.

There was a good fire going in the grate and the remains of a meal on the table. A lady of Jean's station and standing should have had a lassie to clear her things away and wash the dishes, but there was none and it was clear enough why not, for how could she entertain her gentlemen caller with a lassie in the house to carry the gossip all round the Ferry?

Jean did all she could to make him feel welcome. I watched as she went out and returned in a moment with a big cut-glass decanter and she poured him out a fearsome whisky. Never in all the years I knew her did she do as much for me. Great was the merriment, and soon enough she went back to the bottle and poured him another, but this time she took one for herself.

And there was worse to come. Off she went to the sideboard and she brought out a box of cigars and then she stood there in front of the fire, lit one and got it going, rolling it around in her lips, watching herself in the mirror over the fireplace as she did it, standing there, legs apart, a fist on her hip like a caricature of a man and then, the bitch, she went and sat on his knee and took the cigar from her own lips and placed it between his, but it was not there long before she took it out and kissed him full on the mouth, one hand at the back of his head, the other waving that damned cigar like a trophy. After that, you might be assured, one thing quickly led to another.

There was an oblong of lamplight shining across the damp grass and they were shining in it, laughing and pawing at one another like apes. I might have stood right at that window and they would never have noticed, but I took care to stay in the shadows. I left my place amongst the trees and went and stood in a gap of darkness between the two downstairs windows, listening because watching was more than I could bear.

"And everything is fixed, isn't it, dear."

"Everything's ready. Just a few loose ends to tie up. I'll catch the early train tomorrow. I'll be back in no time."

"And then?"

"Canada. You and I, man and wife in charge of the sweetest, richest gold mine in the territories. Together forever."

And then more laughter and the sounds of glasses being filled and Jean's bright giggles and the savouring of kisses and "Come on. Hurry. Hurry," and more laughter but a different, hungrier kind this time and then the sound of them moved from the room on my right, where she sat and took her meals, to the room on my left, where she had her bed. They left the lamp to burn itself dry on the table and they did not bother to light one in her bedroom, but I saw through the darkness as if it had been noontime. That room, all its familiar furniture, the breathless little gasps, boots dropped on the floor, shirts, corsets, underwear flung across the room, the rattle of buttons as trousers were draped on the bed end, the sighs and groans, the slap of flesh on flesh, that same squeak, squeak, squeak of the bed sawing at my brain, the cries wilder and yet more fevered every moment and – this was the worst of all – not once did she say, "Not a word, or I'll say you forced me." Not once. Never.

No, when it was done and the bed gave its final victorious squeak and they collapsed together in a tangled knot of hot exhaustion, this is what she said: "They are so grateful." She said that to him and she laughed.

I would be a liar if I pretended to know how I got through that night or why I stood there against the wall of Elmgrove hardly moving, for hour after hour, afraid to make a sound lest it should rouse the two sleepers on the other side of that thin pane of glass. I breathed yet more softly than the ticking clock. The stone of the wall was rough and gritty under my fingers. My tears were hot and salt.

When the clock struck four there was a movement from indoors, the sounds of someone dragging themselves up from

330

sleep, and more warm and affectionate mutterings. Then the sounds of someone stumbling round in the dark.

"There are matches on the chest of drawers, dear."

"No need. We left the lamp burning next door."

The toilet flushed. The window next to me brightened as he trimmed the wick. In the bedroom I heard Jean rise. She was going to the hook on the back of the door where her dressing gown always hung. I knew that, though I could not see it. How many hundred, hundred times had I seen her do it in the past.

"Right. I must go if I'm to catch the early train."

"Goodbye, my own dear one. I'll be ready."

"Tomorrow night."

Around the corner, I heard the sound of the front door opening and closing and then his boots on the path as he walked towards the gate. Even if he had looked back, he could not have seen me standing there. I waited for a moment, thinking to follow and smash his brains out with my truncheon on some shadowy street corner – I had no better plan – but before I could move, the wheels of a cart came rumbling and grinding along the street and I heard the scrape of a shovel in the gutter. The gate banged shut. Footsteps went ringing off up the road. There was the noise of a shovel being flung into the cart, a squeak of harness, a slap of reins, hoofs and wheels in the other direction. I waited, listening until the only sound I could hear was the silence pressing against my ears, and then I quietly kicked my footprints out of the earth at the wall and left by the front gate. No one saw me go and the street was empty. Though I hunted for him along Strathern Road, the young man with the yellow moustache was gone. I heard the far metallic singing of the tram and I knew he had escaped me, so I turned back towards home. I needed sleep and there were only a few hours until my duty began for another day.

52

THAT DAY WAS long. I came on duty at seven o'clock and there was nothing in the night log and not a single prisoner in the cells. Nothing happened all day. It takes a long time for nothing to happen. I made a lot of tea and left it all undrunk. Mr Sempill hid in his office.

I spent the time dozing in my chair, dreaming fitfully about the night before and going round and round in my head about Jean, wondering how I might save her from herself. I had to make her see sense. I had to make her understand that there was still a way that she and I could be together, as we were intended to be. I could not allow her to make a fool of herself with that rogue, and I knew, if I could but speak to her, she would see reason.

But Jean was wandering up and down Strathern Road, frantically looking for the young man with the yellow moustache in every tramcar that passed.

I left the office at 7 p.m. My way lay to the east. Elmgrove was in the west. I went west along the Dundee Road. Grove Road is a respectable area. At that hour residents are in their homes with the doors bolted. No one saw me come.

I clearly recall how Mr Trench flitted round Elmgrove that first day he arrived in Broughty Ferry, like a bear in a bowler hat, making notes of one thing and another, observing, imagining. He called it "making up stories". He was weighing the evidence and inventing little plays in his head, trying to imagine a set of circumstances which would leave behind the evidence he could see before his eyes. Poor Mr Trench. He exhausted his powers of invention with the final story. There was no sign of a forced entry, so Miss Milne must have gone into the garden for a moment, leaving the door open for an intruder. Rubbish. I simply walked in through the kitchen. She had left her keys often enough at the police office; it was a simple matter to have copies cut, and Jean's keys jangled in my pocket alongside my own. I liked to have them. They were a comfort to me.

And when I came into the hall, there was Jean, hard at work. Mr Trench decided that the intruder must have dragged Jean's luggage out into the hall to ransack it, but long experience has taught me that the simplest answer is usually the best. She was packing to go away.

Indeed, she was so busy that at first she did not notice me and then when she looked up from her work there was such a look on her face, a sudden startlement to see me there all unbidden, and then, what? Not quite disgust and not quite pity. A weariness, I suppose.

"You are going away with him," I said.

She said nothing. She simply stayed, kneeling there in front of that trunk, with a pair of drawers in her hands, folding them and refolding aimlessly. The air stirred with the scent of lavender.

I reached out and stilled her hands, but she left them folded together there, inside that piece of linen. "Show me," I said. I took her hand and drew her to her feet. "Show me your ring."

She held out her hand, as women do, a little bent at the wrist, fingers together, presenting the ring, an affected look of supreme boredom on her face.

"So you are going to be married?"

"Yes. Yes, John."

"To him?"

She looked at me, quizzically.

"The man who was here last night."

Her hand flew to her lips in shock, as if she was horrified at such an accusation, despite all I knew of her. Still she said nothing.

"You might have married me."

She said nothing.

"I asked you."

"That was a long time ago."

"But it's not too late. It's not too late. You are packing up to go. I understand why we cannot stay in the Ferry, but we can go now, together. America. Patagonia. They want men to farm there. I'm not on duty tomorrow. We can have a day's start before we are missed."

"John." That was all she said, but the chill pity in her voice was like a razor.

"I have given you my whole life. There was never anyone but you. I might have had a wife. I might have had children, but you came and you twisted me into this. This."

Miss Milne sighed a little sadly and considered for a moment before she began to speak. "There is no more to be said. And you needn't think to threaten me or hold me to ransom—"

"I'd never do that."

"You can forget about trying to blacken my name. I will be gone from this place before long. You can say what you like about me, it won't matter. I think you've done very well out of our understanding, John, but you must see that I'm entitled to a little happiness. It's my right with a man who—"

"He's a swindler."

"Now, John, I can't have that. I can't let you say such things about the man I am to marry."

"He's only after your money."

"John, stop that! I will not have it. But, since you mention it, I think I have a little money in my bedroom. I'd like you to take it. Just as a parting gift. You might buy some small souvenir to remind you of happier times."

"I don't want your money."

She was icy again. "Well in that case, I don't think there is much to add. He will be here soon. You should be gone before he arrives. It's for the best, John. You know it is." She stood there for a moment or two, that tiny woman, her chin in the air, daring me, defying me. "It's for the best. Say it, John. Say it."

And I struck her across the face, all my weight behind a great, back-handed slap and I screamed: "NO, MISS MILNE!" Two blows in quick succession, back and fore, east and west, her face spinning, her neck snapping round. "NO, MISS MILNE! NO, MISS MILNE!"

There was an upper set of false teeth lying on the right-hand corner of the doormat at the entrance to the drawing room and there was the lower set flung right across to the other side of the hall, lying on the third step of the stair.

Miss Milne staggered and fell to her knees. Her face was half collapsed, her toothless mouth folded in on itself, her skin already blazing from my slaps, and she was suddenly ancient and withered. She tried to flee, gripped by sheer terror, but it was as if she were unravelling before my eyes. Her hair came unpinned and fell down and a great wad of it tumbled off her head and rolled away and what was left was thin and feeble and old. She made a terrified animal sound with one hand at her mouth, as if to hide its awful, gaping emptiness, and she lunged for the stair, not because there was safety on the upper floor but because it was the only way to escape me. She was quick, as quick as fear can drive a woman on, but I reached out to her with a shout of fury, my one great hand gripping her tiny ankle and I pulled her back to me and she went down, hard, on the edge of the step and there was a sound like wood splitting.

I didn't know what to do and I did not care. I simply grabbed her by the ankles and dragged her back down the stair. My fury was inexhaustible. It had raged untended for thirty years, a great, boiling furnace of hurt, and now Jean Milne had opened the furnace door. Who could she blame if the flames engulfed her?

The curtains in the hall were tied back with cords. I took them off and used one to tie her ankles as she lay there on the carpet. Mr Trench surmised as to how the other landed halfway up the stair. It was there because I threw it there, that's all. Still my fury was unabated. I set about to wreck the place. I swept my arms across her damned, stupid, pointless, dainty little tables. I scattered her ever-so-artistic floral arrangements from one side of the room to the other, I kicked her as I passed, hot tears streaming down my face, hot, gasping sobs burning my throat. A pair of garden secateurs left lying carelessly amongst the cut branches went flying and hit the wall, and I grabbed them and snipped through the cables of her fancy telephone device. Why? How would Mr Trench explain that? Viciousness, that's all. What they call in the charge sheets "malicious mischief". I did it because I could, and when that was done, I went reeling off looking for more to destroy.

There on the sideboard was a box of cigars, not quite full. His cigars. I took one out. I cast about for a match but I found none, so I opened the drawer. There were the matches. I took one out and split the end with my teeth and I used it as a spike to open the end of the cigar.

I called to Jean lying in the lobby. "That's me smoking your fancy man's cigars," I said. I struck the match and lit the cigar. I took my time. "What do you think of that?"

She did not answer.

"I said: 'What do you think of that?' Miss Milne. When a young gentleman makes a remark, it is considered polite to answer."

Still she said nothing, and all my rage returned again and boiled over, and there, in the drawer, I saw the carving set with its big bone-handled fork. With my cigar in one hand and the carving fork in the other, I went back to where Jean lay in the middle of the carpet and stood over her.

Mr Trench imagined a little piece of madness, where Jean was stabbed by an imaginary attacker, stabbed here and there as she fled, stabbed seventeen times in a matter of moments. Madness. My madness was greater. Seventeen times. "I said: That's me smoking . . ."

In the soft, white flesh of her forearm.

". . . your fancy man's cigars . . ."

In her shoulder.

". . . Miss Milne . . ."

In her breast.

". . . What do you think . . ."

Pressing the points of the fork against her clothing, pressing, watching the cloth dent and pucker, pressing all my weight behind it until it pierced right through.

". . . of that?"

Seventeen times. Not all at once. I took my time.

I sat on the bottom of the stairs watching her. It was obvious she was dying. Hitting her head on the stairs had been enough. She was dying, and I wanted to be with her as it happened. I wanted to see it and share it. I wondered if she knew.

I lost interest in the fork. I threw it away. But I went back for another cigar and the matches. It was dark. I struck a match. The light was beautiful. The shadows were beautiful.

The places where the light met the shadows were the most beautiful of all. I looked at Jean lying there, tied up, bleeding gently, dying so softly. The match went out. I threw it at her. I struck another and I held that one in a different place, watching different shadows flaring on the walls. I threw that one at her too and watched the shadows leap as it flared on the carpet beside her and died away. I remember wondering if it failed in her last breath. I struck another match and got down on my hands and knees, holding it close to her mouth, watching it waver in her faint breathing. I blew cigar smoke into her mouth and laughed.

Mr Trench made no explanation for the matches that littered the floor of Elmgrove. The explanation was simple. I liked to strike matches. And Mr Trench ignored the brass vase filled with piss. He made no attempt to explain it, though I recorded it faithfully in my statement. It's obvious. I could not leave Jean, even for a moment.

I wanted to be with Jean at the end, but it was dark and I was very tired. As my great love for her drained away, exhaustion seemed to flood in to take its place. I slept, there on the stairs, with my face pressed against the bannister rail, and I woke up weeping without knowing why. I struck another match and held it high and moved it from side to side. There were not many left.

I sat in the dark holding an unlit match in my fingers, promising myself that I would light this one after twenty minutes, counting the seconds up to sixty, counting the minutes on my fingers and starting again until it lasted half an hour, and then there was the grating crunch of the sandpaper and the tiny firework pop and the blinding flare of light and, for just moments, the light and Jean and the blood flooded my brain again. It was so lovely.

When the final match was gone I left my place on the stairs and went to lie down beside her. We slept together there on the floor for the last time. It was the first time we had ever passed a night together.

The noise of Postie Slidders dropping his letters into the big iron box at the kitchen door roused me in the morning. I was lying on my side, just as Jean was, my head resting on my arm, just as hers was. I woke up and looked into her ruined face. I had loved her for thirty years and it was almost all gone. This was grief.

I lay beside her for a while, touching her hair, crooning to her, comforting her, wishing she would die. Everything was so lovely, the light from behind the curtains over the door, the shine of those holly boughs scattered on the floor, the colours of the carpet. Everything so bright with the life of the world as Jean lay dying beside me. From where I lay on the floor I saw a dribble of blood on the wall by the stair, just where I had sat in the darkness. It caught my eye. I went to examine it. It was lovely too. A perfect crimson teardrop, dragging its way down the wall. I touched it. I had to touch it, and the skin on the surface broke like a bubble and the dribble of blood left inside ran away quickly over the wallpaper and stopped again. I'm not a fool. I pressed my finger in the mark and smeared it away.

It was then that Jean gave a long moan, and when I turned, her eyes were open and she was looking at me, looking right at me with recognition, moaning, and the tip of her tongue was working between her lips, like some hideous lizard.

I knew then that she might not die. She might live. So I had to kill her. There was the fork lying on the floor. I went to the drawing room looking for the knife. Jean's moans were growing louder and wilder. There was no time. I came back to her, and when I came back, I had the poker. Jean was clawing weakly at the carpet, little twitching grabs, trying to crawl away like the wounded thing she was. I stood over her, one boot on either side of her body, and I laid the poker gently on her head, measuring, testing. I lifted the poker over my head. She knew it was coming. She made a shrill noise, like a trapped rabbit, and I smashed the brass end of it down on her skull. But still she did not die. She howled. She howled. I hit her again. Harder and quickly again and again. I wanted it to be over. Again. Again. Again. Again. The poker broke. It was over.

I sat down on the stairs to recover myself. I threw the poker away.

What a fool Mr Sempill was with his damned stupid notions of the random killer. If some intruder had killed her in a sudden fury, what need to tie her up? And if he had tied her up, what need to kill her, unless she recognised him? It was so obvious, and yet he was the Chief Constable and I was the sergeant.

Sitting there on the step, looking down at Jean's body, I saw the picture had changed. Where there had been darkness and shadows, there was morning light filling the room. There were beautiful patterns of blood on the walls, fern shapes, garlands, arching up to the roof. Everything was different. Everything had to be looked at again. It was necessary to look at everything and remember it, for Jean's sake.

I don't know how long that took. I watched the light moving round the room. I saw the shadows moving like the hands on a clock. By the middle of the afternoon, I was sick of it. I went to the kitchen and washed my hands under the running tap. When I came back to the lobby, I couldn't bear to look at Jean any longer. I turned my eyes away and went straight to her bedroom. In the drawer of her wardrobe I found a folded sheet. I took it and spread it over her head to hide it. There was a bulging purse lying in the drawer. I left it where it was. The stump of my cigar was lying on the step where it fell from my fingers. I threw it in the dead fireplace for Mr Trench to discover, sat down with Jean and waited for the kindness of dark to cover us.

I forgot to wind my watch, so I do not know what time it was when the young man with the yellow moustache returned at last.

He simply walked in through the front door like the master of the house, calling out: "Jean? Jean? Why are you in the dark?"

I heard him fumbling with the gasolier, lifting up the shade to light the gas. When he struck the match I saw him. He saw me, sitting there on the step, my policeman's uniform soaking up the shadows, my face shining pale as the moon, and then he looked down and saw Jean and the wreck of the room and the glass shade fell from his hand and broke.

"Light the gas before we're all killed," I said. "Don't try to run."

He did as he was told.

"You did this," I said.

"I didn't. No. I just arrived. You must have seen me come in. I just got here. Oh God, help us."

"You did this."

"No. No!" There was terror in his voice.

"Yes, you did. You're responsible. None of this would ever have happened but for you. You made this happen."

I think then he began to understand and he cringed away from me like the little coward he was.

"She will be missed very soon and then there will be a hue and cry the length of the land and we will find you, we will track you down and we will drag you back and your arms will be tied behind you and they will put a bag on your head and a rope round your neck and the floor will fall away under your feet and, if you are very, very lucky, your neck will break. You did this and you will be punished."

All he could say was "No" in a little squeaking whisper.

I took him by the lapels of his fancy, shiny coat and pressed my face close to his. "Yes," I said. "Yes. Yes. I've had a long time here with Jean, all alone in this big house. Plenty of time to leave a few little clues. Is there a printed pamphlet offering shares in a gold mine forgotten in a drawer? Does it have the printer's name? Would he remember who paid for the job? Is there a ticket for a cruise in the Highlands? Is there a receipt, maybe a receipt for a ring? You've been here before. Your fingerprints are everywhere. Do you remember where? Do you remember what you touched – apart from her, of course." He was whimpering and trembling in my hands. "If you run, you will be caught. You will be caught and you will hang. But I'm a sportsman. I'll give you time. Feel free to see if you can find the clues. Clean up as much as you like."

I let go of his coat. "I have left my key in the back door," I told him. "I won't be needing it again." And then I left the way he had come, down the path to home. I heard the door lock at my back as I went. I took his cigars with me, of course.

AFTERWORD

All stories are fiction but they are not all inventions. Everybody named in this story existed and almost all of the places mentioned still exist today. I made up nothing except conversations. All the evidence, the circumstances, the witness statements – everything – is there in the police files and in newspaper reports, right up until the moment of Warner's release, when the file closes.

As far as the police are concerned, the case remains unsolved. There were obvious gaps in the investigation, and when they fitted together they led me to a solution. There really was a Sergeant Fraser, but I changed his name because I still live in Broughty Ferry and for all I know his grandchildren do too.